GREAT CITY

"It's a hell of a feeling being lost in a great city," the man said slowly. "And the world is full of great cities." His voice was deep and solemn. He spoke slowly, staring straight ahead, and his words seemed to emanate from a trance. "The human mind is a great city in which a guy is always lost. He spends his lifetime groping, trying to locate himself."

—from "World Full of Great Cities" by Joseph Heller

BANTAM LITERATURE

BIG CITY STORIES BY MODERN AMERICAN WRITERS edited by Tom and Susan Cahill

FIFTY GREAT AMERICAN SHORT STORIES edited by Milton Crane

FIFTY GREAT ESSAYS edited by Elizabeth and Edward Huberman

FIFTY GREAT EUROPEAN SHORT STORIES edited by Edward and Elizabeth Huberman

FIFTY GREAT POETS edited by Milton Crane

FIFTY GREAT SHORT STORIES edited by Milton Crane

GREAT BRITISH SHORT NOVELS edited by Robert Donald Spector

GREAT BRITISH SHORT STORIES edited by Edward and Elizabeth Huberman

GREAT RUSSIAN SHORT NOVELS translated by Andrew R. MacAndrew

MODERN EUROPEAN POETRY edited by Willis Barnstone

SEVENTY-FIVE SHORT MASTERPIECES edited by Roger B. Goodman

THE VOICE THAT IS GREAT WITHIN US edited by Hayden Carruth

BIG CITY STORIES
BY MODERN AMERICAN WRITERS
Edited by
Tom and Susan Cahill

BIG CITY STORIES BY MODERN AMERICAN WRITERS
A Bantam Book / published September 1971
2nd printing
3rd printing
4th printing

All rights reserved.
Copyright © 1971 by Bantam Books, Inc.

COPYRIGHTS AND ACKNOWLEDGMENTS

The copyright notices are listed below and on the page following, which constitutes an extension of this copyright page.

"Encounter on a Rooftop," by William Melvin Kelley. From his A Different Drummer. Copyright © 1959, 1962 by William Melvin Kelley. Reprinted by permission of Doubleday & Co., Inc.

"World Full of Great Cities," by Joseph Heller. Copyright © 1955 by Manvis Publications, Inc. Reprinted by permission of Robert Lantz-Candida Donadio Literary Agency, Inc.

"Luther," by Jay Neugeboren. From his Corky's Brother. Copyright © 1966, 1969 by Jay Neugeboren. Reprinted by permission of Farrar, Straus & Giroux, Inc.

"Hoods I Have Known," by Sondra Spatt Olsen. From MADEMOISELLE. Copyright © 1956 by Street and Smith Publications, Inc. Reprinted by permission of Sondra Spatt Olsen.

"Sonny's Blues," by James Baldwin. From his Going to Meet the Man. Copyright © 1957 by James Baldwin. Reprinted by permission of The Dial Press.

"A Lot You Got to Holler," by Nelson Algren. From his Neon Wilderness. Copyright 1947 by Nelson Algren and reprinted with his permission and that of Doubleday & Co., Inc.

"Hector Rodriguez," edited by Jeremy Larner. From his The Addict in the Street. Copyright © 1964 by Grove Press, Inc., and reprinted with their permission.

"The Screamers," by LeRoi Jones. From his Tales. Copyright © 1967 by LeRoi Jones. Reprinted by permission of The Sterling Lord Agency.

"Georgy," by Jon Lomberg. From In Growing Up in America edited by Robert A. Rosenbaum. Copyright © 1969 by Jon Lomberg and reprinted with his permission.

"Black Is My Favorite Color," by Bernard Malamud. From his Idiots First. Copyright © 1963 by Bernard Malamud. Reprinted by permission of Farrar, Straus & Giroux, Inc.

"A Story for Teddy," by Harvey Swados. From his A Story for Teddy. Copyright © 1965 by Harvey Swados and reprinted with his permission.

"Beautiful Light and Black Our Dreams," by Woodie King, Jr. Copyright © 1963 by THE NEGRO DIGEST. Reprinted by permission of Woodie King, Jr.

"The Enormous Radio," by John Cheever. From his The Enormous Radio and Other Stories. Copyright 1953 by John Cheever. Reprinted by permission of Funk & Wagnalls.

"City Boy," by Leonard Michaels. From his Going Places. Copyright © 1967, 1969 by Leonard Michaels. Reprinted by permission of Farrar, Straus & Giroux, Inc.

"October in the Railroad Earth," by Jack Kerouac. From EVERGREEN REVIEW #2. Copyright © 1957 by Jack Kerouac. Reprinted by permission of The Sterling Lord Agency.

"Christ in Concrete," by Pietro Di Donato. Copyright 1937, 1939 by Esquire-Coronet, Inc. Reprinted by permission of the author's estate and his agents, Scott Meredith Literary Agency, Inc.

"The Man Who Went to Chicago," by Richard Wright. From his Eight Men. Copyright 1945 by L. B. Fischer Publishing Corporation under the title "Early Days in Chicago." Reprinted by permission of Paul R. Reynolds, Inc.

"Pete: A Quarter Ahead," by John Rechy. From his City of Night. Copyright © 1963 by John Rechy. Reprinted by permission of Grove Press, Inc.

"In a While Crocodile," by William Eastlake. From his

Portrait of An Artist With 26 Horses. Copyright © 1959 by William Eastlake. Reprinted by permission of The Harold Matson Company, Inc.

"A New Day," by Charles Wright. From Best Short Stories by Negro Writers edited by Langston Hughes. Copyright © 1967 by Little, Brown & Company, Inc. Reprinted by permission of Robert Lantz-Candida Donadio Literary Agency, Inc.

"An Act of Prostitution," by James Alan McPherson. From his Hue and Cry. Copyright © 1968, 1969 by James Alan McPherson. Reprinted by permission of Little, Brown & Company, Inc.

"A Policeman's Journal" by T. Mike Walker. From his Voices From the Bottom of the World. Copyright © 1969 by T. Mike Walker. Reprinted by permission of Grove Press, Inc.

"Cry for Me," by William Melvin Kelley. From his Dancers on the Shore. Copyright © 1962 by Fawcett Publications, Inc. Reprinted by permission of Doubleday & Company, Inc.

"Laughs, etc.," by James Leo Herlihy. From his A Story That Ends With a Scream and Eight Others. Copyright © 1963, 1964, 1965 by James Leo Herlihy. Reprinted by permission of Simon & Schuster, Inc.

"Daddy Wolf," by James Purdy. From his Children Is All. Copyright © 1960 by James Purdy. Reprinted by permission of New Directions Publishing Corporation.

"Judgement Day," by Flannery O'Connor. From her Everything That Rises Must Converge. Copyright © 1956, 1957, 1958, 1960, 1961, 1962, 1964, 1965 by the Estate of Mary Flannery O'Connor. Reprinted by permission of Farrar, Straus & Giroux, Inc.

"A Pedestrian Accident," by Robert Coover. From his Pricksongs and Descants. Copyright © 1969 by Robert Coover. Reprinted by permission of E. P. Dutton & Co., Inc.

"The Watchers," by Florence Engel Randall. From HARPER'S Magazine, 1965. Copyright © 1965 by Harper's Magazine, Inc. Reprinted by permission of Theron Raines.

"The Police Band," by Donald Barthelme. From his Unspeakable Practices, Unnatural Acts. Copyright © 1964, 1968 by Donald Barthelme. Reprinted by permission of Farrar, Straus & Giroux, Inc.

"Tomorrow and Tomorrow and Tomorrow," by Kurt Vonnegut, Jr. From his Welcome to the Monkey House. Copyright 1950, 1951, 1953, © 1954, 1955, 1956, 1958, 1960, 1961, 1962, 1964, 1966, 1968 by Kurt Vonnegut, Jr. A Seymour Laurence Book. Reprinted by permission of Delacorte Press.

This book may not be reproduced in whole or in part, by mimeograph or any other means, without permission. For information address: Bantam Books, Inc.

Published simultaneously in the United States and Canada

Bantam Books are published by Bantam Books, Inc., a National General company. Its trade-mark, consisting of the words "Bantam Books" and the portrayal of a bantam, is registered in the United States Patent Office and in other countries. Marca Registrada. Bantam Books, Inc., 666 Fifth Avenue, New York, N.Y. 10019.

PRINTED IN THE UNITED STATES OF AMERICA

Contents

INTRODUCTION — viii

GROWING UP

WILLIAM MELVIN KELLEY/Encounter on a Rooftop — 3
JOSEPH HELLER/World Full of Great Cities — 15
JAY NEUGEBOREN/Luther — 26
SONDRA SPATT/Hood's I Have Known — 42
JAMES BALDWIN/Sonny's Blues — 55
NELSON ALGREN/A Lot You Got to Holler — 85
JEREMY LARNER (ed.)/Hector Rodriguez — 97
LEROI JONES/The Screamers — 106

LOVING

JON LOMBERG/Georgy — 115
BERNARD MALAMUD/Black Is My Favorite Color — 120
HARVEY SWADOS/A Story for Teddy — 130
WOODIE KING, JR./Beautiful Light and Black Our Dreams — 155
JOHN CHEEVER/The Enormous Radio — 164
LEONARD MICHAELS/City Boy — 175
JACK KEROUAC/October in the Railroad Earth — 185

WORKING

PIETRO DI DONATO/Christ in Concrete	201
RICHARD WRIGHT/The Man Who Went to Chicago	215
JOHN RECHY/Pete: A Quarter Ahead	245
WILLIAM EASTLAKE/In a While Crocodile	262
CHARLES WRIGHT/A New Day	273
JAMES ALAN MCPHERSON/An Act of Prostitution	278
T. MIKE WALKER/A Policeman's Journal	292
WILLIAM MELVIN KELLEY/Cry for Me	301

DYING

JAMES LEO HERLIHY/Laughs, etc.	319
JAMES PURDY/Daddy Wolf	327
FLANNERY O'CONNOR/Judgement Day	335
ROBERT COOVER/A Pedestrian Accident	353

LOOKING AHEAD

FLORENCE ENGEL RANDALL/The Watchers	375
DONALD BARTHELME/The Police Band	386
KURT VONNEGUT, JR./Tomorrow and Tomorrow and Tomorrow	389

SELECTED BIBLIOGRAPHY   403

Introduction

There are such things as city writers. In their work the city, whether celebrated or damned, is not merely the backdrop for the action, but a real presence. The urban environment exerts a strong influence on the shape and style of their art and plays an actor's role in the movement of the story. The city may be the catalyst of the action or the ingredient without which the story could not happen. But none of the stories in this book could be imagined outside their urban setting.

For classification's sake city writers might be divided into two groups. One group could be called the Urbane School: the wits, the deliberately complex, the arcanely allusive, those whose knowing audience are Ph.D. candidates and Bloomsbury Groups. At its best the Urbane School reflects the city's capacity for embracing any taste, however rare, and any scent, however exotic, and brings under some control the baffling complexities of urban experience. *Ulysses* is its undisputed masterpiece. At its weakest the Urbane School delights merely in sophistication for its own sake. Its jaded palate salivates for all things elegantly perverse and *recherché*, and in its self-admiring smugness human compassion gets lost. Of this side of the Urbane spectrum Gore Vidal is an apt representative. In any case, whether at its most magnificent or silliest, the Urbane School is largely represented, not by short stories, but by novels, and is therefore little in evidence here.

The other group of city writers might be called the Big City School. These are blood-and-guts, almost always popular (in some sense), sometimes crass, often concerned with the city's rich and festering underbelly rather than with its polished and elegant surfaces, occasionally trapped by an excess of sentiment, usually focused on a small or strange subject, and never dull. From the past, Walt Whitman, Stephen Crane, Frank Norris, Theodore Dreiser, and to an extent, Nathanael West are well-known examples. James Leo Herlihy is a fine current representative. The cheap strain in this group—the sloppy, easy depiction of the melodrama of being human—is exemplified by O. Henry and Jimmy Breslin on bad days.

The stories in this book come mostly from the Big City School, though we have used no rigid guidelines in making the selections. (Robert Coover and Donald Barthelme, for instance, lean more toward the Urbane School.) Most of these stories were written within the last five or ten years, though Baldwin, Algren, Richard Wright, and others are older voices. Many of the stories are written in traditional forms, but there are several in the contemporary mode, having a chronologically distorted or nonlinear development and a narrative presented in an elliptical rather than a highly representational style. The stories by LeRoi Jones, Leonard Michaels, Donald Barthelme, Jack Kerouac, and Robert Coover, all leading experimentalists, serve to expose the reader to new trends in fiction. A few selections (Rechy's, Walker's, and Larner's) are really not short stories but defined and fairly complete chapters from episodic novels, or, in Larner's case, a taped interview. Two of these city stories have not been written by city writers, and one, "In a While Crocodile," does not even take place in a city. But William Eastlake's reporter brings the city with him to the Indian reservation. And Flannery O'Connor, in the only story she ever wrote which takes place in a city, catches a glimpse of urban life perhaps best described by a Southern ruralist. All the selections are by American authors.

More and more the modern short story writer has chosen the city as the fictional place in which to explore the meanings of human experience because there—in the parks, on the rooftops, at the demonstrations—are found in abundant variety the sort of subject that makes the short story what it is. In *The Lonely Voice,* Frank O'Connor's study of the modern short story, the Irish writer has called that subject "a submerged population group." The identities within the group change from writer to writer and from generation to generation. In the past it was Maupassant's prostitutes, Chekhov's doctors and teachers, and Sherwood Anderson's midwestern provincials. Today it may be Rechy's homosexuals, Jones's blacks, Walker's cops. But one characteristic, according to O'Connor, binds all these different groups together:

> Always in the short story there is this sense of outlawed figures wandering about the fringes of society, superimposed sometimes on symbolic figures whom they caricature and echo— Christ, Socrates, Moses. . . . As a result there is in the short story at its most characteristic something we do not often find in the novel—an intense awareness of human loneliness.

Though these fringe populations are not to be found in cities alone (as O'Connor's rural stories bear witness), many of the stories that follow eloquently pinpoint the loneliness of the individual who moves through the great human sea of the city.

In each story the environment is, in LeRoi Jones's words, "total, i.e., social, cultural, and physical, and not merely scenery." Whether the humans shape the environment or the environment shapes the particular forms of humanity, these stories are incomprehensible without reference to environment. In many stories the urban environment proves inhuman, deadly to the growth and delicately balanced existence of our kind. But sometimes it is full of revelation ("Encounter on a Rooftop"), ecstasy ("The Screamers" and "Cry for Me"), sweet warmth and freedom ("Georgy"), hope ("A New Day"), and even salvation ("Luther"). For one writer the city inevitably suffocates its victims ("Daddy Wolf"), for another it is a world of infinite variety, a holy celebration ("October in the Railroad Earth"). But to each story the city is indispensable.

GROWING UP

Encounter on a Rooftop
William Melvin Kelley

Whenever I get to thinking about the evil in the world, I always think about my friend, Stinger Riley. This is not because Stinger is evil, although there are a lot of people who have said so. It's just because he seems to have had it all figured out from the beginning, from the time we were in the third grade and had to go around on Wednesday afternoons with the rest of the Catholic kids for religious instructions at the nuns' high school. Stinger always went through the motions with the rest of us, but I could tell that he wasn't having any. He didn't even believe in God. And, because I didn't give him credit for an overdose of brains, I used to think he came by this attitude out of plain badness. But gradually, as we got older and moved into high school, I became aware that Stinger lived by a set of fairly sophisticated truths: that men are born savages, are selfish and prone to what is called evil; that they are sometimes idealists and invent gods; that they get scared and invent redeemers and heavens; that they are sadistic and invent devils and hells; and that they are damned fools and spend their lives trying to reconcile good and evil, gods and men, life and death. But I wasn't convinced that he had thought these things out, consciously and systematically, until one day just a couple of years ago when we were walking around Central Park Reservoir and he got off the one and only theological disquisition of his life. And it ran something like this:

"You know how it is, Bas, when you try to figure out life and what the hell we're doing here. Maybe you start off thinkin' about what a bunch of bastards people are, and just how in hell they got that way. I mean, were they always such bastards? And this gets you to thinkin' about Adam and Eve and the Garden of Eden and the first sin and all that noise, and that's where the cheese gets bindin'. Because you've got to decide which side you're on. And it's easy to get on God's side. All you've got to say is that He's a great guy and gave people free will just to be big about it, and that sin and evil got into things because people used their free will the wrong way. And that's okay and explains why people are such nasty bastards. But then, Bas, you are just figurin' you've got it knocked when you remember about hurricanes, clap, mosquitoes, cancer, earthquakes, piss-ants, volcanoes, and tidal waves, and these are a blow in the ass. Because nobody's free will invented them. So you think about it some more, taking it from all sides and finin' it all down to the short hair, and it gets to look like God ain't so good after all, or maybe He just ain't. And that's when you decide that there's evil in the world just because there is, and that people are nasty bastards just because that's what most of them naturally are."

Now, I'm not trying to tell you that Stinger did this sort of thinking in the third grade, but I insist that he did have it figured out vaguely, working from an instinctive awareness that the body, not the soul, was the basic reality and that it held all the important secrets. For, all his life, he has acted with a certain consistency, without tensions or guilt. He goes along enjoying what he sees and whatever is offered. He takes the good with the bad, deciding which is which for himself, and he scratches it where it itches if it itches at all. He's the happiest man I know.

I didn't meet Stinger until I was skipped into the third grade in January of my second year in school. We sat side by side then, and so we were more or less thrown together. And we became friends right away. Stinger got his nickname on account of his dexterity with a three-inch hatpin and, as far as I know, I was the only one in the third grade who was spared the rigors of his steel. He was a hell-raiser, impulsive and without inhibition. I was quiet, generally cautious, and given even that early to calculating odds and consequences. But we had a profound regard for one another's talents. Stinger was in awe, for example, of the ease with which I learned, concluding that I must be genius if I could skip a whole year of schooling. I was equally in awe of his gift for social relations, his ability to charm everybody with far less effort than it took me to tell someone my name. It wasn't this clear to us in the third grade, of course, and it was to be some time before I realized that Stinger's great talent was a simple matter of sex.

Everybody else said sex was evil. Stinger didn't think so, and, being a year older than I and precocious anyway, he was concerned with it from the very beginning. One result was that I got curious about this great evil pretty early.

But I had no talent for it, and I didn't begin to understand for a long, long time. And this was not really Stinger's fault; he did try. I made inquiry once about why it was necessary for girls and boys to have separate toilets, and Stinger did the best he could with it. But I received the information with such apparent confusion and lack of comprehension that he soon gave it up as a bad job. We remained friendly, but he developed a certain respect or delicacy with regard to me that seemed to preclude any inclination on his part either to ridicule my ignorance or dispel any of it.

It didn't help any that at this time Stinger and I were being forced to undergo training as altar boys at the parish church. I took it seriously and Stinger didn't, but this doesn't mean that I was pious. The ceremonies of the Church didn't mean any more to me than to Stinger. But the Church and Father Cassidy scared me, and I had a great fear of offending either one of them. I would serve Father Cassidy's Mass in the winter, when the air was cold in the church and the pews were almost empty, and I would ring the bell at the elevation of the Host and, looking at its whiteness, begin to imagine that I had committed all manner of terrible sins. I would quake until the ordeal was over, and scurry out of the church, and from under Father Cassidy's hard eyes, as fast as I could get rid of my surplice.

Stinger was not so troubled. His only comment on the Mass was that it took too damned long and that all the kneeling made his knees hurt. He used to yawn, wiggle, belch, and scratch throughout the ceremony, and when I would tell him to be careful, he'd say that God wasn't watching. I would insist that God most assuredly was watching, but this never seemed to worry him. Sometimes I would tell him about the fires of purgatory, and he would begin to wince and look worried, but it had no lasting effect.

And Stinger mistook my fear for piety and, typically, respected it as such. So I got no lessons in sex that I didn't ask for and sometimes not even then. And I guess things would have stayed that way for a long time had it not been for the lady on the roof. I met this lady during the summer between the third and fourth grades. And when I told Stinger about her the following fall, he thought it was the greatest story he had ever heard, and he had me tell it to him over and over again. And it changed everything between Stinger and me, because, after the lady on the roof, I was adjudged fully qualified to receive even the most delicate sexual information. This despite the fact that even after Stinger's patient explanations, I still had no clear idea as to what the lady had been up to, if indeed, as Stinger darkly hinted, she had been up to anything. You have got to judge for yourself.

I remember it was a hot day and Sean, my grandfather, was cleaning the hallway on the fifth floor. I was sitting on the steps watching him. He was mopping, bent over, the sweat dripping from his forehead onto the wet floor. I was watching the drops of sweat, waiting in fascination until the black, soggy mass of the mop swept over them and they disappeared without a trace.

Every few minutes he would stop and take a red bandanna from his pocket. He would wipe his face and tell me that it was pretty damned hot. I already knew this but didn't say so.

After a while he stopped mopping and said that he had to help the man with the ashes from the hot-water heater and that I should wait for him until he got back. Then he walked by me and down the stairs. I sat there and listened to his footsteps until he was all the way down into the cellar.

I waited and waited and the time went by very slowly. I got hot and itchy and tired. So I got up and walked down the hall to where the stairs went up to the roof. The door at the top of the stairs was propped open and a slow breeze was coming through. I sat down on the bottom step and it was much cooler there.

And I sat for what seemed like another hour at least, but Sean did not come, and I began to get hot again, so I moved up the stairs a couple of steps. Later I moved up a couple more. This went on, it getting hotter and hotter and the breeze feeling nicer and nicer as I got nearer the top, until I was sitting on the top step.

There I could lean back and look right out onto the roof. It was the first time I had seen it, being under positive assurance from Sean that if I ever went out on it I would invariably fall off the edge and get all smashed to a bloody pulp on the sidewalk. I remember this and it worried me. So I leaned back and looked for the edge of the roof, trying to see around the big red chimney that was opposite the door. And I saw a bare foot sticking out from behind the chimney.

It looked like a big foot and there was a little chain, like the one on my Blessed Virgin medal, around the ankle. I watched this foot awhile. The toes were pointing downward toward the roof. Several times the foot went up in the air and in behind the chimney. But it always came down again.

I got to wondering where the other one was. I thought that maybe it was a one-legged man. Then I saw the toes of the other foot right against the chimney sticking out a little beyond it.

So I started to slither out a little further to see what else there was, still on my back and pushing myself with my legs, and I banged my head against the open roof door. It hurt, but I did not cry out. I rubbed my head with my eyes closed tight. Then I thought that since I was all the way out on the roof now anyway, I might just as well stand up and take a good look.

So I got up quietly and looked around. I couldn't see much of anything except the sky and other roofs and New Jersey way over on the other side of the river. But I could see the edge of the roof. It was a good block away. I decided I could walk over to the chimney without running the risk of falling off. I was wearing sneakers and made no noise. I eased my way around the side of the chimney where I had seen the feet. I got right up to the corner. The toes of one foot were still sticking out from behind it a little. I leaned forward around the toes and took a look.

The feet belonged to a lady who was lying on her stomach on a white blanket, and her hair was long and brown and hung down over her shoulders. And she had no clothes on.

I pulled my head back again and thought about this for a minute. I guessed that she lived in one of the apartments in the building. I also guessed that she did not have much sense. Nobody else I knew went around with no clothes on, and Sean had told me that you could get locked up for not covering your parts in public. I decided I would tell this lady a few things. I stepped out from behind the chimney.

"Hey, lady," I said. I almost whispered because I was scared. She did not move, so I reached over and tapped her near foot.

"Hey, lady," I said again.

This time she whirled around and grabbed for a towel that was lying near her head. I recognized her as a lady who lived on the fourth floor. I did not know her name. She stopped as soon as she saw me. She dropped the towel over her bottom and smiled. It was a nice smile, as though I had done something only a little wrong.

"Don't ever sneak up on anybody like that, Bascomb," she said.

"I wasn't sneaking. How did you know my name is Bascomb?"

"Oh, I find out all kinds of things." And she turned her head around again and brushed her hair back and began to look at a magazine propped up in front of her. I stood there looking, but she appeared to have forgotten me.

"Hey, lady," I said. I walked around and stood by her side. "Don't you know you can get locked up for not covering your parts in public?"

She laughed out loud and turned to look at me. I remember that her teeth were very even and straight and looked snow-white against her tanned face.

"What do you know about parts?" She spoke as she laughed. Her eyes flashed in the sunlight.

"My grandfather told me. Sean, I mean."

"Your grandfather!" She jumped and stopped laughing and reached for a bathrobe that was folded up alongside of her. "Where's your grandfather?"

"He's downstairs."

"How far down?"

"All the way down into the cellar."

"Good." She put the robe down. "What does your grandfather say?"

"He says you can get locked up for not covering your parts in public."

"He's right."

"So then, why don't you cover them?"

"Well, they are covered." She readjusted the towel without looking back. "Can you see anything?"

I made a short inspection. "Not now, I guess. But when I came up here first I could see your backside, and if I'd been a cop I'd have run you in."

"What for?" Now she was laughing again. I began to figure that she was really dumb. Somebody was going to lock her up for sure.

"For not covering your parts in public, that's what for."

"Well, I'm not in public, am I?"

This one stopped me for a minute. But only for a minute.

"I'm here and I'm public," I told her shortly.

"Oh no," she said quickly, shaking her head and making her hair slide back and forth across her bare shoulders. "You're strictly private. You're a friend of mine."

"How can I be a friend of yours if I don't even know your name?"

"How will it be if I tell you my name?"

"All right, I guess."

"Okay. My name is Lilly Vale. Now are we friends?"

"I guess so." I knew I had been trapped but it was too late. And I hated to see the law in point lose its effect by my rapid transition from public to private. But I did not see how I could get around it now. So I went back to my question. She was looking at her magazine again.

"What are you doing up here, lady?"

"Why don't you call me Lilly?"

"Lilly."

"I'm taking a sunbath."

"A sunbath?"

"That's right."

"Is it like a water bath any?"

"Sure."

"Do you scrub?"

"Oh no. You just lie here."

"Don't use soap?"

"No soap."

"And no water?"

"No water."

This, I decided, was the way to take a bath. I would have to tell Sean about it. And it cleared up a few things for me.

"Is that why you've got no clothes on, because you're taking a bath?"

"That's right."

"Is it fun?"

"Oh sure."

"How long do you have to lie there before you are clean?"

"Not too long. Matter of fact, I'm done on this side now." She looked back at her legs. Then she reached down and secured the towel around her bottom, turned over, and sat up. And for the first time I saw her breasts. I stood fascinated by them as she reached for a bottle of sun oil and rubbed it on them and on her shoulders, arms, and stomach. When she had finished, she lay back and put one arm over her eyes. Her breasts stood straight up, like the tops of two fire hydrants.

"Hey, lady." I spoke softly. "What are those?"

"What are what?" she said gently, not moving.

"These things." I bent down and touched the near breast. She jumped a little. Then she peeked out at me from under her arm.

"Oh, you've seen things like those before." She smiled.

"No, I haven't."
"Why, sure. Haven't you seen your mother's?"
"My mother hasn't got any."
"Sure she has."
"I never saw any."
"Well, she has. You look next time."
"Next time what?"
"How should I know? Just next time. Next time you take a bath with her."
"I don't take any baths with her."
"Didn't you ever?"
"No. I took a bath with my brother Tim once."
"Well, that isn't the same thing."
"He took up all the room."
"Do you always take a bath alone?"
"Yes. But Sean scrubs me."
"Your grandfather? Doesn't your mother take care of you?"
"No. She takes care of my father and my brother Tim."
"Oh." Then she turned away and closed her eyes and said something about a strange family.
"Hey, lady."
"Why don't you call me Lilly like I told you?"
"I forgot."
"Suppose I called you 'boy'?"
"I am a boy."
"I know. But you've got a name. Don't you like to be called by your name?"
"I guess so."
"Well, I like to be called by mine."
"All right. Lilly."
"That's better."
"Well, can I?"
"Can you what?"
"Can I touch them?"
"Touch what?" Then she saw where I was looking. She rose on one elbow. "You mean my . . . Oh no! That wouldn't be nice."
"Why wouldn't it be nice?"
"It just wouldn't. I mean, little boys just don't go around touching ladies' things."
"I'm not a little boy. I'm eight."
"Oh, I didn't mean it that way. Big boys don't go around feeling them either."

"Why don't they?"

"Well, because. Because it's bad, that's all. Bad."

"What do you mean, bad?"

"How should I know what I mean?"

"Bad like a sin?"

"Sure. I guess so. Bad like a sin." Then she smiled and lay back on her blanket. "Though I guess it depends on who does it and all."

"Would it be a sin if I did it?"

She closed her eyes and still smiled and said something about the mouths of babes and how she would be hung for a liar. Then she laughed out loud, causing her breasts to shake.

"How old did you say you were?" she asked.

"Eight."

"And you never, I mean, nobody's ever told you about girls?"

"Sean told me about girls. He said they have all got empty heads. He's going to tell me more about them someday, he said."

"I'd like to hear that." And she laughed again.

"And my best friend Stinger told me too."

"What did he tell you?"

"He said girls go to the toilet different."

"Do you know why?"

"No."

"Aren't you curious?"

"What's that?"

"I mean don't you want to know why girls go to the toilet different?"

"Girls do everything different. I don't care."

"Well, I'll be damned." She shook her head back and forth.

"So then would it be a sin if I touched them?"

"You really want to touch them, don't you?"

"Yes. Really."

"Well, after everybody else that's touched them, I don't see why I should draw the line with you."

"Can I do it now?"

"Sure. Go ahead."

So I knelt down beside her and took the point of the near breast between my fingers. Then I squeezed.

"Does that hurt?" I asked. It was a clinical question.

"No." She spoke softly, her arm over her eyes. "Feels fine. What's it feel like to you?"

"Feels like Sean's nose."

She roared with laughter. I let go for a minute so I could watch them. They were very pretty. Like jello.

"What are these things for?" I asked.

"Well, let's see. They're for little babies to play with."

"Have you got any little babies?"

"Nope."

"So then who plays with yours?"

"Oh, you'd be surprised. Only big babies play with mine." I thought about this for a minute. But I did not know what to say, so I leaned over and started to feel them again.

"What do you call them?" I asked.

"Oh, different things. Anything from louse to a son of a . . . Oh! You mean—my things!"

"Yes, these things."

"Oh sure. Well, most people just call them—call them knobs."

"Knobs? Like on a radio?"

"Sure. That's it."

"They're pretty big knobs."

"Thanks, kid. I like them that way."

"Can I feel them all over?"

"Haven't you had enough?"

"No."

"How come you talk so nice? How come you never say 'yeah' and 'naw' like other kids?"

"Because Sean says he will paddle my backside if I do."

This made her laugh again.

Then I could feel them getting harder, and I saw that the tips were sharper now and standing up, and that they looked bigger all over.

"They're getting big," I said solemnly.

"Yes, they are." But she did not look.

"How big do they get?"

"Oh, that's as big as they get. You're doing a fine job."

Then, all at once, there were voices and footsteps in the hallway below. Not wanting to, but thinking of Sean and of getting caught on the roof, I lifted my hands from Lilly's breasts.

"Don't stop," she said.

"I think I have to go now."

"Why do you have to go?" She raised her arm from her eyes and looked at me. Then she heard the voices too. Her face became tense at once. "Is that your grandfather?"

I listened. I did not hear Sean. "No, I don't think it is. It sounds like two ladies."

Lilly smiled. "That's good."

"I think I'd better go now." I spoke uneasily and began to move away, inching backward on my knees.

"What's your hurry, Bascomb?" She lifted herself to one elbow. "It isn't your grandfather."

"Yes. But I think I better go anyway."

"Don't you want to touch them any more?"

"No. I don't. Thank you."

Then I started to stand up. Lilly reached out and took me by the wrist.

"Now just a minute." She spoke gently. I tried to pull away but her grip was too strong.

"Let me go," I said.

"If I let go now, do you promise you won't tell anybody about what you've done? Not even your grandfather?"

"I promise."

Then she let go of my wrist and I backed away, still on my knees. She turned and reached for her bathrobe. The towel had fallen away from her hips. I could see her whole body. And her belly was very white down near where her legs began. I watched her as she put on the robe, her body all tan except for the white patch on her belly. Then she noticed me watching her.

"Okay, free show's over. Get along now."

"Yes. I'm going." I got up and walked over by the chimney and looked back at her. She was standing up now, combing her long brown hair with swift, hard strokes, and it shimmered in the sunlight. She was looking out and down in the direction of the Hudson River.

"Good-by, Lilly," I said quietly.

"Good-by," she said over her shoulder, and she half turned, causing the robe to fall away from her breasts, and they were pretty in the sun.

"Thanks for letting me feel your knobs, Lilly."

"Oh sure, kid, sure. Any time. Any time you got the price."

Her voice didn't carry in the breeze, and she turned away from me as she spoke, but I am fairly sure that those were her words. And I thought about them as I walked down the stairs and wondered what she meant by the price. I decided that she must have meant that the next time I felt her knobs it was going to cost me something.

But I never felt Lilly's knobs again. She moved out shortly

after the incident, and I watched her walking down West 107th Street, carrying her straw suitcase. When she turned the corner onto Broadway I hollered to her and waved. But she didn't hear me, and I felt bad about it because she looked lonely.

As I said, this story made a great impression on Stinger. As time went by, I came to understand how rare and wonderful an experience it had been, but I don't think I ever got quite the kick out of it that Stinger did. Its value to me was in the fact that it served to put Stinger in a mood for talking about sex, and I listened to whatever he had to say with great eagerness, feeding an insatiable curiosity.

World Full of Great Cities
Joseph Heller *

The boy left his last telegram with the receptionist in the lawyer's office and walked down Beekman Place to the apartment house. He rode the elevator to the sixth floor, found the door he wanted, rang the bell, and waited. After a few seconds the door opened, and a blonde woman looked out at him. She opened the door wide when she saw him. She remained motionless in the doorway, studying him coldly from head to foot. She was a beautiful woman, and the boy felt his face color as he lowered his eyes and waited for her to speak.

"Where'd you park your bicycle?" she asked finally.

"We don't have bicycles," the boy said. "I had to walk."

"Is that why you got here so fast?"

"I came as soon as I could," the boy said. "I had to make four stops before I came here."

"I wasn't being sarcastic. You came sooner than we expected. Can you wait a few minutes? My husband is busy."

"I can wait," the boy said.

"Come inside then." The woman stepped back and he followed her into the apartment. As he moved inside, he noted immediately how expensively decorated the room was. He stared about him with wondrous respect at the large room and at the rich furnishings that met his gaze wherever he looked. There were several photographs about the room, and behind her he noticed a cigarette burning in a silver ash tray.

"How do you like it?" the woman asked caustically.

"I'm sorry," the boy said. "I was just looking around."

"Don't be sorry. You can look around all you want. It's a privilege we extend to the proletariat."

She walked across the room, picked up the cigarette, and crushed it out. She turned slowly and looked at him.

"I bet it's just like your own home."

The boy remained silent. He stood in the center of the room,

---

* Mr. Heller wrote this story in 1949 while an undergraduate at New York University.

feeling warm and uncomfortable, and moved his cap slowly in his hands.

"Isn't it?" the woman persisted.

"No," the boy answered softly.

"Why isn't it? I suppose your home is nicer."

The boy didn't speak.

"Is it?"

"My home isn't as nice as this," the boy said.

The woman turned from him and picked a cigarette from an ivory box. On the table there were some glasses, a bottle of whiskey, and a bottle of club soda. She lighted her cigarette and turned, exhaling smoke through the side of her mouth.

"It's a beautiful place, isn't it?" she asked in a softer tone.

"Yes," he said. "It's very beautiful."

"I suppose you think anybody can be happy living here." When he didn't answer, she asked, "Don't you?"

"I don't know." The boy looked down at the floor.

"Don't rationalize. You know damn well they can. Don't you realize the power of money?"

The boy looked up and met her eyes. "Why are you picking on me?" he asked. "I didn't do anything to you."

The woman raised her hand and rubbed it across her cheek, leaving a pallid mark that disappeared instantly, and she pursed her lips together in a nervous expression of regret. "I'm sorry. I didn't mean to pick on you. I'm upset. I have to talk to you until my husband comes and I don't know what to say."

The boy smiled apologetically, realizing she was under some strain. She was very beautiful and he was sorry for her.

"What's your name?" she asked.

"Sidney."

A man called from another room, "Who is it?"

"It's the messenger," the woman answered.

"How does he look?"

The woman looked at the boy. He stood without moving, turning his cap slowly in his hands and wondering what they wanted of him.

"He's pretty," the woman said. "But he's very young."

There was the sound of footsteps on tile, and a thin middle-aged man entered the room, wearing a deep blue dressing gown with a towel around his neck and holding an electric shaver in his hands. He nodded coldly to the boy as he studied him. The woman sat down in a corner of the sofa. She kicked off her shoes and tucked her legs up behind her.

The man frowned. "He looks effeminate."

"That would be just my luck," the woman said bitterly.

"I'll send him back." The man stepped toward the boy and smiled. "Look, go back to the office and tell them to send an older boy. We have a special errand and we need an older boy. Do you understand?"

The boy nodded and turned to go.

"Let him stay," the woman said. "I think it will be better with him. I think I'll feel a little safer."

"Do you really think so?"

The woman nodded.

"All right." He turned to the boy. "I'll be with you in a few minutes. Sit down and wait. Give him a drink," he said to the woman and left the room.

"Sit down, Sidney." The boy walked across the room and sat down in a chair facing her. "And don't look so uncomfortable. No one is going to hurt you."

He placed his cap on a table near the chair and looked about the room self-consciously. There was a photograph of a good-looking boy in a football uniform, and he wondered if he was her son. She looked too young to be his mother.

"What's the matter?" the woman asked.

"Nothing," the boy said.

"Don't be afraid of me. Do you want a drink?"

He shook his head.

"I didn't think so. You're too young to drink."

"I drink," the boy said.

"Whiskey?"

"Sometimes," he lied. "I like beer, though."

"I have some in the kitchen. Do you want a bottle?"

"No, thanks. We're not allowed to drink when we're working."

"Do you smoke?"

"We're not allowed to smoke either."

"You go ahead and smoke," the woman said. "Do they pay you well?"

"Pretty well."

"How much do you make a week?"

"I don't make so much," the boy explained. "I only work after school. The ones that work all week make a lot."

"You're going to make a lot today," the woman said, sitting up as she crushed her cigarette out. She poured some whiskey into a glass and added a bit of soda. She stared soberly into the glass for a few seconds as she swirled it around in quick circles. Then she raised the glass and emptied it. The boy watched her face. She swallowed without expression.

"Sidney," she said, setting the glass down, "you're a very pretty boy. I'll bet the girls in school go wild over you."

The boy turned away, flushing with embarrassment.

"Do you go with girls?"

He nodded.

"I'll bet you have a lot of them."

"I have a few," the boy answered. He felt good because she thought so.

"Do you get much?"

The boy thought he had misunderstood her and turned to her questioningly.

"Do you get much?" she said again.

The boy's face burned with shame, and he stared down at a patch of rug between the legs of a round table that stood before the large window.

"You don't have to answer if you don't want to."

"I don't want to."

"All right, don't. If you're still a virgin, it's your own fault. The girls in school are wild about you."

"No, they aren't," the boy said, smiling shyly.

"Yes, they are. You look around and you'll see. You're a very pretty boy, Sidney. I'd like to see you on a cold day. I bet your lips and cheeks turn crimson when it's cold."

Sidney grinned with guilt. He had already noticed how red his lips and cheeks became on cold days and how good-looking he was compared to other boys his age. He had been kept close to home while his father was alive. Now he was forced to work in the city, and the world about him was beginning to unfold slowly in a vast and puzzling panorama, delighting him with each new revelation. He pointed to the picture of the boy in the football uniform.

"Is that your son?" he asked.

"No," the woman said. "It's Mr. Ingall's son." When he looked puzzled, she explained, "I'm his second wife."

"Oh."

"He used to stay here six months during the year, but now he's away at college. He hasn't been here for almost six years."

She reached forward and took another cigarette, tapping it nervously against the back of her hand. She picked up the lighter and turned to him, hesitating, and her face became really soft for the first time.

"You're a nice boy, Sidney," she said slowly. "The girls are crazy about you. I was your age once and I know. Get as many as you can before it's too late. That's what they're here for. Take them while you can and you'll never regret it. Neither will they." She stopped speaking when she saw how distressed he looked. "What's the matter?"

"I don't know," he mumbled.

"Are you always afraid to talk to girls?"

"No," he answered.

"Then what is it? Don't you ever discuss such things with them?"

"No grown-up woman ever talked to me about it before."

"Is it because I'm older or because I'm so nice looking?"

"Both, I guess."

"Do you think I'm nice looking?" she asked.

He nodded, blushing.

"Beautiful?"

He nodded again. He looked toward the foyer, wondering when the man would return.

"What do you like about me?"

"Everything, I guess."

"There must be something special you like. Is it my face, or my breasts, or the way you imagine my thighs are shaped?"

The boy felt himself perspiring and looked away at a table in the corner.

"Well? Which is it?"

"I wish you wouldn't talk like that," he said.

"All right," the woman said. "I won't talk like that. How would you like to go to bed with me?"

He turned to her with surprise, angry now and afraid, because he remembered her husband was in the next room. "I have to go," he said, and stood up. "I have to get back to the office."

"All right, Sidney," she said, with a shrug. "Sit down. I won't bother you." He sat down slowly, watching her suspiciously. "What's the matter?" she asked. "Don't I appeal to you?"

"Not that way," the boy answered in a low voice.

"Why not? If you saw me walking on the street, I'd appeal to you. Wouldn't I?"

He turned away. She was the most beautiful woman he had ever spoken to, and he knew that if he ever did see her walking on the street, he would stop and stare after her until she disappeared from sight.

"I guess I just don't interest you," the woman said wearily.

A silence fell, and the boy sat with his hands in his lap, trying not to stare at her pretty face or the full curves of her body. The man entered briskly with a nervous smile.

"Well, how's it going?" he asked.

"I don't think Sidney likes me," the woman said.

"Of course he likes you. You're probably just scaring him to death. Go inside and get ready. And hurry up. We can't keep him here all day."

She handed him her cigarette and walked from the room. The man turned to Sidney and smiled. He was somewhere in his late forties, with deep serious eyes, and his face, clean shaven now, was marked with deep lines running down from the sides of his nostrils to the corners of his mouth. His voice was soft and smooth, calm and serious. He led Sidney to the center of the room and they sat down facing each other.

"Do they mind if you stay out long on an errand?" he asked.

"I can't stay too long," Sidney said.

"Can you fix it up someway if we keep you?"

"I don't know," the boy answered.

The man reached into the pocket of his dressing gown and removed two bills. He held one out. Sidney took it hesitantly and put it away, noting, as he folded it, that it was a ten-dollar bill.

"That's for waiting so long," the man said. "I'll give you the other one when you do what we want."

"What do you want me to do?" the boy asked suspiciously.

"Didn't she tell you?"

"No."

"Well, don't worry about it. It isn't anything much." He poured a drink. "Do you want one?"

"No, thanks," the boy said. "What do you want me to do?"

"We'll tell you when she comes in." He swallowed the whiskey, making a wry face, and set the glass down. "What do you think of her?"

"She's very pretty," the boy answered.

"She's beautiful," the man said. "Beautiful. Do you like her?"

The boy nodded cautiously.

"She's beautiful," the man repeated. He seemed very depressed, very tired. He started to pour another drink, stopped himself, and set the bottle down. "She's an actress," he said.

The boy was thrilled. It was a new experience talking to an actress. "Are you an actor?"

"I work in television," the man said. He stared thoughtfully before him for several moments. "She's very unhappy," he said, slowly looking up. "We're both very unhappy."

The boy listened with interest.

"That's why we called you. It's an experiment. Would you want to help us?"

"I'd like to if I can," the boy said.

"All right. Maybe you can. How old are you?"

"I was just sixteen."

"Christ, you're just a kid. A happy, oblivious kid. You're a good-looking boy. I'll bet you make out all right with the girls, don't you?"

The boy didn't answer.

"You can talk to me," the man said. "I'm not a woman. Have you had much experience with girls?"

"I go with them a lot," the boy admitted.

"Are they fast?"

"Some of them are," Sidney answered. "Some aren't."

"Do you like the fast ones?"

Sidney grinned sheepishly. "What do you think?"

"Are they pretty?"

"A few are. Most of them aren't."

"You'll find that all through life. Are any of them as pretty as her?"

"No," the boy said. "None are that pretty."

The man leaned forward. "She's really a beautiful girl, isn't she?" he asked, watching the boy closely.

"Yes," he answered. "She is."

"How would you like to make love to her?" the man asked.

The boy turned away quickly. There was a strong undercurrent of desperation in the man's manner. It was strange and intense, and the boy was afraid because it was new to him and he did not know what it meant. The man's eyes were fixed upon him as he waited for a reply.

"I'd like a girl as pretty as her," the boy admitted, in a low, hesitant voice.

The man started to say something but fell silent and watched him for a while. He leaned back in the chair, drumming his fingers slowly on his knee.

"Do you ever get lost when you're working?" he asked.

"I used to at first," Sidney said. "I still do sometimes when they send me uptown."

"It's a hell of a feeling, isn't it?"

"It isn't so bad. The first time I was a little scared. Now I just ask somebody. It sure is a big city."

"It's a hell of a feeling being lost in a great city," the man said slowly. "And the world is full of great cities." His voice was deep and solemn. He spoke slowly, staring straight ahead, and his words seemed to emanate from a trance. "The human mind is a great city in which a guy is always lost. He spends his lifetime groping, trying to locate himself."

The boy listened solemnly, too impressed to reply.

"We're still strangers when we die," the man continued, "lost in a great big city."

He stood up and walked slowly to the window. He stared out at the afternoon without moving, and the boy felt that he had forgotten his presence. The man said quietly:

"It's a horrible picture when you think of it that way. A naked arm in every brain groping its way through a great black city. Can't you just see a world of naked, groping arms?"

He turned and looked at the boy. He had his hand to his forehead, running his fingers slowly around his temple. "I can feel the arm in my own head. I get headaches. I can almost feel the fingers probing through the tissues." He looked at the boy with surprise, as though just discovering he was there. "Do you know what I'm talking about?"

"I think so," the boy said.

"No you don't. You're too young. And it's just as well." He walked into the foyer. "Goddammit, Helen," he called out, "hurry up. The kid doesn't have all day."

He walked across the room and seated himself in a chair facing the sofa. He poured some whiskey into a glass and held it between his legs, staring down at the floor. After a few seconds the woman returned. The boy sat up with surprise when he saw her. She had changed into a blue dressing gown and slippers, and when she walked across the room and sat down on the sofa, he could see the lithe round lines of her body rippling beneath the shiny film of material.

"Well?" she asked, looking at the man.

"Tell him," he said. "This is your idea."

"I thought you were going to."

"Do you want me to?"

The woman nodded. The man raised the glass to his lips and drained it. The boy watched his face curl into an expression of distaste. He waited fearfully. The man set the glass on a table and turned to the woman.

"You do it," he said.

"All right," the woman said, and turned to Sidney. "Have you ever seen a naked woman before?"

The boy gasped and looked away quickly. He felt the silence grow in the room and start to tingle and then ring in his ears.

"For chrisakes, don't be coy. Have you or haven't you?"

"No," the boy answered faintly.

"Would you like to see one now?"

Through the corner of his eye the boy watched the folds of her gown, terrified, not knowing what she was going to do. He shook his head. He felt panic rise within him, and the seconds crawled ominously.

"All right, Helen," the man said, "I'll do it. You sure as hell have no tact." He turned and looked at the boy. "Here's what we want you to do. We want you to make believe that Helen is one of your girl friends. Okay?"

The boy's breath caught in his throat. "What do you mean?"

"You know what I mean. Sit down and neck with her. We want you to make believe she's one of your fast girl friends."

The boy leaped to his feet violently, shaking his head again. His face was hot and damp, his body cold with terror. "No!" he said, blurting the word out. "I won't do it. Here." He groped in his pocket. "Here's your money back."

"Forget the damned money," the man said. "That's yours. Why won't you do it?"

"Because it isn't right, that's why."

The man shook his head slowly and forced a laugh. "You don't understand. It isn't anything wrong." He pointed to the photograph of the boy in football clothes. "You see that boy?" he asked. Sidney nodded. "That's our son. Mine and Helen's. He's dead now. She misses him. You know how mothers are. We just want you to kiss her, to sort of take his place."

The boy remembered what the woman had told him and knew the man was lying, but the fear left him slowly. He remembered how pathetically the man had turned from the window with his fingers on his forehead.

"You mean you want me to kiss her like she was my mother?" he asked.

"No. Just make believe she's one of your girl friends, the one you like best. That's all."

Sidney glanced at the woman. She was watching him with a tight, hopeful, pleading expression. The boy suddenly felt sorry for her. The man leaned forward, waiting for the boy to decide.

"All right," the boy said. "I'll kiss her if she says it's all right."

The woman smiled weakly and nodded. "It's all right."

The man stood up and walked to the liquor tray. The woman rose, beckoning the boy to approach, and he walked to her slowly. Behind him he heard the light splash of whiskey spilling into the glass. He came to a stop before her. She was an inch or two taller, and he looked up at her, trembling with fear and uncertainty. She held up her arms.

"Don't be afraid," she murmured tenderly, with a strange, sad smile.

The man stood to the side, motionless, watching with rigid attention. "Go ahead," he said, when the boy glanced his way. "It's all right."

The boy swallowed nervously. He leaned forward and kissed her on the mouth. The woman slid her arms around him. The boy raised his hands slowly to her shoulders. As he felt his fingers touch her, he pulled his face away quickly and stepped back with alarm.

"What's the matter?" the man demanded.

"He's afraid," the woman said.

"No wonder. You look like you're gonna scratch his eyes out. Smile at him."

The woman turned to the boy and smiled again. Her face grew soft and appealing, and deeply sorrowful. The boy felt a tide of affection grow, and he smiled back slowly. He stepped near her. She took his arms and placed them around her. She pulled his face against her own and slid her arms around him in a tight grip. Then she began kissing him about his mouth. The boy was too frightened to move. Her lips moved about his face more and more rapidly and then left him entirely.

"He's not doing anything!" the woman cried, tearing her face away for a moment and then throwing it back against his neck. Her shoulders shook and the boy knew she was crying. He heard and felt the giant sobs rolling through the body in his arms.

The man ran up behind him and began beating his hands on his back, shouting, "Kiss her! God damn you! Kiss her! Kiss her!"

He pushed him hard with both hands, and the boy and the woman tumbled to the sofa. The woman was weeping loudly. The boy stared and saw that her face was wracked with despair. Suddenly, she put her hands on his shoulders and shoved him away violently. He fell to the floor on his knees. He rose quickly and scampered across the room in panic, away from the man, who was glaring down at the woman with a wild, fiery expression, his fists clenched.

"It's no use!" she cried. "He's too young."

The man whirled upon the boy. "Go back to the office," he shouted angrily. "Tell them to send an older boy. Do you understand? An older boy. We want an older boy."

The boy nodded. He ran to the table and grabbed his cap, glancing quickly at the woman, whose loud, hysterical cries were tearing through the apartment. The man caught him when he started to the door.

"Wait a minute. Don't tell anybody anything. Forget what happened. Do you understand?"

"Tell them!" the woman cried. "Tell everybody!"

"Shut up, Helen. For Godsake, shut up."

The woman rose and ran to the boy, her face haggard with hysteria. "Tell everybody, Sidney," she sobbed. "Tell the whole damned world."

"Helen, shut up," the man pleaded, catching her shoulders. "Please shut up."

The boy watched her, unable to move. Her face was like chalk, shaking and cruelly distorted as she fought to break away.

The man raised his hand and slapped her across the face. She was stunned and stopped struggling. He backed her up slowly and set her down gently in a chair. He watched her sadly for a moment. Then he turned to the boy and walked him slowly to the door.

"Don't tell anyone a thing," he said quietly. He pushed the other ten-dollar bill into the boy's hand. "Forget all about it. Do you understand?"

The boy could hear the woman sobbing softly. Behind the man he could see her shoulders shaking in the chair.

"Remember now. Don't tell anyone. Okay?"

The boy nodded.

The man opened the door. "You'll forget all about it, won't you?"

The boy nodded again and stepped into the hall.

The door slammed shut.

Luther
Jay Neugeboren

Luther arrived at Booker T. Washington Junior High School (Columbus Avenue and 107th Street, Manhattan) in September of 1955, six months before I did. I met him at the end of February, the third week I taught there, when one of the assistant principals asked me to cover the cafeteria during fifth period for a teacher who had to be at a conference. "Good luck with the animals," I remember him saying.

I was on my guard when I entered the cafeteria; perhaps even a trifle scared. The stories I had been hearing in the teachers' lounge had prepared me to expect anything. During the winter months the students were not allowed to leave the lunchroom and the results of keeping them penned in—the fights, the food-throwing, the high-pitched incessant chattering in Spanish, the way the Negro and Puerto Rican boys and girls chased each other around the tables—such things did, I had to admit, give the room a zoo-like quality.

The day I was assigned, however, was a Catholic holy day and many of the students were absent. Those who remained filled a little less than half of the large room and though they were noisy, it was relatively easy to keep them in order. Luther sat at a table by himself, near the exit to the food-line. Occasionally, I noticed, a few boys would come and sit next to him. The third time I patrolled his area, however, his table was empty and he stopped me.

"Hey, man," he said, poking me in the arm to get my attention, "you new here?"

He had a stack of about ten cookies in his other hand and he put one into his mouth as he waited for an answer. When I told him that I was not new, he nodded and looked at me. "You have any trouble yet?"

"No," I said, as sternly as possible. Despite my feelings of sympathy for the students, I knew that if I ever hoped to get anywhere with them, I had to appear tough and confident. "No," I repeated, almost, I recall, as if I were challenging him. "I haven't."

Luther cocked his head to one side then and smiled slowly. "You will," he said, and went back to his cookies.

In the teachers' lounge, the first time I told the story, somebody asked if the boy who had stopped me was a little Negro kid, very black, with a slight hunchback. I said he was. The teachers laughed. "That's Luther," one of them said.

"He's batty," said another. "Just leave him be."

I repeated the story endlessly. It was the first anecdote of my teaching experience that excited admiration and some sort of reaction from those I told it to, and this was important to me then. I had no more direct encounters with Luther that term, though I did see him in the halls, between classes. I always smiled at him and he would smile back—or at least I thought he did. I could never be sure. This bothered me, especially the first time it happened. Through my retelling of the story, I realized, he had become so real to me, so much a part of my life that I think I took it for granted that our encounter had assumed equal significance in his life. The possibility that he had not even repeated the story to a single one of his friends disturbed me.

Once or twice during the term I spotted him wandering around the halls while classes were in session, slouching down the corridor, his body pressed against the tile walls. When I asked the other teachers if he was known for cutting classes, they told me again to just leave him be—that the guidance counselor had suggested that the teachers let him do what he wanted to. He was harmless, they said, *if* you left him alone. Those teachers who had him in their classes agreed with the guidance counselor. Left alone, he didn't annoy them. When he wanted to, he worked feverishly—and did competent work; but when he did not want to work he would either sit and stare, or just get up, walk out of the room, and wander around the building. He was, they concluded, a mental case.

I returned to Booker T. Washington Junior High School the following September, and Luther turned up in one of my English classes. He had changed. He was no longer small, having grown a good five inches over the summer, and he was no longer quiet. When classwork bored him now he would stand up, and instead of leaving the room, would begin telling stories. Just like that. He had his favorite topics, too—his cousin Henry who had epilepsy, Willie Mays, what was on sale at the supermarket, the football team he played on, the stories in the latest *Blackhawk* comic book. When he ran out of stories, he would pull *The National Enquirer* out of his back pocket and begin reading from it, always starting with an item in the "Personals" columns that had caught his eye. I never knew what to do. When I would yell at him to sit down and be quiet, he would wave his hand at me, impatiently, and continue. Moreover, no expression on his face, nothing he ever said, indicated that he thought he was doing anything wrong. An hour after disrupting a class, if I would see him in the corridor, he would give me a big smile and a hello. After a while, of course, I gave up even trying to interrupt him. I listened with the other students—laughing, fascinated, amazed.

I tried to remember some of his stories, but when I retold them they never seemed interesting, and so I purposely gave Luther's class a lot of composition work, trying to make the topics as imaginative as possible—with the hope, of course, that he would use one of them to let loose. But all of the topics, he declared, were "stupid" and he refused to write on any of them. Then, when I least expected it, when I assigned the class a "How To—" composition, he handed one in. It was typewritten on a piece of lined notebook paper, single-spaced, beginning at the very top of the page and ending just at the first ruled line. It was titled: "How To Steal Some Fruits":

> How To Steal Some Fruits, by Luther
> Go to a fruit store and when the fruitman isn't looking take some fruits. Then run. When the fruitman yells "Hey you stop taking those fruits" run harder. That is how to steal some fruits.

The next day he sat quietly in class. When I looked at him, he looked down at his desk. When I called on him to answer a question, he shrugged and looked away. At three o'clock, however, no more than five seconds after I had returned from escorting my official class downstairs, he bounded into my room, full of life, and propped himself up on the edge of my desk.

"Hey man," he said. "How'd you like my composition? It was deep, wasn't it?"

"Deep?"

"Deep, swift, *cool*—you know."

"I liked it fine," I said, laughing.

"Ah, don't put me on, man—how *was* it?"

"I liked it," I repeated, my hands clasped in front of me. "I mean it."

His face lit up. "You mean it? I worked hard on it, Mister Carter. I swear to God I did." It was the first time, I remember, that he had ever addressed me by my name. He stopped and wiped his mouth. "How'd you like the typing? Pretty good, huh?"

"It was fine."

"Christ, man," he said, stepping down from my desk and moving to the blackboard. He picked up a piece of chalk and wrote his name, printing it in capital letters. "How come you so tight? Why don't you loosen up? I ain't gonna do nothing. I just want to know about my composition. That's all."

I felt I could reach him, talk to him. I wanted to—had wanted to for some time, I realized, but he was right. I was tight, uncomfortable, embarrassed. "Where'd you get a typewriter?" I offered.

He smiled. "Where I get fruits," he replied, then laughed and clapped his hands. I must have appeared shocked, for before I could say anything, he was shaking his head back and forth. "Oh, man," he said. "You are really deep. I swear. You really are." He climbed onto my desk again. "You mind talking?"

"No," I said.

"Good. Let me ask you something—you married?"

"No," I said. "Do you think I should be married?"

"It beats stealing fruits," he said, and laughed again. His laugh was loud and harsh and at first it annoyed me, but then his body began rocking back and forth as if his comment had set off a chain of jokes that he was telling himself silently, and before I knew it I was laughing with him.

"I really liked the composition," I said. "In fact, I hope you don't mind, but I've already read it to some of the other teachers."

"No shit."

"They thought it was superb."

"It's superb," he said, shaking his head in agreement. "Oh, it's superb, man," he said, getting up again and walking away. His arms and legs moved in different directions and he seemed so loose that when he turned his back to me and I noticed the way his dirty flannel shirt was stretched tightly over his misshapen back, I was surprised—as if I'd noticed it for the first time. He walked around the room, muttering to himself, tapping on desks with his fingertips, and then he headed for the door. "I'm superb," he said. "So I be rolling on my superb way home—."

"Stay," I said.

He threw his arms apart. "You win!" he declared. "I'll stay." He came back to my desk, looked at me directly, then rolled his eyes and smiled. "People been telling stories to you about me?"

"No."

"None?" he questioned, coming closer.

"All right," I said. "Some—."

"That's all right," he said, shrugging it off. He played with the binding of a book that was on my desk. Then he reached across and took my grade book. I snatched it away from him and he laughed again. "Oh man," he exclaimed. "I am just so restless!—You know what I mean?"

He didn't wait for an answer, but started around the room again. The pockets of his pants were stuffed and bulging, the cuffs frayed. The corner of a red and white workman's handkerchief hung out of a back pocket. He stopped in the back of the room, gazed into the glass bookcase, and then turned to me and leaned back. "You said to stay—what you got to say?"

The question was in my mind, and impulsively I asked it: "Just curious—do you remember me from last year?"

"Sure," he said, and turned his back to me again. He looked in the bookcase, whirled around and walked to the side of the room, opening a window. He leaned out and just as I was about to say something to him about it, he closed it and came back to the front of the room. "Man," he exclaimed, sitting on my desk again. "Were you ever scared that day! If I'd set off a cherry bomb you'd have gone through the fan." He put his face closer to mine. "Man, you were scared green!"

"Was I scared of you, Luther?" I asked, looking straight into his eyes.

"Me? Nah. Nothing to be scared of." He hopped off the desk and wiped his name off the blackboard with the palm of his hand; then he started laughing to himself. He looked at me, over his shoulder. "Bet I know what you're thinking now," he said.

"Go ahead—."

"You're thinking you'd like to *help* a boy like me. Right? You're getting this big speech ready in your head about—."

"No," I interrupted. "I wasn't."

He eyed me suspiciously. "You sure?"

"I'm sure."

"Not even with compositions? Oh man, if you'd help me with compositions, before we'd be through with me, I'd be typing like a whiz." He banged on a desk with his palms, and then his fingers danced furiously on the wood as he made clicking noises inside his mouth. "Ding!" he said, swinging the carriage across. "Ain't it fun to type!"

"Okay," I said. "Okay. Maybe I was thinking that I would like to help you."

"I knew it, man," he said, to himself. "I just knew it."

"You have a good mind, Luther—much better than you let on."

"I do, I do," he muttered, chuckling. I stood up and went to the closet to get my coat. "Okay. What do I get if I work for you?" he asked.

I shrugged. "Nothing, maybe. I can't promise anything."

"I *like* that, man," he said.

"Could you call me Mister Carter?" I asked, somewhat irritably. "I don't call you, 'hey, you'—."

"Okay, Mister Carter," he said. He took my coat sleeve. "Let me help you on with your coat, Mister Carter."

We walked out of the room and I locked the door. "You ain't a *real* social worker like the others," he commented as we started down the stairs. He held the door open for me. "I do like that."

I nodded.

"Playing it close to the vest again, huh? Tight-mouthed."

"Just thinking," I said.

When we were outside he asked me what he had to do.

"For what?" I asked.

"To get you to help me to be somebody, to educate myself —all that stuff."

"Do what you want to do," I said. "Though you might start by doing your homework. Then we'll see—."

"I know," he said, cocking his head to one side again. "If I play ball with you you'll play ball with me. Right? Okay, okay. I know."

Then he was gone, running down the street, his arms spread wide as if he were an airplane, a loud siren-like noise rising and falling from him as he disappeared from view.

The next few months were without doubt the most satisfying to me of any during the eight years I've been a teacher. Luther worked like a fiend. He was bright, learned quickly, and was not really that far behind. He did his homework, he paid attention in class, he studied for tests, and he read books. That was most important. On every book he read I asked him to write a book report: setting, plot, theme, characters, and his opinion of the book—and once a week, on Thursday afternoons, we would get together in my room for a discussion. During the remainder of the term he must have gone through at least forty to fifty books. Most of them had to do with sports, airplanes, and insects. For some reason he loved books about insects. All the reports came to me typed, and on some he drew pictures—"illustrations" he called them, which, he claimed, would be a help to me in case I had not read the book.

When we would finish talking about books, I would help him with his other subjects, and his improvement was spectacular. I looked forward to my sessions with him, to his reports, to just seeing him—yet from day to day, from moment to moment, I always expected him to bolt from me, and this pleased me. Every time he came to me for a talk I was truly surprised.

When the term ended he asked if I would continue to help him. I said I would. He was not programmed for any of my English classes during the spring term, but we kept up with our weekly discussions. As the weather improved, however, he read less and less; I didn't want him to feel as if he *had* to come see me every Thursday, and so, about a week before the opening of the baseball season, I told him that I thought he had reached the point where he could go it alone. "When you feel like talking, just come knocking—" I said. "We don't need a schedule." He seemed relieved, I thought, and I was proud that I had had the sense to release him from any obligation he might have felt.

Then, suddenly, I didn't see him anywhere for three weeks. I asked his home-room teacher about him and she said she hadn't seen him either; she had sent him a few postcards, but had received no reply. That very night—it was almost as if he had been there listening, I thought—he telephoned me at home.

"Is this Mister Carter? This is Luther here."

"Hi, Luther," I said.

"I looked you up in the telephone book. You mind me calling you at home?"

"No, no. I don't mind."

"Okay," he said, breathing hard. "I just wanted to let you know not to worry about me because I'm not in school. Okay?"

"Sure," I said. "Sure."

"I had some things to take care of—you know?"

"Sure," I said.

"Man, you *know* you're itching to ask me *what?*" He laughed. "You are deep. I'll be back Monday."

That was all. On Monday, as he had promised, he returned to school and came to visit me in my room at three o'clock. We talked for a while about the way the pennant race was going, and then he said, "Okay, let's cut the jazz, man. I got something to say to you." He seemed very intense about it and I told him that I was listening carefully. He pointed a finger at me. "Now, we stopped our sessions, right?"

"Right," I said.

"And the day after we stopped, I began to play the hook for three straight weeks, right?"

"Right."

"Okay. Now you can tell me it ain't so, but I'll bet you'll be thinking it was your fault. It ain't. If you want the truth, I ain't done a stick of work all term for *any* teacher—so don't go thinking that I stopped being a good student cause we stopped our meetings."

He let out a long breath. "I'm glad you told me," I said.

"Shit, man," he said, getting up and going to the door. "Don't say anything, huh? Why you got to say something all the time?" He came toward me. *"Why?"* He was almost screaming and I slid my chair back from the desk. He shook his head frantically. "Why, man?" he said. He reached into his side-pocket and I started to stand up. Abruptly, he broke into laughter. "Oh man, you are deep! You are just so deep!" He clapped his hands and laughed at me some more. "Ra-ta-tat-tat!" he said as he banged on a desk. "You're real sweet, man! Just so sweet! Ra-ta-tat-tat! Comin' down the street!" He sat down in one of the seats. "But don't you worry none. I got seven liberry cards now and books growing out the ceiling. I got a liberry card for Luther King and one for Luther Queen and one for Luther Prince and one for Luther Jones and one for Luther Smith and one for Luther Mays and one for Luther B. Carter." He banged on the top of the desk with his fist, then drummed with his fingers again. "But don't you worry none—ra-ta-tat-tat—just don't you worry—."

"I'm not," I said.

"That's all," he said, and dashed out of the room.

He attended classes regularly for about two weeks and then disappeared again for a week. He returned for a few days, stayed away, returned. The pattern continued. In the halls when we saw each other he would always smile and ask if I was worrying and I would tell him I wasn't. Once or twice, when he was absent, he telephoned me at home and asked me what was new at school. He got a big charge out of this. Then another time, I remember, he came riding through the schoolyard on a bicycle during sixth period, when I was on patrol. "Don't report me, man!" he yelled and rode right back out, waving and shouting something in Spanish that made everybody laugh.

Near the end of May, the assistant principal in charge of the eighth grade called me into his office. He knew I was friendly with Luther, he said, and he thought that I might talk to the boy. For the past six or seven months, he told me, Luther had been in and out of juvenile court. "Petty thefts," the assistant principal explained. I wasn't surprised; Luther had hinted at this many times. I had never pressed him about it, however, not wanting to destroy our relationship by lecturing him. The assistant principal said he didn't care whether I said anything to Luther or not. In fact, he added, he would have been just as happy to get rid of him—but that before he was shipped off to a 600-school or put away somewhere else, he wanted to give me an opportunity to do what I could. More for me, he said, than for Luther.

About a week after this, on a Friday, Luther telephoned me.

"How've you been?" I asked.

"Superb, man," he said. "Hey listen—we ain't been seeing much of each other lately, have we?"

"No—."

"No. Okay. Listen—I got two tickets to see the Giants play tomorrow. You want to come?" I didn't answer immediately. "Come on—yes or no—tickets are going fast—."

"I'd like to," I said. "Yes. Only—only I was wondering where you got the money for the tickets?" I breathed out, glad I had said it.

Luther just laughed. "Oh man, you're not gonna be like that, are you? You been listening to too many stories again. That judge from the court must of been gassing with you. Tell you what—you come to the game and I'll tell you where I got the tickets. A deal?"

"A deal."

"Meet you in front of the school at eleven o'clock—I like to get there early to see Willie go through batting practice.

Batting practice—that's more fun than the game, sometimes. You know?"

He was waiting for me when I got there a few minutes before eleven the following day. "Let's go," he said, flourishing the tickets. "But don't ask me now, man—let's enjoy the game first. Okay?"

I did enjoy the game. The Giants were playing the Cardinals and to Luther's delight, Willie Mays had one of his better days, going three-for-four at bat, and making several brilliant plays in the field. For most of the game, I was truly relaxed. Along about the eighth inning, however, I began to think about the question again—to wonder when would be the best time to ask it. Luther, it seemed, had forgotten all about it. The Giants were winning 5–2.

"Oh man," he said. "If only that Musial don't do something, we're home free. Look at Willie!" he exclaimed. "Ain't he the greatest that ever lived. He is just so graceful! You know? How you like to see a team of Willie Mayses out there? Wow!" Wes Westrum, the Giant catcher, grounded out, short to first, and the eighth inning was over. "One to go, one to go," Luther said. Then he jabbed me in the arm with his finger. "Hey listen—I been thinking. Instead of an All-Star game every year between the leagues, what they ought to do one year is have the white guys against our guys. What you think?"

I shrugged. "I don't know," I said.

"Sure," he said. "Listen—we got Willie in center. Then we put Aaron in right and Doby in left. He's got the raw power. Some outfield, huh? Then we got Campy catching and Newcombe pitching. You can't beat that. That Newcombe—he's a mean son of a bitch, but he throws. Okay. I been thinking about this a long time—." He used his fingers to enumerate. He was excited, happy. "At first base we put Luke Easter, at second—Junior Gilliam, at short—Ernie Banks, and at third base we bring in old Jackie Robinson just to give the team a little class—you know what I mean? Man, what a line-up! Who could you match it with?"

When I said I didn't know, Luther eyed me suspiciously. "C'mon—Musial, Mantle, Williams, Spahn—you name 'em and I'll match 'em, man for man, your guys against ours." He stopped and cheered as a Cardinal popped out to Whitey Lockman at first. "What's the matter—don't you like the idea? Ha! Face it, man, we'd wipe up the field with you.

Swish! Swish!" He laughed and slapped me on the knee. "Hey, I know what's bugging you, I bet—." He leaned toward me, cupping his hand over his mouth, and whispered in my ear. "Tell the truth now, would you have ever offered to help me if I wasn't colored?"

"Would I—?" I stopped. "Sure," I said. "Of course I would. Of course—."

Luther smiled; triumphantly, dubiously. "Look," I said. "As long as we're asking questions, let me ask you something."

"About the tickets, right?"

"No," I said. "Forget the tickets. No long lectures, either. Just a question. Just one: how come you steal?"

"Oh man," he said, laughing. "That's an easy one!—Because I'm not getting what I want and when you don't get what you want, man, you got to take. Don't you know that?"

I stared at him, not sure I had heard right. He winked at me. "Enjoy the ballgame, man! Say hey, Willie!" he shouted, as Mays caught a fly ball, bread-basket style, for the second out. "Ain't he the sweetest!"

A minute later the game was over and the players were racing across the field toward the clubhouse in center field, trying to escape the fans who scrambled after them. "They won't get Willie," Luther said. "He's too swift, too swift."

When we were outside I thanked Luther and told him how much I had enjoyed the game. "How about a Coke or something?" I offered.

"Nah," he said. "I got things to do." He extended his hand quickly and I shook it, the first time we had ever done that. "Okay. You go get spiffed up and get a wife. Time you were married." He tossed his head back and laughed. "Ain't you married yet? No, no. *Smile,* man—how you gonna get a wife, never smiling." He started away, through the crowd. "Stay loose," he called back. "Don't steal no fruits."

I never questioned him again about stealing, but even if I had wanted to, I wouldn't have had much opportunity. He did not come to see me very often the rest of that year. When he returned to school in September of 1958 for his last year of junior high school, he had grown again. But not up. He never did go higher than the five-five or five-six he had reached by that time. He had taken up weightlifting over the summer, however, and his chest, his neck, his arms—they had all broadened incredibly. Instead of the dirty cotton and flannel shirts he had worn the two previous years, he now walked through the halls in laundry-white T-shirts, the sleeves rolled up to the shoulder, his powerful muscles exposed. There were always a half-dozen Negro boys following him around now also and they all dressed the way he did—white T-shirts, black chino pants, leather wrist straps, and—hanging from their necks on pieces of string—miniature black skulls.

The guidance counselor for the ninth grade came to me one day early in the term and asked me if I could give him any evidence against Luther. He claimed that Luther and his gang were going around the school, beating and torturing those students who refused to "loan" them money. All of the students, he said, were afraid to name Luther. "The kid's a born sadist," he added. I told him I didn't know anything.

The term progressed and the stories and rumors increased. I was told that the police in Luther's neighborhood were convinced that he and his gang were responsible for a series of muggings that had occurred. I tried not to believe it, but Luther all but gave me conclusive proof one afternoon, right before Christmas. He came into my room at three o'clock, alone, and said he had something for me. He said he trusted me not to tell anybody about it or show it to anyone. I said I wouldn't.

"Okay, man—here it is—." His eyes leapt around the room, frenzied, delirious. He took a little card from his wallet. "You might need this sometime—but don't ask me no questions. Ha! And don't you worry none. I'm doing okay. Expanding all the time. Don't you worry." I took the card from him. "See you now, Mister Carter. See you, see you."

He left and I looked at the card. Across the top was printed: THE BLACK AVENGERS, and below it was written: "Don't touch this white man. He's okay." It was signed by Luther and under his name he had drawn a skull and crossbones. I put the card in my wallet.

In January, to no one's great surprise, Luther was sent away to reform school in upstate New York. I was never exactly clear about the precise event that had led to it—the policeman assigned to our school said it had to do with brutally beating an old man; Luther's friends said it had to do with getting caught in a gang war. They claimed the fight was clean but that the cops had framed Luther. There was nothing in the papers, Luther had not contacted me, and I did not find out about it all until he had already been shipped off.

I received a postcard from him that summer. It was brief.

I hate it here. I can't say anymore or they'll beat shit out of me. I hate it. I'm reading some. I'll visit you when I get out and we'll have a session.

I answered the card with a letter. I told him I was sorry about where he was and that I'd be glad to talk to him whenever he wanted. I gave him some news of the school and included some current baseball clippings. I asked him if there was anything he needed and if there was anybody in his family he wanted me to get in touch with. I told him that in return for the time he'd taken me to the baseball game I had ordered a subscription to *Sport* magazine for him.

He replied with another post card.

Visiting day this summer is August 21. I'd like for you to come.

When I arrived, he seemed glad to see me, but I remember that he was more polite than he had ever been before, and more subdued. I wondered, at the time, if they were giving him tranquillizers. I was only allowed an hour with him and we spent most of that time just walking around the grounds— the school was a work-farm reformatory—not saying anything.

The visit, I could tell, was a disappointment to him. I don't know what he expected of me, but whatever it was, I didn't provide it. I wrote him a letter when I got home, telling him I had enjoyed seeing him and that I'd be glad to come again if he wanted me to. He didn't answer it, and I heard no more from him for a year and a half.

Then one day in the spring of 1961, just about the time of the Bay of Pigs invasion of Cuba, I remember, he popped into my room at school. He looked horrible. His face was unshaven, his clothes were filthy and ragged, his eyes were glazed. Underneath his clothes, his body had become flabby and he bent over noticeably when he walked. At first I didn't recognize him.

When I did, I was so glad to see him, I didn't know what to do. "Luther—for crying out loud!" I said, standing up and shaking his hand. "How the hell are you?"

He smiled at me. "I'm superb, man—can't you tell from looking at me?" He laughed then, and I laughed with him.

"You've gotten older," I said.

"Past sixteen," he said. "That means I don't got to go to school no more—"

He waited, but I didn't offer an opinion. "How about going down with me and having a cup of coffee? I'm finished here for the day—just getting through with mid-terms."

"Nah," he said, looking down and playing with his hands. "I gotta meet somebody. I'm late already. But I was in the neighborhood so I thought I'd come let you know I was still alive." He came to my desk and looked down. He shook his head as if something were wrong.

"What's the matter?" I asked.

"Don't see no wedding ring on your finger yet." He looked straight into my face. "Hey, man—you ain't a fag, are you?"

"No," I said, laughing. "Not that I know of—."

He laughed, his mouth opening wide. "Okay. That's all the gas for today. I'll see you, man."

During the next few months he visited me several times. Sometimes he looked good, sometimes bad—but I never could find out what he was doing with his days. He never gave a straight answer to my questions. More and more, I felt that he was asking me for some kind of help, but when I would touch on anything personal or even hint that I wanted to do something for him, with him, he would become defensive.

I didn't see him over the summer, but the following fall he came by periodically. He seemed to be getting a hold on himself, and sometimes he would talk about going to night school. Nothing came of the talk, though. In November he was arrested and sent to Riker's Island—to P.S. 616, the combination prison-school for boys between the ages of sixteen and twenty. His sentence was for eighteen months and during the first three months I visited him twice. Both times all he wanted to do was to talk about the English class we had had, and the stories and compositions he had made up. He said he was trying to remember some of them for the English teacher he had there, but couldn't do it all the time. He seemed to be in terrible shape, and I didn't have much hope for him.

So I was surprised when I began getting postcards from him again. "I am studying hard," the first one said. "There is a Negro who comes here to help me. I like him. I will be a new man when I come out. Yours sincerely, Luther." It was neatly and carefully written. The ones that followed were the same and they came at regular intervals of about five weeks. He told me about books he was reading, most of them having to do with Negro history, and about how he was changing. "Improving" was the word he used most.

I answered his cards as best I could, and offered to come

see him again, but he never took up any of my offers. When his eighteen months were up, I expected a visit from him. He never came. Sometimes I wondered what had become of him, but after the first few months passed and I didn't hear from him, I thought about him less and less. A year passed—two since we had last seen each other at Riker's Island—and then we met again.

I spotted him first. It was a beautiful summer night and I had gone up to Lewisohn Stadium for a concert. It had been good, I was relaxed and happy as I walked out of the stadium. Luther was standing at the corner of Amsterdam Avenue and 138th Street. He was wearing a dark blue suit, a white shirt and a tie. He was clean shaven, his hair was cut short and he looked healthy and bright. He was stopping people and trying to sell them newspapers.

"How are you, Mister Carter?" he asked, when I walked up to him. His eyes were clear and he seemed very happy to see me. "Interested in buying a newspaper to help the colored people? Only a dime—."

"No thanks," I said. The paper he was selling, as I had expected, was *Muhammad Speaks*, the newspaper of the Black Muslims. "You look fine," I added.

"Thanks—excuse me a second." He turned and sold a copy to somebody. People snubbed him but this didn't stop him from smiling or trying. I waited. When the crowd had gone, he asked me where I was going. "Home," I said. "Cup of coffee first?"

"No thanks," he said. "Thanks, but no thanks."

"When did all this start?" I asked, motioning to the newspapers.

"At Riker's Island," he said. He put up a hand, as if to stop my thoughts from becoming words. "I know what you're thinking, what you hear on TV and read in the newspapers about us—but don't believe everything. We're essentially a religious organization, as you may or may not know."

"I know," I said.

"And it's meant a lot to me—I couldn't have made it without their help. They—they taught me to *believe* in myself." His eyes glowed as he twisted his body toward me. "Can you understand that?" It seemed very important to him that I believe him. "*Can* you?" He relaxed momentarily and shrugged. "I don't believe everything they teach, of course, but I follow their precepts: I don't smoke, I don't drink, I don't curse, I don't go out with women who aren't Muslims

—I feel good *inside*, Mister Carter. Things are straightening themselves out." He paused. "It hasn't been easy."

"I know," I said, and smiled.

He nodded, embarrassed, I thought. "I'm going back to school also—."

"I'm glad."

"Even my body feels good! I'm lifting weights again, too," he said. Then he laughed and the sound tore through the warm night. His eyes were flashing with delight. "Oh man— someday I'll be the head of a whole damned army! Me and my old hunchback." He laughed again, pleased with himself. Then his laughter subsided and he patted me on the shoulder. "Oh man, you are still so deep, so deep. Don't worry none, Mister Carter. I don't go around advocating no violence." He chuckled. "I've got to go," he said, extending a hand. "It's been good seeing you again. Sure you don't want to buy a copy?"

"I'm sure," I said, shaking his hand. "Good luck to you, Luther. I'm glad to see you the way you are now—."

"Thanks." We looked at each other for a minute and he smiled warmly at me. Then I started toward the subway station. When I had crossed the street he called to me.

"Hey—Mister Carter—!"

I turned.

"Let me ask you something—do you still have that card I gave you?" He howled at this remark. "Oh man, I'd save that card if I were you! I'd do that. You never know when you might need it. You never know—."

I started back across the street, toward him. He tossed his head back and roared with laughter. "You never know, you never know," he repeated, and hurried away from me, laughing wildly. I stared at him until he disappeared in the darkness. Then I just stood there, dazed, unable to move—I don't know for how long. Finally I made myself turn around, and as I walked slowly toward the lights of Broadway all I could feel was the presence of his muscular body, powerful, gleaming, waiting under his white shirt, his clean suit.

Hoods I Have Known
Sondra Spatt

Whenever I reminisce about old beaux, I begin with poor Larry Dinhofer, who sat behind me in the eighth grade and asked me to the P.S. 333 prom because I asked him to my graduation party. From gratitude for that first invitation, Larry's mother bought me a monstrous bottle of Sweet Primrose toilet water, which I have kept to this day. The primroses or whatever they were have become so fermented through the years that I now use it for rubbing alcohol and think "Dinhofer" whenever I have an ache in my back. But strictly speaking, although memorable, Larry was not my first but only my first respectable beau. Before Larry I had an unrespectable romance, long suppressed, a seventh-grade affair with the dirty, untrustworthy Danny Tooey, who was a hood.

Perhaps I should explain about hoods. Hoods in Brooklyn are boys who go to school only by the grace of the truant officer, "hood" being short for "hoodlum." "Juvenile delinquent" is a much longer word and not half as piquant. Our seventh-grade hoods were comparatively unaggressive. They never did much but loaf at the back of the class and throw spitballs at each other, sometimes at the teacher. They wore dungarees or chartreuse pants with pistol pockets in imitation of the Avenue E Boys, who were model hoods and real court cases. Our hoods, although harmless, grew aggressive-looking sideburns and great masses of curly black or blond hair. All of them shaved. Danny Tooey was the biggest, tallest, hairiest of the lot and the one who had been left back most often. He was fifteen.

When Danny was first left back into our class, we ignored each other. Our social milieux, even in school, were different. I sat in the front of the room, covered my books, raised my hand in answer to all questions and agreed with the teacher on all points. I had already set my eye on the General Excellence Award at graduation. Danny, as I have already pointed out, never did anything in school except pledge allegiance to the flag, proving that hoods were untrustworthy but not unpatriotic.

Danny did not cover books; he destroyed them. Miss Malcolm thought well-bound books in hoody hands a waste, so Danny scattered the leaves of his worn-out volumes like nuts in May, sometimes maliciously, more often from the sort of pure disinterest playboys show when they run their Jaguars off cliffs in the movies. No one had ever called upon Danny to read from these books, you see. It was *l'acte gratuit*.

When I fell into disgrace, Danny was the first hood whose friendship I won. I was in with the leader of the gang, so to speak. I had been the Winged Messenger of the seventh grade and scurried around corridors clutching notes from Miss Malcolm with the expression postmen have when they meet up with the sleet or snow or fog people have been telling them about. I took my messenger position seriously, even though the notes, whenever I paused to open them, revealed nothing more serious than a date for tea or a lift to the beauty parlor. One day Miss Malcolm decided to affix a postscript to a note that she'd dispatched with me and came around a corner unexpectedly, giving both of us a shock.

"Since you have proved yourself a criminal, I'm going to treat you that way," she announced pontifically before the class, and made me clean out my desk and remove my books and self to the back of the room.

As a criminal, I found myself in a peculiar position. It had only been a note asking for more toilet supplies for the teachers' rest room, and hardly worth the drastic punishment, I felt. It was a mundane confidence I'd broken, though Miss Malcolm had mysteriously underlined "toilet supplies" for some reason I could not fathom. Nevertheless, I was disgraced, not only with the teacher but with all my friends. From that day on Miss Malcolm would not call on me in class, even though I was the only one who knew the three most important Atlantic fishing ports and waved my arm wildly like a drowning Atlantic fisherman. She instructed the class to ignore me too. My friends from the front of the room, oh, perfidy, had been waiting all these years, I found, praying that I would fall from grace. They simply would not turn their heads or accept my notes.

Instead of being crushed by my fate I was confident and not at all apologetic. After all, I was the star pupil. And what would Miss Malcolm do without me when we reached the difficult Middle Atlantic States? As for my friends, "those schmoey kids" as I called them, my contempt for them was boundless. I vowed if I ever achieved my pure state again I'd make them suffer.

Miss Malcolm seated Danny and me in a double seat, thinking, dear woman, that close contact with a hood was the worst punishment anyone could inflict on a clean, well-brought-up little girl. She expected me to cry and beg to be let back, at least to the class middle. That was because Miss Malcolm herself was afraid of that hairy creature who slouched into class with disquieting tread and rumbled unintelligible answers deep in his throat. "Urghs" was Danny's favorite comment, and it frightened Miss Malcolm.

When I arrived at the last seat, last row, Danny didn't know quite what to think. I was obviously a pseudo hood and not destined to stay very long. Danny didn't rumble anything at me but regarded me mildly, even amusedly, that first afternoon. "You staying here, little girl?" he asked sarcastically as I piled my books in the desk. His tone implied that I didn't look dangerous enough to merit such a position. I don't think Danny fully realized the moral turpitude of note-reading.

No, I didn't think I was going to stay with Danny long either, at first. But days went by, and Miss Malcolm's gaze never glided past the dividing line—Raymond de Fato, who occasionally threw a spitball but wore a tie. I began to grow more and more uncomfortable. The classroom was long and crowded. Because of scufflings and murmurings around me I couldn't hear anything that was going on past Raymond; Raymond wouldn't tell me, and even if I did hear no one would call on me. But I could not go to Miss Malcolm begging to be let back. I was proud.

I began to bring *Jane Eyre* to school and spent the whole day reading ferociously. But even that splendid book couldn't make up for the fact that I was missing the Middle Atlantic States. Nor did snubbing Miss Malcolm every day in front of the coatroom bring the desired satisfaction. I couldn't complain at home because my mother thought I should beg for mercy. She said I was "a stubborn fool" and "just like your father." I was an outcast and everybody knew it.

I would have been completely miserable if Danny hadn't decided to take me into his group.

Danny began making the first overtures by looking on with me as I read *Jane Eyre*. Of course I was surprised. Until then it had been mere peaceful coexistence. I didn't even know

Danny could read. He'd just sat for days looking at me sardonically from under his tousle of black curls. Occasionally he had cocked an eyebrow at me and his entire broad and grimy brow had moved.

"Dat looks like a good book," he said to me one day, looking interested, and I immediately lent him my four-color pencil to doodle with. From then on we were friends. Even the good girls in my class didn't read Brontë because they couldn't understand words like "choler" and "lineaments." Such praise from a hood made me glow with pleasure.

Our friendship was sealed next day, when we had an examination. Danny gave me his rabbit foot for keeps. It was for luck, he explained, and you could write the answers on a little piece of paper in the claw.

"Are you sure you don't want it?" I remember asking diffidently. "You probably need it more than I do."

"Oh, I can copy off you—dat's all right," he said.

I really didn't want that rabbit foot. A crib sheet was a little too far out on the road to dishonesty for a former star pupil, and I knew my New England products backward and forward anyway. Still, I accepted the foot for luck and as a token. I still remember the softness of it, and the little sharpnesses that were the nails.

The next thing Danny did was introduce me to the boys. This was difficult, but he managed to get them to ask me to lend them pencils. They were the shiest hoods imaginable. There were really ten of us in the back, but I only got to know five: Danny, Harry la Marca, Alan Brodnik, Ronny Abry and Jo-Jo Begoyne.

These were the Destry Road Boys. Because of his age, ability and the fact that he had been approached by the Avenue E Boys for possible merger, Danny was definitely the leader. He ruled with an iron hand. Once Harry and Jo-Jo had a fight in the back of the room, and they might have ripped each other to pieces if Danny hadn't broken it up. They moved silently, slowly, crouching a little by the door to the gym. "You never seen a shiv fight before?" Danny asked when he saw my wonder afterward, and he showed me the knives, six inches long.

"Dose guys are gonna get into real trouble one day—dey're only tirteen—dey don't have any sense," he said. During the fight Miss Malcolm had gone on with the class in the front of the room as though nothing was happening. After twenty years of dealing with crime Miss Malcolm had found her method—the silent or you-don't-exist treatment.

The boys got a great deal of pleasure out of telling me about shiv fights and how the Avenue E Boys got away with robbing a candy store. The Destry Road Boys had never gotten away with anything because they had never pulled anything, except turning in false alarms, which any five-year-old can do. They were a small-time bunch and they knew it. Our neighborhood, Newton Park, was just too quiet and genteel to start any trouble, and there wasn't any point going over to Avenue E to find some because Danny wouldn't let them. "You want to get your heads knocked off?" he asked. Danny was the most cautious, perhaps because he was the only gang leader I've ever known. He'd been around and he knew that it was safest to do nothing and if anybody asked you anything to just mumble along.

I found that I too could expound to the boys on topics they hadn't heard before, usually last month's lessons. I think I may have been more interesting than Miss Malcolm, because when I told them about Cortes in Mexico and killing the great chief Montezuma, their eyes gleamed and they clasped imaginary sword handles. Alan Brodnik expressed a desire to make a poniard or a rapier in shop that week. "Swords, dat's all you guys need," Danny said in disgust, but I could see that he was interested too.

"Why didn't dey make a deal wit Montezuma and get a percentage?" he asked me once when I got involved with the more intricate dealings. "A percentage is better. Dopey Spaniards." I could see that Danny had everything all figured out.

I had been sitting in the back of the room for a week and a half when I began to notice a perceptible change in Danny. He began to wear white polo shirts instead of his old, saggy yellow one and smelled faintly of Ivory soap. His face was clean and his hair was somehow higher, pulled together into a compact pompadour. Danny even turned his club jacket inside out so that the plain black showed instead of the worn fuchsia silk with its huge black "Destry Boys" lettering. " 'Stoo flashy," Danny said, and that afternoon, after lunch, all the boys had their jackets turned around too.

Soon, whenever Danny and I read together because of Danny's pageless volumes, his fingers curled around my white-clean covers were white-clean too. The fingers also turned the pages exactly right, which proved that Danny could actually read as fast as I did. I began to think that Danny wasn't really a hood, or was just pretending, or that being a hood wasn't so bad at all if only the teacher would notice you. If we listened very carefully, Danny and I, we could hear Miss Malcolm's voice reading *Evangeline* far off, and once, when we got to the part that goes

Black were her eyes as the berry that grows on the thorn by the wayside—
Black, yet how softly they gleamed beneath the brown shade of her tresses!
Sweet was her breath as the breath of kine that feed in the meadows . . .

Danny bent over and whispered. "She looks like you."

Since I was definitely blond and blue-eyed, and since Danny had never whispered before in his life, I began to think something was wrong. Or, if Danny was becoming poetic, something might be right. But anyway—something. Yes, I thought rather priggishly, Danny has probably never sat next to a good poetry-reading little girl in his life; my presence has probably opened the door to a whole new world of clean-smelling respectability.

It occurred to me that I might tame Danny and turn him into a star pupil, thus killing two birds with one stone and getting me a seat in Respectability too. Why, I could probably persuade Danny to take elocution lessons. Then he could learn to pronounce "th" and other things and Miss Malcolm would understand him. I had a little difficulty myself sometimes. And if I could convince his mother to get him some crisp white shirts and a tie. . . . Maybe my mother would iron them for him if Mrs. Tooey was busy.

Ronny, Harry, Alan and Jo-Jo, although they showed no immediate signs of conversion, might still follow their leader out of hood-hood and I would have a whole gang to my credit. I could learn to iron shirts myself. Soon I would walk down Destry Road to be pointed at and stared at by the citizenry. "There's the girl who saves hoods," ladies would say as they waited on line by the fruit counter at Willy's. "Can you come and talk to my boy after school?" "Dere's dat dame." The Avenue E Boys would scowl and lurk behind the gum machine in front of Harry's. "She's the one who's been takin' our best material. Why, Danny Tooey, he could've been the best hood in Brooklyn, he's studyin' for the ministry."

Yes, I would save Danny. I determined to bring my *Believe-It-Or-Not* Ripley book to school immediately so Danny could begin assimilating the mass of interesting facts so necessary to star pupils. We would sit in the first row, side by side.

Alas. While I had been making plans for reformation, I had overlooked the real reason for Danny's behavior, which was, of course, sex. Danny Tooey wanted me to be more than just a friend. On Friday morning, May 11, Danny asked me to go to the movies with him the next evening, May 12. Not in the afternoon. In the evening. It was a sword-fighting picture, he said, and I would like it. I was shocked. Respectable seventh-grade girls, especially me, didn't wear lipstick or go out with boys; eighth-grade girls could wear lipstick and go out, if they didn't make too much fuss about it. But no decent girl ever went anywhere, morning or evening, with a hood.

Oh, yes, there were a few. But they were scrawny and inky-haired and went to P.S. 293 and only appeared hanging around outside by the homogenized-bagel man at three o'clock. They weren't decent either. Because when the boys didn't show up, they would flirt with the homogenized-bagel man, and when he wasn't there they would go to Harry's and stand in front of the gum machine. And they would make remarks like "Look who's here," whenever someone passed. The Avenue E Dolls, an auxiliary of the Boys, set the fashion in this case, and any girl hood who didn't have long black hair had to grow it or dye it quick, or run the risk of not being à la mode hood. A la mode hood also meant doe eyes, ultrabright lipstick, gold bangle earrings, cheap, tight skirts and the black and white uniform: black bra and white sweater or white bra and black sweater. And no slip. These girls didn't need to wear bras and I did. Only I didn't, and always felt self-conscious when I passed Harry's Candy Store in my light lawn dresses.

No, I couldn't possibly go out with Danny. I might convert him, but I couldn't go out with him. He probably would want me to kiss him in the movies. I knew what went on in the Destry Theatre; I went every Saturday night with my mother and father; I knew. Those hoods. Surely Danny with all his hoodish savoir-faire knew that a girl in a pinafore dress, long blond braids and well-fed expression was highly inappropriate for the leader of a gang. It was just the lure of the unknown, and was, of course, impossible.

I told Danny politely that I appreciated the thought but didn't think my mother would let me go out since I was only eleven years old. I had skipped several grades, I explained. Danny was very understanding about it and said I certainly looked older. At the end of the day I gave him my *Believe-It-Or-Not* Ripley book for keeps, saying that my mother had refused permission at lunchtime but that this was for him, blushing all the while, I suppose. Danny was very embarrassed. He didn't blush, at first only mumbled "Urghs," but later came over to me at the coatroom and said: "Tanks. I don't know how to make just retribution." He was sweet about the whole thing.

Actually, I hadn't told my mother about Danny's invitation at all. I doubted whether she'd think the connection savory. But I thought about this, my almost first date, all the way home from school and all weekend. In fact, I couldn't stop thinking about it. No sooner would I settle down with my favorite book than the name Tooey would intrude itself into my mental stream. I felt the irresistible urge to write Danny Tooey, Danny or just plain D. T. on all my clean book covers. Finally, in desperation, I wrote Yeoot Ynnad very small in the top of my stationery box. Such a thing had never happened to me before.

I decided to look up similar occurrences in my library, my highest source of wisdom. But mine proved an unprecedented occurrence. Heathcliff had been bad and Cathy had decided to be his girl friend, but he hadn't reformed and they had both died. That was the best I could find. But still . . . Jane Eyre wouldn't marry Mr. Rochester when he was already married to Bertha, so it didn't seem right for me to go out with Danny while he was still a hood. But after he reformed . . . it would probably take till eighth grade and then we could go out legitimately. Girls in the eighth grade not only went out, they could kiss too.

My mother noticed my mood of sorrowful melancholy, interspersed with come-hither glances and a slight puckering motion of the lips, and wrongly attributed my strange behavior to worry about the Middle Atlantic States. She instructed me to sue for Miss Malcolm's favor immediately or she would come up to school herself. Poor Mamma. How was she to know? After all, I had been a terrible bookworm, and I was only eleven years old.

When I went to the movies Saturday night with my parents I tried to reconstruct Danny's features. All that hair made it difficult; it was all I could reconstruct. Underneath Danny was handsome, I decided, and the features of the man on the screen melted, dimmed and turned Tooeyesque in the darkness. What if it had not been my father sitting next to me, wheezing slightly from the air conditioning? What if it had been . . . To this day I can give no accurate description of Danny. The years have blurred even that blurry face. No matter how handsome and hairy and suave the fifteen-year-old Danny may have been, I hardly think he could have looked as I still picture him today—the precise image of Clark Gable.

Coming out of the Destry after the show, I managed to walk into an embarrassing situation. There stood Alan Brodnik, leaning against the fire hydrant, his arms round a girl. Alan looked at me appealingly and removed his arms. I made no comment, walked by without turning my head. My heart was sad though, oh, sad. For what if it had been Yeoot Ynnad?

When I arrived at school Monday morning I found our backseat idyl broken. No longer could we peruse the same book like lion and lamb. Danny and I breathed hard and stared in whatever direction was opposite; we both mumbled. At last I had enough courage to ask Danny if he had learned anything interesting from the *Believe-It-Or-Not* Ripley book. He only looked at me vaguely and mumbled "Urghs." He had retrogressed.

Danny continued shy all day and did not speak to me. But he gave long, piteous glances and drew girls' heads in ink on the backs of his hands. This was terrible. I decided to follow Danny after school and make him talk to me. It was only to find out something of his home life for future reform, I told myself. When three o'clock and Danny and Harry, Jo-Jo, Alan and Ronny broke upon the homogenized-bagel man, I was there too.

The boys looked at me curiously. All the other little girls were retreating away from school as fast as they could go, backs straight and heads held high. Was it true? Was it true? Jo-Jo winked at Harry. Danny said nothing but asked me if I wanted salt on my bagel. No, don't buy me bagels, don't, I felt like crying out. I don't *want* to be your girl friend. I just want to find out about your home life. However, I took one with salt.

Danny seemed relaxed and at ease now. He spoke animatedly, even vivaciously, and I could catch nearly every word he was saying. He took my arm and headed me, yes, toward Harry's Candy Store. The boys followed. I would not go to Harry's Candy Store, I told myself firmly, I would not under any conditions go to Harry's Candy Store. . . .

On the way to the candy store, Danny told me about his job as utility man, whatever that was, on a small fishing boat out of Sheepshead Bay. The boat and Danny left every day at three in the morning and didn't return till eight-thirty, just in time to drop Danny off for school. "Dat's why I'm so sleepy in da mornings," Danny explained.

When he was sixteen, next year, he wouldn't have to come to school any more and could be a full-time fisherman. How exciting, I thought, thinking of *Captains Courageous*, but then I remembered. If Danny left school, he'd never reach eighth grade, and what would happen to his "th's" and his white shirts and . . . our date for the movies. Even if he became a fisherman—? what if there were a fish famine or something? Without me Danny would have to go back to being a hood. I would not let that happen. I would persuade Danny not to leave school. I would go with him to Harry's Candy Store every day and stand around with him near the gum machine.

When we reached Harry's, there were no girls from 293 around, thank goodness. Danny did nothing worse than hitch himself up on the wooden rack that held the newspapers and let his feet dangle on the New York *Post*. He'd been working since he was ten, he said, and it was all right. Except when the weather was bad and he didn't get paid. Or just got paid in fish. His Aunt Bella didn't like fish he added a little glumly; she hated fish.

Aunt Bella's strong aversion to fish was all I ever found out about Danny Tooey's home life. "Look who's here," Danny said next, and when I looked, there stood Miss Malcolm.

"I want to talk to you, dear," she said.

Miss Malcolm and I walked home together. We had a long, intimate conversation on the way, though I couldn't imagine why. I still hadn't apologized, and I certainly wasn't going to. I suppose Miss Malcolm had come out of school at three and seen her ex-star pupil in informal conversation with a recognized hood. Poor Miss Malcolm. She thought she'd been responsible for starting me on a life of crime.

"You don't know it, dear, but I've been watching you," she said. I clutched my stationery box, but she only took my arm as we crossed the street as though I was her little girl.

"I've noticed how unhappy you've been at the back of the room. You've just been moping around and moping around, haven't you?"

I made no reply. I wondered what Miss Malcolm wanted me to do for not telling my mother about Harry's Candy Store. Yes, blackmail was on my mind. I had the makings of a first-class hood.

"You've been unhappy because you've wanted to come up to me and apologize for reading my note, haven't you?"

We were nearing my home. I thought about walking Miss Malcolm right past it and right on down to Sheepshead Bay. We could go down to the pier and watch the fishing boats come in. My Lord, I really was a fiendish child, now that I think of it.

"But you've been afraid. You've been afraid I was going to say something unkind, weren't you?"

She patted me kindly on the arm. I thought of how I had walked past her every morning on my way to the coatroom, my head held high.

"But you know, I wouldn't have said anything unkind. Because I like you, dear. I think you're my best pupil."

I still didn't say anything. I was her best pupil. I wondered what Miss Malcolm was planning to study next. It must be something harder than the Middle Atlantic, because three people had raised their hands that day and she didn't need me.

"And because I know you've wanted to apologize for a long time, tomorrow morning I am going to let you come back to the first seat, first row."

I couldn't stop the pleasure that I felt.

I didn't know why I had been reinstated but I was glad. Justice, as I had always maintained, does triumph. And oh, what I would do to all those schmoey kids. I was a nasty-good little girl.

Miss Malcolm came inside the house to meet my mother and we all had tea. I didn't mind taking the enemy inside. Danny would approve, I was sure. And from my influential position, what couldn't I do for my friends. Soon I would convince Miss Malcolm of Danny's merits—and then . . .

"Do you think seventh-grade girls are too young to go out?" I remember asking Miss Malcolm as Mamma poured tea.

Alas, again. All my plans were in vain. The end of the affair came next day.

As Miss Malcolm announced the happy news and I carried my books away from our scarred double seat to my honored one, Danny stared at me sullenly without saying a word. He didn't say good-by, but on my last trip to the front of the room he piled his *Believe-It-Or-Not* Ripley book on top of my grammar and the stationery box with the secret Yeoot Ynnad. He looked at me as though from across a million rows of double seats. Then he turned back to carving his name on the desk.

Hurt and bewildered, I couldn't understand Danny's heartlessness. I followed him out of the school building at three, lingered shyly by the homogenized-bagel man, but he just walked away. His back was slouched and his hair was no longer kempt. He was whistling.

After this I never went near Danny or any of the other boys again. And when Larry Dinhofer asked me for a date to the senior prom I pretended that he was the first. But I always kept track of the Destry Road Boys, secretly, ashamedly. I felt a strong sense of communion with them and liked to think that my short stay had done them all good. Alan and Ronny and Harry went on to high school with me, but were put in special RX classes where they could sit around all day and throw spitballs without being disturbed by anyone. They just had a happy, lazy time. Occasionally I'd glimpse them having refreshments in front of the school. It was a different, nonhomogenized-bagel man, but the same boys all right. When I passed they would stare but never make any sign of recognition.

Although none of the Destry Boys ever made Honor Society or anything like that, they never got any more delinquent than they were. As it turned out, only one boy from P.S. 333 ever ended up in jail, and that was Larry Dinhofer. He robbed a liquor store, and he had always worn white cuffs and sat in the first row, and no one I know has ever found a logical explanation. So Larry does belong among the hoods I've known after all. Alan Brodnik, bless him, was the only Destry Boy whose degenerate career I followed after high school. I've lost touch with him since, but the last I heard he'd turned up at Brooklyn College carrying *Tropic of Capricorn* and wearing a neat black goatee and a red velvet cummerbund. I never could quite understand that one either.

As for Danny, I never saw him after graduation. In fact, I don't think he stayed around that long but left after his sixteenth birthday sometime in March. I believe he gave the Destry Road Boys to Jo-Jo because he was the smartest. By that time my wounded feelings had healed, since I'd decided what had motivated him. It was all due to Danny's pure moral philosophy or something, I deduced, that was stronger than mere romance. Hoods didn't do anything but pledge allegiance to the flag. Star pupils sat in the first row. We just couldn't be friends. It was against all established codes, and Danny supported codes. I had to admire that.

Someone I know says she thinks she saw someone who looked like Danny in a summer theatre production in Woodstock last year. She said that he was still big and had a lot of hair but that he spoke English perfectly. She said he was sweet and looked like Marlon Brando. Despite what my friend says, I don't like to think Danny became an actor. I don't like to think that at all. It makes me sad and a little embarrassed, for that would mean after all my seventh-grade heartbreak and eleven-year-old plans somebody else had reformed Danny after all. I'd rather have him be a fisherman. I'd rather have him be a hood.

Sonny's Blues
James Baldwin

I read about it in the paper, in the subway, on my way to work. I read it, and I couldn't believe it, and I read it again. Then perhaps I just stared at it, at the newsprint spelling out his name, spelling out the story. I stared at it in the swinging lights of the subway car, and in the faces and bodies of the people, and in my own face, trapped in the darkness which roared outside.

It was not to be believed and I kept telling myself that, as I walked from the subway station to the high school. And at the same time I couldn't doubt it. I was scared, scared for Sonny. He became real to me again. A great block of ice got settled in my belly and kept melting there slowly all day long, while I taught my classes algebra. It was a special kind of ice. It kept melting, sending trickles of ice water all up and down my veins, but it never got less. Sometimes it hardened and seemed to expand until I felt my guts were going to come spilling out or that I was going to choke or scream. This would always be at a moment when I was remembering some specific thing Sonny had once said or done.

When he was about as old as the boys in my classes his face had been bright and open, there was a lot of copper in it; and he'd had wonderfully direct brown eyes, and great gentleness and privacy. I wondered what he looked like now. He had been picked up, the evening before, in a raid on an apartment downtown, for peddling and using heroin.

I couldn't believe it: but what I mean by that is that I couldn't find any room for it anywhere inside me. I had kept it outside me for a long time. I hadn't wanted to know. I had had suspicions, but I didn't name them, I kept putting them away. I told myself that Sonny was wild, but he wasn't crazy. And he'd always been a good boy, he hadn't ever turned hard or evil or disrespectful, the way kids can, so quick, so quick, especially in Harlem. I didn't want to believe that I'd ever see my brother going down, coming to nothing, all that light in his face gone out, in the condition I'd already seen so many others. Yet it had happened and here I was, talking about algebra to a lot of boys who might, every one of them for all I knew, be popping off needles every time they went to the head. Maybe it did more for them than algebra could.

I was sure that the first time Sonny had ever had horse, he couldn't have been much older than these boys were now. These boys, now, were living as we'd been living then, they were growing up with a rush and their heads bumped abruptly against the low ceiling of their actual possibilities. They were filled with rage. All they really knew were two darknesses, the darkness of their lives, which was now closing in on them, and the darkness of the movies, which had blinded them to that other darkness, and in which they now, vindictively, dreamed, at once more together than they were at any other time, and more alone.

When the last bell rang, the last class ended, I let out my breath. It seemed I'd been holding it for all that time. My clothes were wet—I may have looked as though I'd been sitting in a steam bath, all dressed up, all afternoon. I sat alone in the classroom a long time. I listened to the boys outside, downstairs, shouting and cursing and laughing. Their laughter struck me for perhaps the first time. It was not the joyous laughter which—God knows why—one associates with children. It was mocking and insular, its intent was to denigrate. It was disenchanted, and in this, also, lay the authority of their curses. Perhaps I was listening to them because I was thinking about my brother and in them I heard my brother. And myself.

One boy was whistling a tune, at once very complicated and very simple, it seemed to be pouring out of him as though he were a bird, and it sounded very cool and moving through all that harsh, bright air, only just holding its own through all those other sounds.

I stood up and walked over to the window and looked down into the courtyard. It was the beginning of the spring and the sap was rising in the boys. A teacher passed through them every now and again, quickly, as though he or she couldn't wait to get out of that courtyard, to get those boys out of their sight and off their minds. I started collecting my stuff. I thought I'd better get home and talk to Isabel.

The courtyard was almost deserted by the time I got downstairs. I saw this boy standing in the shadow of a doorway, looking just like Sonny. I almost called his name. Then I saw that it wasn't Sonny, but somebody we used to know, a boy from around our block. He'd been Sonny's friend. He'd never been mine, having been too young for me, and, anyway, I'd never liked him. And now, even though he was a grown-up man, he still hung around that block, still spent hours on the street corners, was always high and raggy. I used to run into him from time to time and he'd often work around to asking me for a quarter or fifty cents. He always had some real good excuse, too, and I always gave it to him, I don't know why.

But now, abruptly, I hated him. I couldn't stand the way he looked at me, partly like a dog, partly like a cunning child. I wanted to ask him what the hell he was doing in the school courtyard.

He sort of shuffled over to me, and he said, "I see you got the papers. So you already know about it."

"You mean about Sonny? Yes, I already know about it. How come they didn't get you?"

He grinned. It made him repulsive and it also brought to mind what he'd looked like as a kid. "I wasn't there. I stay away from them people."

"Good for you." I offered him a cigarette and I watched him through the smoke. "You come all the way down here just to tell me about Sonny?"

"That's right." He was sort of shaking his head and his eyes looked strange, as though they were about to cross. The bright sun deadened his damp dark brown skin and it made his eyes look yellow and showed up the dirt in his kinked hair. He smelled funky. I moved a little away from him and I said, "Well, thanks. But I already know about it and I got to get home."

"I'll walk you a little ways," he said. We started walking. There were a couple of kids still loitering in the courtyard and one of them said goodnight to me and looked strangely at the boy beside me.

"What're you going to do?" he asked me. "I mean, about Sonny?"

"Look. I haven't seen Sonny for over a year, I'm not sure I'm going to do anything. Anyway, what the hell *can* I do?"

"That's right," he said quickly, "ain't nothing you can do. Can't much help old Sonny no more, I guess."

It was what I was thinking and so it seemed to me he had no right to say it.

"I'm surprised at Sonny, though," he went on—he had a funny way of talking, he looked straight ahead as though he were talking to himself—"I thought Sonny was a smart boy, I thought he was too smart to get hung."

"I guess he thought so too," I said sharply, "and that's how he got hung. And how about you? You're pretty goddamn smart, I bet."

Then he looked directly at me, just for a minute. "I ain't smart," he said. "If I was smart, I'd have reached for a pistol a long time ago."

"Look. Don't tell *me* your sad story, if it was up to me, I'd give you one." Then I felt guilty—guilty, probably, for never having supposed that the poor bastard *had* a story of his own, much less a sad one, and I asked, quickly, "What's going to happen to him now?"

He didn't answer this. He was off by himself some place. "Funny thing," he said, and from his tone we might have been discussing the quickest way to get to Brooklyn, "when I saw the papers this morning, the first thing I asked myself was if I had anything to do with it. I felt sort of responsible."

I began to listen more carefully. The subway station was on the corner, just before us, and I stopped. He stopped, too. We were in front of a bar and he ducked slightly, peering in, but whoever he was looking for didn't seem to be there. The juke box was blasting away with something black and bouncy and I half watched the barmaid as she danced her way from the juke box to her place behind the bar. And I watched her face as she laughingly responded to something someone said to her, still keeping time to the music. When she smiled one saw the little girl, one sensed the doomed, still-struggling woman beneath the battered face of the semi-whore.

"I never *give* Sonny nothing," the boy said finally, "but a long time ago I come to school high and Sonny asked me me how it felt." He paused, I couldn't bear to watch him, I watched the barmaid, and I listened to the music which seemed to be causing the pavement to shake. "I told him it felt great." The music stopped, the barmaid paused and watched the juke box until the music began again. "It did."

All this was carrying me some place I didn't want to go. I certainly didn't want to know how it felt. It filled everything the people, the houses, the music, the dark, quicksilver barmaid, with menace; and this menace was their reality.

"What's going to happen to him now?" I asked again.

"They'll send him away some place and they'll try to cure him." He shook his head. "Maybe he'll even think he's kicked the habit. Then they'll let him loose"—he gestured, throwing his cigarette into the gutter. "That's all."

"What do you mean, that's *all*?"

But I knew what he meant.

"*I mean, that's all*." He turned his head and looked at me, pulling down the corners of his mouth. "Don't you know what I mean?" he asked, softly.

"How the hell *would* I know what you mean?" I almost whispered it, I don't know why.

"That's right," he said to the air, "how would *he* know what I mean?" He turned toward me again, patient and calm, and yet I somehow felt him shaking, shaking as though he were going to fall apart. I felt that ice in my guts again, the dread I'd felt all afternoon; and again I watched the barmaid, moving about the bar, washing glasses, and singing. "Listen. They'll let him out and then it'll just start all over again. That's what I mean."

"You mean—they'll let him out. And then he'll just start working his way back in again. You mean he'll never kick the habit. Is that what you mean?"

"That's right," he said, cheerfully. "*You* see what I mean."

"Tell me," I said at last, "why does he want to die? He must want to die, he's killing himself, why does he want to die?"

He looked at me in surprise. He licked his lips. "He don't want to die. He wants to live. Don't nobody want to die, ever."

Then I wanted to ask him—too many things. He could not have answered, or if he had, I could not have borne the answers. I started walking. "Well, I guess it's none of my business."

"It's going to be rough on old Sonny," he said. We reached the subway station. "This is your station?" he asked. I nodded. I took one step down. "Damn!" he said, suddenly. I looked up at him. He grinned again. "Damn it if I didn't leave all my money home. You ain't got a dollar on you, have you? Just for a couple of days, is all."

All at once something inside gave and threatened to come pouring out of me. I didn't hate him any more. I felt that in another moment I'd start crying like a child.

"Sure," I said. "Don't sweat." I looked in my wallet and didn't have a dollar, I only had a five. "Here," I said. "That hold you?"

He didn't look at it—he didn't want to look at it. A terrible, closed look came over his face, as though he were keeping the number on the bill a secret from him and me. "Thanks," he said, and now he was dying to see me go. "Don't worry about Sonny. Maybe I'll write him or something."

"Sure," I said. "You do that. So long."
"Be seeing you," he said. I went on down the steps.

And I didn't write Sonny or send him anything for a long time. When I finally did, it was just after my little girl died, he wrote me back a letter which made me feel like a bastard.

Here's what he said:

> Dear brother,
> You don't know how much I needed to hear from you. I wanted to write you many a time but I dug how much I must have hurt you and so I didn't write. But now I feel like a man who's been trying to climb up out of some deep, real deep and funky hole and just saw the sun up there, outside. I got to get outside.
> I can't tell you much about how I got here. I mean I don't know how to tell you. I guess I was afraid of something or I was trying to escape from something and you know I have never been very strong in the head (smile). I'm glad Mama and Daddy are dead and can't see what's happened to their son and I swear if I'd known what I was doing I would never have hurt you so, you and a lot of other fine people who were nice to me and who believed in me.
> I don't want you to think it had anything to do with me being a musician. It's more than that. Or maybe less than that. I can't get anything straight in my head down here and I try not to think about what's going to happen to me when I get outside again. Sometime I think I'm going to flip and *never* get outside and sometime I think I'll come straight back. I tell you one thing, though, I'd rather blow my brains out than go through this again. But that's what they all say, so they tell me. If I tell you when I'm coming to New York and if you could meet me, I sure would appreciate it. Give my love to Isabel and the kids and I was sure sorry to hear about little Gracie. I wish I could be like Mama and say the Lord's will be done, but I don't know it seems to me that trouble is the one thing that never does get stopped and I don't know what good it does to blame it on the Lord. But maybe it does some good if you believe it.
>
> Your brother,
> Sonny

Then I kept in constant touch with him and I sent him whatever I could and I went to meet him when he came back to New York. When I saw him many things I thought I had forgotten came flooding back to me. This was because I had begun, finally, to wonder about Sonny, about the life that

Sonny lived inside. This life, whatever it was, had made him older and thinner and it had deepened the distant stillness in which he had always moved. He looked very unlike my baby brother. Yet, when he smiled, when we shook hands, the baby brother I'd never known looked out from the depths of his private life, like an animal waiting to be coaxed into the light.

"How you been keeping?" he asked me.

"All right. And you?"

"Just fine." He was smiling all over his face. "It's good to see you again."

"It's good to see you."

The seven years' difference in our ages lay between us like a chasm: I wondered if these years would ever operate between us as a bridge. I was remembering, and it made it hard to catch my breath, that I had been there when he was born; and I had heard the first words he had ever spoken. When he started to walk, he walked from our mother straight to me. I caught him just before he fell when he took the first steps he ever took in this world.

"How's Isabel?"

"Just fine. She's dying to see you."

"And the boys?"

"They're fine, too. They're anxious to see their uncle."

"Oh, come on. You know they don't remember me."

"Are you kidding? Of course they remember you."

He grinned again. We got into a taxi. We had a lot to say to each other, far too much to know how to begin.

As the taxi began to move, I asked, "You still want to go to India?"

He laughed. "You still remember that. Hell, no. This place is Indian enough for me."

"It used to belong to them," I said.

And he laughed again. "They damn sure knew what they were doing when they got rid of it."

Years ago, when he was around fourteen, he'd been all hipped on the idea of going to India. He read books about people sitting on rocks, naked, in all kinds of weather, but mostly bad, naturally, and walking barefoot through hot coals and arriving at wisdom. I used to say that it sounded to me as though they were getting away from wisdom as fast as they could. I think he sort of looked down on me for that.

"Do you mind," he asked, "if we have the driver drive alongside the park? On the west side—I haven't seen the city in so long."

"Of course not," I said. I was afraid that I might sound as though I were humoring him, but I hoped he wouldn't take it that way.

So we drove along, between the green of the park and the stony, lifeless elegance of hotels and apartment buildings, toward the vivid, killing streets of our childhood. These streets hadn't changed, though housing projects jutted up out of them now like rocks in the middle of a boiling sea. Most of the houses in which we had grown up had vanished, as had the stores from which we had stolen, the basements in which we had first tried sex, the rooftops from which we had hurled tin cans and bricks. But houses exactly like the houses of our past yet dominated the landscape, boys exactly like the boys we once had been found themselves smothering in these houses, came down into the streets for light and air and found themselves encircled by disaster. Some escaped the trap, most didn't. Those who got out always left something of themselves behind, as some animals amputate a leg and leave it in the trap. It might be said, perhaps, that I had escaped, after all, I was a school teacher; or that Sonny had, he hadn't lived in Harlem for years. Yet, as the cab moved uptown through streets which seemed, with a rush, to darken with dark people, and as I covertly studied Sonny's face, it came to me that what we both were seeking through our separate cab windows was that part of ourselves which had been left behind. It's always at the hour of trouble and confrontation that the missing member aches.

We hit 110th Street and started rolling up Lenox Avenue. And I'd known this avenue all my life, but it seemed to me again, as it had seemed on the day I'd first heard about Sonny's trouble, filled with a hidden menace which was its very breath of life.

"We almost there," said Sonny.

"Almost." We were both too nervous to say anything more.

We live in a housing project. It hasn't been up long. A few days after it was up it seemed uninhabitably new, now, of course, it's already rundown. It looks like a parody of the good, clean, faceless life—God knows the people who live in it do their best to make it a parody. The beat-looking grass lying never hold out the streets, and they know it. The big windows around isn't enough to make their lives green, the hedges will fool no one, they aren't big enough to make space out of no space. They don't bother with the windows, they watch the TV screen instead. The playground is most popular with the children who don't play at jacks, or skip rope, or roller skate, or swing, and they can be found in it after dark. We moved in partly because it's not too far from where I teach, and partly for the kids; but it's really just like the houses in which Sonny and I grew up. The same things happen, they'll have the same things to remember. The moment Sonny and I started into the house I had the feeling that I was simply bringing him back into the danger he had almost died trying to escape.

Sonny has never been talkative. So I don't know why I was sure he'd be dying to talk to me when supper was over the first night. Everything went fine, the oldest boy remembered him, and the youngest boy liked him, and Sonny had remembered to bring something for each of them; and Isabel, who is really much nicer than I am, more open and giving, had gone to a lot of trouble about dinner and was genuinely glad to see him. And she's always been able to tease Sonny in a way that I haven't. It was nice to see her face so vivid again and to hear her laugh and watch her make Sonny laugh. She wasn't, or, anyway, she didn't seem to be, at all uneasy or embarrassed. She chatted as though there were no subject which had to be avoided and she got Sonny past his first, faint stiffness. And thank God she was there, for I was filled with that icy dread again. Everything I did seemed awkward to me, and everything I said sounded freighted with hidden meaning. I was trying to remember everything I'd heard about dope addiction and I couldn't help watching Sonny for signs. I wasn't doing it out of malice. I was trying to find out something about my brother. I was dying to hear him tell me he was safe.

"Safe!" my father grunted, whenever Mama suggested trying to move to a neighborhood which might be safer for children. "Safe, hell! Ain't no place safe for kids, nor nobody."

He always went on like this, but he wasn't, ever, really as bad as he sounded, not even on weekends, when he got drunk. As a matter of fact, he was always on the lookout for "something a little better," but he died before he found it. He died suddenly, during a drunken weekend in the middle of the war, when Sonny was fifteen. He and Sonny hadn't ever got on too well. And this was partly because Sonny was the apple of his father's eye. It was because he loved Sonny so much and was frightened for him, that he was always fighting with him. It doesn't do any good to fight with Sonny. Sonny just moves back, inside himself, where he can't be reached. But the principal reason that they never hit it off is that they were so much alike. Daddy was big and rough and loud-talking, just the opposite of Sonny, but they both had—the same privacy.

Mama tried to tell me something about this, just after Daddy died. I was home on leave from the army.

This was the last time I ever saw my mother alive. Just the same, this picture gets all mixed up in my mind with pictures I had of her when she was younger. The way I always see her is the way she used to be on a Sunday afternoon, say, when the old folks were talking after the big Sunday dinner. I always see her wearing pale blue. She'd be sitting on the sofa. And my father would be sitting in the easy chair, not far from her. And the living room would be full of church folks and relatives. There they sit, in chairs all around the living room, and the night is creeping up outside, but nobody knows it yet. You can see the darkness growing against the windowpanes and you hear the street noises every now and again, or maybe the jangling beat of a tambourine from one of the churches close by, but it's real quiet in the room. For a moment nobody's talking, but every face looks darkening, like the sky outside. And my mother rocks a little from the waist, and my father's eyes are closed. Everyone is looking at something a child can't see. For a minute they've forgotten the children. Maybe a kid is lying on the rug, half asleep. Maybe somebody's got a kid in his lap and is absent-mindedly stroking the kid's head. Maybe there's a kid, quiet and big-eyed, curled up in a big chair in the corner. The silence, the darkness coming, and the darkness in the faces frighten the child obscurely. He hopes that the hand which strokes his forehead will never stop—will never die. He hopes that there will never come a time when the old folks won't be sitting around the living room, talking about where they've come from, and what they've seen, and what's happened to them and their kinfolk.

But something deep and watchful in the child knows that this is bound to end, is already ending. In a moment someone will get up and turn on the light. Then the old folks will remember the children and they won't talk any more that day. And when light fills the room, the child is filled with darkness. He knows that every time this happens he's moved just a little closer to that darkness outside. The darkness outside is what the old folks have been talking about. It's what they've come from. It's what they endure. The child knows that they won't talk any more because if he knows too much about what's happened to *them,* he'll know too much too soon, about what's going to happen to *him.*

The last time I talked to my mother, I remember I was restless. I wanted to get out and see Isabel. We weren't married then and we had a lot to straighten out between us.

There Mama sat, in black, by the window. She was humming an old church song, *Lord, you brought me from a long ways off*. Sonny was out somewhere. Mama kept watching the streets.

"I don't know," she said, "if I'll ever see you again, after you go off from here. But I hope you'll remember the things I tried to teach you."

"Don't talk like that," I said, and smiled. "You'll be here a long time yet."

She smiled, too, but she said nothing. She was quiet for a long time. And I said, "Mama, don't you worry about nothing. I'll be writing all the time, and you be getting the checks...."

"I want to talk to you about your brother," she said, suddenly. "If anything happens to me he ain't going to have nobody to look out for him."

"Mama," I said, "ain't nothing going to happen to you *or* Sonny. Sonny's all right. He's a good boy and he's got good sense."

"It ain't a question of his being a good boy," Mama said, "nor of his having good sense. It ain't only the bad ones, nor yet the dumb ones that gets sucked under." She stopped, looking at me. "Your Daddy once had a brother," she said, and she smiled in a way that made me feel she was in pain. "You didn't never know that, did you?"

"No," I said, "I never knew that," and I watched her face.

"Oh, yes," she said, "your Daddy had a brother." She looked out of the window again. "I know you never saw your Daddy cry. But *I* did—many a time, through all these years."

I asked her, "What happened to his brother? How come nobody's ever talked about him?"

This was the first time I ever saw my mother look old.

"His brother got killed," she said, "when he was just a little younger than you are now. I knew him. He was a fine boy. He was maybe a little full of the devil, but he didn't mean nobody no harm."

Then she stopped and the room was silent, exactly as it had sometimes been on those Sunday afternoons. Mama kept looking out into the streets.

"He used to have a job in the mill," she said, "and, like all young folks, he just liked to perform on Saturday nights. Saturday nights, him and your father would drift around to different places, go to dances and things like that, or just sit around with people they knew, and your father's brother would sing, he had a fine voice, and play along with himself on his guitar. Well, this particular Saturday night, him and your father was coming home from some place, and they were both a little drunk and there was a moon that night, it was bright like day. Your father's brother was feeling kind of good, and he was whistling to himself, and he had his guitar slung over his shoulder. They was coming down a hill and beneath them was a road that turned off from the highway. Well, your father's brother, being always kind of frisky, decided to run down this hill, and he did, with that guitar banging and clanging behind him, and he ran across the road, and he was making water behind a tree. And your father was sort of amused at him and he was still coming down the hill, kind of slow. Then he heard a car motor and that same minute his brother stepped from behind the tree, into the road, in the moonlight. And he started to cross the road. And your father started to run down the hill, he says he don't know why. This car was full of white men. They was all drunk, and when they seen your father's brother they let out a great whoop and holler and they aimed the car straight at him. They was having fun, they just wanted to scare him, the way they do sometimes, you know. But they was drunk. And I guess the boy, being drunk, too, and scared, kind of lost his head. By the time he jumped it was too late. Your father says he heard his brother scream when the car rolled over him, and he heard the wood of that guitar when it give, and he heard them strings go flying, and he heard them white men shouting, and the car kept on a-going and it ain't stopped till this day. And, time your father got down the hill, his brother weren't nothing but blood and pulp."

Tears were gleaming on my mother's face. There wasn't anything I could say.

"He never mentioned it," she said, "because I never let him mention it before you children. Your Daddy was like a crazy man that night and for many a night thereafter. He says he never in his life seen anything as dark as that road after the lights of that car had gone away. Weren't nothing, weren't nobody on that road, just your Daddy and his brother and that busted guitar. Oh, yes. Your Daddy never did really get right again. Till the day he died he weren't sure but that every white man he saw was the man that killed his brother."

She stopped and took out her handkerchief and dried her eyes and looked at me.

"I ain't telling you all this," she said, "to make you scared or bitter or to make you hate nobody. I'm telling you this because you got a brother. And the world ain't changed."

I guess I didn't want to believe this. I guess she saw this in my face. She turned away from me, toward the window again, searching those streets.

"But I praise my Redeemer," she said at last, "that He called your Daddy home before me. I ain't saying it to throw no flowers at myself, but, I declare, it keeps me from feeling too cast down to know I helped your father get safely through this world. Your father always acted like he was the roughest, strongest man on earth. And everybody took him to be like that. But if he hadn't had *me* there—to see his tears!"

She was crying again. Still, I couldn't move. I said, "Lord, Lord, Mama, I didn't know it was like that."

"Oh, honey," she said, "there's a lot that you don't know. But you are going to find it out." She stood up from the window and came over to me. "You got to hold on to your brother," she said, "and don't let him fall, no matter what it looks like is happening to him and no matter how evil you gets with him. You going to be evil with him many a time. But don't you forget what I told you, you hear?"

"I won't forget," I said. "Don't you worry, I won't forget. I won't let nothing happen to Sonny."

My mother smiled as though she were amused at something she saw in my face. Then, "You may not be able to stop nothing from happening. But you got to let him know you's *there*."

Two days later I was married, and then I was gone. And I had a lot of things on my mind and I pretty well forgot my promise to Mama until I got shipped home on a special furlough for her funeral.

And, after the funeral, with just Sonny and me alone in the empty kitchen, I tried to find out something about him.

"What do you want to do?" I asked him.

"I'm going to be a musician," he said.

For he had graduated, in the time I had been away, from dancing to the juke box to finding out who was playing what, and what they were doing with it, and he had bought himself a set of drums.

"You mean, you want to be a drummer?" I somehow had the feeling that being a drummer might be all right for other people but not for my brother Sonny.

"I don't think," he said, looking at me very gravely, "that I'll ever be a good drummer. But I think I can play a piano."

I frowned. I'd never played the role of the older brother quite so seriously before, had scarcely ever, in fact, *asked* Sonny a damn thing. I sensed myself in the presence of something I didn't really know how to handle, didn't understand. So I made my frown a little deeper as I asked: "What kind of musician do you want to be?"

He grinned. "How many kinds do you think there are?"

"Be *serious*," I said.

He laughed, throwing his head back, and then looked at me. "I *am* serious."

"Well, then, for Christ's sake, stop kidding around and answer a serious question. I mean, do you want to be a concert pianist, you want to play classical music and all that, or—or what?" Long before I finished he was laughing again. "For Christ's *sake*, Sonny!"

He sobered, but with difficulty. "I'm sorry. But you sound so—*scared!*" and he was off again.

"Well, you may think it's funny now, baby, but it's not going to be so funny when you have to make your living at it, let me tell you *that*." I was furious because I knew he was laughing at me and I didn't know why.

"No," he said, very sober now, and afraid, perhaps, that he'd hurt me, "I don't want to be a classical pianist. That isn't what interests me. I mean"—he paused, looking hard at me, as though his eyes would help me to understand, and then gestured helplessly, as though perhaps his hand would help—"I mean, I'll have a lot of studying to do, and I'll have to study *everything*, but, I mean, I want to play *with*—jazz musicians." He stopped. "I want to play jazz," he said.

Well, the word had never before sounded as heavy, as real, as it sounded that afternoon in Sonny's mouth. I just looked at him and I was probably frowning a real frown by this time. I simply couldn't see why on earth he'd want to spend his time hanging around nightclubs, clowning around on bandstands, while people pushed each other around a dance floor. It seemed—beneath him, somehow. I had never thought about it before, had never been forced to, but I suppose I had always put jazz musicians in a class with what Daddy called "good-time people."

"Are you *serious?*"

"Hell, *yes*, I'm serious."

He looked more helpless than ever, and annoyed, and deeply hurt.

I suggested, helpfully: "You mean—like Louis Armstrong?"

His face closed as though I'd struck him. "No. I'm not talking about none of that old-time, down home crap."

"Well, look, Sonny, I'm sorry, don't get mad. I just don't altogether get it, that's all. Name somebody—you know, a jazz musician you admire."

"Bird."

"Who?"

"Bird! Charlie Parker! Don't they teach you nothing in the goddamn army?"

I lit a cigarette. I was surprised and then a little amused to discover that I was trembling. "I've been out of touch," I said. "You'll have to be patient with me. Now. Who's this Parker character?"

"He's just one of the greatest jazz musicians alive," said Sonny, sullenly, his hands in his pockets, his back to me. "Maybe *the* greatest," he added, bitterly, "that's probably why *you* never heard of him."

"All right," I said, "I'm ignorant. I'm sorry. I'll go out and buy all the cat's records right away, all right?"

"It don't," said Sonny, with dignity, "make any difference to me. I don't care what you listen to. Don't do me no favors."

I was beginning to realize that I'd never seen him so upset before. With another part of my mind I was thinking that this would probably turn out to be one of those things kids go through and that I shouldn't make it seem important by pushing it too hard. Still, I don't think it would do any harm to ask: "Doesn't all this take a lot of time? Can you make a living at it?"

He turned back to me and half leaned, half sat, on the kitchen table. "Everything takes time," he said, "and—well, yes, sure, I can make a living at it. But what I don't seem to be able to make you understand is that it's the only thing I want to do."

"Well, Sonny," I said, gently, "you know people can't always do exactly what they *want* to do—"

"*No,* I don't know that," said Sonny, surprising me. "I think people *ought* to do what they want to do, what else are they alive for?"

"You getting to be a big boy," I said desperately, "it's time you started thinking about your future."

"I'm thinking about my future," said Sonny, grimly. "I think about it all the time."

I gave up. I decided, if he didn't change his mind, that we could always talk about it later. "In the meantime," I said, "you got to finish school." We had already decided that he'd have to move in with Isabel and her folks. I knew this wasn't the ideal arrangement because Isabel's folks are inclined to be dicty and they hadn't especially wanted Isabel to marry me. But I didn't know what else to do. "And we have to get you fixed up at Isabel's."

There was a long silence. He moved from the kitchen table to the window. "That's a terrible idea. You know it yourself."

"Do you have a *better* idea?"

He just walked up and down the kitchen for a minute. He was as tall as I was. He had started to shave. I suddenly had the feeling that I didn't know him at all.

He stopped at the kitchen table and picked up my cigarettes. Looking at me with a kind of mocking, amused defiance, he put one between his lips. "You mind?"

"You smoking already?"

He lit the cigarette and nodded, watching me through the smoke. "I just wanted to see if I'd have the courage to smoke in front of you." He grinned and blew a great cloud of smoke to the ceiling. "It was easy." He looked at my face. "Come on, now. I bet you was smoking at my age, tell the truth."

I didn't say anything but the truth was on my face, and he laughed. But now there was something very strained in his laugh. "Sure. And I bet that ain't all you was doing."

He was frightening me a little. "Cut the crap," I said. "We already decided that you was going to go and live at Isabel's. Now what's got into you all of a sudden?"

"*You* decided it," he pointed out. "*I* didn't decide nothing." He stopped in front of me, leaning against the stove, arms loosely folded. "Look, brother. I don't want to stay in Harlem no more, I really don't." He was very earnest. He looked at me, then over toward the kitchen window. There was something in his eyes I'd never seen before, some thoughtfulness, some worry all his own. He rubbed the muscle of one arm. "It's time I was getting out of here."

"Where do you want to *go*, Sonny?"

"I want to join the army. Or the navy, I don't care. If I say I'm old enough, they'll believe me."

Then I got mad. It was because I was so scared. "You must

be crazy. You goddamn fool, what the hell do you want to go and join the *army* for?"

"I just told you. To get out of Harlem."

"Sonny, you haven't even finished *school*. And if you really want to be a musician, how do you expect to study if you're in the *army?*"

He looked at me, trapped, and in anguish. "There's ways. I might be able to work out some kind of deal. Anyway, I'll have the G.I. Bill when I come out."

"*If* you come out." We stared at each other. "Sonny, please. Be reasonable. I know the setup is far from perfect. But we got to do the best we can."

"I ain't learning nothing in school," he said. "Even when I go." He turned away from me and opened the window and threw his cigarette out into the narrow alley. I watched his back. "At least, I ain't learning nothing you'd want me to learn." He slammed the window so hard I thought the glass would fly out, and turned back to me. "And I'm sick of the stink of these garbage cans!"

"Sonny," I said, "I know how you feel. But if you don't finish school now, you're going to be sorry later that you didn't." I grabbed him by the shoulders. "And you only got another year. It ain't so bad. And I'll come back and I swear I'll help you do *whatever* you want to do. Just try to put up with it till I come back. Will you please do that? For me?"

He didn't answer and he wouldn't look at me.

"Sonny. You hear me?"

He pulled away. "I hear you. But you never hear anything *I* say."

I didn't know what to say to that. He looked out of the window and then back at me. "OK," he said, and sighed. "I'll try."

Then I said, trying to cheer him up a little, "They got a piano at Isabel's. You can practice on it."

And as a matter of fact, it did cheer him up for a minute. "That's right," he said to himself. "I forgot that." His face relaxed a little. But the worry, the thoughtfulness, played on it still, the way shadows play on a face which is staring into the fire.

But I thought I'd never hear the end of that piano. At first, Isabel would write me, saying how nice it was that Sonny was so serious about his music and how, as soon as he came in from school, or wherever he had been when he was supposed to be at school, he went straight to that piano and stayed there until suppertime. And, after supper, he went back to that piano and stayed there until everybody went to bed. He was at the piano all day Saturday and all day Sunday. Then he bought a record player and started playing records. He'd play one record over and over again, all day long sometimes, and he'd improvise along with it on the piano. Or he'd play one section of the record, one chord, one change, one progression, then he'd do it on the piano. Then back to the record. Then back to the piano.

Well, I really don't know how they stood it. Isabel finally confessed that it wasn't like living with a person at all, it was like living with sound. And the sound didn't make any sense to her, didn't make any sense to any of them—naturally. They began, in a way, to be afflicted by this presence that was living in their home. It was as though Sonny were some sort of god, or monster. He moved in an atmosphere which wasn't like theirs at all. They fed him and he ate, he washed himself, he walked in and out of their door; he certainly wasn't nasty or unpleasant or rude, Sonny isn't any of those things; but it was as though he were all wrapped up in some cloud, some fire, some vision all his own; and there wasn't any way to reach him.

At the same time, he wasn't really a man yet, he was still a child, and they had to watch out for him in all kinds of ways. They certainly couldn't throw him out. Neither did they dare to make a great scene about that piano because even they dimly sensed, as I sensed, from so many thousands of miles away, that Sonny was at that piano playing for his life.

But he hadn't been going to school. One day a letter came from the school board and Isabel's mother got it—there had, apparently, been other letters but Sonny had torn them up. This day, when Sonny came in, Isabel's mother showed him the letter and asked where he'd been spending his time. And she finally got it out of him that he'd been down in Greenwich Village, with musicians and other characters, in a white girl's apartment. And this scared her and she started to scream at him and what came up, once she began—though she denies it to this day—was what sacrifices they were making to give Sonny a decent home and how little he appreciated it.

Sonny didn't play the piano that day. By evening, Isabel's mother had calmed down but then there was the old man to deal with, and Isabel herself. Isabel says she did her best to be calm but she broke down and started crying. She says she just watched Sonny's face. She could tell, by watching him, what was happening with him. And what was happening was that they penetrated his cloud, they had reached him. Even if their fingers had been a thousand times more gentle than human fingers ever are, he could hardly help feeling that they had stripped him naked and were spitting on that nakedness. For he also had to see that his presence, that music, which was life or death to him, had been torture for them and that they had endured it, not at all for his sake, but only for mine. And Sonny couldn't take that. He can take it a little better today than he could then but he's still not very good at it and, frankly, I don't know anybody who is.

The silence of the next few days must have been louder than the sound of all the music ever played since time began. One morning, before she went to work, Isabel was in his room for something and she suddenly realized that all of his records were gone. And she knew for certain that he was gone. And he was. He went as far as the navy would carry him. He finally sent me a postcard from some place in Greece and that was the first I knew that Sonny was still alive. I didn't see him any more until we were both back in New York and the war had long been over.

He was a man by then, of course, but I wasn't willing to see it. He came by the house from time to time, but we fought almost every time we met. I didn't like the way he carried himself, loose and dreamlike all the time, and I didn't like his friends, and his music seemed to be merely an excuse for the life he led. It sounded just that weird and disordered.

Then we had a fight, a pretty awful fight, and I didn't see him for months. By and by I looked him up, where he was living, in a furnished room in the Village, and I tried to make it up. But there were lots of other people in the room and Sonny just lay on his bed, and he wouldn't come downstairs with me, and he treated these other people as though they were his family and I weren't. So I got mad and then he got mad, and then I told him that he might just as well be dead as live the way he was living. Then he stood up and he told me not to worry about him any more in life, that he *was* dead as far as I was concerned. Then he pushed me to the door and the other people looked on as though nothing were happening, and he slammed the door behind me. I stood in the hallway, staring at the door. I heard somebody laugh in the room and whistling to keep from crying, I kept whistling to myself, *You then the tears came to my eyes. I started down the steps, going to need me, baby, one of these cold, rainy days*.

I read about Sonny's troubles in the spring. Little Grace died in the fall. She was a beautiful little girl. But she only lived a little over two years. She died of polio and she suffered. She had a slight fever for a couple of days, but it didn't seem like anything and we just kept her in bed. And we would certainly have called the doctor, but the fever dropped, she seemed to be all right. So we thought it had just been a cold. Then, one day, she was up, playing, Isabel was in the kitchen fixing lunch for the two boys when they'd come in from school, and she heard Grace fall down in the living room. When you have a lot of children you don't always start running when one of them falls, unless they start screaming or something. And, this time, Grace was quiet. Yet, Isabel says that when she heard that *thump* and then that silence, something happened in her to make her afraid. And she ran to the living room and there was little Grace on the floor, all twisted up, and the reason she hadn't screamed was that she couldn't get her breath. And when she did scream, it was the worst sound, Isabel says, that she'd ever heard in all her life, and she still hears it sometimes in her dreams. Isabel will sometimes wake me up with a low, moaning, strangled sound and I have to be quick to awaken her and hold her to me and where Isabel is weeping against me seems a mortal wound.

I think I may have written Sonny the very day that little Grace was buried. I was sitting in the living room in the dark, by myself, and I suddenly thought of Sonny. My trouble made his real.

One Saturday afternoon, when Sonny had been living with us, or, anyway, been in our house, for nearly two weeks, I found myself wandering aimlessly about the living room, drinking from a can of beer, and trying to work up the courage to search Sonny's room. He was out, he was usually out whenever I was home, and Isabel had taken the children to see their grandparents. Suddenly I was standing still in front of the living room window, watching Seventh Avenue. The idea of searching Sonny's room made me still. I scarcely dared to admit to myself what I'd be searching for. I didn't know what I'd do if I found it. Or if I didn't.

On the sidewalk across from me, near the entrance to a barbecue joint, some people were holding an old-fashioned revival meeting. The barbecue cook, wearing a dirty white apron, his conked hair reddish and metallic in the pale sun, and a cigarette between his lips, stood in the doorway, watching them. Kids and older people paused in their errands and stood there, along with some older men and a couple of very tough-looking women who watched everything that happened on the avenue, as though they owned it, or were maybe owned by it. Well, they were watching this, too. The revival was being carried on by three sisters in black, and a brother. All they had were their voices and their Bibles and a tambourine. The brother was testifying and while he testified two of the sisters stood together, seeming to say, amen, and the third sister walked around with the tambourine outstretched and a couple of people dropped coins into it. Then the brother's testimony ended and the sister who had been taking up the collection dumped the coins into her palm and transferred them to the pocket of her long black robe. Then she raised both hands, striking the tambourine against the air, and then against one hand, and she started to sing. And the two other sisters and the brother joined in.

It was strange, suddenly, to watch, though I had been seeing these street meetings all my life. So, of course, had everybody else down there. Yet, they paused and watched and listened and I stood still at the window. "*'Tis the old ship of Zion,*" they sang, and the sister with the tambourine kept a steady, jangling beat, "*it has rescued many a thousand!*" Not a soul under the sound of their voices was hearing this song for the first time, not one of them had been rescued. Nor had they seen much in the way of rescue work being done around them. Neither did they especially believe in the holiness of the three sisters and the brother, they knew too much about them, knew where they lived, and how. The woman with the tambourine, whose voice dominated the air, whose face was bright with joy, was divided by very little from the woman who stood watching her, a cigarette between her heavy, chapped lips, her hair a cuckoo's nest, her face scarred and swollen from many beatings, and her black eyes glittering like coal. Perhaps they both knew this, which was why, when, as rarely, they addressed each other, they addressed each other as Sister. As the singing filled the air the watching, listening faces underwent a change, the eyes focusing on something within; the music seemed to soothe a poison out of them; and time seemed, nearly, to fall away from the sullen, belligerent, battered faces, as though they were fleeing back to their first condition, while dreaming of their last. The barbecue cook half shook his head and smiled, and dropped his cigarette and disappeared into his joint. A man fumbled in his pockets for change and stood holding it in his hand impatiently, as though he had just remembered a pressing appointment further up the avenue. He looked furious. Then I saw Sonny, standing on the edge of the crowd. He was carrying a wide, flat notebook with a green cover, and it made him look, from where I was standing, almost like a schoolboy. The coppery sun brought out the copper in his skin, he was very faintly smiling, standing very still. Then the singing stopped, the tambourine turned into a collection plate again. The furious man dropped in his coins and vanished, so did a couple of the women, and Sonny dropped some change in the plate, looking directly at the woman with a little smile. He started across the avenue, toward the house. He has a slow, loping walk, something like the way Harlem hipsters walk, only he's imposed on this his own half-beat. I had never really noticed it before.

I stayed at the window, both relieved and apprehensive. As Sonny disappeared from my sight, they began singing again. And they were still singing when his key turned in the lock.

"Hey," he said.

"Hey, yourself. You want some beer?"

"No. Well, maybe." But he came up to the window and stood beside me, looking out. "What a warm voice," he said.

They were singing *If I could only hear my mother pray again!*

"Yes," I said, "and she can sure beat that tambourine."

"But what a terrible song," he said, and laughed. He dropped his notebook on the sofa and disappeared into the kitchen. "Where's Isabel and the kids?"

"I think they went to see their grandparents. You hungry?"

"No." He came back into the living room with his can of beer. "You want to come some place with me tonight?"

I sensed, I don't know how, that I couldn't possibly say no. "Sure. Where?"

He sat down on the sofa and picked up his notebook and started leafing through it. "I'm going to sit in with some fellows in a joint in the Village."

"You mean, you're going to play, tonight?"

"That's right." He took a swallow of his beer and moved back to the window. He gave me a sidelong look. "If you can stand it."

"I'll try," I said.

He smiled to himself and we both watched as the meeting across the way broke up. The three sisters and the brother, heads bowed, were singing *God be with you till we meet again.*

The faces around them were very quiet. Then the song ended. The small crowd dispersed. We watched the three women and the lone man walk slowly up the avenue.

"When she was singing before," said Sonny, abruptly, "her voice reminded me for a minute of what heroin feels like sometimes—when it's in your veins. It makes you feel sort of warm and cool at the same time. And distant. And—and sure." He sipped his beer, very deliberately not looking at me. I watched his face. "It makes you feel—in control. Sometimes you've got to have that feeling."

"Do you?" I sat down slowly in the easy chair.

"Sometimes." He went to the sofa and picked up his notebook again. "Some people do."

"In order," I asked, "to play?" And my voice was very ugly, full of contempt and anger.

"Well"—he looked at me with great, troubled eyes, as though, in fact, he hoped his eyes would tell me things he could never otherwise say—"they *think* so. And *if* they think so—!"

"And what do *you* think?" I asked.

He sat on the sofa and put his can of beer on the floor. "I don't know," he said, and I couldn't be sure if he were answering my question or pursuing his thoughts. His face didn't tell me. "It's not so much to *play*. It's to *stand* it, to be able to make it at all. On any level." He frowned and smiled: "In order to keep from shaking to pieces."

"But these friends of yours," I said, "they seem to shake themselves to pieces pretty goddamn fast."

"Maybe." He played with the notebook. And something told me that I should curb my tongue, that Sonny was doing his best to talk, that I should listen. "But of course you only know the ones that've gone to pieces. Some don't—or at least they haven't *yet* and that's just about all *any* of us can say." He paused. "And then there are some who just live, really, in hell, and they know it and they see what's happening and they go right on. I don't know." He sighed, dropped the notebook, folded his arms. "Some guys, you can tell from the way they play, they on something *all* the time. And you can see that, well, it makes something real for them. But of course," he picked up his beer from the floor and sipped it and put the can down again, "they *want* to, too, you've got to see that. Even some of them that say they don't—*some*, not all."

"And what about you?" I asked—I couldn't help it. "What about you? Do *you* want to?"

He stood up and walked to the window and remained silent for a long time. Then he sighed. "Me," he said. Then: "While I was downstairs before, on my way here, listening to that woman sing, it struck me all of a sudden how much suffering she must have had to go through—to sing like that. It's *repulsive* to think you have to suffer that much."

I said: "But there's no way not to suffer—is there, Sonny?"

"I believe not," he said and smiled, "but that's never stopped anyone from trying." He looked at me. "Has it?" I realized, with this mocking look, that there stood between us, forever, beyond the power of time or forgiveness, the fact that I had held silence—so long!—when he had needed human speech to help him. He turned back to the window. "No, there's no way not to suffer. But you try all kinds of ways to keep from drowning in it, to keep on top of it, and to make it seem—well, like *you*. Like you did something, all right, and now you're suffering for it. You know?" I said nothing. "Well you know," he said, impatiently, "why *do* people suffer? Maybe it's better to do something to give it a reason, *any* reason."

"But we just agreed," I said, "that there's no way not to suffer. Isn't it better, then, just to—take it?"

"But nobody just takes it," Sonny cried, "that's what I'm telling you! *Everybody* tries not to. You're just hung up on the *way* some people try—it's not *your* way!"

The hair on my face began to itch, my face felt wet. "That's not true," I said, "that's not true. I don't give a damn what other people do, I don't even care how they suffer. I just care how *you* suffer." And he looked at me. "Please believe me," I said, "I don't want to see you—die—trying not to suffer."

"I won't," he said, flatly, "die trying not to suffer. At least, not any faster than anybody else."

"But there's no need," I said, trying to laugh, "is there? in killing yourself."

I wanted to say more, but I couldn't. I wanted to talk about will power and how life could be—well, beautiful. I wanted to say that it was all within; but was it? or, rather, wasn't that exactly the trouble? And I wanted to promise that I would never fail him again. But it would all have sounded—empty words and lies.

So I made the promise to myself and prayed that I would keep it.

"It's terrible sometimes, inside," he said, "that's what's the trouble. You walk these streets, black and funky and cold, and there's not really a living ass to talk to, and there's nothing shaking, and there's no way of getting it out—that storm inside. You can't talk it and you can't make love with it, and when you finally try to get with it and play it, you realize *nobody's* listening. So *you've* got to listen. You got to find a way to listen."

And then he walked away from the window and sat on the sofa again, as though all the wind had suddenly been knocked out of him. "Sometimes you'll do *anything* to play, even cut your mother's throat." He laughed and looked at me. "Or your brother's." Then he sobered. "Or your own." Then: "Don't worry. I'm all right now and I think I'll *be* all right. But I can't forget—where I've been. I don't mean just the physical place I've been, I mean where I've *been*. And *what* I've been."

"What have you been, Sonny?" I asked.

He smiled—but sat sideways on the sofa, his elbow resting on the back, his fingers playing with his mouth and chin, not looking at me. "I've been something I didn't recognize, didn't know I could be. Didn't know anybody could be." He stopped, looking inward, looking helplessly young, looking old. "I'm not talking about it now because I feel *guilty* or anything like that—maybe it would be better if I did, I don't know. Anyway, I can't really talk about it. Not to you, not to anybody," and now he turned and faced me. "Sometimes, you know, and it was actually when I was most *out* of the world, I felt that I was in it, that I was *with* it, really, and I could play or I didn't really have to *play*, it just came out of me, it was there. And I don't know how I played, thinking about it now, but I know I did awful things, those times, sometimes, to people. Or it wasn't that I *did* anything to them —it was that they weren't real." He picked up the beer can; it was empty; he rolled it between his palms: "And other times—well, I needed a fix, I needed to find a place to lean, I needed to clear a space to *listen*—and I couldn't find it, and I—went crazy, I did terrible things to *me*, I was terrible *for* me." He began pressing the beer can between his hands, I watched the metal begin to give. It glittered, as he played with it, like a knife, and I was afraid he would cut himself, but I said nothing. "Oh well. I can never tell you. I was all by myself at the bottom of something, stinking and sweating and crying and shaking, and I smelled it, you know? *my* stink, and I thought I'd die if I couldn't get away from it and yet, all the same, I knew that everything I was doing was just locking me in with it. And I didn't know," he paused, still flattening the beer can, "I didn't know, I still *don't* know, something kept telling me that maybe it was good to smell your own stink, but I didn't think that *that* was what I'd been trying to do—and—who can stand it?" and he abruptly dropped the ruined beer can, looking at me with a small, still smile, and then rose, walking to the window as though it were the lodestone rock. I watched his face, he watched the avenue. "I couldn't tell you when Mama died—but the reason I wanted to leave Harlem so bad was to get away from drugs. And then, when I ran away, that's what I was running from—really. When I came back, nothing had changed, *I* hadn't changed, I was just—older." And he stopped, drumming with his fingers on the windowpane. The sun had vanished, soon darkness would fall. I watched his face. "It can come again," he said, almost as though speaking to himself. Then he turned to me. "It can come again," he repeated. "I just want you to know that."

"All right," I said, at last. "So it can come again. All right."

He smiled, but the smile was sorrowful. "I had to try to tell you," he said.

"Yes," I said. "I understand that."

"You're my brother," he said, looking straight at me, and not smiling at all.

"Yes," I repeated, "yes. I understand that."

He turned back to the window, looking out. "All that hatred down there," he said, "all that hatred and misery and love. It's a wonder it doesn't blow the avenue apart."

We went to the only nightclub on a short, dark street, downtown. We squeezed through the narrow, chattering, jampacked bar to the entrance of the big room, where the bandstand was. And we stood there for a moment, for the lights were very dim in this room and we couldn't see. Then, "Hello, boy," said a voice and an enormous black man, much older than Sonny or myself, erupted out of all that atmospheric lighting and put an arm around Sonny's shoulder. "I been sitting right here," he said, "waiting for you."

He had a big voice, too, and heads in the darkness turned toward us.

Sonny grinned and pulled a little away, and said, "Creole, this is my brother. I told you about him."

Creole shook my hand. "I'm glad to meet you, son," he said, and it was clear that he was glad to meet me *there,* for

Sonny's sake. And he smiled, "You got a real musician in *your* family," and he took his arm from Sonny's shoulder and slapped him, lightly, affectionately, with the back of his hand.

"Well. Now I've heard it all," said a voice behind us. This was another musician, and a friend of Sonny's, a coal-black, cheerful-looking man, built close to the ground. He immediately began confiding to me, at the top of his lungs, the most terrible things about Sonny, his teeth gleaming like a lighthouse and his laugh coming up out of him like the beginning of an earthquake. And it turned out that everyone at the bar knew Sonny, or almost everyone; some were musicians, working there, or nearby, or not working, some were simply hangers-on, and some were there to hear Sonny play. I was introduced to all of them and they were all very polite to me. Yet, it was clear that, for them, I was only Sonny's brother. Here, I was in Sonny's world. Or, rather: his kingdom. Here, it was not even a question that his veins bore royal blood.

They were going to play soon and Creole installed me, by myself, at a table in a dark corner. Then I watched them, Creole, and the little black man, and Sonny, and the others, while they horsed around, standing just below the bandstand. The light from the bandstand spilled just a little short of them and, watching them laughing and gesturing and moving about, I had the feeling that they, nevertheless, were being most careful not to step into that circle of light too suddenly: that if they moved into the light too suddenly, without thinking, they would perish in flame. Then, while I watched, one of them, the small, black man, moved into the light and crossed the bandstand and started fooling around with his drums. Then—being funny and being, also, extremely ceremonious—Creole took Sonny by the arm and led him to the piano. A woman's voice called Sonny's name and a few hands started clapping. And Sonny, also being funny and being ceremonious, and so touched, I think, that he could have cried, but neither hiding it nor showing it, riding it like a man, grinned, and put both hands to his heart and bowed from the waist.

Creole then went to the bass fiddle and a lean, very bright-skinned brown man jumped up on the bandstand and picked up his horn. So there they were, and the atmosphere on the bandstand and in the room began to change and tighten. Someone stepped up to the microphone and announced them.

Then there were all kinds of murmurs. Some people at the bar shushed others. The waitress ran around, frantically getting in the last orders, guys and chicks got closer to each other, and the lights on the bandstand, on the quartet, turned to a kind of indigo. Then they all looked different there. Creole looked about him for the last time, as though he were making certain that all his chickens were in the coop, and then he —jumped and struck the fiddle. And there they were.

All I know about music is that not many people ever really hear it. And even then, on the rare occasions when something opens within, and the music enters, what we mainly hear, or hear corroborated, are personal, private, vanishing evocations. But the man who creates the music is hearing something else, is dealing with the roar rising from the void and imposing order on it as it hits the air. What is evoked in him, then, is of another order, more terrible because it has no words, and triumphant, too, for that same reason. And his triumph, when he triumphs, is ours. I just watched Sonny's face. His face was troubled, he was working hard, but he wasn't with it. And I had the feeling that, in a way, everyone on the bandstand was waiting for him, both waiting for him and pushing him along. But as I began to watch Creole, I realized that it was Creole who held them all back. He had them on a short rein. Up there, keeping the beat with his whole body, wailing on the fiddle, with his eyes half closed, he was listening to everything, but he was listening to Sonny. He was having a dialogue with Sonny. He wanted Sonny to leave the shoreline and strike out for the deep water. He was Sonny's witness that deep water and drowning were not the same thing—he had been there, and he knew. And he wanted Sonny to know. He was waiting for Sonny to do the things on the keys which would let Creole know that Sonny was in the water.

And, while Creole listened, Sonny moved, deep within, exactly like someone in torment. I had never before thought of how awful the relationship must be between the musician and his instrument. He has to fill it, this instrument, with the breath of life, his own. He has to make it do what he wants it to do. And a piano is just a piano. It's made out of so much wood and wires and little hammers and big ones, and ivory. While there's only so much you can do with it, the only way to find this out is to try; to try and make it do everything.

And Sonny hadn't been near a piano for over a year. And

he wasn't on much better terms with his life, not the life that stretched before him now. He and the piano stammered, started one way, got scared, stopped; started another way, panicked, marked time, started again; then seemed to have found a direction, panicked again, got stuck. And the face I saw on Sonny I'd never seen before. Everything had been burned out of it, and, at the same time, things usually hidden were being burned in, by the fire and fury of the battle which was occurring in him up there.

Yet, watching Creole's face as they neared the end of the first set, I had the feeling that something had happened, something I hadn't heard. Then they finished, there was scattered applause, and then, without an instant's warning, Creole started into something else, it was almost sardonic, it was *Am I Blue*. And, as though he commanded, Sonny began to play. Something began to happen. And Creole let out the reins. The dry, low, black man said something awful on the drums, Creole answered, and the drums talked back. Then the horn insisted, sweet and high, slightly detached perhaps, and Creole listened, commenting now and then, dry, and driving, beautiful and calm and old. Then they all came together again, and Sonny was part of the family again. I could tell this from his face. He seemed to have found, right there beneath his fingers, a damn brand-new piano. It seemed that he couldn't get over it. Then, for awhile, just being happy with Sonny, they seemed to be agreeing with him that brand-new pianos certainly were a gas.

Then Creole stepped forward to remind them that what they were playing was the blues. He hit something in all of them, he hit something in me, myself, and the music tightened and deepened, apprehension began to beat the air. Creole began to tell us what the blues were all about. They were not about anything very new. He and his boys up there were keeping it new, at the risk of ruin, destruction, madness, and death, in order to find new ways to make us listen. For, while the tale of how we suffer, and how we are delighted, and how we may triumph is never new, it always must be heard. There isn't any other tale to tell, it's the only light we've got in all this darkness.

And this tale, according to that face, that body, those strong hands on those strings, has another aspect in every country, and a new depth in every generation. Listen, Creole seemed to be saying, listen. Now these are Sonny's blues. He made the little black man on the drums know it, and the bright, brown man on the horn. Creole wasn't trying any longer to get Sonny in the water. He was wishing him Godspeed. Then he stepped back, very slowly, filling the air with the immense suggestion that Sonny speak for himself.

Then they all gathered around Sonny and Sonny played. Every now and again one of them seemed to say, amen. Sonny's fingers filled the air with life, his life. But that life contained so many others. And Sonny went all the way back, he really began with the spare, flat statement of the opening phrase of the song. Then he began to make it his. It was very beautiful because it wasn't hurried and it was no longer a lament. I seemed to hear with what burning he had made it his, with what burning we had yet to make it ours, how we could cease lamenting. Freedom lurked around us and I understood, at last, that he could help us to be free if we would listen, that he would never be free until we did. Yet, there was no battle in his face now. I heard what he had gone through, and would continue to go through until he came to rest in earth. He had made it his: that long line, of which we knew only Mama and Daddy. And he was giving it back, as everything must be given back, so that, passing through death, it can live forever. I saw my mother's face again, and felt, for the first time, how the stones of the road she had walked on must have bruised her feet. I saw the moonlit road where my father's brother died. And it brought something else back to me, and carried me past it, I saw my little girl again and felt Isabel's tears again, and I felt my own tears begin to rise. And I was yet aware that this was only a moment, that the world waited outside, as hungry as a tiger, and that trouble stretched above us, longer than the sky.

Then it was over. Creole and Sonny let out their breath, both soaking wet, and grinning. There was a lot of applause and some of it was real. In the dark, the girl came by and I asked her to take drinks to the bandstand. There was a long pause, while they talked up there in the indigo light and after awhile I saw the girl put a Scotch and milk on top of the piano for Sonny. He didn't seem to notice it, but just before they started playing again, he sipped from it and looked toward me, and nodded. Then he put it back on top of the piano. For me, then, as they began to play again, it glowed and shook above my brother's head like the very cup of trembling.

A Lot You Got to Holler
Nelson Algren

It's a Barnum and Bailey World

I think I started stealing right after the old man threw Aunt out of the house. I was about eight, and used to look forward to her visit all week. She would dangle me on her knee, kiss me, and give me small coins: pennies and nickels and dimes. I remember her smell, the leather touch of her purse, and the warm touch of her hand when she pressed the coins into my hand. That smell, that purse, those kisses, and those coins were all something that belonged peculiarly to her, as she belonged peculiarly to me; for I never received, nor ever expected, those things from anyone else.

The last time I heard her voice was in the hallway, and sensed that she was pleading to kiss me good night. But the old man was in a high-wheeled huff and made her leave without saying good-by. Years later I learned she didn't even have a place to stay that night.

It must have been the next morning that I saw a neighbor woman's purse on a dresser and put it down the front of my shirt without even opening it. They found me sleeping under the back porch with the purse under my cheek like a pillow.

The old man gave me a sound whaling for stealing; but all the while he was slapping me around I had the conviction that I hadn't really done what I was being slapped around for. I felt that, if Aunt were there, she would say I hadn't done anything wrong. I felt, for the first time, that everything was wrong, all wrong.

I first began to believe, about that time, that Aunt was really my mother. It was a screwy, kid's sort of hope, and a hope that finally came true: I must have been about twelve when I learned that the old man had left her and married her younger sister. Don't ask me what he was thinking of, but that's what he did. When I was born, and Aunt had no way of taking care of me, he and the younger sister took me in. I guess the old man figured that was the cheapest way out. He always figured the cheapest way, no matter how much it cost in the long run or who had to pay off. That's how it was that I grew up remembering my mother as "Aunt" and calling my aunt "Ma."

And everything, in remembering her, was hooked up with the smell of her purse and the small coins of love it had carried: I didn't grow up thinking of pennies and nickels and dimes as such; I thought of them always, without fully realizing it, as love-pennies, love-nickels, and love-dimes. When I saved them, as a kid, I wasn't really saving money. Because when I'd realize that money was all they came to I'd break the bank and get rid of them at the nearest candy store as fast as I could spend. If the candy store was closed I'd give them away.

It wasn't always stealing either. Once, when I was about nine, I was going down Division Street flipping a dime. It slipped through my fingers and rolled off the curb into the gutter. When I stooped to pick it up I saw a quarter lying beside it. I looked to see if it had Aunt's picture on it: it was years before I really ceased to believe that the woman's head on a quarter wasn't hers.

And for the next two weeks all I did was walk down Division flipping that lucky dime. I couldn't tell you yet whether I was looking for Aunt or another quarter. When I didn't find either I tried new sidewalks and strange streets. I got to know the whole Near Northwest Side that way. Then I lost the dime. And that, in a small way, was like losing Aunt all over.

But I began dreaming up other ways of finding quarters. Toward spring I decided that lots of kids must have lost money skating on the pond at Eckert Park during the winter. I went over there on the first day that the ice was melting and surveyed the slush inch by inch, although the soles of my shoes were paper-thin. I found four pennies, three dice, and a tin of Prince Albert tobacco. The tin was rusted but the tobacco tasted interesting.

I was sick by evening and, in a fever, confessed about chewing the tobacco. That's the only time I remember admitting doing something wrong without getting whipped. I was too sick to whip.

But sick as I was, I didn't squeal about the four pennies. They were hidden. I was going to return them to Aunt, and I would have died before telling. I remember having a vague and feverish conviction that they were hers, because all the pennies and nickels in the world, somehow, really belonged to her.

By evening the doctor had to come: it wasn't the Prince Albert entirely. I'd caught cold from wading in the slush and it had gone into flu. That was the epidemic of 1917, I guess. Something has always happened to ruin my get-rich-quick schemes.

Toward the end of that summer I was coming home from a swimming pool in Little Italy, about a mile away, where kids could swim for a penny. I remember that my swimming suit was still wet under my clothes and that I took a short cut across the Northwestern tracks. There was a long board fence bounding the coalyard there, in those years, and as I passed a place where a board was missing a kid poked his head out and hissed, "Hey, you, c'mere," as though he'd been expecting me. I'd never seen the kid before. He was about seven, I guess.

He squatted down in the weeds and came up with a green bandanna in which lay eight singles and some small change. "That's your part," he tells me, and gives me half the bills and half the change. He'd taken it all out of a Northwestern caboose, and he knew it was stealing as well as I. That was why he'd called me: to share his guilt.

Only, I didn't feel guilty. I'd already had my beating for stealing, so what I had in my hand had been well paid for. I felt as though somebody, maybe God, had owed me this for a long time and it was only in the natural run of things that it should come my way at last. And as I stood there the warmth of the coins, that had been lying in summer sunlight, spread from my palm through my whole body; for Aunt's warmth was in all coins. When I closed my fist over them I was enclosing her hand, and in that moment they became so precious to me that my fingernails dug into the flesh as if I never wanted to open my hand again. Then I thought of the old man and flattened the bills and stuffed them into my rolled sleeves. I don't know where I got the idea to do that, but kids raised on crowded corners get cunning pretty early.

I wandered around looking for kids I knew and found half a dozen ragged strays lagging beer corks on the corner of Ellen Street. With a prissy-looking eleven-year-old blonde watching in solemn disapproval. I knew her. She lived next door and spent half her life, it seemed to me, on the alert for me to do something wrong in order to report it to the old man. If I spent a penny a mile away she'd learn of it and I'd become entangled in such a web of lies, trying to duck another beating, that I wouldn't know myself what the truth was.

So I stood there, with the most money I'd ever had in my life and just as unable to buy anything with it as though all the ice-cream parlors had closed for keeps. My bathing suit began to itch.

Kids are sly all right. There wasn't any use waiting for her to leave. She'd find out anyhow. So when no one was looking I dropped a dollar in the dirt and hollered, "Oh boy! Look what I found!" The lagging stopped.

"Augie found a dollar! We were all here'n nobody seen it but Augie! Augie the lucky eagle-eye!"

So here we all go to the ice-cream store, with the kids crowding around me and the prissy blonde following like a little Pinkerton. I bought two cones for myself first and alternated at licking them—one chocolate and one vanilla. I didn't like strawberry even then.

I don't think all the kids got cones, because there must have been at least forty swarming into the store by that time.

The blonde got one though. A strawberry double-header.

When the lagging was resumed and the excitement had subsided I felt a crying need for more ice cream. It was getting toward suppertime but I hated going home, even to rid myself of the itching bathing suit; I felt a couple more cones would keep me going to all hours.

This time I played it safe. I only used a half dollar, which seemed then only half as wrong.

"Look! A halfer! Am I lucky today you!"

"Is he lucky today you. Lucky Augie the eagle-eye!"

And so back to the ice-cream store.

When I came out of the house the next morning half a dozen kids were waiting for me. Kids I'd never seen before, from way over on Chicago Avenue. They didn't say anything, but they followed me so closely it was impossible to lose a penny without being seen in the act. And, of course, the twenty-four-hour Pinkerton, the eye that never slept, a little taller than any of the other kids, still shadowing me and still as grave as ever.

The sprouts followed my very eyes: if I glanced toward a telephone pole they would race there and search the alley for yards around. The blonde didn't search. She was hep. She just watched my pockets and my hands.

It didn't do her any good, because I started lagging beer corks with the other kids until her interest wandered to other suspects on whom she was keeping book. And that evening I *earned* seventy-five cents selling the *Saturday Evening Blade* on the corner of Milwaukee Avenue and Ashland.

The same kids were waiting for me the next morning, and I spent every dime of the *Saturday Evening Blade* money on them before noon, to maintain my far-flung reputation as an easy spender. Six bits in a single morning broke all local records for loose living. And you can guess the rest: as soon as she'd finished another strawberry double-header the Pinkerton raced to Ma. "Augie steals money every day," she told the old lady.

"A lot you got to holler, Sissie," I told her. "You helped me spend it." I knew it wasn't any use saying I'd earned it selling the *Blade*. It was a beating either way.

Every time I was whipped unjustly I became lonely for Aunt, and the next morning I started out looking for her, to tell her how it was that nobody bothered you when you spent stolen money, except to help you spend it; but that the pay-off came when you were caught spending money you'd earned honestly. I couldn't figure that out, beyond feeling that my mistake had been in going to work at all. If I'd gone searching around that broken board in the coalyard fence, it seemed to me, instead of fooling around with the *Blade*, I might have done better. At least I wouldn't have been licked.

I had no idea where she lived, and so just wandered around looking at houses and occasionally ringing a doorbell in some blind hope that that might be the place she lived. I knew better than to ask Ma where Aunt lived, because all Ma did when I mentioned Aunt was to bawl.

It got so late that I was afraid to go home without some excuse. I'd been up and down streets and alleys the whole morning and most of the afternoon. And now the red headlines of the *Blade*, which had been featuring kidnap stories, came to my mind. Toward dark I stopped in an alley, found a piece of glass, and gave myself a long scratch down my right arm. The kidnapers had done that, I would tell Ma, when I was struggling to get away.

That's one you'll have to figure out for yourself; but I don't think I really did it to pass myself off as a kidnaped kid. Nor entirely to get out of a beating, either. I think that, at bottom, I had the hope of getting sympathy out of the old man.

It turned out to be the worst beating I'd ever had, and I know I never tried for anyone's sympathy again. After that, I'm sure, I was entirely on my own. After that, so far as myself and the old man were concerned, it was strictly warfare.

But I still feel that, if I could, somehow, have seen Aunt that day, things might have turned out different. I think she might have kept things from getting mixed up, at least until I was grown enough to figure them out for myself. But I didn't see her, and when things got mixed up that day they stayed mixed for keeps.

We grew out of the beer-cork stage into lagging for ten-a-penny pictures of baseball players. Like the beer corks, some of these had a larger value than others: I remember trading an entire strip of ten to get just one of Joe Jackson. And a month later, when Jackson had been kicked out of organized baseball, I had to give one of him, one of Buck Weaver, and two Happy Felschs just to get one Ray Schalk—who'd been on the original strip I'd traded for Shoeless Joe in the first place.

When we started lagging for pennies we forgot about the baseball players, and nobody cared any more whether Ray Schalk was a good guy or a bad guy anyhow. The feeling grew that he may have been a sucker.

Who'd gotten the pay roll? that's what we wanted to know now.

We drifted into the crap games behind the Anderson School, and when the cops started breaking them up the attraction became irresistible. Once a dozen of us spent an afternoon in the Racine Avenue Station because the kid we'd set up as a lookout had wandered off to match nickels with the corner newsie. It was a hot afternoon, and our numbers gave us courage. We heckled the cops, and were really proud of being jailbirds. How did we kill the afternoon when the cops ignored us? You guessed it again. I lost forty-six cents.

When I got home Sissie had already told my old man where I'd been. But the whipping was nothing at all compared to the sense of manhood attained by an afternoon in the clink. It was the most exciting thing that had ever happened to us. For days we bragged to each other about our various parts in the escapade: who was the most scared, who wasn't scared at all, and whose brother, right now, was doing ninety days in County. For us the kid whose brother was doing a stretch was as distinguished as a kid in another neighborhood whose brother was a college football star.

This was all in the days when newspapers were a penny apiece and we had a lot of dodges around the stands. When the race-track and baseball fans handed you a nickel, they'd grab the sheet and stare at the results, with one hand held out blindly for their change. The dodge was to lay a penny in the waiting hand, click a second penny on the first and the third on the second; but the last penny was just clicked, without dropping it. The fellow would shove the change in his pocket and never know he'd been gypped.

Sometimes, if a customer didn't have anything smaller than a nickel or a dime, we'd plead that we had no change and go into the nearest saloon to get it. Then we'd duck out the Ladies' Entrance, leaving the sucker waiting in front.

When the streetcar was waiting for a red light we'd run up alongside the car and some guy would stick his hand out for a paper. If he offered a nickel or a dime we'd fumble and dig for that change until the car started, and then run beside the car with the change trying to reach the fellow's hand but never, somehow, quite making it. That only failed me once. A guy got off at the next stop and came back for the change. A tinhorn.

Around Christmas the big paper guys had cards printed and sold them to us little paper guys for a nickel apiece. The cards read, if I remember rightly:

> *Christmas comes but once a year*
> *And when it comes it brings good cheer*
> *So open your purse without a tear*
> *And remember the newsboy standing here.*

Sometimes that one was good for as much as a quarter. But this was the pay-off: we had to ask for the card back, because it cost us a nickel, and the customer would be thinking it was his, that he'd bought it. We called the big paper guys the Knothole Wonders, I don't remember why.

There were no stands in those days; the papers were just piled on the corners with stones on them, and every corner pile was run by some big guy. If a little guy sold a paper, it had to be in the middle of the block. But I remember selling a paper to a woman on the corner of Robey and Division, right under a big guy's nose.

I never tried that again. I had to buy the paper back from the big guy—and got a kick that was positively terrific. It lifted me off the ground and scattered my papers for yards. I didn't even take time to howl while gathering them up in the rush of noontime traffic—I was so afraid of losing those papers. But when I got home it really began hurting, and I cried all night.

And every time I saw the big paper guy, for a year after, I would still feel that kick. Sometimes I can still feel it.

And sometimes one of the big guys would make a deal with one of the little guys. He would say, "Hey, sprout, you want to buy me out tonight?" That meant buying him out around midnight, when the final lull began, at the wholesale price.

I made a deal like that once, but along about 1 A.M. it turned bitterly cold, and I had more papers left than I could sell in a week of Saturday nights. I was stuck. So I started to bawl, too cold to stand still and too afraid to go home. Just wandered around, wiping my nose on my sleeve and bawling, making people pause to ask what the matter was. I sold out, bawling the whole time. And had enough tears left over to help one of the other kids get rid of his papers too. I must have been nine or ten by that time.

If there wasn't anything in the headlines to yell about we just hollered, "Big Whitehouse scandal! Big Whitehouse scandal!" I thought the Whitehouse was the Derby Hotel, where the big guys went to see the big girls. It had white doors and a long white marble desk.

One afternoon when I was about thirteen I delivered a couple papers up there, to the third floor, and saw a woman in a kimono come down the hall whom I took for Aunt. I said, "Hello, Aunt," with such a hope of happiness in me I've never felt since. I don't think I'll ever come that close again. But she didn't answer and she didn't look around, and I had to believe it wasn't her after all.

But in later years I figured it this way: if it really *hadn't* been her, she would have turned when I called. She would have turned her head to see who'd called her. I figure now she was afraid to turn her head.

I went up there a number of times after that, under the pretense of delivering a paper, and wandered the long plush-carpeted hall listening to the laughter of women behind many doors, hoping always to hear Aunt's laughter. It was dark in the hallway, that was why she hadn't recognized me, I had decided. It had been so long since I'd seen her, I'd grown so much taller, that was why she hadn't recognized me. I spent so much time up there that the desk man made me leave the papers at the desk. He thought I was up to something else.

That's how it's always been: I was always in the clear so long as I was truly guilty. But the minute my motives were honest someone would finger me.

Another way we used to raise money was to go to the market and get those big empty barrels—not the casks, the barrels. The bigger guys could carry them, but we little guys rolled them. They rolled easy, and the meat packers paid us a nickel each for them. We couldn't find enough of them, naturally; so we'd steal them from one packer and sell them to another.

I must have been about fourteen when I made sudden friends with a kid who had a nice home. I don't remember the kid, but I remember the home, which was clean and bright all day, and his mother, who was handsome. It was a third-floor flat somewhere, with lots of plants in the front room with the sunlight on them. He had a puppy and we used to play with it up there. It's the first memory I have of being happy, playing with that pup in that pleasant place.

We must have been making a lot of noise, because this kid's mother walked past and said jokingly, to make us be a little quiet, "Why don't you kids just throw that dog out of the window?" I was so happy at just being there, so overwhelmed with an eagerness to please, that I picked up the pup, walked to the window and threw it out. Just like that.

I can still see that poor damned pup sprawling and turning and pawing for a foothold in mid-air on its way down to the pavement. And felt, suddenly, that I was falling too.

I was falling all right. But I was sixteen before I hit the ground. It happened the week after the old man told me that Aunt was dead, and I guess a kid still has a right to tears at that age. But I didn't shed one. I had some twisted idea that that would give the old man some sort of satisfaction. I just dummied up on him.

He was so puzzled because I didn't bawl, or even look like I felt bad, that he followed me out of the room to tell me that she was really my mother.

"I knew that eight years ago," I told him straight. "I knew she was my old lady the night you threw her out. But you were never my old man." Of course he was all right. I was just trying to make him feel like he was trying to make me feel.

He started blowing up and told me to get out. I knew he didn't mean it, because I was bringing him the rent. "If I left now," I told him, "you'd have me locked up. I'll wait till I'm of age. Then I'll see you in hell with your back broke."

"I'll be glad to get rid of you now," he tells me. "You're going to go bad, you might as well go now and get a good start."

"And you won't have me locked up for running away?"

"Why should I?" he asks. "All you been to me is trouble."

"What do you think you've been to me?" I asked him then. "A father? A lot you got to holler." And I grabbed my cap and left.

I took a room with Little Johnny Polish over on Western Avenue. Johnny called himself a juke-box mechanic, and he had a car. We went around fixing jukes whenever we got on the shorts. We really fixed them, too. Only, sometimes we'd make a mistake and hit some juke we'd already fixed once. We did that once in a bookie, of all places.

A tavern with a bookie in the back. I thought it looked familiar, but Johnny didn't say anything so we went right ahead. On the way out the bartender, who knew Johnny, called him over and said something, looking a little white. When we got in the car Johnny looked white too and I really wheeled out of there.

"They're gettin' tired of us in there," Johnny said after a while. "That's a syndicate box."

We didn't go near that joint again and were more careful altogether. We operated out of the neighborhood until the syndicate cooled off. And sometimes we'd have so many dimes, nickels, and quarters up in the room that we wouldn't even bother to divide them. We got a scale and weighed them. I remember we figured eleven ounces to the dollar.

The first time I took a fall I was alone, having coffee at a restaurant on Damen and Division. They sat down, one on either side of me, and the first thing that popped into my head was that they were syndicate men dressed like coppers. Something like that had happened in the neighborhood before.

They were real cops though. I had to sweat it out at Eleventh and State overnight and stand the showup before I found out that all it was was the old man. He'd reneged on his word to me, just as he had with Aunt. He'd given me out as a runaway and I had to put in twenty days at Juvenile.

All I remember of that stretch is this: when we came in

we were given a copy of the rules, told to make the best of things, and that was all the interest any of us received there.

The night I got out I slugged a peanut machine—one of those El platform jobs. It was in the dark, at the far end of the platform, and all I went up to the thing for was to get a handful of peanuts. But when I put my hand on the lever I felt the warmth of the day still trapped in the metal, and the warmth of Aunt's hand pressing pennies into my hand— before I knew what I was doing I'd slugged the glass with my naked fist.

It was absolutely crazy and I don't understand it myself to this day. I cut the hell out of my hand and a woman at the cashier's cage heard the tinkle of the glass. I would have been a lot smarter to have slugged her instead of the peanuts.

That was the only time I used raw-jaw methods. Rip-and-tear is all right for kids, but there's no future in it.

Johnny Polish laughed his head off over that one when he came up to see me at County. Then he had the ward superintendent put in the fix and all I got was thirty days. I was paroled to my old man. What a laugh.

I've never figured out to myself why I pinned everything onto the old man. Sometimes I think I started blaming him before I was born almost. It wasn't anything I tried figuring at all, it was just the way I *felt*, so deep down that it was beyond all figuring.

I used to wake up nights thinking of the night he'd given her the bum's rush when she didn't have a place to go. Except, perhaps, the Derby Hotel. When I thought of *that* I think I could have killed him as quick as stepping on a roach. And that easy.

And yet by that time it wouldn't have done me any more good than stepping on a roach. When I came out of County I had him where I could have stepped on him any time. Like it says in the song, I had him in the palm of my hand.

All I did was lay around the house smoking cigarettes and playing the radio loud and never letting the old man tune in the Polish hour, because that was the one program, I knew, which he understood and enjoyed. In fact it was the only thing he enjoyed and the one thing he'd bought the radio for. I'd turn on Spike Jones and he'd sit in the kitchen and drink and take it out on Ma. That was their business, so long as they stayed in the kitchen. He wanted me home, he'd told the police. So now he had me there. He wasn't in much of a position to tell them he'd changed his mind.

Some nights I'd have half the neighborhood in the front room. Little Johnny'd bring up a couple of neighborhood tramps and the joint would really jump. One night, just to get his goat, we started a strip-poker game. The old man lost his head and called the squad.

Little Johnny asked them in, and they saw who was there beside the tramps: the ward super, two precinct captains, Little Johnny, a Jew mouthpiece we called Noseberg O'Brien, and a bailiff from the Criminal Court. They asked us to be a little quiet about it and we slipped them a fin apiece, and they backed off. With all the writs and corpuses Noseberg O'Brien had in his hat, they were lucky to get out with their jobs, coming into a private home without a warrant like that.

After the party broke up I told the old man, polite-like, in Polish, that if he ever did a thing like that again they'd find him under the sink with his little toes turned up. Under the sink, with the rest of the pipes. But letting a roach go don't make you like him any more the next time you see him come crawlin'.

He *begged* me to leave then, and promised he wouldn't have me brought back.

"What's the use?" I said. "You'd have me locked up all over again is all."

"This time I won't," he said. And that time I knew he meant it at last. He had a stomachful of Little Augie by then.

I stayed home that night, and when I was packing, in the morning, he stuck his mug in the door and watched awhile, to see that I wasn't taking anything that belonged to him.

"You gonna die in jail, Augie," he tells me after a while, just to say something.

"You never cared where I lived," I told him, "a lot you got to holler where I die."

And I remembered how she had wanted to say good-by to me one night in this same house and he hadn't let her.

I didn't even say so long.

Hector Rodriguez
Jeremy Larner (ed.)

I started taking narcotics in the Bronx, when I was eleven. I was curious, but I wasn't using them that much—I was just taking marijuana once in a while and snorting; I wasn't shooting it up, I was just skinning it then. Skinning is just where you hit anywhere in your body and shoot the dope in. That's with heroin. And snorting is where you snort it up your nose, just like if you're sniffing something. And burning marijuana, that's just like smoking a cigarette, the only thing you inhale it, you don't let it out, you just try to hold it in.

I was using it up there, and then when I moved down here, I was still using it, you know, but I didn't have no habit or nothing. Like when I started going to school, I would go to school high, and I learned how to read a little high. You know, like I wanted to learn something, the things I need in life, but the teachers wouldn't teach me. They used to ignore me, and pay attention to the other kids. Then when I didn't want to learn, they used to come and try to teach me how to learn. Like I couldn't see that; it used to burn me up. I used to go to school high and start nodding all over the classroom, get drowsy, and that's when I started staying out of school; I didn't go to school no more than three or four months in a year.

That's when I started mainlining, when I got to be fifteen; I started mainlining like a dog. Then when I was sixteen, about three or four months ago, I told my mother I was on narcotics. She started crying, but I told her don't cry, if I was another kid I would probably keep it to myself and die by myself. All I want you to do is give me your signature. That way I can go away to Riverside and help myself. The day that I was going away my mother came and gave me some money, my sister gave me some money, and my mother said, I can't see you go, and I said, well go home, 'cause I can't see myself go, 'cause I love you and I know I done one of the most stupidest mistakes in my life. My mother left crying and that hurt me, you know, but I had to take it like a man, because I knew that I stepped into something that was bigger than myself.

Then when I went to Riverside, it wasn't that bad kicking, because they give you medication to calm down your sickness, and that way you can kick in peace. I was wrapped up in a blanket for five days with cold sweats, and when they came to bring my food I couldn't eat. Then after five days I started out with soup and milk, and I couldn't hold that in my system. After that when I started eating, I started going down to my social worker, having my team meetings.

I was on Team Two. Mr. W. was my social worker, Mr. Z. was my psychiatrist; then I had Mr. P. my psychologist, and I had a few other people there that I forgot their names. I used to go down and tell them my troubles and when they asked me how come I started using narcotics, I told them I was curious, because that was the truth; it wasn't because I had a problem or nothing, I was just curious, I played it stupid. I used to see my friends using it, I used to see them having fun, and I wanted to know what it was. When I got my hands on it I started to like it, so then it was too late to back out of it. So then I turned myself over to Riverside. They understood it, and at first they wanted to keep me six months, but I told them I wanted to come out, I wanted to start straight, see if I could get me a job, you know, to help out my parents. With a job I could occupy my time, kill time, stay away from everything. So they let me out, and every Thursday at six o'clock I got to check into the after-care clinic. I'm on three years' probation, and if I get caught with narcotics, I get taken in again, and this time they hit me with six months. And if I keep getting in trouble, they give me a year or send me upstate.

Marijuana smells like tea and olive seasoning mixed up together. Once you got it in you it makes you feel drowsy and it makes you forget about things you don't even want to know about. Or it just brings you out so you can have a gay time. If you want to jump around, you jump around; if you want to sit down and just be in a world of your own, you just sit down and look for your own kicks on it. Like if you see somebody and they come talk to you and something strikes you funny, you just crack up laughing. And you sit down, talk to a girl or boy, you know, like you got some company. You just stay sitting down in a corner and nobody can bother you, no trouble, no nothing. Since marijuana isn't habit-forming you can take it any time you feel like it. If you're in a good mood, you want to get gay, you haven't got nothing to do, you just go and buy yourself a couple of sticks, if you know anybody that sells it. You need to know the right person, 'cause you can go ask a cop for all I know, you need to know the right connection. If you get it, you just take it and there you are, in your own world.

I used to get it uptown, anywhere in Prospect Avenue, right in the streets. Like if you see a junkie and you know him, you just ask him where can I cop some pot? If he knows he'll take you, he'll cop for you. I paid 75 cents a stick, or a dollar for a bomb. A bomb is about as big as a Pall Mall and as fat as a Pall Mall. Like a regular cigarette. The other one is skinnier. I used to smoke it anywhere, like I coulda smoked it in a hallway, smoke it in my house, and if I wanted to just start walking down the street smoking it without nobody seeing me. Just cuff it up in my hand without nobody seeing me and keep on smoking it, just like if I'm smoking a cigarette. Like I would light up a cigarette and light up a joint, start smoking the joint, and everytime I would see a cop or a person coming up I would hide it in my hand or in my pocket and just take out the cigarette, keep on walking. That way nobody would suspect.

I was eleven when I started with marijuana and heroin, too. I stole the heroin off of some guys. I seen them put it up on a roof. I didn't like them because they push me around too much. And I said I don't know what it is, but the only way I can get even with them is by taking it. And I got two of my friends, you know, they were brothers; one of them was twelve and the other was thirteen, like they would shoot up and all. So I took it; since I had seen them doing it, I knew what it was already, more or less. I went and took it and then I knew what it felt like and I liked it. Then from there on I kept on using it.

When you snort heroin, you know, it got a bad bitter taste, like a taste that would turn your stomach inside out. It got some way-out taste. I couldn't snort because I couldn't take that taste; so I started shooting up. Shooting up you don't get the taste; all you get is a fast rush and a boss feeling, you know, like then you got a higher kick than marijuana. You feel drowsy, sit in a corner nodding, nobody to bother you, you're in your own world, in other words. You ain't got no problems whatsoever, you think freely, you don't think about things you were thinking about before shooting up, like you're in your own world, nobody to bother you or nothing.

The first time I skinned, like I wouldn't hit the vein, just pick up the spike and shove it in. Skin-popping, it takes quite a while before you feel it—take a couple of minutes, but it still do the same effect. Skin-popping you don't get no tracks or nothing. Now mainlining you get tracks, and you're hitting directly in the vein. You get a faster habit and while you're mainlining you can feel the stuff faster. Tracks are marks, black marks, like a long black streak coming down your arm directly over your vein; that comes from hitting in the same place so much. Now when you skin-pop you hit all over your body; you can't keep up with tracks. You lose them; they just keep falling off.

I was fifteen when I started mainlining. I got a set of works: a spike, a whisky bottle cap with a bobby pin around it to make like a handle, an eyedropper, and a baby's pacifier. Now when you cook the stuff you just put it inside the bottle cap, draw it up with the eyedropper, tie the dropper to the spike and just shoot it in your veins. You need water to cook it up—a lot of guys carry a little bottle. You have a special spot to shoot up, that's where you have your water stashed. You measure out the heroin into the water, light a match, and cook it up in the cooker just like when you're heating up a bowl of soup or something. They got a piece of cotton inside the cooker to help them draw it all up. They put the spike on the dropper, strap their arm up and wait till the veins come up and then just hit directly. You put the spike in slow, and the only way you know you got a hit is by watching the blood come up; then you just take off the strap and squeeze it in. Then you feel that rush all over your body and you got your high.

Once you squeeze it in, the drug circulates with your blood, it will come around your system, and all of a sudden your eyes will feel like they gonna close up on you. You feel drowsy, your mouth will dry up on you, your spit will turn into cotton balls, right?; then you just start nodding all over the place, take out the works, clean 'em and hide 'em. Then you got that boss feeling, man, like you're your own boss, there ain't nobody can tell you what to do in this world.

If you're weak-minded, if you get a habit, your body will like cramp up on you, your skin'll start shrinking up, you'll start getting sick and need a fix, you'll start sweating at the same time you'll feel cold, you'll be wrapped up in blankets. You'd do anything just to get a fix. For me to get my habit without mainlining it took me six months. I just kept on using it, and I kept on getting the money, right?, so I didn't have to worry about me getting sick. When I started to get sick and I needed the money for a fix, I would go tell my Mom, look I have to buy my girl a present, this and that, and my Mom would fall for it. She would give me the money, I would run down for a shot, take off, and my body would feel relieved, feel at ease. You know, I don't cramp up, then I feel boss. Then when I had money I got my works, and anybody want to use them have to give me a taste of their junk, and somehow I kept up with my habit. Till I finally realized that I didn't want to use it no more, I wanted to straighten up, I wanted to go to work, help out my parents.

I have my own works, right? Now you're using junk yet you ain't got your own works. Well, you will come to use mine, 'cause you can't snort and you need a shoot-up. Now I'll tell you you have to give me a fix before using my works. You ain't got no choice, you have to give me a fix or go on without one. I had a bathroom in Henry Street and then I had a roof in Henry Street. Inside the bathroom they got that box upstairs, the clean water, fresh water comes down to wash out the bowl; well we just take a canful and bring it down. I had a special rule, you know: nobody could come up and get me till after nine o'clock in the morning, 'cause I was out all night. I had two sets of works—the one at home and the one I lend out to the people. Now sometimes I tell them, look, I've already shot up, I don't want to shoot up, just put a little bit inside of this bag—and I'll go shoot that home. Then we would shoot up in that bathroom or up on the roof. After that I would stash the works downstairs where nobody could see me, go home and during the night when I'm sick I have my own works home. I would lock myself in the bathroom where nobody see me and shoot up there, all by myself.

That bowl, you know, in the bathroom—I used to move it, and we had like a loose brick where I stash them; and the minute I move it back in place it look like it was built there and nobody could move it. Now before I hide them I tell my fellas, okay now go downstairs, and I start walking upstairs. They would think that I'm hiding upstairs and I would just watch them leave, and then I would just run down and hide them, go upstairs and come down through the next building. That way they wouldn't know where I had them.

The works that I had home, I used to clean up the spike and wrap it up in a piece of aluminum paper. Then I would wrap up the cooker in a piece of aluminum paper. The eyedropper I would wrap up in a piece of bag paper, and put it all inside a box of Marlboro, you know, an empty pack of cigarettes, keep those home. Now the other works I used to wrap them up the same but wrap them up in a hanky and stash them. I kept this up till I was ready to go to Riverside, then I threw the works away, flushed them down the bowl piece by piece.

During a day I would take up two at a time; altogether it would come out to about sixteen fellas. Now you know if I was high, I wasn't gonna shoot up sixteen times, so I say okay, just start putting what you gonna give me inside this bag; then I just used to save it all up, and the next day I have my fix. I didn't have to worry about getting money or nothing.

The others couldn't get works. I had to steal my spike out of the hospital. Like when I went to the hospital for my penicillin shot when I had the Asiatic Flu, as the nurse walked out I seen where she threw the spike, inside a big jug full of alcohol. I just put my hand in and grabbed a whole bunch of spikes. I came out and I sold a whole lot of them to a whole lot of guys. And they lost them. But I still had two of them left, and I had my two sets of works, one home and one at the bathroom. And everybody after they lost theirs started coming to me. And I just kept collecting fixes.

I kept earning, I wouldn't sell nothing out. I figured if I sold something, I would spend the money, and later on like I be sick and nobody will come to give me a fix and I be stuck right there. So I used to keep taking in but I wouldn't give none out. A bag would be about a square inch—of that bag they would give me about a third. Now I would shoot up about four bags a day, right? The rest I would save and then I would have me about two more bags. I had it in my house stashed under the bureau. Or in the bathroom under the toilet bowl. I looked a long time before I found that place.

If one of them was nervous and he couldn't hit himself, if he would ask me I would hit him myself. I hit a lot of guys in my days. Now if a fella is capable to hit his own self, I would let him, I would let him judge his own self. Now I tell you I used to hit my own self. I wouldn't let no one hit me, I wouldn't take the chance. They might be nervous and run right through my vein, and who's gonna get messed up? Me.

In the morning, that's when everybody comes out sick, you know, to cop, and that's when I used to be ready with my works, just waiting for these people to come over my way. They used to come, boom! I would be collecting right there and then. They meet me in Henry Street. I wouldn't take nobody up to my house to shoot up, because I didn't want my parents to get a bad name. If I had a bad name why mess it up for my parents? I have to clear that up in my own ways. I would wait next to La Guardia Park, let 'em meet me there. When they come on I would say okay, go ahead, you know where to meet me. When they walk I would just run ahead, have the works and everything ready. I had a short-cut and I'd be there waiting for them.

About the junk itself, it is different depending on where and who you get it from. Now if one of these big operators, you know, the brain of the gang, if he would go and cop, and if he cops a piece that already been cut, he won't have to mess around with it unless he want to mess it up, you know, to make a little more out of it. Now if he go and cop a pure piece, that piece ought to be cut six and one, but he would come down and cut it two and one, make it nice and strong. Right there and then you got good junk, good heroin. Now if he were going to mess it up to get more junk than what he's supposed to get, he'll cut it up six and four, he'll loosen it up and make it weak, like guys won't cop off of him every day. By six and four I mean cutting it one spoon of pure heroin and six or four of sugar. They say it's supposed to be six and one, but if the dealer is wise, he wants everybody to keep coming to him, and he wants to give them a nice count so they can fall out, he will go and cut it two and one, or three and one, make it nice and strong.

Uptown they had this broad, you know, she was a woman already, she was married and she had three kids. She was a junkie and every time she would send somebody out to cop for her—'cause she wouldn't take the chance of going and buying for herself—they would beat her out of her money. And she started marking down the people who started doing that. And she lost her head. So she went and bag up a couple of bags full of rat poison, and when the guys came, you know, she told 'em, well I'm dealing now; and when they cop off her she say, well this guy didn't beat me or nothing, he didn't take my money, so she gave him a good bag. And she say, why this guy beat me, six times, so far he got 150 of my money. Boom! We'll give him a bag of rat poison and mess him up. Now if the guy taste it and know it's rat poison he can't do nothing about it, 'cause he beat her. If he shoots it up he's gonna die instantly.

I taste every bit of junk myself before I use it. I wouldn't take the chance—somebody could be sick, and they might want to get my money so they could get their real cure, and they might sell me a bag of Ajax or a bag of rat poison. And if I wouldn't taste it, if I would play stupid, I would just shoot it up, and like I would go out. Because rat poison cooks up. Now Ajax it cakes up on you, like it bubbles up, and I know if it's junk or not. I make a practice of tasting it, so I know what I'm getting and no one beats me for my money or tries to mess me up.

I had two overdoses in my life. One of them I had in Henry Street when I shot up, but it didn't hit me then, I didn't feel nothing till I walk downstairs. Boom! As soon as I hit the street I passed out. A guy took me up to his house, to his girl's house, and they woke me up. Then the second time I took too much, we were driving around inside a car and we were shooting up inside the car. I wind up in Jackson Park, unconscious, I done passed out, and the guys took me all the way back to Henry Street, took me up to a girl's house, gave me a salt shot, made me drink milk, forced milk down my system while I was out. Then they gave me some more salt shots and started slapping me out of it. Then when I opened one eye, they started walking me around. I was bleeding through my nose like a dog. After I woke up I thought I wasn't myself, because I was more than high. I still had that junk inside my system, and I was drowsy all over the street, I couldn't see where I was going.

It's very dangerous. If you go and shoot up someplace by yourself and you take an O.D. and you ain't got nobody to give you a salt shot, to help you out one-two-three, you'll die right there. You'll have white foam coming out of your mouth, you'll be bleeding. . . . This boy called Bobby, he died in a bathroom up here in Henry Street. He took an O.D. It was where Paul used to live. Paul came down and he was dead and Paul just stepped right over him. I know a lot of people died of overdoses.

I almost got yellow jaundice twice. I was here in Henry Street, and I was nodding. My friend came up and told me, hey, like your face is real yellow, man. Your whole body is yellow. Then when I went to the bathroom, my urinal came out like the color of tea. And the fellas told me, you know you could have yellow jaundice, and I told them no. And they looked at my eyes, made me stick out my tongue, and they said could you eat? And I told them no, and they said you got the reflex towards yellow jaundice, but we can't say for sure you got it. And like I didn't have it. I almost had it those two times, but I didn't get it. I didn't make it because I cut out in time.

I knew this Italian fellow who died of yellow jaundice in Bellevue. Like I knew George from Monroe Street. He had yellow jaundice, his eyes were all yellow; all you could see was a little black pit and the rest was all yellow. He went to the hospital and he came out all right, thank God. And a guy almost got his arm contaminated, they almost had to cut it off, because he blew air inside. He put air inside his veins and puffed them up. He was in the hospital for quite a while.

I've been walking around since I've been back, but I ain't seen none of the fellows who used to use my works. Except one, and he got popped the other day. He got picked up. I'm lucky I kicked.

The Screamers
LeRoi Jones

Lynn Hope adjusts his turban under the swishing red green yellow shadow lights. Dots. Suede heaven raining, windows yawning cool summer air, and his musicians watch him grinning, quietly, or high with wine blotches on four-dollar shirts. A yellow girl will not dance with me, nor will Teddy's people, in line to the left of the stage, readying their *Routines*. Haroldeen, the most beautiful, in her pitiful dead sweater. Make it yellow, wish it whole. Lights. Teddy, Sonny Boy, Kenny & Calvin, Scram, a few of Nat's boys jamming long washed handkerchiefs in breast pockets, pushing shirts into homemade cummerbunds, shuffling lightly for any audience.
"The Cross-Over,"
Deen laughing at us all. And they perform in solemn unison a social tract of love. With no music till Lynn finishes "macking" with any biglipped Esther screws across the stage. White and green plaid jackets his men wear, and that twisted badge, black turban/on red string conked hair. (OPPRESSORS!) A greasy hipness, down-ness, nobody in our camp believed (having social-worker mothers and postman fathers; or living squeezed in lightskinned projects with adulterers and proud skinny ladies with soft voices). The theory, the spectrum, this sound baked inside their heads, and still rub sweaty against those lesser lights. Those niggers. Laundromat workers, beauticians, pregnant short-haired jail bait separated all ways from "us," but in this vat we sweated gladly for each other. And rubbed. And Lynn could be a common hero, from whatever side we saw him. Knowing that energy, and its response. That drained silence we had to make with our hands, leaving actual love to Nat or Al or Scram.

He stomped his foot, and waved one hand. The other hung loosely on his horn. And their turbans wove in among those shadows. Lynn's tighter, neater, and bright gorgeous yellow stuck with a green stone. Also, those green sparkling cubes dancing off his pinkies. A-boomp bahba bahba, A-boomp bahba bahba, A-boomp bahba bahba, A-boomp bahba bahba, the turbans sway behind him. And he grins before he lifts the horn, at Deen or drunk Becky, and we search the dark for girls.

Who would I get? (Not anyone who would understand this.) Some light girl who had fallen into bad times and ill-repute for dating Bubbles. And he fixed her later with his child, now she walks Orange St. wiping chocolate from its face. A disgraced white girl who learned to calypso in vocational school. Hence, behind halting speech, a humanity as paltry as her cotton dress. (And the big hats made a line behind her, stroking their erections, hoping for photographs to take down south.) Lynn would oblige. He would make the most perverted hopes sensual and possible. Chanting at that dark crowd. Or some girl, a wino's daughter, with carefully vaselined bow legs would drape her filthy angora against the cardboard corinthian, eying past any greediness a white man knows, my soft tyrolean hat, pressed corduroy suit, and "B" sweater. Whatever they meant, finally, to her, valuable shadows barely visible.

Some stuck-up boy with "good" hair. And as a naked display of America, for I meant to her that same oppression. A stunted head of greased glass feathers, orange lips, brown pasted edge to the collar of her dying blouse. The secret perfume of poverty and ignorant desire. Arrogant too, at my disorder, which calls her smile mysterious. Turning to be eaten by the crowd. That mingled foliage of sweat and shadows: *Night Train* was what they swayed to. And smelled each other in The Grind, The Rub, The Slow Drag. From side to side, slow or jerked staccato as their wedding dictated. Big hats bent tight skirts, and some light girls' hair swept the resin on the floor. Respectable ladies put stiff arms on your waist to keep some light between, looking nervously at an ugly friend forever at the music's edge.

I wanted girls like Erselle, whose father sang on television, but my hair was not straight enough, and my father never learned how to drink. Our house sat lonely and large on a half-Italian street, filled with important Negroes. (Though it is rumored they had a son, thin with big eyes, they killed because he was crazy.) Surrounded by the haughty daughters of depressed economic groups. They plotted in their projects for mediocrity, and the neighborhood smelled of their despair. And only the wild or the very poor thrived in Graham's or could be roused by Lynn's histories and rhythms. America had choked the rest, who could sit still for hours under popular songs, or be readied for citizenship by slightly bohemian social workers. They rivaled pure emotion with wind-up record players that pumped Jo Stafford into Home Economics rooms. And these carefully scrubbed children of my parents' friends fattened on their rhythms until they could join the Urban League or Household Finance and hound the poor for their honesty.

I was too quiet to become a murderer, and too used to extravagance for their skinny lyrics. They mentioned neither cocaine nor Bach, which was my reading, and the flaw of that society. I disappeared into the slums, and fell in love with violence, and invented for myself a mysterious economy of need. Hence, I shambled anonymously thru Lloyd's, The Nitecap, The Hi-Spot, and Graham's desiring everything I felt. In a new English overcoat and green hat, scouring that town for my peers. And they were old pinch-faced whores full of snuff and weak dope, celebrity fags with radio programs, mute bass players who loved me, and built the myth of my intelligence. You see, I left America on the first fast boat.

This was Sunday night, and the Baptists were still praying in their "faboulous" churches. Though my father sat listening to the radio, or reading pulp cowboy magazines, which I take in part to be the truest legacy of my spirit. God never had a chance. And I would be walking slowly toward The Graham, not even knowing how to smoke. Willing for any experience, any image, any further separation from where my good grades were sure to lead. Frightened of post offices, lawyers' offices, doctors' cars, the deaths of clean politicians. Or of the imaginary fat man, advertising cemeteries to his "good colored friends." Lynn's screams erased them all, and I thought myself intrepid white commando from the West. Plunged into noise and flesh, and their form become an ethic.

Now Lynn wheeled and hunched himself for another tune. Fast dancers fanned themselves. Couples who practiced during the week talked over their steps. Deen and her dancing clubs readied *avant-garde* routines. Now it was *Harlem Nocturne,* which I whistled loudly one Saturday in a laundromat, and the girl who stuffed in my khakis and stiff underwear asked was I a musician. I met her at Graham's that night and we waved, and I suppose she knew I loved her.

Nocturne was slow and heavy and the serious dancers loosened their ties. The slowly twisting lights made specks of human shadows, the darkness seemed to float around the hall.

Any meat you clung to was yours those few minutes without interruption. The length of the music was the only form. And the idea was to press against each other hard, to rub, to shove the hips tight, and gasp at whatever passion. Professionals wore jocks against embarrassment. Amateurs, like myself, after the music stopped, put our hands quickly into our pockets, and retreated into the shadows. It was as meaningful as anything else we knew.

All extremes were popular with that crowd. The singers shouted, the musicians stomped and howled. The dancers ground each other past passion or moved so fast it blurred intelligence. We hated the popular song, and any freedman could tell you if you asked that white people danced jerkily, and were slower than our champions. One style, which developed as Italians showed up with pegs, and our own grace moved toward bellbottom pants to further complicate the cipher, was the honk. The repeated rhythmic figure, a screamed riff, pushed in its insistence past music. It was hatred and frustration, secrecy and despair. It spurted out of the diphthong culture, and reinforced the black cults of emotion. There was no compromise, no dreary sophistication, only the elegance of something that is too ugly to be described, and is diluted only at the agent's peril. All the saxophonists of that world were honkers, Illinois, Gator, Big Jay, Jug, the great sounds of our day. Ethnic historians, actors, priests of the unconscious. That stance spread like fire thru the cabarets and joints of the black cities, so that the sound itself became a basis for thought, and the innovators searched for uglier modes. Illinois would leap and twist his head, scream when he wasn't playing. Gator would strut up and down the stage, dancing for emphasis, shaking his long gassed hair in his face and coolly mopping it back. Jug, the beautiful horn, would wave back and forth so high we all envied him his connection, or he'd stomp softly to the edge of the stage whispering those raucous threats. Jay first turned the mark around, opened the way further for the completely nihilistic act. McNeeley, the first Dada coon of the age, jumped and stomped and yowled and finally sensed the only other space that form allowed. He fell first on his knees, never releasing the horn, and walked that way across the stage. We hunched together drowning any sound, relying on Jay's contorted face for evidence that there was still music, though none of us needed it now. And then he fell backwards, flat on his back, with both feet stuck up high in the air, and he kicked and thrashed and the horn spat enraged sociologies.

That was the night Hip Charlie, the Baxter Terrace Romeo, got wasted right in front of the place. Snake and four friends mashed him up and left him for the ofays to identify. Also the night I had the grey bells and sat in the Chinese restaurant all night to show them off. Jay had set a social form for the poor, just as Bird and Dizzy proposed it for the middle class. On his back screaming was the Mona Lisa with the mustache, as crude and simple. Jo Stafford could not do it. Bird took the language, and we woke up one Saturday whispering *Ornithology*. Blank verse.

And Newark always had a bad reputation, I mean, everybody could pop their fingers. Was hip. Had walks. Knew all about The Apple. So I suppose when the word got to Lynn what Big Jay had done, he knew all the little down cats were waiting to see him in this town. He knew he had to cook. And he blasted all night, crawled and leaped, then stood at the side of the stand, and watched us while he fixed his sky, wiped his face. Watched us to see how far he'd gone, but he was tired and we weren't, which was not where it was. The girls rocked slowly against the silence of the horns, and big hats pushed each other or made plans for murder. We had not completely come. All sufficiently eaten by Jay's memory, "on his back, kicking his feet in the air, Go-ud Damn!" So he moved cautiously to the edge of the stage, and the gritty Muslims he played with gathered close. It was some mean honking blues, and he made no attempt to hide his intentions. He was breaking bad. "Okay, baby," we all thought, "Go for yourself." I was standing at the back of the hall with one arm behind my back, so the overcoat could hang over in that casual gesture of fashion. Lynn was moving, and the camel walkers were moving in the corners. The fast dancers and practicers making the whole hall dangerous. "Off my suedes, motherfucker." Lynn was trying to move us, and even I did the one step I knew, safe at the back of the hall. The hippies ran for girls. Ugly girls danced with each other. Skippy, who ran the lights, made them move faster in that circle on the ceiling, and darkness raced around the hall. Then Lynn got his riff, that rhythmic figure we knew he would repeat, the honked note that would be his personal evaluation of the world. And he screamed it so the veins in his face stood out like neon. "Uhh, yeh, Uhh, yeh, Uhh, yeh," we all screamed to push him further. So he opened his eyes for a second, and really made his move. He looked over his shoulder at the other turbans, then marched in time with his riff, on his toes across the stage. They followed; he marched across to the other side, repeated, then finally he descended, still screaming, into the crowd, and as the sidemen followed, we made a path for them around the hall. They were strutting, and all their horns held very high, and they were only playing that one scary note. They moved near the back of the hall, chanting and swaying, and passed right in front of me. I had a little cup full of wine a murderer friend of mine made me drink, so I drank it and tossed the cup in the air, then fell in line behind the last wild horn man, strutting like the rest of them. Bubbles and Rogie followed me, and four-eyed Moselle Boyd. And we strutted back and forth pumping our arms, repeating with Lynn Hope, "Yeh, Uhh, Yeh, Uhh." Then everybody fell in behind us, yelling still. There was confusion and stumbling, but there were no real fights. The thing they wanted was right there and easily accessible. No one could stop you from getting in that line. "It's too crowded. It's too many people on the line!" some people yelled. So Lynn thought further, and made to destroy the ghetto. We went out into the lobby and in perfect rhythm down the marble steps. Some musicians laughed, but Lynn and some others kept the note, till the others fell back in. Five or six hundred hopped-up woogies tumbled out into Belmont Avenue. Lynn marched right in the center of the street. Sunday night traffic stopped, and honked. Big Red yelled at a bus driver, "Hey, baby, honk that horn in time or shut it off!" The bus driver cooled it. We screamed and screamed at the clear image of ourselves as we should always be. Ecstatic, completed, involved in a secret communal expression. It would be the form of the sweetest revolution, to huckle-buck into the fallen capital, and let the oppressors lindy hop out. We marched all the way to Spruce, weaving among the stalled cars, laughing at the dazed white men who sat behind the wheels. Then Lynn turned and we strutted back toward the hall. The late show at the National was turning out, and all the big hats there jumped right in our line.

Then the Nabs came, and with them, the fire engines. What was it, a labor riot? Anarchists? A nigger strike? The paddy wagons and cruisers pulled in from both sides, and sticks and billies started flying, heavy streams of water splattering the marchers up and down the street. America's responsible immigrants were doing her light work again. The knives came out, the razors, all the Biggers who would not be bent, counterattacked or came up behind the civil servants smashing at them with coke bottles and aerials. Belmont writhed under the dead economy and splivs floated in the gutters, disappearing under cars. But for a while, before the war had reached its peak, Lynn and his musicians, a few other fools, and I, still marched, screaming thru the maddened crowd. Onto the sidewalk, into the lobby, halfway up the stairs, then we all broke our different ways, to save whatever it was each of us thought we loved.

LOVING

Georgy
Jon Lomberg

Hare

Rama

Hare

Rama

Rama

Rama

Hare

Hare

But her real name I later found out was Ellen something and she was from Georgia though now she lived on Long Island but she told me her name was Georgy and names and origins didn't seem so important on that day when you'd turn around and poof! magic you'd be in love with the person who was there and you'd smile or give them a ruby crystal or a kiss and stay with them for a second or an hour but what's time anyway? I first saw her sometime shortly before or after Beth, unlooked-for and unexpected, came into my arms, weeping dirty smelling starved and frightened, a black witch from the North who tripped out in brilliant and tragic bursts, sucking her retinue of Beth-people along with her into the savage pits wherein she wandered. But she wasn't marching for Peace in Vietnam or chanting the Hare Rama and I didn't want to be a Beth-person any more because I wanted colors she could never give. I invited her to come with me, on a joint trip I would lead, but she fled leaving an uptown address scrawled on my hand where I could bring her wine and pastry the next morning if I chose to serve her again.

The Sheep Meadow is a big place and hard to fill but it was filled that morning. Frantic organizers (organizers!) had planted signs all around —Mothers, Businessmen, Students, Indians, Veterans—to try and get everyone in order, but I would march where I happened to be and couldn't bother with a place in line, so Paul and I, eventually separating from Sean and Ronnie and Helene and the others of our tribe, wandered toward the rock where I had met them all

Hare	when the sun rose on Easter and where we
Krishna	heard now again as before as if it had been sung
	and droned continuously since we were last
Hare Hare	there the beloved Hare Rama Hare Rama Rama
	Rama Hare Krishna Hare Krishna Krishna
	Krishna Hare Hare chanted to bells and drums
Krishna	by friends there. The people from the Con-
Krishna	sciousness Center were up on the rock and I
Krishna	saw the pretty mustached and somewhat effete
	in tight boots man beating his tambourine and
	dancing. I waved and shouted hello to him and
Hare	he waved back though he didn't recognize me.
	A person carried a big sign with the chant in-
Hare	scribed on it for the ones who didn't know and
	everyone learned and sang and grooved glad-
Hare	ness. Costumes beautiful tissue clothes spring
	silk-screened Love incantation Victorian even-
Rama	ing gown plush and gallons of beads from Haiti
	and Samarkand and Fourth Street and my
Hare	wide white Robin Hood Don Giovanni hat soar-
Rama	ing me up and through and into. Paul's mus-
Rama	tache bounced as he did singing Hare Rama
	Hare Rama Krishna Rama Krishna Krishna
Rama	Hare Hare and I laughed at his Paulness and he
	at me.
Hare	Turning at a moment Georgy appeared and
Hare	smiled and was young and nice and rather
Hare	askewedly pretty and she wanted my smile as
Krishna	she threw balloons at me and I taught her
	the chant. Unadorned she glowed through
Hare	clothes of Long Island sloppy, though beautiful
Krishna	nakedness would have been better and I took
Krishna	the bells from my feet and gave them to her and
	as we hopped, I in my hat and she in her bells,
Krishna	we rang and were dashing together.
Hare	Later separated I saw her again in the long
Hare	line of march down Park Avenue now with Red-
Hare	beard, and Paul and I, each with arms around
Rama	walking and kissing new friends, waved to her
	and she to us happy in the rediscovery though
Hare	none would not have been mourned because we
Rama	had met once and would not forget.
Hare	Before the UN the Hare Rama began again
Krishna	in a huge singing circle with clappers on the

outside and dancers   Rama
in the middle, great vibrating shouts Hare and smiles Hare   Hare Krishna and everyone stopping to curl their fingers Rama in
            Hare   Krishna Hare
the chant of Om which is Krishna Krishna Krishna the breath of the universe rhythm sounding through all and is in curves of grass and stars Rama Rama and I was Wounded Eagle fluttering in diminishing circles to the cement around
            Rama Rama
around Hare Hare one arm strong and waving and the other
            Krishna Hare
in tight Hare Rama with Georgy and Redbeard and Paul laughing and hugging Krishna small circle within
            Krishna
the circle whirling whirling whirling Hare Hare Rama circle of family anyone could join chanting and kissing until it Hare Rama began Hare Rama to Hare Rama Hare rain Ramaramarama

Then walking down Park to the Village in a line strung out the width of the sidewalk: Paul, his George Harrison mustache streaming water and hoarse from so much singing; the two lithe and happy models with whom we had marched before; Redbeard, tall and rangy in high boots looking like Strider or a Dunedain; me, under my curving hat wing; Georgy, ringing every other step; and a new person in a black cape who played on a flute and whose cloak spread out to shield Georgy and part of my right side from the rain. Arms around each other, tightly laughing in step and chanting together.

Later at Reenee's house, the two models and the cloaked stranger gone now, sitting and smoking pot and playing. Georgy took the pipe and drew enormous puffs, which she immediately let escape through the other side of her mouth, and Redbeard smiled to me and to her, gently, "Inhale it and hold it in more." She

Rama	talked to me about her name and about her parents and sad and dead home life high school and then realized that she was away from that
Hare	here and with family.
Rama	Finally Redbeard's exit into the night and Reenee and Paul and Georgy and I sleeping naked together on one immense double bed, all
Rama	clothes fallen away leaving our natural breasts and arms and hair and loving parts all Reenee's and mine and Paul's and Georgy's and the bells
Rama	around her ankle still jingling and that her too. Listening to one another's gasps and
Hare	joy washing all through the air as though each orgasm at the same time belonged to the in-
Hare	dividual and to the family, a little family that had been built that night just by chance and would dissolve in the morning probably for-
Krishna	ever. Getting up in the night to make chili and then sleep, touches and caresses all around and a bright and happy morning.
Hare	Gentle glide down peace at Sean's later that day with more of the tribe, Day-glo paint for my hitchhiking sign and toast with honey and
Krishna	eggs and the I Ching and games and intricate Magic Marker designs drawn on each others' backs. Reading Thor comics by the side of the highway next to the George Washington Bridge with Reenee and Ronnie the filmmaker who sat with Georgy since I had earlier presented
Krishna	her to him ceremoniously and solemnly, smoking more pot, this almost discovered by police who slowed down to watch us until Reenee and I skipped away kissing, playful lovers, with all the pot in her pocket, lovers in the park. Evening coming, time to go, hitchhike to Con-
Krishna	necticut and good-by to Reenee and Ronnie and Paul and Sean. And Georgy.
	She wrote me once, telling me that she went home soon after I left, about the cop that stopped and smiled at her bells ching-ching in
Hare	the subway, about the math test she flunked, about going over to Reenee's to help her paint and playing with her kitten. I wanted to write back but couldn't decipher the home address

and I was a little sad because children are to be treasured and helped to grow to a better maturity, to find new thoughts to color the frames her mind was building. Reenee later told me she had been grounded by her parents because of her new friends, but that is no barrier. She will grow and flower and find new Jons and Pauls and Reenees where she goes and hope, happiness.

Hare Hare Rama Rama Krishna Krishna Krishna Rama Hare Hare

Black Is My Favorite Color
Bernard Malamud

Charity Sweetness sits in the toilet eating her two hardboiled eggs while I'm having my ham sandwich and coffee in the kitchen. That's how it goes only don't get the idea of ghettoes. If there's a ghetto I'm the one that's in it. She's my cleaning woman from Father Divine and comes in once a week to my small three-room apartment on my day off from the liquor store. "Peace," she says to me, "Father reached on down and took me right up in Heaven." She's a small person with a flat body, frizzy hair, and a quiet face that the light shines out of, and Mama had such eyes before she died. The first time Charity Sweetness came in to clean, a little more than a year and a half, I made the mistake to ask her to sit down at the kitchen table with me and eat her lunch. I was still feeling not so hot after Ornita left but I'm the kind of a man—Nat Lime, forty-four, a bachelor with a daily growing bald spot on the back of my head, and I could lose frankly fifteen pounds—who enjoys company so long as he has it. So she cooked up her two hardboiled eggs and sat down and took a small bite out of one of them. But after a minute she stopped chewing and she got up and carried the eggs in a cup in the bathroom, and since then she eats there. I said to her more than once, "Okay, Charity Sweetness, so have it your way, eat the eggs in the kitchen by yourself and I'll eat when you're done," but she smiles absentminded, and eats in the toilet. It's my fate with colored people.

Although black is still my favorite color you wouldn't know it from my luck except in short quantities even though I do all right in the liquor store business in Harlem, on Eighth Avenue between 110th and 111th. I speak with respect. A large part of my life I've had dealings with Negro people, most on a business basis but sometimes for friendly reasons with genuine feeling on both sides. I'm drawn to them. At this time of my life I should have one or two good colored friends but the fault isn't necessarily mine. If they knew what was in my heart towards them, but how can you tell that to anybody nowadays? I've tried more than once but the language of the heart either is a dead language or else nobody understands it the way you speak it. Very few. What I'm saying is, personally for me there's only one human color and that's the color of blood. I like a black person if not because he's black, then because I'm white. It comes to the same thing. If I wasn't white my first choice would be black. I'm satisfied to be white because I have no other choice. Anyway, I got an eye for color. I appreciate. Who wants everybody to be the same? Maybe it's like some kind of a talent. Nat Lime might be a liquor dealer in Harlem, but once in the jungle in New Guinea in the Second War, I got the idea when I shot at a running Jap and missed him, that I had some kind of a talent, though maybe it's the kind where you have a marvelous idea now and then but in the end what do they come to? After all, it's a strange world.

Where Charity Sweetness eats her eggs makes me think about Buster Wilson when we were both boys in the Williamsburg section of Brooklyn. There was this long block of run-down dirty frame houses in the middle of a not-so-hot white neighborhood full of pushcarts. The Negro houses looked to me like they had been born and died there, dead not long after the beginning of the world. I lived on the next street. My father was a cutter with arthritis in both hands, big red knuckles and swollen fingers so he didn't cut, and my mother was the one who went to work. She sold paper bags from a second-hand pushcart in Ellery Street. We didn't starve but nobody ate chicken unless we were sick or the chicken was. This was my first acquaintance with a lot of black people and I used to poke around on their poor block. I think I thought, brother, if there can be like this, what can't there be? I mean I caught an early idea what life was about. Anyway I met Buster Wilson there. He used to play marbles by himself. I sat on the curb across the street, watching him shoot one marble lefty and the other one righty. The hand that won picked up the marbles. It wasn't so much of a game but he didn't ask me to come over. My idea was to be friendly, only he never encouraged, he discouraged. Why did I pick him out for a friend? Maybe because I had no others then, we were new in the neighborhood, from Manhattan. Also I liked his type. Buster did everything alone. He was a skinny kid and his brothers' clothes hung on him like worn-out potato sacks. He was a beanpole boy, about twelve, and I was then ten. His arms and legs were burnt out matchsticks. He always wore a brown wool sweater, one arm half unraveled, the other went down to the wrist. His long and narrow head had a white part cut straight in the short woolly hair, maybe with a ruler there, by his father, a barber but too drunk to stay a barber. In those days though I had little myself I was old enough to know who was better off, and the whole block of colored houses made me feel bad in the daylight. But I went there as much as I could because the street was full of life. In the night it looked different, it's hard to tell a cripple in the dark. Sometimes I was afraid to walk by the houses when they were dark and quiet. I was afraid there were people looking at me that I couldn't see. I liked it better when they had parties at night and everybody had a good time. The musicians played their banjos and saxophones and the houses shook with the music and laughing. The young girls, with their pretty dresses and ribbons in their hair, caught me in my throat when I saw them through the windows.

But with the parties came drinking and fights. Sundays were bad days after the Saturday night parties. I remember once that Buster's father, also long and loose, always wearing a dirty gray Homburg hat, chased another black man in the street with a half-inch chisel. The other one, maybe five feet high, lost his shoe and when they wrestled on the ground he was already bleeding through his suit, a thick red blood smearing the sidewalk. I was frightened by the blood and wanted to pour it back in the man who was bleeding from the chisel. On another time Buster's father was playing in a crap game with two big bouncy red dice, in the back of an alley between two middle houses. Then about six men started fist-fighting there, and they ran out of the alley and hit each other in the street. The neighbors, including children, came out and watched, everybody afraid but nobody moving to do anything. I saw the same thing near my store in Harlem, years later, a big crowd watching two men in the street, their breaths hanging in the air on a winter night, murdering each other with switch knives, but nobody moved to call a cop. I didn't either. Anyway, I was just a young kid but I still remember how the cops drove up in a police paddy wagon and broke up the fight by hitting everybody they could hit with big nightsticks. This was in the days before LaGuardia. Most of the fighters were knocked out cold, only one or two got away. Buster's father started to run back in his house but a cop ran after him and cracked him on his Homburg hat with a club, right on the front porch. Then the Negro men were lifted up by the cops, one at the arms and the other at the feet, and they heaved them in the paddy wagon. Buster's father hit the back of the wagon and fell, with his nose spouting very red blood, on top of three other men. I personally couldn't stand it, I was scared of the human race so I ran home, but I remember Buster watching without any expression in his eyes. I stole an extra fifteen cents from my mother's pocketbook and I ran back and asked Buster if he wanted to go to the movies. I would pay. He said yes. This was the first time he talked to me.

So we went more than once to the movies. But we never got to be friends. Maybe because it was a one-way proposition —from me to him. Which includes my invitations to go with me, my (poor mother's) movie money, Hershey chocolate bars, watermelon slices, even my best Nick Carter and Merriwell books that I spent hours picking up in the junk shops, and that he never gave me back. Once he let me go in his house to get a match so we could smoke some butts we found, but it smelled so heavy, so impossible, I died till I got out of there. What I saw in the way of furniture I won't mention—the best was falling apart in pieces. Maybe we went to the movies all together five or six matinees that spring and in the summertime, but when the shows were over he usually walked home by himself.

"Why don't you wait for me, Buster?" I said. "We're both going in the same direction."

But he was walking ahead and didn't hear me. Anyway he didn't answer.

One day when I wasn't expecting it he hit me in the teeth. I felt like crying but not because of the pain. I spit blood and said, "What did you hit me for? What did I do to you?"

"Because you a Jew bastard. Take your Jew movies and your Jew candy and shove them up your Jew ass."

And he ran away.

I thought to myself how was I to know he didn't like the movies. When I was a man I thought, you can't force it.

Years later, in the prime of my life, I met Mrs. Ornita Harris. She was standing by herself under an open umbrella at the bus stop, crosstown 110th, and I picked up her green glove that she had dropped on the wet sidewalk. It was in the end of November. Before I could ask her was it hers, she grabbed the glove out of my hand, closed her umbrella, and stepped in the bus. I got on right after her.

I was annoyed so I said, "If you'll pardon me, Miss, there's no law that you have to say thanks, but at least don't make a criminal out of me."

"Well, I'm sorry," she said, "but I don't like white men trying to do me favors."

I tipped my hat and that was that. In ten minutes I got off the bus but she was already gone.

Who expected to see her again but I did. She came into my store about a week later for a bottle of scotch.

"I would offer you a discount," I told her, "but I know you don't like a certain kind of a favor and I'm not looking for a slap in the face."

Then she recognized me and got a little embarrassed.

"I'm sorry I misunderstood you that day."

"So mistakes happen."

The result was she took the discount. I gave her a dollar off.

She used to come in about every two weeks for a fifth of Haig and Haig. Sometimes I waited on her, sometimes my helpers, Jimmy or Mason, also colored, but I said to give the discount. They both looked at me but I had nothing to be ashamed. In the spring when she came in we used to talk once in a while. She was a slim woman, dark but not the most dark, about thirty years I would say, also well built, with a combination nice legs and a good-size bosom that I like. Her face was pretty, with big eyes and high cheek bones, but lips a little thick and nose a little broad. Sometimes she didn't feel like talking, she paid for the bottle, less discount, and walked out. Her eyes were tired and she didn't look to me like a happy woman.

I found out her husband was once a window cleaner on the big buildings, but one day his safety belt broke and he fell fifteen stories. After the funeral she got a job as a manicurist in a Times Square barber shop. I told her I was a bachelor and lived with my mother in a small three-room apartment on West Eighty-third near Broadway. My mother had cancer, and Ornita said she was very sorry.

One night in July we went out together. How that happened I'm still not so sure. I guess I asked her and she didn't say no. Where do you go out with a Negro woman? We went to the Village. We had a good dinner and walked in Washington Square Park. It was a hot night. Nobody was surprised when they saw us, nobody looked at us like we were against the law. If they looked maybe they saw my new lightweight suit that I bought yesterday and my shiny bald spot when we walked under a lamp, also how pretty she was for a man of my type. We went in a movie on West Eighth Street. I didn't want to go in but she said she had heard about the picture. We went in like strangers and we came out like strangers. I wondered what was in her mind and I thought to myself, whatever is in there it's not a certain white man that I know. All night long we went together like we were chained. After the movie she wouldn't let me take her back to Harlem. When I put her in a taxi she asked me, "Why did we bother?"

For the steak, I wanted to say. Instead I said, "You're worth the bother."

"Thanks anyway."

Kiddo, I thought to myself after the taxi left, you just found out what's what, now the best thing is forget her.

It's easy to say. In August we went out the second time. That was the night she wore a purple dress and I thought to myself, my God, what colors. Who paints that picture paints a masterpiece. Everybody looked at us but I had pleasure. That night when she took off her dress it was in a furnished room I had the sense to rent a few days before. With my sick mother, I couldn't ask her to come to my apartment, and she didn't want me to go home with her where she lived with her brother's family on West 115th near Lenox Avenue. Under her purple dress she wore a black slip, and when she took that off she had white underwear. When she took off the white underwear she was black again. But I know where the next white was, if you want to call it white. And that was the night I think I fell in love with her, the first time in my life though I have liked one or two nice girls I used to go with when I was a boy. It was a serious proposition. I'm the kind of a man when I think of love I'm thinking of marriage. I guess that's why I am a bachelor.

That same week I had a holdup in my place, two big men —both black—with revolvers. One got excited when I rang open the cash register so he could take the money and he hit me over the ear with his gun. I stayed in the hospital a couple of weeks. Otherwise I was insured. Ornita came to see me. She sat on a chair without talking much. Finally I saw she was uncomfortable so I suggested she ought to go home.

"I'm sorry it happened," she said.

"Don't talk like it's your fault."

When I got out of the hospital my mother was dead. She was a wonderful person. My father died when I was thirteen and all by herself she kept the family alive and together. I sat shive for a week and remembered how she sold paper bags on her pushcart. I remembered her life and what she tried to teach me. Nathan, she said, if you ever forget you are a Jew a goy will remind you. Mama, I said, rest in peace on this subject. But if I do something you don't like, remember, on earth it's harder than where you are. Then when my week of mourning was finished, one night I said, "Ornita, let's get married. We're both honest people and if you love me like I love you it won't be such a bad time. If you don't like New York I'll sell out here and we'll move someplace else. Maybe to San Francisco where nobody knows us. I was there for a week in the Second War and I saw white and colored living together."

"Nat," she answered me, "I like you but I'd be afraid. My husband woulda killed me."

"Your husband is dead."

"Not in my memory."

"In that case I'll wait."

"Do you know what it'd be like—I mean the life we could expect?"

"Ornita," I said, "I'm the kind of a man, if he picks his own way of life he's satisfied."

"What about children? Were you looking forward to half-Jewish polka dots?"

"I was looking forward to children."

"I can't," she said.

Can't is can't. I saw she was afraid and the best thing was not to push. Sometimes when we met she was so nervous that whatever we did she couldn't enjoy it. At the same time I still thought I had a chance. We were together more and more. I got rid of my furnished room and she came to my apartment —I gave away Mama's bed and bought a new one. She stayed with me all day on Sundays. When she wasn't so nervous she was affectionate, and if I know what love is, I had it. We went out a couple of times a week, the same way—usually I met her in Times Square and sent her home in a taxi, but I talked more about marriage and she talked less against it. One night she told me she was still trying to convince herself but she was almost convinced. I took an inventory of my liquor stock so I could put the store up for sale.

Ornita knew what I was doing. One day she quit her job,

the next she took it back. She also went away a week to visit her sister in Philadelphia for a little rest. She came back tired but said maybe. Maybe is maybe so I'll wait. The way she said it it was closer to yes. That was the winter two years ago. When she was in Philadelphia I called up a friend of mine from the Army, now a CPA, and told him I would appreciate an invitation for an evening. He knew why. His wife said yes right away. When Ornita came back we went there. The wife made a fine dinner. It wasn't a bad time and they told us to come again. Ornita had a few drinks. She looked relaxed, wonderful. Later, because of a twenty-four hour taxi strike I had to take her home on the subway. When we got to the 116th Street station she told me to stay on the train, and she would walk the couple of blocks to her house. I didn't like a woman walking alone on the streets at that time of the night. She said she never had any trouble but I insisted nothing doing. I said I would walk to her stoop with her and when she went upstairs I would go back to the subway.

On the way there, on 115th in the middle of the block before Lenox, we were stopped by three men—maybe they were boys. One had a black hat with a half-inch brim, one a green cloth hat, and the third wore a black leather cap. The green hat was wearing a short coat and the other two had long ones. It was under a street light but the leather cap snapped a six-inch switchblade open in the light.

"What you doin' with this white son of a bitch?" he said to Ornita.

"I'm minding my own business," she answered him, "and I wish you would too."

"Boys," I said, "we're all brothers. I'm a reliable merchant in the neighborhood. This young lady is my dear friend. We don't want any trouble. Please let us pass."

"You talk like a Jew landlord," said the green hat. "Fifty a week for a single room."

"No charge fo' the rats," said the half-inch brim.

"Believe me, I'm no landlord. My store is 'Nathan's Liquors' between Hundred Tenth and Eleventh. I also have two colored clerks, Mason and Jimmy, and they will tell you I pay good wages as well as I give discounts to certain customers."

"Shut your mouth, Jewboy," said the leather cap, and he moved the knife back and forth in front of my coat button. "No more black pussy for you."

"Speak with respect about this lady, please."

I got slapped on my mouth.

"That ain't no lady," said the long face in the half-inch brim, "that's black pussy. She deserve to have evvy bit of her hair shave off. How you like to have evvy bit of your hair shave off, black pussy?"

"Please leave me and this gentleman alone or I'm gonna scream long and loud. That's my house three doors down."

They slapped her. I never heard such a scream. Like her husband was falling fifteen stories.

I hit the one that slapped her and the next I knew I was laying in the gutter with a pain in my head. I thought, goodbye, Nat, they'll stab me for sure, but all they did was take my wallet and run in three different directions.

Ornita walked back with me to the subway and she wouldn't let me go home with her again.

"Just get home safely."

She looked terrible. Her face was gray and I still remembered her scream. It was a terrible winter night, very cold February, and it took me an hour and ten minutes to get home. I felt bad for leaving her but what could I do?

We had a date downtown the next night but she didn't show up, the first time.

In the morning I called her in her place of business.

"For God's sake, Ornita, if we got married and moved away we wouldn't have that kind of trouble that we had. We wouldn't come in that neighborhood any more."

"Yes, we would. I have family there and don't want to move anyplace else. The truth of it is I can't marry you, Nat. I got troubles enough of my own."

"I coulda sworn you love me."

"Maybe I do but I can't marry you."

"For God's sake, why?"

"I got enough trouble of my own."

I went that night in a cab to her brother's house to see her. He was a quiet man with a thin mustache. "She gone," he said, "left for a long visit to some close relatives in the South. She said to tell you she appreciate your intentions but didn't think it will work out."

"Thank you kindly," I said.

Don't ask me how I got home.

Once on Eighth Avenue, a couple of blocks from my store, I saw a blind man with a white cane tapping on the sidewalk. I figured we were going in the same direction so I took his arm.

"I can tell you're white," he said.

A heavy colored woman with a full shopping bag rushed after us.

"Never mind," she said, "I know where he live."

She pushed me with her shoulder and I hurt my leg on the fire hydrant.

That's how it is. I give my heart and they kick me in my teeth.

"Charity Sweetness—you hear me?—come out of that goddamn toilet!"

A Story for Teddy
Harvey Swados

What is it that drives us to consider the girls of our youth, those we enjoyed for a day or a month, those whose scruples we strove and strained to overcome, those who scorned us, those who fled? I am not sure, since even the easy nostalgia arising from the memory of success must give way to other emotions when defeats and not victories come to mind. In the case of Teddy, it was an accident, a typically New York accident, which brought her back to me not long ago, but it is only as a result of my own deliberate life as a writer, and the painful, endless effort to understand, that she has come back with such clarity that I can close my eyes now and see not merely as much but more than I saw twenty years ago.

When I try to recall how I first came to know Teddy, I think back to a double date early in the war, arranged by an acquaintance. Teddy was his date, but my own I cannot visualize in any way—she was surely one of those girls who sit near the telephone, waiting to be fixed up by an attractive cousin. Teddy must have been that cousin. Within an hour of our having met, while the other two danced (we were in some collegiate hangout in Yorkville), I was urging her to go out with me.

Teddy colored. With her fingertips she pushed her ginger ale glass toward my bourbon glass. "You're pretty fast."

"I have to be."

Teddy was not very strong on repartee, and I fancied that I was ruthless. She was just eighteen, went to college at night, was taking courses in child psychology, and worked by day as a steno for some agency that helped soldiers' families, like Travelers Aid. She lived with her little brother and their widowed mother in an apartment house in a remote fastness of the Bronx. All that mattered to me was that she was lovely.

As for me, I was twenty-three and terribly world-weary. I had worked as a copy boy on the old New York *Sun* the year between college and the Merchant Marine, long enough to learn my way around town. I had only three months before finishing boot camp and shipping out, and I was anxious to waste as little time as possible.

Teddy was not sharp and competitive, like the girls I had known at Ohio State and around Manhattan. She was simple, unambitious, and vulnerable. She made no pretense of being smart or well read, but she was gentle and modest and virginal, and utterly unsophisticated—you might have thought she was the one from Ashtabula instead of me. Her skin was clean and glowing, her blond hair tumbled over her forehead, her lavender eyes were soft and troubled.

I picked up her small, defenseless hand, ostensibly so that I could admire her charm bracelet, from which dangled a little Scottie and a windmill with revolving sails; she had gotten it from her father for her fourteenth birthday. Squeezing her still childish fingers, I said, with a self-pity that was realer than she could imagine, "I've only got my weekends—and not too many of them—before I ship out. Won't you meet me next Saturday? In the afternoon, as soon as I can get in? Say at two-thirty, under the clock at the Biltmore?"

All that week I thought about Teddy. In the clapboard barracks where, like college boys all over America, I was learning with a thrill of despair that my fellow citizens from farm and factory were foul-mouthed, ignorant, and bigoted, it was difficult enough to remember that girls like Teddy still existed. Teddy, snub-nosed and sincere, in awe of me because I came from out of town and had hitchhiked to California and back, and eager to help me forget that hell-hole where I alternately sweated and froze; such a girl took on the proportions of a prize, one I had been awarded without even being fully eligible.

When I pushed my way into the Biltmore lobby through the swirling Saturday crowds, I was struck speechless at the sight of Teddy, already waiting for me. Not only was she unaware that she had breached the code by arriving early, but she did not even seem to notice how she was being sized up by a group of nudging sailors. She was nervous, yes, but only —I could tell—because she was looking for me. The tip of her blunt little nose was pinker than her cheeks, and she dabbed at it with a handkerchief that she took from the pocket of her fur-trimmed plaid coat as she squinted this way and that, searching for me. I realized for the first time that she was nearsighted.

I hung back for just a moment, then stepped forward and called out her name.

With a glad cry she hastened toward me. "I was afraid I might have missed you in all this crowd."

"I was afraid you wouldn't show up at all."

"Silly." This was a word Teddy used often. But she was pleased, and as she pressed my arm I could smell her perfume, light and girlish. "What are we going to do?"

I wanted to show her off. Outside, I led her over to Fifth Avenue, then north, and we paused now and then in the faltering late-October sunlight to look in the shop windows. With Teddy at my side I felt once again a part of the life of the city, secure for the moment at least, as I had not felt wandering forlornly with my false liberty, or hanging, miserable, around the battered ping-pong tables of the USO, waiting for nothing.

At 53rd Street we headed west and stopped at the Museum of Modern Art. The bulletin board announced an old Garbo movie. I turned to Teddy.

"We're just in time for the three-o'clock showing."

"Don't you have to be a member or something?" Teddy looked at me uneasily.

I was still learning how provincial some of these New York girls could be. I led Teddy through the revolving glass doors and took unhesitating advantage of my uniform to get us two tickets; skirting the crowd waiting for the elevator, we skipped down the stairs to the auditorium.

The movie was *The Story of Gösta Berling*. I remember very little about it other than the astonishingly plump whiteness of the youthful Garbo's arms, for I was burningly aware of Teddy's forearm alongside mine. After a while I took her hand and held it through the picture. As our body warmth flowed back and forth, coursing between us like some underground hot spring, I peered covertly at her. She was staring intently—too intently—at the screen; and I knew, as I knew the thud of my own pulse in my ears, that I would never be content with simply sitting at her side. I would have to possess her. Somewhere near the end of the movie, reasonably certain that no one would be observing us, I raised her hand to my mouth, palm up, and pressed it full against my lips. At that she turned her head and gazed at me tremulously.

"You mustn't," she whispered.

She meant the contrary, I was positive. Giddily, I allowed her to retrieve her hand, and when the picture ended I slipped her coat over her shoulders and led her up the stairs to the main gallery.

"I'll show you my favorite picture here," I said. We stood

before the big canvas that used to be everybody's favorite in those old days before everybody went totally abstract. It was by Tchelitchew, it was called *Hide and Seek,* and it's too bad it didn't get burned up in the fire they had not long ago. It consisted mostly of an enormous, thickly foliated tree, like an old oak, aswarm with embryolike little figures, some partly hidden, some revealed, some forming part of the tree itself.

Teddy appraised it carefully. Finally she said, "You know what it reminds me of? Those contests I used to enter. Find seven mystery faces hidden in the drawing and win a Pierce bicycle."

I was nettled. "Did you win?"

"Sure. But instead of giving me the girl's twenty-six-inch bike, they'd send me huge boxes of Christmas cards to sell."

By the time Teddy and I were walking south on Lexington, with the wind comfortably at our backs, we had exchanged considerable information about our childhoods, none of hers important enough for me to recall now except that her father had dropped dead in the street during his lunch hour, in the garment center, two years earlier.

"Where are we going?" she asked, clinging to my arm.

"I thought we'd eat in an Armenian restaurant. Unless you don't care for Armenian food."

"I never tasted it. Not that I know of."

No other girl that I knew would have admitted it. Not in that way. We hastened to 28th Street, to a basement restaurant with candlelit tables and a motherly proprietress.

I thought I was doing not badly at all. Over the steaming glasses of tea and the nutty baklava Teddy's eyes glowed, and she held my hand tightly on the crumpled linen cloth. Her face was still unformed, but I observed, for the first time, that her cheekbones slanted, almost sharply, beneath the soft freshness of her delicate skin, and in the shadow cast by the uncertain candle there was a suggestion of a cleft in her chin. I couldn't wait to be alone with her, and I judged that the time had come for me to tell her about my friends in the Village who sometimes loaned me their little apartment for my weekend liberties, as they had this weekend.

"Phil is in four-F with a hernia, but he's nervous about being reclassified, so he's been trying to line up a Navy commission in Washington. Charlene—that's his wife—just found out she can't have children. She's planning to start her own nursery school in Washington if Phil gets into Navy Intelligence."

"If they're your friends," Teddy said gravely, "they must be nice."

I winced for her. Now I know a little better; don't we all flatter ourselves by thinking that way of our friends, when all too often it is simply not true? Phil was not nice; he was a climber. His ambition, combined with his terror of death, drove him to get that commission.

But to Teddy I explained, earnestly and wholeheartedly, "Phil is an anthropologist, and Charlene paints. They've been to Mexico, and their place is full of things like beaten silver masks and temple fragments."

"It sounds lovely."

"Let's go. It's not far—just down on Jane Street."

Teddy was not quick, but she was not stupid either. "Will there be anyone there?"

I knew at once that I had moved too fast. And lying could only make things worse. "They probably won't be back from Washington before tomorrow."

"In that case I think I'd better not." Teddy flushed, and forced herself to look at me. "You're not angry, are you?"

"I wasn't planning on assaulting you," I said, trying hard not to sound sullen. "I mean, the place isn't an opium den."

"I know. It's just that I don't think it would be a good idea."

When we were out on the street once again, walking west into a fall rain as fine as spray from an atomizer, Teddy stopped suddenly before a darkened courtyard and looked up at me anxiously.

"I didn't mean to hurt your feelings. I guess I'm just not very sophisticated about those things."

Pressing her against the wrought-iron picket fence before which she stood, her head tilted, trying to catch some light in my eyes or across my face which would tell her what I was feeling, I folded her in my arms and kissed her for the first time.

I kissed her again, and a third time, and maybe I wouldn't have been able to stop, but Teddy passed her hand across her forehead to brush back her damp hair and said, laughing somewhat shakily, "Don't you know that it's raining?"

So we went on to the Village Vanguard, and then to Romany Marie's, where Teddy assured me, after she had had her fortune told, that this had been the loveliest evening she had ever spent. Like a dream, she said—the whole day had been like a dream.

At about two o'clock in the morning I offered to see her home. She insisted, as we stood arguing by the mountain of

Sunday papers at the Sheridan Square newsstand, that she wouldn't think of my riding the subway all the way up to the East Bronx for an hour and then all the way back for another hour. Not when I had to get up almost every morning at five-thirty, do calisthenics, and practice lowering lifeboats into the icy waters of Sheepshead Bay. I yielded, but not before I had gotten her promise that we would meet that afternoon at the Central Park Zoo, where she had to take her younger brother. I stood at the head of the subway stairs and watched, bemused, as she tripped down them, as lightly and swiftly as if she were still a child, hurrying so as not to be late for school.

At the zoo I found Teddy as easily as if we had been alone in that vast rectangle of rock and grass, instead of being surrounded as we were by thousands of Sunday strollers. She was standing in front of the monkey cages with her younger brother, Stevie, a solemn-looking mouth-breather with glasses and the big behind that many boys acquire during the final years of childhood. She whirled about at my touch, her face already alight with pleasure.

"Did you sleep well, Teddy?"

"Like a baby. Such sweet dreams!" And she introduced me to her brother.

What he wanted was to attend a war-bond rally at Columbus Circle, where they were going to display a Jap Zero and a movie star. I think the star was Victor Mature; in any case, on the way to see him and the captured airplane I pulled Teddy aside and asked her if we couldn't cut out for a couple of hours and run down to Phil's apartment.

She stared at me. "Honestly, I think you have a one-track mind."

"Phil and Charlene are in from Washington," I explained hastily. "They'd like to meet you."

"But I'm hardly even dressed to meet *you!*" In dismay she pointed to her loafers, her sweater and skirt, her trench coat, but I succeeded in persuading her.

While we stood in line to see the airplane, Teddy asked Stevie if he'd mind if we left him alone for a while. He barely heard her. He promised to wait for her through the Army Band concert, and we hurried off to the downtown bus. All the way to the Village Teddy kept me busy reassuring her that we wouldn't be barging in where we weren't wanted.

Phil's place was strewn not only with the various sections of the Sunday *Times* but with a crowd of weary weekend loungers who hadn't been there when I left that morning: an unmilitary Army officer and his hung-over girl friend, a dancer in blue jeans from the apartment across the hall who was studying the want ads while she picked at her bare toes, a nursery-school-teacher friend of Charlene's who was arguing heatedly with her in the kitchen about child development. The radio on the bookcase was blasting away with the New York Philharmonic.

Teddy sat primly on a corner of the studio couch with her knees pressed together and a paper napkin spread over them, sipping coffee and nibbling on a Triscuit and speaking only when spoken to. Phil got me off in the john at one point and said, grinning and shaking his head and winking in his nervous way, "You'll never make that girl."

I was annoyed, but I wasn't exactly sure why. "What makes you say that?"

"Aside from the fact that she's a virgin and terrified of you and your highbrow friends, she's too clean. I'll swear she uses those soaps they advertise in *The American Girl*."

"How would you know about *The American Girl*?"

"I've got a little sister."

I thought of the contests that Teddy used to enter—Find 7 Hidden Faces—and I found myself hurrying back to her side with her trench coat.

"Yes, let's go," she said. "I'm getting worried about Stevie. If my mother knew, she'd kill me."

"I wouldn't let her do that," I replied manfully.

"I'd like to see you stop her," Teddy said to me over her shoulder on our way out. "You don't know my mother."

I didn't know quite how to answer that, so I busied myself with finding a cab—no mean trick in those days, when they weren't allowed to cruise. I didn't want to know her mother, but on the other hand I wasn't about to come out and say so. When we were settled in the taxi that I had gone several blocks to find, Teddy said mournfully, "Your friends are very talented people."

That made me a little suspicious. "Most of them aren't my friends. And besides, who's talented?"

"Well, take that Army lieutenant. He's an artist. He told me so."

"Rollini? He paints camouflage on the sides of airplane hangars. I don't see that that's such a big deal."

"You know what I mean. I just don't think I fit in with

those people. I can't do anything special." She gestured helplessly. "Look at me."

The cab swung sharply onto Sixth Avenue, and Teddy was flung into my arms. I kissed her while her mouth was still open to say something else.

"Wait," she panted, breaking free. "I want to ask you something." She huddled up, very small, out of my reach in a corner of the cab. "Do you really like me?"

"Like you?" I asked. "My God, you're the most beautiful girl I've ever known. All week in those cruddy barracks I keep telling myself—"

She interrupted my protestations. "That's not what I mean. I wasn't fishing for compliments. I didn't ask you if you thought I was pretty, I asked you how much you liked me."

Teddy knew as well as I how hard that would be for me to answer. Maybe that was why she didn't stop me when I reached out for her once again, wanting to substitute caresses for words. Only when we were within a few blocks of Columbus Circle did she part from me again, her forehead wrinkled and her lower lip trembling just the slightest bit.

"I just don't understand," she said wonderingly and not very happily. "It's all wrong."

What was I going to tell her—that I wanted to make love to her? She knew that already. Before I could say anything we were caught up and blocked in the traffic of the bond rally that was on the point of breaking up. Teddy darted out of the cab door, calling over her shoulder, "I'll write you!" as she dashed off in search of Stevie. While I stood there in the eddying crowd, paying the driver, the band broke into "Praise the Lord and Pass the Ammunition," and I saw Stevie the mouth-breather, standing with his jaw agape and staring at the trombones through his eyeglasses.

Before the week was over I had my letter from Teddy. I am not going to try to reproduce it here. I will only say that it can best be described as a love letter and that it was so gauche, so overwritten, so excruciatingly true ("I am simply not used to going out with boys like you") and at the same time so transparently false ("my brother Stevie thinks the world of you") that it was immediately, painfully, terribly clear to me that I would never be able to answer in kind, and that there was no sense in my deluding myself into believing that I would. I hope it does not make me sound completely impossible if I add that her words not only released me from thinking seriously about her; they also made it all but impossible for me to think of anything but conquering her.

What inflamed me all the more was that shortly after I found Teddy's provocative letter on my bunk, my entire platoon was restricted to the base for the weekend. Trapped in that raw, artificial place, in its womanless wooden huts thrown up hastily to house some thousands of frightened boys being converted into sailors of a sort, I spent my mornings bobbing on a whaleboat in the bay, rowing in ragged unison with my freezing mates, and my afternoons ostensibly learning knots and braiding lines but actually lost in an erotic reverie of Teddy—of her slim arms, her tumbling hair, her pulsing lips—gone all wanton and yielding.

By the time we finally met again, I had memorized every line of her, from her slanting cheekbones to her small feet that toed out the least bit—and I could hardly remember what she looked like. We were constrained then, two weeks after the bond rally, not only by what had passed between us but by the heedless souls shoving us away from each other in the 42nd Street entrance to the Times Square subway station. It was the worst possible place for a boy and a girl to meet on a Saturday afternoon, in that blowing surf of old newspapers and candy wrappers, with the hot, rancid smell of nut stands assailing us. We hardly knew what to say to each other.

She smiled at me nervously, and I was emboldened to take her by the hand. "Let's get out of here." Willingly she mounted the stairs with me to the street, but when we came out onto the sidewalk the raw rain had turned to sleet; it cut at our faces like knives. I cursed the world, the war, the weather.

"But if you were stationed at that Merchant Marine camp in St. Petersburg," Teddy pointed out, "we would never have met."

"Oh great," I said. "Now you're going to do the Pollyanna routine."

"I didn't mean it like that," Teddy replied humbly.

"I want to kiss you, that's all. Are we supposed to stand out here in public and freeze to death while I make love to you? Come on, Teddy, let's go down to my friends' apartment. Like civilized people, like folks. What do you say?"

She could tell I wasn't going to push it too hard, so she laughed and tucked her arm in mine. "Come on, Mr. One-Track Mind, let's get out of the sleet."

It was driving down hard, and we had to run into a doorway,

which turned out to be the entrance to a second-floor chess-and-checkers parlor. When Teddy laughed, still gasping a little and shaking off wetness like a puppy, and said, "I wonder what it's like up there," I took her by the arm and led her up the stairs. It never ceased to amaze me how a New York girl could know so little.

Teddy hadn't played much chess, only with her brother (their father had taught them), so I showed her a few openings, but she was frankly more interested in sizing up the habitués.

Later, while we were having a drink at an Eighth Avenue hotel bar (I teased Teddy into having a Pink Lady instead of her usual ginger ale), I asked her if she'd ever eaten a real Chinese dinner. She looked a little disappointed. "We have Chinks in the Bronx almost every Saturday. Sometimes we even take it home with us."

"I'm not talking about chop suey, Teddy. I'm talking about the greatest cooking this side of Paris."

As if I'd ever eaten in Paris, much less in Peking! But that made no difference. I knew a real restaurant down on Doyers Street, and when we got there the headwaiter even remembered me. Or at least he claimed to, which was just as good; and when he followed the bird's-nest soup with platters of crisp glazed duck, Teddy gazed at me in awe.

Afterward we walked off the dinner through the dim, narrow streets of Chinatown, echoing with soft, slurring voices, and then took a subway back up to midtown in order to see Noël Coward's *Blithe Spirit*. We were fortunate to get tickets, and made it just after the curtain had gone up, groping our way to our seats.

Teddy poked frantically in her purse and came up at last with a pair of shell-rimmed eyeglasses. She was seeing bright comedy on the stage for the first time; I was seeing her in glasses for the first time. For both of us it was a revelation. She thought the play was brilliant; I thought she was delicious.

When the play let out, we stopped in at Jimmy Ryan's on 52nd Street, ostensibly for a drink, but actually so that Teddy could see how casually I greeted the boys who were playing there—Pee Wee, and George Brunies, and Zutty Singleton—poker-faced at the drums like Joe Louis—and Art Hodes, whose daily jazz program, I told Teddy, I used to follow on WNYC. But since Teddy's musical background was confined to André Kostelanetz and Lily Pons, she was only impressed, and not overwhelmed, by my acquaintance with the great. I took her across the street to hear Billie Holiday.

We stood at the bar, Teddy's back against my chest, and stared through the throat-tearing smoke at Billie, who sang "My Man" and "Strange Fruit" and "Gloomy Sunday."

Teddy's eyes were wet and shining. She raised her head. "You're opening a whole new world for me."

That was precisely what I was trying to do, but it bothered me to have her put it so patly. It reinforced my conviction that she would always be like that, forever, and that there was no point in my even considering that she might ever be otherwise.

She went on, "And I don't know that it's such a good thing. For either of us. Why should we kid ourselves? It's not going to be my world—it never will."

It was a somewhat melancholy note on which to end the evening, but in a way I preferred that. It struck me that it would be almost diabolically patient to let Teddy stew overnight, torn between guilt and gratitude. The next day was to be the climactic one. I forced myself to kiss her more lightly in parting than I wanted to, and we agreed to meet the next day by the lions in front of the Public Library.

For a change the weather was on my side. The wind was brisk, and Teddy had tied her print scarf around her blond hair babushka-style—it accentuated the slope of her cheekbones when she laughed—but the sun was out. We walked all the way up to the Frick Collection and were lucky enough to get in to the Sunday concert. Teddy had never even heard of the institution and made no attempt to conceal her ignorance.

Although she knew no more of chamber music than she did of jazz, Schubert stirred her, and she held tight to my arm throughout "Death and the Maiden," breathing softly and shallowly while she squinted (no glasses in the daytime) at the musicians. When the recital was over, we walked on up to the Metropolitan Museum, which Teddy hadn't visited since she was ten.

I led her directly to El Greco's *View of Toledo*. "This is worth the trip, this and the Courbets inside. Better to see just these than to get a headache from looking at too many."

How insufferable I must have been, lecturing Teddy first on music, then on painting, about which I knew so little! But she smiled at me gratefully, and let me know by the way in which she clung to me that I was both patient and wise.

As we left the Metropolitan and walked south through Central Park, darkness caught up with us and the wind came up too. Our breaths frosting, we hurried on across Central Park South against the traffic, skipping in and out of the dimmed, blurry headlights until we had gained the rococo refuge of Rumpelmayer's.

Warm, snug, soothed, we spooned up the great blobs of whipped cream floating on our hot chocolates and laughed over inconsequential things, and then suddenly, as if by common accord, we both stopped. I stared into Teddy's lavender eyes, so soft and moist that I wanted to kiss them closed, and she opened her mouth but without speaking, as if she dared not utter whatever it was that she wanted to say.

"I must kiss you," I murmured.

She nodded dumbly.

We went outside. In the dimout across the street the aging men who took you on carriage rides through the park and along Fifth Avenue were adjusting the straps on their horses' feedbags and hoisting blankets over their hides to protect them from the chilly evening. I signaled the leader of the line.

Teddy said apprehensively, "This must be terribly expensive."

Without answering, I raised her up into the carriage and climbed in after her. The driver tucked us in with a warm comforter, swung himself aboard behind us, clucked to his horse, and we were off.

Teddy and I turned to each other so precipitately that we bumped foreheads, searching, in the sudden dark of the covered carriage, for each other's lips. We rode on through the lamplit evening, clinging to each other, kissing, until the current that flowed between us warmed not only our lips but our cheeks and our hands, our fingers and the tips of our fingers.

"You have been so nice to me, so nice to me," Teddy whispered.

I responded by kissing her into silence. It was only after a long time that she could protest, trembling in my arms and frowning, "You shouldn't kiss me like that."

"Like what?"

"You know. It's not right, that's all."

"Nobody can see."

"Silly! I mean, I think it's for married people, or anyway for engaged couples, and like that."

We weren't engaged or like that—the very thought was enough to frighten me out of my ardor—but I had every intention of our becoming lovers, and the sooner the better. "There's only one way," I whispered into her ear, "for you to stop me."

"What's that?"

"Kiss me back the way I kiss you."

Before she could express her shock, I had stopped her mouth again. We must have been near 72nd Street on the west side of the park before we drew apart, panting.

"You know where I'm going to take you to dinner?" I asked.

"Where?"

"Phil and Charlene's. And I'm going to cook it myself. Wait till you taste my soufflé! On the way down we'll pick up some French pastries, and—"

"They're not there, are they?"

"Who?" As if I didn't know.

"Phil and his wife. Because if they're not there, I'm not going. I don't think you ought to take advantage of the fact that you're so attractive and I'm so weak."

I forced myself to be calm and reasonable. "Teddy, darling, what's so terrible about our being alone together for a while?"

"I don't trust myself. Any more than I trust you." She uttered the words with as much heartfelt emotion as though she had invented them—as though no one before her had ever even expressed such thoughts. And she looked more ravishing, more flowerlike than I had ever seen her before, her lips fuller than usual, a little swollen perhaps, her eyes staring piteously at me, her hair escaping from her scarf in little tendrils that clung to her forehead.

"Is it so awful," I demanded, "for two people who care about each other to be alone together?"

"But what you care about isn't me, it's getting me alone." Teddy paused, as if to give me time for a fervent denial.

I could say nothing. I was not the noblest or the most honorable twenty-three-year-old left in the United States, but I was incapable of promising engagement rings to young girls in return for their favors. And this much at least Teddy understood about me. The damnable truth was that I couldn't even imagine myself falling in love with, much less marrying, a girl who would make a big issue out of protecting her virtue. And on top of it all, I had been keyed up for what was going to be a triumph. I still wanted Teddy very badly, but it was obvious that I had failed completely.

After a long while she said, "I think I'd better go home."

She wanted to be contradicted, as with her other assertion that we had left hanging in the air, but I could no more find it in me to protest this time than before. I was too hurt and too shamed.

But so was Teddy, and when we had been brought back in jolting silence to our starting point, she jumped out and began to walk away toward the Sixth Avenue subway so swiftly that after I paid the driver I had to run for the better part of a block before I caught up with her.

"Please, if you insist on going, let me see you home."

"There's no need. Really. And I don't want you to think I'm angry with you, because I'm not. I had a perfectly lovely time. You'll never know how much I loved it—every minute of it. I'm just angry with myself, that's all. You and I are very different, and it's my fault, not yours. I should have faced it right at the beginning."

Still dumb, I shook her extended hand and watched her hurry off toward the subway and the Bronx.

Three days later I stood by my bunk staring at a letter from Teddy, incongruously pink and girlish on the coarse blue of my Navy blanket. For a moment I was afraid to touch it. Finally I tore it open.

It was the letter of a pen pal, jolly and comradely. A friend had given her two tickets to the Columbia-Brown game this coming Saturday. (I was learning that when a girl says a friend she means a boy—otherwise she specifies.) Wouldn't I please be her guest, so she could repay me just a little for all the fun I'd shown her?

If I had been older probably I would have said no. But I was desperately lonely in those barracks, graduation time was nearing for my platoon, and I thought, If I say no, she'll think I'm still pouting. And besides, hope revived: If I turned her down, how would I ever know for sure that she hadn't changed her mind and was using the football game as an excuse, a means of saying I'm sorry, I was wrong, you were right, I'll do whatever you want?

So I awaited the weekend as fervently as I had all the others, and to calm myself on the long, long subway ride up to Baker Field I did a crossword puzzle. Teddy met me by the entrance on the Columbia side, as she had said she would—but so much more real, so much more beautiful than my imaginings of her, that I could almost have believed I not only wildly wanted her but wildly loved her too.

It was apparent immediately, though, that we were to be pals. Teddy was dressed for late November, and for this last game of the season, in plaid flannel skirt and a heavy mackinaw and little fuzzy earmuffs. She looked adorable. When she arranged her small lap robe across our knees I reached around her waist and hugged her tightly to me, but all I could feel were layers of wool and bulky insulation.

"It's my brother's mackinaw. Do you recognize it?"

"It looks better on you than on him."

"This stadium must seem pretty tiny to you after those Big Ten games with seventy and eighty thousand people in the stands."

It did, it did. I could hardly take any of it seriously, the scrimmages, the end runs, the quick collisions, the slow roars, the cheerleading. And especially not the athletes, so puny compared to the hulks on football scholarships with whom I had eaten in my Ohio coop. Not when so many other young men my age were burning and drowning, trapped in torpedoed tankers less than a hundred miles from where we sat cheering. But then it was going to be a long war—everyone promised us that—and these boys on the field would get their chance to die, some of them before the next year was out.

As we shoved our way through the crowds onto the street, weaving in and out of the crawling cars, Teddy turned to me, her face glowing. I had never seen her prettier—or happier.

"That was fun, wasn't it?"

"What's next on the program?"

She laughed. "Know anything about bowling?"

"I know what you're up to," I said. "You're trying to wear me out."

We went to an alley she knew of in Washington Heights where a young crowd hung out—refined, she said, not bums or low-class. To me they looked like high-school graduates waiting to be drafted and their kid sisters. No doubt their younger brothers were working as pin boys. We drank two Cokes and bowled two games. Teddy was a little clumsy, but I loved watching her strain forward eagerly, frowning over the progress of her ball down the alley.

If only, I thought, if only. But I couldn't even plead with her, not when she was content to be surrounded by dozens of shouting kids her own age. Why keep pushing her? I asked myself. Why not leave her to her games and her soft drinks and her soldier pen pals in Greenland, North Africa and Australia?

We had steaks—black market, to judge from the price if not the taste—at a restaurant on upper Broadway, and as I chewed I mumbled, "We've had football and we've had bowling; now all we need is swimming to make our day complete."

"The St. George pool has mixed swimming tonight. Let's go!"

"I see enough water all week. We have to jump into the damned bay with rubber suits on; sometimes they dump out a couple barrels of oil and set them on fire to make it more interesting to swim through."

"I didn't think," she said, crestfallen. "Anyway, it's too cold."

Of course when she spoke like that I had to insist we go. We rode the Seventh Avenue subway all the way down to Brooklyn, got off at Clark Street and went up by elevator straight into the hotel without even setting foot on the street. We parted for the first time all day at the lockers, urging each other to hurry.

I got to the pool first. Teddy came in a moment later, a little shy, tugging at the nether parts of her rented tank suit as she stepped forward on the damp tiles, her pink-tinted toes curling gingerly upward. Her body was slight, paler than mine, and vulnerable. Her embarrassment only increased my own; I turned my eyes away and dived into the water at the deep end. But she slipped in after me and came up alongside me, dripping and cheerful.

"Isn't it great? I'll race you down to the shallow end!"

Actually, although Teddy thrashed bravely, she couldn't swim very well. But she splashed me happily, slipping loose from my grasp when I reached out to paddle her. Laughing and gasping she hauled herself out of the pool and flung herself upon the tiles. She grinned down at me as I hung from the lip of the pool, my legs dangling in the water.

"I'm so glad we came. You were sweet to bring me. Isn't this more fun than all that other stuff? You know what I mean."

"No," I said, "it's not."

Teddy's little bosom was rising and falling regularly; the droplets of water clinging to her bare arms and legs glistened under the lights. I was infinitely touched by the way in which the fine golden down smoothed itself around the soft flesh of her thighs and her forearms. I had never seen her with so little clothing. Her body was not only tender and almost childishly graceful; it was so appealing that it was physically painful for me to survey it without being able to touch it, and I shrank down into the water.

"Why?" she asked. "What's wrong?"

"Everything." I reached up and took hold of her ankle. It was so fine that my thumb and forefinger nearly girdled it, and it seemed to me that I could feel every little interlocking bone as she flexed it in an instinctive frightened withdrawal. "Do you know what I'd be doing now if there was no one in the pool but us?"

Teddy giggled. "There'd still be those people up in the balcony, looking down at us."

"I mean if we had the pool entirely to ourselves . . . I wouldn't even start by kissing you. First I'd peel your suit off."

Her grin faded. She withdrew her foot from my grasp and pulled her knees up tight against her chest, hugging them as if she had taken a sudden chill, or perhaps wanted to hide from me as much of herself as she could.

"I'd pull you down here into the water, both of us naked," I said desperately. "I'd hold you against me so we could feel every inch of each other. I'd run my hands up and down your back, and I'd—"

"Listen," she broke in nervously, "why don't you come up here and sit next to me and we'll talk about something else?"

"Because I'm in such a state I'm ashamed to get out of the water, that's why. Now are you satisfied?"

"I don't know what you're talking about."

"Well, if you don't you're even more childish than I thought."

At that she colored all the way down to the base of her throat. She turned her head swiftly, anxiously, to either side, as if to make sure that the handful of Saturday-night swimmers, mostly older women, could not overhear us.

"Please don't be angry with me," she said. She released her hold on her legs and leaned forward so that she could speak softly, confidentially. The front of her shapeless gray tank suit fell away from her chest, and I found myself gazing raptly into the shadow between her small breasts. She spoke so eagerly that she disregarded my gaze. "If you could get those urges satisfied elsewhere—I mean with some other girls, some other kind of girls—then you and I could just have fun like we did today. Couldn't we?"

"You're joking."

"No, no, I'm not. Not really. I mean, if you wanted it like that—" she sucked in her breath and laughed jaggedly— "maybe I could find a girl who would—you know—do those other things for you. Then you could get off that one track you're always on with me."

I didn't know whether to laugh or to cry. All I could think of to say was, "Here I'm telling you that you're adorable, that it's you I want and not some stranger, but nothing registers. It's obvious that you don't care about me, or you wouldn't say such fantastic things."

"No," Teddy muttered, not looking at me, "it's you who don't care for me. Do you think, if you loved me, that we'd—" She broke off with a quick shudder. The little golden hairs were standing upright on her arms and legs. "See," she said sadly, "I'm all goose pimples. I'm going to take a hot shower. We've done enough for one day, haven't we?"

I remained in the barracks after that, brooding, waiting to ship out into the North Atlantic. I made no effort to get in touch with Teddy. Finally, since I had time on my hands for the first time in months, and access to a typewriter in the Master at Arms' office, where I often stood night watch alone, I wrote a short story.

It was a bitter story, of course, about a young serviceman who, because he is denied physical intimacy by the girl who claims to love him, goes recklessly to his death, a snarl upon his lips.

I made two copies. The first went to *The New Yorker*. After debating with myself for a day or so, I wrote across the face of the carbon copy, *Here is the most I can offer you for Christmas, something I made for you myself, from the bottom of my heart.* I signed my name and mailed it to Teddy.

Within two days the original came back from *The New Yorker*. I stuck it in a fresh envelope and shipped it off to the *Atlantic Monthly*, where I knew from experience that it would rest long enough for me to go off to sea under the happy illusion that it was being seriously considered.

I heard nothing at all from Teddy. After a few days I could stand it no longer, and one night I rang her up from the pay phone in the rec room. She answered, but from her tone, a little frightened when she recognized my voice, I was sure that her mother was there.

"Teddy," I said, "I've been worried by your silence. Are you all right?"

"Yes, I am. Are you?"

"Yes, of course. Is your mother there with you?"

"I don't see what difference that makes." Then she said what her mother must have been coaching her to say, against the moment when I should phone again. "My mother feels I shouldn't see you any more. And I think she's right."

I was so shocked that I forgot to ask about my story. I stammered, "But all I wanted was to see you one last time before I ship out. Does that seem so unfair? For us just to get together this Saturday afternoon?"

"If you had any respect for my wishes," she said stiffly, "you wouldn't press it any further."

I muttered goodbye and slammed down the receiver. But the next day, after a night spent cursing myself for not having let it rest with my sardonically inscribed story, I received a note from Teddy.

She apologized for the way she had spoken (I was right; her mother had been listening) and went on to add that if I still wanted to say goodbye she'd look for me on Saturday at one o'clock in the waiting room of Penn Station. She would tell her mother she was going shopping at Macy's.

It was Teddy's willingness to deceive her mother that encouraged in me the wild hope that maybe my story had accomplished what my physical presence and my pleading had been unable to do. But when I dashed into Penn Station, Teddy came up to me unexpectedly and offered me only her hand and not her lips.

The hand was gloved, but I had the feeling that her fingers would be cold; her lips were pale and bloodless and she smiled at me tremulously.

"You look well," she said. "I'm sorry I can't stay very long."

People were bumping into us in their anxiety to reach the escalator. The vaulted terminal was bleak, drafty and—to me at that moment—terrifying.

"My God, Teddy," I said, "you can't just shake my hand and walk away." I pointed to the bag hanging from her left hand. "You've done your Macy's shopping already. That ought to satisfy your mother. Can't we get out of here? Please?"

"If we could just be happy one last time—like we were for a little while . . ."

"Come with me." I took her by the hand. "I know a good French restaurant near here. While we eat you can talk and I can sit and admire you."

"You'll have to promise that you won't get personal like that."

"Supposing I get personal not like that?"

By the time we reached the restaurant we were laughing

together; you might have thought we were just getting to know each other. But in a matter of minutes the laughter had faded away and we were face to face more nakedly than we had ever been before.

We entered the restaurant and passed through the long, narrow bar where three elderly Frenchmen were having their apéritifs. We seated ourselves in the glassed-in garden dining room in the rear courtyard and ordered our hors d'oeuvres. Suddenly Teddy pouted, as one does when one remembers a forgotten obligation. Then she reached into the red-and-green, holiday-decorated shopping bag and handed me back my story.

I stared at her, my spoonful of pickled beets suspended in air.

"Teddy," I said at last, "that was a present. A Christmas present. You don't give back presents."

"I have to. I just can't accept it."

"But why?"

"It, uh . . ." Teddy swallowed. "It was insulting, that's why. Here, take it, please. Then we won't have to talk about it."

"The hell we won't. Do you know how hard I worked on it? Maybe it's not the greatest story in the world, but it's the best I have in me, and you might at least have acknowledged it, even if you didn't like it."

"But I did. I do." Teddy gazed at me in agony. "It's just that you shouldn't have put down all those intimate details."

"I can't believe that you felt like that when you first read it," I began, and then I stopped. A suspicion formed in my mind. "Wait a minute. Did you show that story to anyone else?"

"Well . . . just to my mother."

"I knew it." I was too sickened to be triumphant. "You might as well give me her literary verdict. I'm sure she had some memorable comment."

"She said it was dirty."

I jumped to my feet and flung down my napkin, knocking a knife and a fork to the floor. My legs seemed to be entangled with my half-tipped-over chair. A French family at the next table looked up in surprise from its *pot au feu*. So did three ladies on the other side of us.

With her knuckles at her lips, Teddy asked, "Where are you going?"

"I'm leaving. What did you expect?"

She began to cry. Ignoring the tears that were welling from

her eyes and dropping onto her artichoke hearts, she whispered, "Please, please, please, don't go. Don't leave me like this."

Frightened by her tears and by the enormity of what I was about to do—walk out on a sobbing girl under the disapproving gaze of a roomful of people—I hesitated.

Teddy went on. "I promise not to say anything more to upset you. All I ever wanted was for us to have fun together, without hurting anybody, before you shipped out."

I sat down. Weeping softly, Teddy told me that I had expected too much of her from the start, that she wasn't like all the other, older girls with whom I had been intimate (there had been only two, but Teddy imagined scores).

"I suppose the trouble was," she mused sadly, somewhat more under control, "that it was all just a little too cold-blooded. If I had felt that you cared for me . . . I couldn't lie to my mother about that. Don't you see, maybe she's not so smart, but she's all I've got, she and Stevie, and I have to live the way she expects me to. The way she wants me to."

If before Teddy had made me enraged, now she was making me squirm. Seeing this, she reached across the table to touch me lightly on the arm and added, "Don't ever think I'm not grateful. You can't imagine how much you've done for me."

Mollified, I disclaimed any special virtue, and we left the restaurant almost as calmly as we had entered it. We strolled up to 42nd Street and then east through Times Square to Bryant Park, stopping under the movie marquees to study the stills of the Ritz Brothers and the Three Stooges, of Lynn Bari and Jean Parker.

We sat on a stone bench under a leafless tree in Bryant Park, discussing books and observing the types on their way into the library. We were careful not to talk about ourselves, or about Christmas, or about what the new year would bring; when we bumped knees, we excused ourselves. But then it began to rain again, the fine but mean rain of a Manhattan December, and as we looked hopelessly at each other and then at the forbidding bulk of the library, I remembered the movie houses on 42nd Street.

"Come on," I said. "I'll take you to see *Intermezzo*."

"I really must go home. I'm expected."

"Not yet." I tugged her off the bench. "You yourself told me Ingrid Bergman is the most beautiful girl in the world. You bragged about seeing her in front of Bloomingdale's."

Laughing and protesting, Teddy allowed me to hurry her

to the theater. But *Intermezzo* was a mistake. We had to sit through the last hour of an anti-Nazi epic, plus a newsreel of Mrs. Thomas E. Dewey launching a Liberty ship, before we were rewarded with Leslie Howard making love to Ingrid Bergman. They went off together to celebrate their illicit passion in a sun-kissed Mediterranean villa, knowing—or at least Ingrid knowing—that it could come to no good end and that she would have to tiptoe out of Leslie's life in order to spare him for his art.

I sat with my arm around Teddy's shoulders, but I might as well have clasped a statue. She held herself absolutely rigid and stared fixedly at the screen through the little shell-rimmed glasses she was no longer self-conscious about wearing, her elbows tight against her sides, her fingers locked together in her lap. By the end of the film I was intoxicated all over again with the odor of Teddy's damp blond hair and lightly fragrant perfume, and she was biting her lips, fighting back the tears as Ingrid took leave of her unsuspecting lover. The theme music swelled to a crescendo, and we groped our way out to the street.

It was almost pitch-dark, the dimout was on, and the rain was driving directly into our faces. Luckily I captured a cab and we tumbled gratefully into it, slammed the door behind us and waved the driver on. Then, to my astonishment, Teddy flung her arms around my neck, held me so tightly I could hardly breathe, and proceeded to kiss me as I had taught her to kiss.

My God, I thought, have I won at the last possible moment? And when the driver called back, "Which way, folks?" I whispered to her, "Let's go down to the apartment. Now!"

I have thought since then that if I had been a bit more mature, more masterful, if I had simply directed the driver down to Jane Street, I might have won out. But I doubt it. For Teddy shook her head fiercely, even while she continued to caress me, and muttered, "No, no, no, I'm going home, I'm saying goodbye to you here."

We remained clasped in each other's arms all the way up to the Bronx. In front of her apartment house, while I stood, distraught, counting bills into the cab driver's hand, Teddy ran a comb unsteadily through her hair and apologized for the expense of the long ride.

"I'm the one who should apologize for never taking you home before," I said. "Let's go on up."

In the back of my mind, I suppose, was the final hope that

Teddy's mother and brother would be out. The old red brick building was shabby, with peeling hallways; but what was worse, it was a walkup, and Teddy lived on the top floor.

We climbed slowly and awkwardly with our arms around each other's waists and on the fourth floor Teddy told me, blushing, that we still had two more flights to go. "The higher you go, see, the cheaper the rent is."

As we moved dreamlike up the last flights, I thought how often she must have flitted up and down all these steps—no wonder she was so slim!

When we reached the top floor she indicated silently the door which was hers: 6B. But before she could say anything I unbuttoned her coat—my pea jacket was already open—and pulled her close to me. As I began to kiss her she went limp. I was kissing her hair, her ears, her eyelids, her cheeks, but when I pressed her lips to mine she did not respond with the ardor which had so surprised me in the taxi; and even though she opened her mouth under the pressure of my lips, she remained absolutely passive, drooping like a flower deprived of sun, her eyes closed, as I raised her unresisting arms and slipped them around my neck.

For some reason this passivity drove me wild, and I tore at her woolen dress, searching for the zipper and the buttons, until I had worked my hands through. Her underthings slithered to my touch, and in a frenzy I pulled up handfuls of her slip until my fingers reached the smooth flesh of her back and her belly. She remained motionless, neither assisting nor opposing me, as I worked open her brassiere and freed her breasts.

My hands roved frantically, attempting with desperate speed to discover what had been denied them for so long. Her body was more delicately wrought than her wistful, pretty face, and I was stunned to feel the sharp, childish wings of her shoulder blades, the fragile bones of her rib cage behind which her heart was throbbing, the pathetic soft buds of her breasts.

Suddenly I was crying. "Teddy, Teddy, Teddy," I whispered, and I felt her give way in my arms. In another moment we would both have sunk to the cold stone floor; but at that instant the steel door of 6B swung open and Teddy's mother flew into the hall like some great bird of prey.

She could have been no older than I am now, but she seemed a dreadful old bag, a harpy, her hair half crammed into a net, her eyes darting venomously out of a craggy face slimed with cold cream. As I released Teddy, she pulled her coat together to cover her gaping dress, and then, yanked forward in her mother's iron grip, stumbled blindly into the sanctuary of their apartment. Her mother flashed me one scornful glance—part rage and part pure triumph—before she slammed the door.

I stood there dripping rain and sweat, too shocked even to be conscious of frustration. My eye was caught by the Macy's shopping bag, stuffed with gaily wrapped Christmas presents, that had fallen from Teddy's hand to the floor. I bent to pick it up when the door opened again. Teddy's mother snatched the bag from me without a word, and before I could open my mouth she had slammed the door.

No doubt it was the shopping bag, decorated with holly and mistletoe, that reminded me of my story, my gift to Teddy. As I made my way slowly down the long flights of steps, pulling myself together to face what had to be faced in the world beyond Teddy, I discovered that I did not have the manuscript she had returned to me. It must have been kicked under the table at the restaurant, and as I swayed out into the dreary street I thought, Well, I'll never see the restaurant, I'll never see the story, I'll never see her. Never again.

I was right, of course; at least in that limited realization I was right, if in nothing else. But a few weeks ago I had to see an editor about a manuscript, and I drove into New York and pulled into a West Side lot. It was a raw wintry day, with the soundless wind rushing papers about the streets to remind one that beyond the solid brick and stone, nature still strove to do you down. I gave myself one more moment of my car heater's warmth before braving the cold, and while I was checking the contents of my briefcase and putting on my hat to protect my bald skull, I was overcome by the eerie sensation of having been here once before, in some different incarnation, younger, hatless, without a briefcase. But in an empty lot?

The attendant rapped on the car window with his knuckles. "What do you say, Mac? I haven't got all day. Leave the key in the car."

"Wait a minute," I said. "Do you live around here?"

"I was born exactly two blocks down the street." He was an underslung, argumentative Italian, remarkable only for his long nose and for his pride in the place of his birth. "Anything you want to know about the neighborhood, ask."

"What used to be here, before the parking lot?"

"Rooming house, like everyplace else on the block. Restaurant on the first floor."

My eyes began to smart. I closed them for a moment. "A French restaurant?"

"French, Italian, what's the difference? A restaurant."

I got out of the car and shuddered in the chill wind as loose sheets of paper plastered themselves against my shins. They were not likely to be pages of the story I had left behind, a story which had surely turned to ashes with the restaurant, and probably long before. The story was gone; so was the little blonde who had sat just here, weeping as she handed it back to me—and so was I, the would-be writer, pompous but still unsure of his craft and his magic charm.

We have all three died, as surely as if the war had done us in; but did we really die forever? Teddy still lives in my mind as she was then, whether she has gained the chairmanship of her P.T.A. or not. And I, too, live again in my mind as I was then, whether or not I have won my way to what I dearly desired to be. Only that well-meant and ill-written manuscript, that rejected gift, deserved to die forever. It is *this* story—called up by the sudden stinging recollection of two young strangers, the boy and girl at the last table of the garden restaurant, yearning for everything but understanding nothing—that is the real story for Teddy.

Beautiful Light and Black Our Dreams
Woodie King, Jr.

His world is all aglow today. And the day itself is beautiful; the sun is shining. Across the street in the park, young men and women are laughing and playing in the warm sun. Now and then pigeons flutter; birds glide in and sing gay songs; both birds and pigeons are drinking from the beautiful fountains. Here and there in the warm sun people are reading their free press. Today she, as the sun, will return after her long absence. He is in the Greek restaurant, across from the park, waiting and dreaming.

"Everyone is so full of dreams, in the light *and* in the dark," he is remembering her saying. And he is thinking of her in light, high above the city in a beautiful glass office, smiling gleefully. He is thinking that on that eleventh floor of that City Building how full of dreams she really is; aglow, he is thinking this.

Today he is sitting again, at the same spot again, waiting for her again. This year he is fifteen minutes early.

He is remembering.

"But what's your dream?" he wanted to ask her that last time when she sat across from him, finishing her lunch. But he did not—not that moment. But he wanted to. He watched her. Face like poisonous exotic fruit. Dark gray eyes, large and always on watch. Lips full and always in that position— that position that caused him to know his heart *could* beat. Queenly; the woman everyone wants. The beauty, part-time actress, secretary six hours a day on the eleventh floor of the new City Building; only one of that beautiful color. Joanne. Watching her finish her lunch with a million dreams in that beautiful head. Beautiful Joanne, so serene. One of the many women born Negro, yet are almost white inside and outside; the kind of Negro woman that has a million dreams of winning beauty contests in Canada or being the first Negro Miss Street & Railway, then being spotted by Stanley Kramer or somebody, anybody. The light kind with the features of the

Caucasian; the kind that all men seem to love because they are, yet they are not.

And yet he is man, it is not those things that made him care for her, love her. For him, it goes farther; to the time when he first saw her.

Start at the beginning. Drift backwards, travel in slow motion through other winters and summers; through time, that element that taught her you. All the way back to the reason for her being across from you, through other tears and laughter.

The beginning,

Once there was a woman named Joanne. . . .

Go on. . . .

. . . I saw her first on the floor of a Little Theater reading her lines from a Greek tragedy. She and an Irish fellow whom she loved (Oh, how she loved him!) played there on that floor in that little white theater. So gay was her laughter, so dry was his. Talking of their trip to Palestine, talking of blue grass in the beautiful Highlands, speaking like Modjeska, saying *gee whiz*, eating pizza, laughing, getting excited, playing . . . wrestling. I would watch her often. I had to. And I wondered why she never looked at me. Was it time?

They read their lines.

And I being dark and invisible to them chose to remain that way. For in a world so white and light, so strange, I felt darkness was forbidden.

Everything about the theater was white. She blended in. I did not: I could not. Often I would pass her. Sometimes she would look up—not at me, but up. Then it changed. We would be apart and our eyes would find each other. Her smiling ceased; no words. Never . . . never words . . . never smiles . . . strange. The Irish did not look up. He looked down always when he was with her.

He came with indifference
And with indifference did I receive him

I dreamed one night that she would tell me I did not belong. The dream occurred in a snowstorm. Far away in a place where the snow never seemed to cease its steady fall. And I was lost in that snow desert, unable to find my way. Then I saw her . . . and the falling snow . . . and she was in a sort of transparent nightgown. I asked her if she was cold; I wanted to protect her from the cold snow, wanted her warm. Her mouth moved. I could hear her voice in an echo, resounding, away . . . away . . . go away . . . away. Then the dream changed. I disappeared, and a gigantic black man in chains, sweat glistening on his back and face, walked slowly towards her singing *any day now*. And his presence made the snow melt, made the sun shine, made her smile. And they danced to songs of Leadbelly, they danced until she became exhausted, until Belafonte sang, until Leadbelly cried. I reappeared and the snow returned and the echo. Away . . . away . . . go away . . . away.

I went away.

A long interval of dream-filled days and nights.

The middle.

Once there was a store downtown. . . .

Slowly . . .

I went in out of the cold white snow. A feeling hit me; something wonderful, more wonderful than life itself in that store. Something as wonderful as the sudden return of summer after a snow-filled winter. My body became fervent. I looked for the cause throughout the large store. It had to be there. It was there, I felt it. Up from the basement, all through it until I saw that black and white checked coat far away, descending.

I saw her. I looked at her across the store, she looked at me. No words. A smile. I found her that winter morning and she saved my summers. Then we knew. We had to know.

I returned.

Winters and summers of tears and laughter, searching.

The end.

The end?

Yes.

Life stops sometimes. And in those times pain is the only substitute. For me, there have been many. I believe this day will bring another.

He cares for her and loves her because time caused it. Time . . . time that puts beginnings, middles, and endings to life and love.

Still remembering.

She turned, flashing glances through every face within the huge immaculate restaurant, then out the large glass window facing Circus Park, the church, the Institute of Technology, North, and a city filled with pure white snow.

"Look at them," she said. "See how they move? They don't know where they are going, none of them, do they?"

He smiled, glad to be with her, nodded his head, agreeing.

"Look at that funny-looking couple with the poodle," he said finally.

They both laughed.

"I know they are cold. I just know it," she said. "Why do they pretend they are warm? It's freezing out there."

"I'm hip," he said. "But I can't really think of anything outside. You're it today."

"Love you," she said.

Silence while they looked at each other.

He wanted to ask her, have your dreams changed since the last ones? He could not—not now.

"They don't even know. One of these days they are going to know who we are, 'ay man?"

He nodded and sipped the hot black coffee.

"We are going to be famous, man, you and I," she said. But not as serious as it had been said in happier winters and summers.

And he thought he knew then.

"Yes. We are going to be famous," he said. "One of these days."

He looked at her long.

"What's your dream now, Joanne Labold?"

"My dream?" she said. "I want to get off the eleventh floor of that damned building. I want to be somebody; want things. Want so much." She turned the spoon in the black coffee. "Sometimes I look from my glass and I want to fly down and kiss my fate. But there will have to be revolutions before my dream comes true. And I can't wait that long. Look at me, my face. Where do I belong? What's my dream? What's your dream? Am I your dream?" She looked at him long, then out the window, North.

"Will my dream end here? Joanne?" He placed his dark hand on her light face. Gently . . . gently . . . gently he moved her face opposite his. And the black porters in white jackets and black ties gazed; the white men in black suits glanced. And all the white blonds, all white and starch, sat rigid while the knives and forks and spoons tinkled and clashed. But he could not hear them. He, in that moment of black agony, heard only the soft white snow, falling.

"Will my dream end *again?*" he repeated himself. And the minute she took to answer seemed like an hour.

"We have some time to talk," she said. "He will meet me here in a short while." She moved the dark hand away from her face slowly. She held it tightly with both hands. "I won't be seeing you again, honest. But I love you, I love you, *love you* . . ."

. . . won't be seeing you again . . .

He knew then. He felt it. It was there. All the turmoil before an erupting emotion; all the rushing to the head of the inside of his soul, leaving the boiling deep, deep, far away in the head, then changing to hot tears—tears that lingered within his hot burning eyes; not coming out to be seen, never coming out to be seen . . . tears . . . tears . . . and he fought them. He noticed her mouth—ugly now—moving, trying to say something. Not hearing her, not wanting to, he looked out the glass into the white, white snow—North. At the cathedral. At the bell that would chime, then the Te Deums that, for him, would never mean glory. After them he would be alone again, without Joanne again; viduity again . . . feeling like a single falling leaf late in the dawn again.

Is this what he had feared?

Her mouth moved. "I had to see you, tell you."

The seconds of silence seemed like years.

"What can I say? He's very nice, you will like him. Anyway, you know him. He's Irish."

"Yes, I know him," he said. His voice was a whisper.

"I know," she whispered. She turned and looked out the glass. And that day she remembered.

She is remembering.

Saturday night, Sunday morning, the end of summer. We attended the play *Long Day's Journey into Night*. How beautifully O'Neill recreates the feeling of impending doom. And I knew there would be a sense of doom in me that night. For I had been searching in a strange black world. And that world had refused me when I needed it most. I wanted to destroy it by becoming a part of the white, blending with the white. The tragedy of nature, he would call it.

Had already told him I loved Alexandros, that he wanted to take me to Paris and Ireland. And as I remember, it was the first time we had ever really talked. Strange. Our first conversation had to be about someone white, about what that someone wanted to do for me. He was hurt because he did not want me to love Alexandros, did not want me to tell him what white could do for me. He tried desperately not to show it. I believe I convinced him that that love was a different love, not like the feeling for him. But I don't think I convinced him. Anyway he took me to see Alexandros in the O'Neill play; he took me to the after-party. He wanted me to be near Alexandros, it seemed. We stayed at the party until four A.M. I glanced at him often, watched him moving through the white party, dark and invisible to them. He never looked at me. I talked to Alexandros all that time. We exhausted ourselves talking about nothing. And when we couldn't think of anything else to say, we made a date for Sunday night. I did not tell him. He knew. We made the date at four A.M. At four A.M. he looked at me across the room through the white crowd.

Sunday morning . . . mourning . . . far away . . . the Te Deums.

We talked. We kissed for the first time that Sunday morning between darkness and dawn. So gentle. Gently . . . gently. Oh God! How wonderful I felt! I felt more love than Dido must have felt. And I fell in love's abyss for the first time. Everything around me was so strange: the darkness and the dawn, the sun and the night, the coldness and the heat, all together at the same time. All my life I had been told, and I felt that I *should* go beyond darkness. And I could. I could change with the seasons. But everything about me changed when we caught the darkness and the dawn. Every little thing became a beautiful phallic symbol, made me think of him, dark and invisible, melting the pretty, pretty snow.

"I know," she said again.

"You shouldn't have told him to meet you here," he said.

"We tried, you know that."

"Tried?" He tried to say something else; no words came. Even his lips felt heavy, thick. He prayed to be what she wanted, but he knew he could never be. "Let's talk about something else. How's your family?"

She looked at him long. Her eyes and pretty face expressionless. Everything about her serene, as if she was at rest, as if she was . . . was . . . inertia.

"I wanted to tell you how it came about; I wanted you to understand."

"I understand," he says. "But do you understand?"

"Don't make me cry," she said. "This had to be."

"Do YOU UNDERSTAND?" he said louder, bitter.

The black porters in white jackets and black ties turned;

the blond people, all white and starch, showed signs of life. And he was slowly dying, again.

"All my life," she said, "I have had to protect myself, be on guard."

"From what?" he shouted.

"The pimps, hustlers, lesbians, and others trying to misuse me." She paused, rubbed his hand, continued without looking at him. "I look unusual—"

"Go on; what else?" he asked.

"More than anything else it is the Negro man."

"I am Negro man," he said, "and I never attempted to misuse you."

"How could I know that? Tell me how could I have known? How could I be sure you were *real?* I always guess at what you are feeling, never knowing where you are, never."

He looked at a white blond, snow white, crisp.

"Are you listening?"

"Yes."

The seconds seemed like hours.

"And man I have been misused!" She lit a cigarette. "Some tell me of movie contracts. And I say, 'Well, Miss Labold, this is *it.*' I spend weeks, sometimes months making sure. Disillusioned. Some tell me they can make me a star in the Ebony Fashion Fairs or put me on the cover or in the center of *Jet* magazine. Always it seemed like the break, my chance. Some seem truthful. And God knows I try, I try to find out. But it's always the same: to them I am an illusion. They want that day and night dream—me. But they don't want the *real* me; they don't want the me that breathes, cries, wakes up in the morning, goes to the bathroom. Men don't want me. They want an illusion."

"Joanne—" he tried to say something.

"Please listen. Please," she continued. "It made me feel like half a woman, not complete in the way I want to be complete. Long ago, Iarbas, I think I discovered—and it may sound funny as hell—men are spiritually weak. They believe in God and nature." She smiled. "You too, man, you too."

"Joanne," he said, "you are trying to get outside your world. The Irish one is not for you. He will never be; he cannot be. Nature and God forbid it. Don't you see? Don't you understand?"

They could find nothing to say for a long time.

"Just as nature and God forbid snow to fall twelve months

of the year, summer must return. You are my summers, Joanne. And if you are leaving because of disillusions, feeling I think you are an illusion, you will return. Like summer."

"So full of dreams," she said. "Love you."

"In light *and* darkness?"

"I think, maybe yes," she said.

The seconds lingered.

"Don't leave me, Joanne," he whispered. "Don't take it away."

"I can never be complete with you bridge people; I cannot make your dream come true. I am human."

"Don't you know you will return, again? Don't you know you cannot—he cannot—take away what is *mine*? By birth you are mine. I know it, he knows it, you know it . . . mine . . . mine . . . mine . . ."

"I love you I love you I love you I love you, Iarbas, I love . . ."

"Don't, Joanne," he remembered saying.

The bell in the church rang. One-two-three-four . . . His heart must have skipped a beat, he felt his chest once, looked out the glass. Hearing the bell sounding in his ears, feeling his heart hitting his chest, feeling his mouth becoming dry; still looking out the glass, looking for that face—looking—searching for that face that would blend with the snow. And she, flashing glances as if really frightened, regaining her composure; putting on her lipstick or looking at herself in her small mirror. And he, still looking out into the snow, hearing the bell, hoping it would cease. Then both looking out the glass; both seeing Alexandros approaching from the far end of the park; approaching, dressed in a black topcoat. And sitting there he could not hear chains dragging from afar, and he could not hear *him* singing *any day now,* but he could hear music from the psaltery. And the music sounded so beautiful in that glen of blue grass in the Highlands far away where he could never be but where she might go and leave him forever. And she could dance her dance to the music of the psaltery; she could play in the blue grass of the high places as she played on that floor in that little theater long ago, she could stop and listen to the bell. The bell. The bell. One-two-three . . . The Te Deums . . . bong-bong-bong-bong-I love you-bong-love you-bong-love-bong-you-bong . . . bong . . .

Alexandros approaching *with indifference.*

She rose, looked at him. "See you."

"See you."

Alexandros there.
She smiling up to him.
. . . *and with indifference did I receive him.*
Both leaving.
He is alone.
Both crossing the snow-filled park. Her checked black and white coat's collar turned up. He, holding her arm, going north. And she speaking something to Alexandros.
He, still sitting in the restaurant, watching her ugly back; watching the tracks of her black overshoes sink deeper and deeper into the pretty, pretty snow. Watching and hoping; hearing her voice, *see you . . . see you . . .* Wishing he could be what she wanted.

He turns and looks into the sun-filled park; at the couples laughing; at the birds and pigeons that lounge and linger there; at the beautiful water fountains that emit all colors of waters—waters that spring so misty and settle so clear; at the cut green grass, so green that it appears blue. And the feeling he holds at this moment should be a bequeathal to the world. It is everyman's.
He sees her. She is running towards him, calling his name. He stands; he smiles. She waves. And watching her he is thinking that winters cannot last forever, but he is also thinking that neither can the warm summers.
There are so many things that nature and God forbid.

The Enormous Radio
John Cheever

Jim and Irene Westcott were the kind of people who seem to strike that satisfactory average of income, endeavor, and respectability that is reached by the statistical reports in college alumni bulletins. They were the parents of two young children, they had been married nine years, they lived on the twelfth floor of an apartment house in the East Seventies between Fifth and Madison Avenues, they went to the theatre on an average of 10.3 times a year, and they hoped someday to live in Westchester. Irene Westcott was a pleasant, rather plain girl with soft brown hair and a wide, fine forehead upon which nothing at all had been written, and in the cold weather she wore a coat of fitch skins dyed to resemble mink. You could not say that Jim Westcott, at thirty-seven, looked younger than he was, but you could at least say of him that he seemed to feel younger. He wore his graying hair cut very short, he dressed in the kind of clothes his class had worn at Andover, and his manner was earnest, vehement, and intentionally naïve. The Westcotts differed from their friends, their classmates, and their neighbors only in an interest they shared in serious music. They went to a great many concerts—although they seldom mentioned this to anyone—and they spent a good deal of time listening to music on the radio.

Their radio was an old instrument, sensitive, unpredictable, and beyond repair. Neither of them understood the mechanics of radio—or of any of the other appliances that surrounded them—and when the instrument faltered, Jim would strike the side of the cabinet with his hand. This sometimes helped. One Sunday afternoon, in the middle of a Schubert quartet, the music faded away altogether. Jim struck the cabinet repeatedly, but there was no response; the Schubert was lost to them forever. He promised to buy Irene a new radio, and on Monday when he came home from work he told her that he had got one. He refused to describe it, and said it would be a surprise for her when it came.

The radio was delivered at the kitchen door the following

afternoon, and with the assistance of her maid and the handyman Irene uncrated it and brought it into the living room. She was struck at once with the physical ugliness of the large gumwood cabinet. Irene was proud of her living room, she had chosen its furnishings and colors as carefully as she chose her clothes, and now it seemed to her that the new radio stood among her intimate possessions like an aggressive intruder. She was confounded by the number of dials and switches on the instrument panel, and she studied them thoroughly before she put the plug into a wall socket and turned the radio on. The dials flooded with a malevolent green light, and in the distance she heard the music of a piano quintet. The quintet was in the distance for only an instant; it bore down upon her with a speed greater than light and filled the apartment with the noise of music amplified so mightily that it knocked a china ornament from a table to the floor. She rushed to the instrument and reduced the volume. The violent forces that were snared in the ugly gumwood cabinet made her uneasy. Her children came home from school then, and she took them to the Park. It was not until later in the afternoon that she was able to return to the radio.

The maid had given the children their suppers and was supervising their baths when Irene turned on the radio, reduced the volume, and sat down to listen to a Mozart quintet that she knew and enjoyed. The music came through clearly. The new instrument had a much purer tone, she thought, than the old one. She decided that tone was most important and that she could conceal the cabinet behind a sofa. But as soon as she had made her peace with the radio, the interference began. A crackling sound like the noise of a burning powder fuse began to accompany the singing of the strings. Beyond the music, there was a rustling that reminded Irene unpleasantly of the sea, and as the quintet progressed, these noises were joined by many others. She tried all the dials and switches but nothing dimmed the interference, and she sat down, disappointed and bewildered, and tried to trace the flight of the melody. The elevator shaft in her building ran beside the living-room wall, and it was the noise of the elevator that gave her a clue to the character of the static. The rattling of the elevator cables and the opening and closing of the elevator doors were reproduced in her loudspeaker, and, realizing that the radio was sensitive to electrical currents of all sorts, she began to discern through the Mozart the ringing of telephone bells, the dialing of phones, and the lamentation of a vacuum cleaner. By listening more carefully, she was able to distinguish doorbells, elevator bells, electric razors, and Waring mixers, whose sounds had been picked up from the apartments that surrounded hers and transmitted through her loudspeaker. The powerful and ugly instrument, with its mistaken sensitivity to discord, was more than she could hope to master, so she turned the thing off and went into the nursery to see her children.

When Jim Westcott came home that night, he went to the radio confidently and worked the controls. He had the same sort of experience Irene had had. A man was speaking on the station Jim had chosen, and his voice swung instantly from the distance into a force so powerful that it shook the apartment. Jim turned the volume control and reduced the voice. Then, a minute or two later, the interference began. The ringing of telephones and doorbells set in, joined by the rasp of the elevator doors and the whir of cooking appliances. The character of the noise had changed since Irene had tried the radio earlier; the last of the electric razors was being unplugged, the vacuum cleaners had all been returned to their closets, and the static reflected that change in pace that overtakes the city after the sun goes down. He fiddled with the knobs but couldn't get rid of the noises, so he turned the radio off and told Irene that in the morning he'd call the people who had sold it to him and give them hell.

The following afternoon, when Irene returned to the apartment from a luncheon date, the maid told her that a man had come and fixed the radio. Irene went into the living room before she took off her hat or her furs and tried the instrument. From the loudspeaker came a recording of the "Missouri Waltz." It reminded her of the thin, scratchy music from an old-fashioned phonograph that she sometimes heard across the lake where she spent her summers. She waited until the waltz had finished, expecting an explanation of the recording, but there was none. The music was followed by silence, and then the plaintive and scratchy record was repeated. She turned the dial and got a satisfactory burst of Caucasian music —the thump of bare feet in the dust and the rattle of coin jewelry—but in the background she could hear the ringing of bells and a confusion of voices. Her children came home from school then, and she turned off the radio and went to the nursery.

When Jim came home that night, he was tired, and he took

a bath and changed his clothes. Then he joined Irene in the living room. He had just turned on the radio when the maid announced dinner, so he left it on, and he and Irene went to the table.

Jim was too tired to make even a pretense of sociability, and there was nothing about the dinner to hold Irene's interest, so her attention wandered from the food to the deposits of silver polish on the candlesticks and from there to the music in the other room. She listened for a few moments to a Chopin prelude and then was surprised to hear a man's voice break in. "For Christ's sake, Kathy," he said, "do you always have to play the piano when I get home?" The music stopped abruptly. "It's the only chance I have," a woman said. "I'm at the office all day." "So am I," the man said. He added something obscene about an upright piano, and slammed a door. The passionate and melancholy music began again.

"Did you hear that?" Irene asked.

"What?" Jim was eating his dessert.

"The radio. A man said something while the music was still going on—something dirty."

"It's probably a play."

"I don't think it *is* a play," Irene said.

They left the table and took their coffee into the living room. Irene asked Jim to try another station. He turned the knob. "Have you seen my garters?" a man asked. "Button me up," a woman said. "Have you seen my garters?" the man said again. "Just button me up and I'll find your garters," the woman said. Jim shifted to another station. "I wish you wouldn't leave apple cores in the ashtrays," a man said. "I hate the smell."

"This is strange," Jim said.

"Isn't it?" Irene said.

Jim turned the knob again. " 'On the coast of Coromandel where the early pumpkins blow,' " a woman with a pronounced English accent said, " 'in the middle of the woods lived the Yonghy-Bonghy-Bò. Two old chairs, and half a candle, one old jug without a handle . . .' "

"My God!" Irene cried. "That's the Sweeneys' nurse."

" 'These were all his worldly goods,' " the British voice continued.

"Turn that thing off," Irene said. "Maybe they can hear *us*." Jim switched the radio off. "That was Miss Armstrong, the Sweeneys' nurse," Irene said. "She must be reading to the little girl. They live in 17-B. I've talked with Miss Armstrong in the Park. I know her voice very well. We must be getting other people's apartments."

"That's impossible," Jim said.

"Well, that was the Sweeneys' nurse," Irene said hotly. "I know her voice. I know it very well. I'm wondering if they can hear us."

Jim turned the switch. First from a distance and then nearer, nearer, as if borne on the wind, came the pure accents of the Sweeneys' nurse again: " ' "Lady Jingly! Lady Jingly!" ' " she said, " ' "Sitting where the pumpkins blow, will you come and be my wife," said the Yonghy-Bonghy-Bò . . .' "

Jim went over to the radio and said "Hello" loudly into the speaker.

" ' "I am tired of living singly," ' " the nurse went on, " ' "on this coast so wild and shingly, I'm a-weary of my life; if you'll come and be my wife, quite serene would be my life . . ." ' "

"I guess she can't hear us," Irene said. "Try something else."

Jim turned to another station, and the living room was filled with the uproar of a cocktail party that had overshot its mark. Someone was playing the piano and singing the Whiffenpoof Song, and the voices that surrounded the piano were vehement and happy. "Eat some more sandwiches," a woman shrieked. There were screams of laughter and a dish of some sort crashed to the floor.

"Those must be the Hutchinsons, in 15-B," Irene said. "I knew they were giving a party this afternoon. I saw her in the liquor store. Isn't this too divine? Try something else. See if you can get those people in 18-C."

The Westcotts overheard that evening a monologue on salmon fishing in Canada, a bridge game, running comments on home movies of what had apparently been a fortnight at Sea Island, and a bitter family quarrel about an overdraft at the bank. They turned off their radio at midnight and went to bed, weak with laughter. Sometime in the night, their son began to call for a glass of water and Irene got one and took it to his room. It was very early. All the lights in the neighborhood were extinguished, and from the boy's window she could see the empty street. She went into the living room and tried the radio. There was some faint coughing, a moan, and then a man spoke. "Are you all right, darling?" he asked.

"Yes," a woman said wearily. "Yes, I'm all right, I guess," and then she added with great feeling, "But, you know, Charlie, I don't feel like myself any more. Sometimes there are about fifteen or twenty minutes in the week when I feel like myself. I don't like to go to another doctor, because the doctor's bills are so awful already, but I just don't feel like myself, Charlie. I just never feel like myself." They were not young, Irene thought. She guessed from the timbre of their voices that they were middle-aged. The restrained melancholy of the dialogue and the draft from the bedroom window made her shiver, and she went back to bed.

The following morning, Irene cooked breakfast for the family—the maid didn't come up from her room in the basement until ten—braided her daughter's hair, and waited at the door until her children and her husband had been carried away in the elevator. Then she went into the living room and tried the radio. "I don't want to go to school," a child screamed. "I hate school. I won't go to school. I hate school." "You will go to school," an enraged woman said. "We paid eight hundred dollars to get you into that school and you'll go if it kills you." The next number on the dial produced the worn record of the "Missouri Waltz." Irene shifted the control and invaded the privacy of several breakfast tables. She overheard demonstrations of indigestion, carnal love, abysmal vanity, faith, and despair. Irene's life was nearly as simple and sheltered as it appeared to be, and the forthright and sometimes brutal language that came from the loudspeaker that morning astonished and troubled her. She continued to listen until her maid came in. Then she turned off the radio quickly, since this insight, she realized, was a furtive one.

Irene had a luncheon date with a friend that day, and she left her apartment at a little after twelve. There were a number of women in the elevator when it stopped at her floor. She stared at their handsome and impassive faces, their furs, and the cloth flowers in their hats. Which one of them had been to Sea Island, she wondered. Which one had overdrawn her bank account? The elevator stopped at the tenth floor and a woman with a pair of Skye terriers joined them. Her hair was rigged high on her head and she wore a mink cape. She was humming the "Missouri Waltz."

Irene had two Martinis at lunch, and she looked searchingly at her friend and wondered what her secrets were. They had intended to go shopping after lunch, but Irene excused herself and went home. She told the maid that she was not to be disturbed; then she went into the living room, closed the doors, and switched on the radio. She heard, in the course of the afternoon, the halting conversation of a woman entertaining her aunt, the hysterical conclusion of a luncheon party, and a hostess briefing her maid about some cocktail guests. "Don't give the best Scotch to anyone who hasn't white hair," the hostess said. "See if you can get rid of that liver paste before you pass those hot things, and could you lend me five dollars? I want to tip the elevator man."

As the afternoon waned, the conversations increased in intensity. From where Irene sat, she could see the open sky above Central Park. There were hundreds of clouds in the sky, as though the south wind had broken the winter into pieces and were blowing it north, and on her radio she could hear the arrival of cocktail guests and the return of children and businessmen from their schools and offices. "I found a good-sized diamond on the bathroom floor this morning," a woman said. "It must have fallen out of that bracelet Mrs. Dunston was wearing last night." "We'll sell it," a man said. "Take it down to the jeweller on Madison Avenue and sell it. Mrs. Dunston won't know the difference, and we could use a couple of hundred bucks . . ." " 'Oranges and lemons, say the bells of St. Clement's,' " the Sweeneys' nurse sang. " 'Half-pence and farthings, say the bells of St. Martin's. When will you pay me? say the bells at old Bailey . . .' " "It's not a hat," a woman cried, and at her back roared a cocktail party. "It's not a hat, it's a love affair. That's what Walter Florell said. He said it's not a hat, it's a love affair," and then, in a lower voice, the same woman added, "Talk to somebody, for Christ's sake, honey, talk to somebody. If she catches you standing here not talking to anybody, she'll take us off her invitation list, and I love these parties."

The Westcotts were going out for dinner that night, and when Jim came home, Irene was dressing. She seemed sad and vague, and he brought her a drink. They were dining with friends in the neighborhood, and they walked to where they were going. The sky was broad and filled with light. It was one of those splendid spring evenings that excite memory and desire, and the air that touched their hands and faces felt very soft. A Salvation Army band was on the corner playing "Jesus Is Sweeter." Irene drew on her husband's arm and held him there for a minute, to hear the music. "They're really such nice people, aren't they?" she said. "They have such nice faces. Actually, they're so much nicer than a lot of the people we know." She took a bill from her purse and walked over and dropped it into the tambourine. There was in her face, when she returned to her husband, a look of radiant melancholy that he was not familiar with. And her conduct at the dinner party that night seemed strange to him, too. She interrupted her hostess rudely and stared at the people across the table from her with an intensity for which she would have punished her children.

It was still mild when they walked home from the party, and Irene looked up at the spring stars. "'How far that little candle throws its beams,'" she exclaimed. "'So shines a good deed in a naughty world.'" She waited that night until Jim had fallen asleep, and then went into the living room and turned on the radio.

Jim came home at about six the next night. Emma, the maid, let him in, and he had taken off his hat and was taking off his coat when Irene ran into the hall. Her face was shining with tears and her hair was disordered. "Go up to 16-C, Jim!" she screamed. "Don't take off your coat. Go up to 16-C. Mr. Osborn's beating his wife. They've been quarrelling since four o'clock, and now he's hitting her. Go up there and stop him."

From the radio in the living room, Jim heard screams, obscenities, and thuds. "You know you don't have to listen to this sort of thing," he said. He strode into the living room and turned the switch. "It's indecent," he said. "It's like looking in windows. You know you don't have to listen to this sort of thing. You can turn it off."

"Oh, it's so horrible, it's so dreadful," Irene was sobbing. "I've been listening all day, and it's so depressing."

"Well, if it's so depressing, why do you listen to it? I bought this damned radio to give you some pleasure," he said. "I paid a great deal of money for it. I thought it might make you happy. I wanted to make you happy."

"Don't, don't, don't, don't quarrel with me," she moaned, and laid her head on his shoulder. "All the others have been quarrelling all day. Everybody's been quarrelling. They're all worried about money. Mrs. Hutchinson's mother is dying of cancer in Florida and they don't have enough money to send her to the Mayo Clinic. At least, Mr. Hutchinson says they don't have enough money. And some woman in this building is having an affair with the superintendent—with that hideous superintendent. It's too disgusting. And Mrs. Melville has heart trouble and Mr. Hendricks is going to lose his job in

April and Mrs. Hendricks is horrid about the whole thing and that girl who plays the 'Missouri Waltz' is a whore, a common whore, and the elevator man has tuberculosis and Mr. Osborn has been beating Mrs. Osborn." She wailed, she trembled with grief and checked the stream of tears down her face with the heel of her palm.

"Well, why do you have to listen?" Jim asked again. "Why do you have to listen to this stuff if it makes you so miserable?"

"Oh, don't, don't, don't," she cried. "Life is too terrible, too sordid and awful. But we've never been like that, have we, darling? Have we? I mean we've always been good and decent and loving to one another, haven't we? And we have two children, two beautiful children. Our lives aren't sordid, are they, darling? Are they?" She flung her arms around his neck and drew his face down to hers. "We're happy, aren't we, darling? We are happy, aren't we?"

"Of course we're happy," he said tiredly. He began to surrender his resentment. "Of course we're happy. I'll have that damned radio fixed or taken away tomorrow." He stroked her soft hair. "My poor girl," he said.

"You love me, don't you?" she asked. "And we're not hypercritical or worried about money or dishonest, are we?"

"No, darling," he said.

A man came in the morning and fixed the radio. Irene turned it on cautiously and was happy to hear a California-wine commercial and a recording of Beethoven's Ninth Symphony, including Schiller's "Ode to Joy." She kept the radio on all day and nothing untoward came from the speaker.

A Spanish suite was being played when Jim came home. "Is everything all right?" he asked. His face was pale, she thought. They had some cocktails and went in to dinner to the "Anvil Chorus" from "Il Trovatore." This was followed by Debussy's "La Mer."

"I paid the bill for the radio today," Jim said. "It cost four hundred dollars. I hope you'll get some enjoyment out of it."

"Oh, I'm sure I will," Irene said.

"Four hundred dollars is a good deal more than I can afford," he went on. "I wanted to get something that you'd enjoy. It's the last extravagance we'll be able to indulge in this year. I see that you haven't paid your clothing bills yet. I saw them on your dressing table." He looked directly at her. "Why did you tell me you'd paid them? Why did you lie to me?"

"I just didn't want you to worry, Jim," she said. She drank

some water. "I'll be able to pay my bills out of this month's allowance. There were the slipcovers last month, and that party."

"You've got to learn to handle the money I give you a little more intelligently, Irene," he said. "You've got to understand that we won't have as much money this year as we had last. I had a very sobering talk with Mitchell today. No one is buying anything. We're spending all our time promoting new issues, and you know how long that takes. I'm not getting any younger, you know. I'm thirty-seven. My hair will be gray next year. I haven't done as well as I'd hoped to do. And I don't suppose things will get any better."

"Yes, dear," she said.

"We've got to start cutting down," Jim said. "We've got to think of the children. To be perfectly frank with you, I worry about money a great deal. I'm not at all sure of the future. No one is. If anything should happen to me, there's the insurance, but that wouldn't go very far today. I've worked awfully hard to give you and the children a comfortable life," he said bitterly. "I don't like to see all of my energies, all of my youth, wasted in fur coats and radios and slipcovers and—"

"Please, Jim," she said. "Please. They'll hear us."

"*Who'll* hear us? Emma can't hear us."

"The radio."

"Oh, I'm sick!" he shouted. "I'm sick to death of your apprehensiveness. The radio can't hear us. Nobody can hear us. And what if they can hear us? Who cares?"

Irene got up from the table and went into the living room. Jim went to the door and shouted at her from there. "Why are you so Christly all of a sudden? What's turned you overnight into a convent girl? You stole your mother's jewelry before they probated her will. You never gave your sister a cent of that money that was intended for her—not even when she needed it. You made Grace Howland's life miserable, and where was all your piety and your virtue when you went to that abortionist? I'll never forget how cool you were. You packed your bag and went off to have that child murdered as if you were going to Nassau. If you'd had any reasons, if you'd had any good reasons—"

Irene stood for a minute before the hideous cabinet, disgraced and sickened, but she held her hand on the switch before she extinguished the music and the voices, hoping that the instrument might speak to her kindly, that she might hear the Sweeneys' nurse. Jim continued to shout at her from the door. The voice on the radio was suave and noncommittal. "An early-morning railroad disaster in Tokyo," the loudspeaker said, "killed twenty-nine people. A fire in a Catholic hospital near Buffalo for the care of blind children was extinguished early this morning by nuns. The temperature is forty-seven. The humidity is eighty-nine."

City Boy
Leonard Michaels

"Phillip," she said, "this is crazy."

I didn't agree or disagree. She wanted some answer. I bit her neck. She kissed my ear. It was nearly three in the morning. We had just returned. The apartment was dark and quiet. We were on the living room floor and she repeated, "Phillip, this is crazy." Her crinoline broke under us like cinders. Furniture loomed all around in the darkness—settee, chairs, a table with a lamp. Pictures were cloudy blotches drifting above. But no lights, no things to look at, no eyes in her head. She was underneath me and warm. The rug was warm, soft as mud, deep. Her crinoline cracked like sticks. Our naked bellies clapped together. Air fired out like farts. I took it as applause. The chairs smirked and spit between their feet. The chandelier clicked giddy teeth. The clock ticked as if to split its glass. "Phillip," she said, "this is crazy." A little voice against the grain and power. Not enough to stop me. Yet once I had been a man of feeling. We went to concerts, walked in the park, trembled in the maid's room. Now in the foyer, a flash of hair and claws. We stumbled to the living room floor. She said, "Phillip, this is crazy." Then silence, except in my head where a conference table was set up, ashtrays scattered about. Priests, ministers and rabbis were rushing to take seats. I wanted their opinion, but came. They vanished. A voice lingered, faintly crying, "You could mess up the rug, Phillip, break something . . ." Her fingers pinched my back like ants. I expected a remark to kill good death. She said nothing. The breath in her nostrils whipped mucus. It cracked in my ears like flags. I dreamed we were in her mother's Cadillac, trailing flags. I heard her voice before I heard the words. "Phillip, this is crazy. My parents are in the next room." Her cheek jerked against mine, her breasts were knuckles in my nipples. I burned. Good death was killed. I burned with hate. A rabbi shook his finger, "You shouldn't hate." I lifted on my elbows, sneering in pain. She wrenched her hips, tightened muscles in belly and neck. She said,

"Move." It was imperative to move. Her parents were thirty feet away. Down the hall between Utrillos and Vlamincks, through the door, flick the light and I'd see them. Maybe like us, Mr. Cohen adrift on the missus. Hair sifted down my cheek. "Let's go to the maid's room," she whispered. I was reassured. She tried to move. I kissed her mouth. Her crinoline smashed like sugar. Pig that I was, I couldn't move. The clock ticked hysterically. Ticks piled up like insects. Muscles lapsed in her thighs. Her fingers scratched on my neck as if looking for buttons. She slept. I sprawled like a bludgeoned pig, eyes open, loose lips. I flopped into sleep, in her, in the rug, in our scattered clothes.

Dawn hadn't shown between the slats in the blinds. Her breathing sissed in my ear. I wanted to sleep more, but needed a cigarette. I thought of the cold avenue, the lonely subway ride. Where could I buy a newspaper, a cup of coffee? This was crazy, dangerous, a waste of time. The maid might arrive, her parents might wake. I had to get started. My hand pushed along the rug to find my shirt, touched a brass lion's paw, then a lamp cord.

A naked heel bumped wood.

She woke, her nails in my neck. "Phillip, did you hear?" I whispered, "Quiet." My eyes rolled like Milton's. Furniture loomed, whirled. "Dear God," I prayed, "save my ass." The steps ceased. Neither of us breathed. The clock ticked. She trembled. I pressed my cheek against her mouth to keep her from talking. We heard pajamas rustle, phlegmy breathing, fingernails scratching hair. A voice, "Veronica, don't you think it's time you sent Phillip home?"

A murmur of assent started in her throat, swept to my cheek, fell back drowned like a child in a well. Mr. Cohen had spoken. He stood ten inches from our legs. Maybe less. It was impossible to tell. His fingernails grated through hair. His voice hung in the dark with the quintessential question. Mr. Cohen, scratching his crotch, stood now as never in the light. Considerable. No tool of his wife, whose energy in business kept him eating, sleeping, overlooking the park. Pinochle change in his pocket four nights a week. But were they his words? Or was he the oracle of Mrs. Cohen, lying sleepless, irritated, waiting for him to get me out? I didn't breathe. I didn't move. If he had come on his own he would leave without an answer. His eyes weren't adjusted to the dark. He couldn't see. We lay at his feet like worms. He scratched, made smacking noises with his mouth.

The question of authority is always with us. Who is responsible for the triggers pulled, buttons pressed, the gas, the fire? Doubt banged my brain. My heart lay in the fist of intellect, which squeezed out feeling like piss out of kidneys. Mrs. Cohen's voice demolished doubt, feeling, intellect. It ripped from the bedroom.

"For God's sake, Morris, don't be banal. Tell the schmuck to go home and keep his own parents awake all night, if he has any."

Veronica's tears slipped down my cheeks. Mr. Cohen sighed, shuffled, made a strong voice. "Veronica, tell Phillip . . ." His foot came down on my ass. He drove me into his daughter. I drove her into his rug.

"I don't believe it," he said.

He walked like an antelope, lifting hoof from knee, but stepped down hard. Sensitive to the danger of movement, yet finally impulsive, flinging his pot at the earth in order to cross it. His foot brought me his weight and character, a hundred fifty-five pounds of stomping *schlemiel,* in a mode of apprehension so primal we must share it with bugs. Let armies stomp me to insensate pulp—I'll yell "Cohen" when he arrives.

Veronica squealed, had a contraction, fluttered, gagged a shriek, squeezed, and up like a frog out of the hand of a child I stood spread-legged, bolt naked, great with eyes. Mr. Cohen's face was eyes in my eyes. A secret sharer. We faced each other like men accidentally met in hell. He retreated flapping, moaning, "I will not believe it one bit."

Veronica said, "Daddy?"

"Who else you no good bum?"

The rug raced. I smacked against blinds, glass broke and I whirled. Veronica said, "Phillip," and I went off in streaks, a sparrow in the room, here, there, early American, baroque and rococo. Veronica wailed, "Phillip." Mr. Cohen screamed, "I'll kill him." I stopped at the door, seized the knob. Mrs. Cohen yelled from the bedroom, "Morris, did something break? Answer me."

"I'll kill that bastid."

"Morris, if something broke you'll rot for a month."

"Mother, stop it," said Veronica. "Phillip, come back."

The door slammed. I was outside, naked as a wolf.

I needed poise. Without poise the street was impossible. Blood shot to my brain, thought blossomed. I'd walk on my hands. Beards were fashionable. I kicked up my feet, kicked the elevator button, faced the door and waited. I bent one elbow like a knee. The posture of a clothes model, easy, poised. Blood coiled down to my brain, weeds burgeoned, I had made a bad impression. There was no other way to see it. But all right. We needed a new beginning. Everyone does. Yet how few of us know when it arrives. Mr. Cohen had never spoken to me before; this was a breakthrough. There had been a false element in our relationship. It was wiped out. I wouldn't kid myself with the idea that he had nothing to say. I'd had enough of his silent treatment. It was worth being naked to see how mercilessly I could think. I had his number. Mrs. Cohen's, too. I was learning every second. I was a city boy. No innocent shitkicker from Jersey. I was the A train, the Fifth Avenue bus. I could be a cop. My name was Phillip, my style New York City. I poked the elevator button with my toe. It rang in the lobby, waking Ludwig. He'd come for me, rotten with sleep. Not the first time. He always took me down, walked me through the lobby and let me out on the avenue. Wires began tugging him up the shaft. I moved back, conscious of my genitals hanging upside down. Absurd consideration; we were both men one way or another. There were social distinctions enforced by his uniform, but they would vanish at the sight of me. "The unaccommmodated thing itself." "Off ye lendings!" The greatest play is about a naked man. A picture of Lear came to me, naked, racing through the wheat. I could be cool. I thought of Ludwig's uniform, hat, whipcord collar. It signified his authority. Perhaps he would be annoyed, in his authority, by the sight of me naked. Few people woke him at such hours. Worse, I never tipped him. Could I have been so indifferent month after month? In a crisis you discover everything. Then it's too late. Know yourself, indeed. You need a crisis every day. I refused to think about it. I sent my mind after objects. It returned with the chairs, settee, table and chandelier. Where were my clothes? I sent it along the rug. It found buttons, eagles stamped in brass. I recognized them as the buttons on Ludwig's coat. Eagles, beaks like knives, shrieking for tips. Fuck'm, I thought. Who's Ludwig? A big coat, a whistle, white gloves and a General MacArthur hat. I could understand him completely. He couldn't begin to understand me. A naked man is mysterious. But aside from that, what did he know? I dated Veronica Cohen and went home late. Did he know I was out of work? That I lived in a slum downtown? Of course not.

Possibly under his hat was a filthy mind. He imagined Veronica and I might be having sexual intercourse. He resented it. Not that he hoped for the privilege himself, in his coat and soldier hat, but he had a proprietary interest in the building and its residents. I came from another world. *The* other world against which Ludwig defended the residents. Wasn't I like a burglar sneaking out late, making him my accomplice? I undermined his authority, his dedication. He despised me. It was obvious. But no one thinks such thoughts. It made me laugh to think them. My genitals jumped. The elevator door slid open. He didn't say a word. I padded inside like a seal. The door slid shut. Instantly, I was ashamed of myself, thinking as I had about him. I had no right. A better man than I. His profile was an etching by Dürer. Good peasant stock. How had he fallen to such work? Existence precedes essence. At the controls, silent, enduring, he gave me strength for the street. Perhaps the sun would be up, birds in the air. The door slid open. Ludwig walked ahead of me through the lobby. He needed new heels. The door of the lobby was half a ton of glass, encased in iron vines and leaves. Not too much for Ludwig. He turned, looked down into my eyes. I watched his lips move.

"I vun say sumding. Yur bisniss vot you do. Bud vy you mek her miserable? Nod led her slip. She has beks unter her eyes."

Ludwig had feelings. They spoke to mine. Beneath the uniform, a man. Essence precedes existence. Even rotten with sleep, thick, dry bags under his eyes, he saw, he sympathized. The discretion demanded by his job forbade anything tangible, a sweater, a hat. "Ludwig," I whispered, "you're all right." It didn't matter if he heard me. He knew I said something. He knew it was something nice. He grinned, tugged the door open with both hands. I slapped out onto the avenue. I saw no one, dropped to my feet and glanced back through the door. Perhaps for the last time. I lingered, indulged a little melancholy. Ludwig walked to a couch in the rear of the lobby. He took off his coat, rolled it into a pillow and lay down. I had never stayed to see him do that before, but always rushed off to the subway. As if I were indifferent to the life of the building. Indeed, like a burglar. I seized the valuables and fled to the subway. I stayed another moment, watching good Ludwig, so I could hate myself. He assumed the modest, saintly posture of sleep. One leg here, the other there. His good head on his coat. A big arm across his stomach, the hand between his hips. He made a fist and punched up and down.

I went down the avenue, staying close to the buildings.

Later I would work up a philosophy. Now I wanted to sleep, forget. I hadn't the energy for moral complexities: Ludwig cross-eyed, thumping his pelvis in such a nice lobby. Mirrors, glazed pots, rubber plants ten feet high. As if he were generating all of it. As if it were part of his job. I hurried. The buildings were on my left, the park on my right. There were doormen in all the buildings; God knows what was in the park. No cars were moving. No people in sight. Streetlights glowed in a receding sweep down to Fifty-ninth Street and beyond. A wind pressed my face like Mr. Cohen's breath. Such hatred. Imponderable under any circumstances, a father cursing his daughter. Why? A fright in the dark? Freud said things about fathers and daughters. It was too obvious, too hideous. I shuddered and went more quickly. I began to run. In a few minutes I was at the spit-mottled steps of the subway. I had hoped for vomit. Spit is no challenge for bare feet. Still, I wouldn't complain. It was sufficiently disgusting to make me live in spirit. I went down the steps flatfooted, stamping, elevated by each declension. I was a city boy, no mincing creep from the sticks.

A Negro man sat in the change booth. He wore glasses, a white shirt, black knit tie and a silver tie clip. I saw a mole on his right cheek. His hair had spots of grey, as if strewn with ashes. He was reading a newspaper. He didn't hear me approach, didn't see my eyes take him in, figure him out. Shirt, glasses, tie—I knew how to address him. I coughed. He looked up.

"Sir, I don't have any money. Please let me through the turnstile. I come this way every week and will certainly pay you the next time."

He merely looked at me. Then his eyes flashed like fangs. Instinctively, I guessed what he felt. He didn't owe favors to a white man. He didn't have to bring his allegiance to the transit authority into question for my sake.

"Hey, man, you naked?"

"Yes."

"Step back a little."

I stepped back.

"You're naked."

I nodded.

"Get your naked ass the hell out of here."

"Sir," I said, "I know these are difficult times, but can't we be reasonable? I know that . . ."

"Scat, mother, go home."

I crouched as if to dash through the turnstile. He crouched, too. It proved he would come after me. I shrugged, turned back toward the steps. The city was infinite. There were many other subways. But why had he become so angry? Did he think I was a bigot? Maybe I was running around naked to get him upset. His anger was incomprehensible otherwise. It made me feel like a bigot. First a burglar, then a bigot. I needed a cigarette. I could hardly breathe. Air was too good for me. At the top of the steps, staring down, stood Veronica. She had my clothes.

"Poor, poor," she said.

I said nothing. I snatched my underpants and put them on. She had my cigarettes ready. I tried to light one, but the match failed. I threw down the cigarette and the matchbook. She retrieved them as I dressed. She lit the cigarette for me and held my elbow to help me keep my balance. I finished dressing, took the cigarette. We walked back toward her building. The words "thank you" sat in my brain like driven spikes. She nibbled her lip.

"How are things at home?" My voice was casual and morose, as if no answer could matter.

"All right," she said, her voice the same as mine. She took her tone from me. I liked that sometimes, sometimes not. Now I didn't like it. I discovered I was angry. Until she said that I had no idea I was angry. I flicked the cigarette into the gutter and suddenly I knew why. I didn't love her. The cigarette sizzled in the gutter. Like truth. I didn't love her. Black hair, green eyes, I didn't love her. Slender legs. I didn't. Last night I had looked at her and said to myself, "I hate communism." Now I wanted to step on her head. Nothing less than that would do. If it was a perverted thought, then it was a perverted thought. I wasn't afraid to admit it to myself.

"All right? Really? Is that true?"

Blah, blah, blah. Who asked those questions? A zombie; not Phillip of the foyer and rug. He died in flight. I was sorry, sincerely sorry, but with clothes on my back I knew certain feelings would not survive humiliation. It was so clear it was thrilling. Perhaps she felt it, too. In any case she would have to accept it. The nature of the times. We are historical creatures. Veronica and I were finished. Before we reached her door I would say deadly words. They'd come in a natural way, kill her a little. Veronica, let me step on your head or we're through. Maybe we're through, anyway. It would deepen her looks, give philosophy to what was only charming in her face. The dawn was here. A new day. Cruel, but change is cruel. I could bear it. Love is infinite and one. Women are not. Neither are men. The human condition. Nearly unbearable.

"No, it's not true," she said.

"What's not?"

"Things aren't all right at home."

I nodded intelligently, sighed, "Of course not. Tell me the truth, please. I don't want to hear anything else."

"Daddy had a heart attack."

"Oh God," I yelled. "Oh God, no."

I seized her hand, dropped it. She let it fall. I seized it again. No use. I let it fall. She let it drift between us. We stared at one another. She said, "What were you going to say? I can tell you were going to say something."

I stared, said nothing.

"Don't feel guilty, Phillip. Let's just go back to the apartment and have some coffee."

"What can I say?"

"Don't say anything. He's in the hospital and my mother is there. Let's just go upstairs and not say anything."

"Not say anything. Like moral imbeciles go slurp coffee and not say anything? What are we, nihilists or something? Assassins? Monsters?"

"Phillip, there's no one in the apartment. I'll make us coffee and eggs . . ."

"How about a roast beef? Got a roast beef in the freezer?"

"Phillip, he's *my* father."

We were at the door. I rattled. I was in a trance. This was life. Death!

"Indeed, your father. I'll accept that. I can do no less."

"Phillip, shut up. Ludwig."

The door opened. I nodded to Ludwig. What did he know about life and death? Give him a uniform and a quiet lobby— that's life and death. In the elevator he took the controls. "Always got a hand on the controls, eh Ludwig?"

Veronica smiled in a feeble, grateful way. She liked to see me get along with the help. Ludwig said, "Dots right."

"Ludwig has been our doorman for years, Phillip. Ever since I was a little girl."

"Wow," I said.

"Dots right."

The door slid open. Veronica said, "Thank you, Ludwig." I said, "Thank you, Ludwig."

"Vulcum."

"Vulcum? You mean, 'welcome'? Hey, Ludwig, how long you been in this country?"

Veronica was driving her key into the door.

"How come you never learned to talk American, baby?"

"Phillip, come here."

"I'm saying something to Ludwig."

"Come here right now."

"I have to go, Ludwig."

"Vulcum."

She went directly to the bathroom. I waited in the hallway between Vlamincks and Utrillos. The Utrillos were pale and flat. The Vlamincks were thick, twisted and red. Raw meat on one wall, dry stone on the other. Mrs. Cohen had an eye for contrasts. I heard Veronica sob. She ran water in the sink, sobbed, sat down, peed. She saw me looking and kicked the door shut.

"At a time like this . . ."

"I don't like you looking."

"Then why did you leave the door open? You obviously don't know your own mind."

"Go away, Phillip. Wait in the living room."

"Just tell me why you left the door open."

"Phillip, you're going to drive me nuts. Go away. I can't do a damn thing if I know you're standing there."

The living room made me feel better. The settee, the chandelier full of teeth and the rug were company. Mr. Cohen was everywhere, a simple, diffuse presence. He jingled change in his pocket, looked out the window and was happy he could see the park. He took a little antelope step and tears came into my eyes. I sat among his mourners. A rabbi droned platitudes: Mr. Cohen was generous, kind, beloved by his wife and daughter. "How much did he weigh?" I shouted. The phone rang.

Veronica came running down the hall. I went and stood at her side when she picked up the phone. I stood dumb, stiff as a hatrack. She was whimpering, "Yes, yes . . ." I nodded my head yes, yes, thinking it was better than no, no. She put the phone down.

"It was my mother. Daddy's all right. Mother is staying with him in his room at the hospital and they'll come home together tomorrow."

Her eyes looked at mine. At them as if they were as flat and opaque as hers. I said in a slow, stupid voice, "You're allowed to do that? Stay overnight in a hospital with a patient? Sleep in his room?" She continued looking at my eyes. I shrugged, looked down. She took my shirt front in a fist like a bite. She whispered. I said, "What?" She whispered again, "Fuck me." The clock ticked like crickets. The Vlamincks spilled blood. We sank into the rug as if it were quicksand.

October in the Railroad Earth
Jack Kerouac

There was a little alley in San Francisco back of the Southern Pacific station at Third and Townsend in redbrick of drowsy lazy afternoons with everybody at work in offices in the air you feel the impending rush of their commuter frenzy as soon they'll be charging en masse from Market and Sansome buildings on foot and in buses and all well-dressed thru workingman Frisco of Walkup?? truck drivers and even the poor grime-bemarked Third Street of lost bums even Negroes so hopeless and long left East and meanings of responsibility and *try* that now all they do is stand there spitting in the broken glass sometimes fifty in one afternoon against one wall at Third and Howard and here's all these Millbrae and San Carlos neat-necktied producers and commuters of America and Steel civilization rushing by with San Francisco *Chronicles* and green *Call-Bulletins* not even enough time to be disdainful, they've got to catch 130, 132, 134, 136 all the way up to 146 till the time of evening supper in homes of the railroad earth when high in the sky the magic stars ride above the following hotshot freight trains—it's all in California, it's all a sea, I swim out of it in afternoons of sun hot meditation in my jeans with head on handkerchief on brakeman's lantern or (if not working) on book, I look up at blue sky of perfect lostpurity and feel the warp of wood of old America beneath me and have insane conversations with Negroes in several-story windows above and everything is pouring in, the switching moves of boxcars in that little alley which is so much like the alleys of Lowell and I hear far off in the sense of coming night that engine calling our mountains.

But it was that beautiful cut of clouds I could always see above the little S.P. alley, puffs floating by from Oakland or the Gate of Marin to the north or San Jose south, the clarity of Cal to break your heart. It was the fantastic drowse and drum hum of lum mum afternoon nathin' to do, ole Frisco with end of land sadness—the people—the alley full of trucks and cars of businesses nearabouts and nobody knew or far from cared who I was all my life three thousand five hundred miles from birth-O opened up and at last belonged to me in Great America.

Now it's night in Third Street the keen little neons and also yellow bulblights of impossible-to-believe flops with dark ruined shadows moving back of torn yellow shades like a degenerate China with no money—the cats in Annie's Alley, the flop comes on, moans, rolls, the street is loaded with darkness. Blue sky above with stars hanging high over old hotel roofs and blowers of hotels moaning out dusts of interior, the grime inside the word in mouths falling out tooth by tooth, the reading rooms tick tock big-clock with creak chair and slantboards and old faces looking up over rimless spectacles bought in some West Virginia or Florida or Liverpool England pawnshop long before I was born and across rains they've come to the end of the land sadness end of the world gladness all you San Franciscos will have to fall eventually and burn again. But I'm walking and one night a bum fell into the hole of the construction job where they're tearing a sewer by day the husky Pacific & Electric youths in torn jeans who work there often I think of going up to some of 'em like say blond ones with wild hair and torn shirts and say "You oughta apply for the railroad it's much easier work you don't stand around the street all day and you get much more pay" but this bum fell in the hole you saw his foot stick out, a British MG also driven by some eccentric once backed into the hole and as I came home from a long Saturday afternoon local to Hollister out of San Jose miles away across verdurous fields of prune and juice joy here's this British MG backed and legs up wheels up into a pit and bums and cops standing around right outside the coffee shop—it was the way they fenced it but he never had the nerve to do it due to the fact that he had no money and nowhere to go and O his father was dead and O his mother was dead and O his sister was dead and O his whereabout was dead was dead—but and then at that time also I lay in my room on long Saturday afternoons listening to Jumpin' George with my fifth of tokay no tea and just under the sheets laughed to hear the crazy music "Mama, he treats your daughter mean," Mama, Papa, and don't you come in here I'll kill you etc. getting high by myself in room glooms and all wondrous knowing about the Negro the essential American out there always finding his solace his meaning in the fellaheen street and not in abstract morality and even when he has a church you see the pastor out front bowing to the ladies on the make you hear his great vibrant voice on the sunny Sunday afternoon sidewalk full of sexual vibratos saying "Why yes Mam but de gospel do say that man was born of woman's womb—" and no and so by that time I come crawling out of my warmsack and hit the street when I see the railroad ain't gonna call me till 5 A.M. Sunday morn probably for a local out of Bay Shore in fact always for a local out of Bay Shore and I go to the wailbar of all the wildbars in the world the one and only Third-and-Howard and there I go in and drink with the madmen and if I get drunk I git.

The whore who come up to me in there the night I was there with Al Buckle and said to me "You wanta play with me tonight Jim, and?" and I didn't think I had enough money and later told this to Charley Low and he laughed and said "How do you know she wanted money always take the chance that she might be out just for love or just out for love you know what I mean man don't be a sucker." She was a goodlooking doll and said "How would you like to oolyakoo with me mon?" and I stood there like a jerk and in fact bought drink got drink drunk that night and in the 299 Club I was hit by the proprietor the band breaking up the fight before I had a chance to decide to hit him back which I didn't do and out on the street I tried to rush back in but they had locked the door and were looking at me thru the forbidden glass in the door with faces like undersea—I should have played with her shurrouruuruuruuruuruuruurkdiei.

Despite the fact I was a brakeman making 600 a month I kept going to the Public restaurant on Howard Street which was three eggs for 26 cents 2 eggs for 21 this with toast (hardly no butter) coffee (hardly no coffee and sugar rationed) oatmeal with dash of milk and sugar the smell of soured old shirts lingering above the cookpot steams as if they were making skidrow lumberjack stews out of San Francisco ancient Chinese mildewed laundries with poker games in the back among the barrels and the rats of the earthquake days, but actually the food somewhat on the level of an oldtime 1890 or 1910 section-gang cook of lumber camps far in the North with an oldtime pigtail Chinaman cooking it and cussing out those who didn't like it. The prices were incredible but one time I had the beefstew and it was absolutely the worst beefstew I ever et, it was incredible I tell you—and as they oft did that to me it was with the most intensest regret that I to convey to the geek back of counter what I wanted but he was a tough sonofabitch, ech, ti-ti, I thought the counterman was kind of queer especially he handled gruffly the hopeless drooldrunks, "What now you doing you think you can come in here and cut like that for God's sake act like a man won't you and eat or get out-t-t-t-"—I always did wonder what a guy like that was doing working in a place like that because, but why some sympathy in his horny heart for the busted wrecks, all up and down the street were restaurants like the Public catering exclusively to bums of the black, winos with no money, who found 21 cents left over from wine panhandlings and so stumbled in for their third or fourth touch of food in a week, as sometimes they didn't eat at all and so you'd see them in the corner puking white liquid which was a couple quarts of rancid sauterne rotgut or sweet white sherry and they had nothing on their stomachs, most of them had one leg or were on crutches and had bandages around their feet, from nicotine and alcohol poisoning together, and one time finally on my way up Third near Market across the street from Breens, when in early 1952 I lived on Russian Hill and didn't quite dig the complete horror and humor of railroad's Third Street, a bum a thin sickly littlebum like Anton Abraham lay face down on the pavement with crutch aside and some old remnant newspaper sticking out and it seemed to me he was dead. I looked closely to see if he was breathing and he was not, another man with me was looking down and we agreed he was dead, and soon a cop came over and looked and agreed and called the wagon, the little wretch weighed about 50 pounds in his bleeding count and was stone mackerel snotnose cold dead as a bleeding doornail—ah I tell you—and who could notice but other half dead deadbums bums bums bums dead dead times X times X times all dead bums forever dead with nothing and all finished and out—there—and this was the clientele in the Public Hair restaurant where I ate many's the morn a 3-egg breakfast with almost dry toast and oatmeal a little saucer of, and thin sickly dishwater coffee, all to save 14 cents so in my little book proudly I could make a notation and of the day and prove that I could live comfortably in America while working seven days a week and earning 600 a month I could live on less than 17 a week which with my rent of 4.20 was okay as I had also to spend money to eat and sleep sometimes on the other end of my Watsonville chaingang run but preferred most times to sleep free of charge and uncomfortable in cabooses of the crummy rack—my

26-cent breakfast, my pride—and that incredible semiqueer counterman who dished out the food, threw it at you, slammed it, had a languid frank expression straight in your eyes like a 1930's lunchcart heroine in Steinbeck and at the steamtable itself labored coolly a junkey-looking Chinese with an actual stocking in his hair as if they'd just Shanghai'd him off the foot of Commercial Street before the Ferry Building was up but forgot it was 1952, dreamed it was 1860 goldrush Frisco —and on rainy days you felt they had ships in the back room.

I'd take walks up Harrison and the boomcrash of truck traffic towards the glorious girders of the Oakland Bay Bridge that you could see after climbing Harrison Hill a little like radar machine of eternity in the sky, huge, in the blue, by pure clouds crossed, gulls, idiot cars streaking to destinations on its undinal boom across shmoshwaters flocked up by winds and news of San Rafael storms and flash boats—there O I always came and walked and negotiated whole Friscos in one afternoon from the overlooking hills of the high Fillmore where Orient-bound vessels you can see on drowsy Sunday mornings of poolhall goof like after a whole night playing drums in a jam session and a morn in the hall of cuesticks I went by the rich homes of old ladies supported by daughters or female secretaries with immense ugly gargoyle Frisco millions fronts of other days and way below is the blue passage of the Gate, the Alcatraz mad rock, the mouths of Tamalpais, San Pablo Bay, Sausalito sleepy hemming the rock and bush over yonder, and the sweet white ships cleanly cutting a path to Sasebo.—Over Harrison and down to the Embarcadero and around Telegraph Hill and up the back of Russian Hill and down to the play streets of Chinatown and down Kearney back across Market to Third and my wild-night neon twinkle fate there, ah, and then finally at dawn of a Sunday and they did call me, the immense girders of Oakland Bay still haunting me and all that eternity too much to swallow and not knowing who I am at all but like a big plump long-haired baby worwalking up in the dark trying to wonder who I am the door knocks and it's the desk keeper of the flop hotel with silver rims and white hair and clean clothes and sickly potbelly said he was from Rocky Mount and looked like yes, he had been desk clerk of the Nash Buncome Association hotel down there in 50 successive heatwave summers without the sun and only palmos of the lobby with cigar crutches in the albums of the South and him with his dear mother waiting in a buried log cabin of graves with all that mashed past historied underground afoot with the stain of the bear the blood of the tree and cornfields long plowed under and Negroes whose voices long faded from the middle of the wood and the dog barked his last, this man had voyageured to the West Coast too like all the other loose American elements and was pale and sixty and complaining of sickness, might at one time been a handsome squire to women with money but now a forgotten clerk and maybe spent a little time in jail for a few forgeries or harmless cons and might also have been a railroad clerk and might have wept and might have never made it, and that day I'd say he saw the bridgegirders up over the hill of traffic of Harrison like me and woke up mornings with same lost, is now beckoning on my door and breaking in the world on me and he is standing on the frayed carpet of the hall all worn down by black steps of sunken old men for last 40 years since earthquake and the toilet stained, beyond the last toilet bowl and the last stink and stain I guess yes is the end of the world the bloody end of the world, so now knocks on my door and I wake up, saying "How what howp howelk howel of the knavery they've meaking, ek and won't let me slepit? Whey they dool? Whand out wisis thing that comes flarminging around my dooring in the mouth of the night and there everything knows that I have no mother, and no sister, and no father and no bot sosstle, but not crib" I get up and sit up and says "Howowow?" and he says "Telephone?" and I have to put on my jeans heavy with knife, wallet, I look closely at my railroad watch hanging on little door flicker of closet door face to me ticking silent the time, it says 4:30 A.M. of a Sunday morn, I go down the carpet of the skidrow hall in jeans and with no shirt and yes with shirt tails hanging gray workshirt and pick up phone and ticky sleepy night desk with cage and spittoons and keys hanging and old towels piled clean ones but frayed at edges and bearing names of every hotel of the moving prime, on the phone is the Crew Clerk, "Kerroway?" "Yeah." "Kerroway it's gonna be the Sherman Local at 7 A.M. this morning." "Sherman Local right." "Out of Bay Shore, you know the way?" "Yeah." "You had that same job last Sunday—Okay Kerroway-y-y-y-y." And we mutually hang up and I say to myself okay it's the Bay Shore bloody old dirty hagglous old coveted old madman Sherman who hates me so much especially when we were at Redwood Junction kicking boxcars and he always insists I work the rear end tho as one-year man it would be easier for me to follow pot but I work rear and he wants me to be right there with a block of wood when a car or cut of cars kicked stops, so they won't roll down that incline and start catastrophes, O well anyway I'll be learning eventually to like the railroad and Sherman will like me some day, and anyway another day another dollar.

And there's my room, small, gray in the Sunday morning, now all the franticness of the street and night before is done with, bums sleep, maybe one or two sprawled on sidewalk with empty poorboy on a sill—my mind whirls with life.

So there I am in dawn in my dim cell—2½ hours to go till the time I have to stick my railroad watch in my jean watchpocket and cut out allowing myself exactly 8 minutes to the station and the 7:15 train No. 112 I have to catch for the ride five miles to Bay Shore through four tunnels, emerging from the sad Rath scene of Frisco gloom gleak in the rainymouth fogmorning to a sudden valley with grim hills rising to the sea, bay on left, the fog rolling in like demented in the draws that have little white cottages disposed realestatically for come-Christmas blue sad lights—my whole soul and concomitant eyes looking out on this reality of living and working in San Francisco with that pleased semi-loin-located shudder, energy for sex changing to pain at the portals of work and culture and natural foggy fear.—There I am in my little room wondering how I'll really manage to fool myself into feeling that these next 2½ hours will be well filled, fed, with work and pleasure thoughts.—It's so thrilling to feel the coldness of the morning wrap around my thickquilt blankets as I lay there, watch facing and ticking me, legs spread in comfy skidrow soft sheets with soft tears or sew lines in 'em, huddled in my own skin and rich and not spending a cent on—I look at my little-book—and I stare at the words of the Bible.—On the floor I find last red afternoon Saturday's *Chronicle* sports page with news of football games in Great America the end of which I bleakly see in the gray light entering—the fact that Frisco is built of wood satisfies me in my peace, I know nobody'll disturb me for 2½ hours and all bums are asleep in their own bed of eternity awake or not, bottle or not—it's the joy I feel that counts for me.—On the floor's my shoes, big lumberboot flopjack workshoes to colomp over rockbed with and not turn the ankle—solidity shoes that when you put them on, yokewise, you know you're working now and so for same reason shoes not be worn for any reason like joys of restaurant and shows.—Nightbefore shoes are on the floor beside the Clunkershoes a pair of blue canvas shoes à la 1952 style, in them I'd trod soft as ghost the indented hill sidewalks of Ah Me Frisco all in the glitter night, from the top of Russian Hill I'd looked down at one point on all roofs of North Beach and the Mexican nightclub neons, I'd descended to them on the old steps of Broadway under which they were newly laboring a mountain tunnel—shoes fit for watersides, embarcaderos, hill and plot lawns of park and tiptop vista.—Workshoes covered with dust and some oil of engines—the crumpled jeans nearby, belt, blue railroad hank, knife, comb, keys, switch keys and caboose coach key, the knees white from Pajaro Riverbottom finedusts, the ass black from slick sandboxes in yardgoat after yardgoat—the gray workshorts, the dirty undershirt, sad shorts, tortured socks of my life.—And the Bible on my desk next to the peanut butter, the lettuce, the raisin bread, the crack in the plaster, the stiff-with-old-dust lace drape now no longer laceable but hard as—after all those years of hard dust eternity in that Cameo skid inn with red eyes of rheumy oldmen dying there staring without hope out on the dead wall you can hardly see thru windowdusts and all you heard lately in the shaft of the rooftop middle way was the cries of a Chinese child whose father and mother were always telling him to shush and then screaming at him, he was a pest and his tears from China were most persistent and worldwide and represented all our feelings in brokendown Cameo tho this was not admitted by bum one except for an occasional harsh clearing of throat in the halls or moan of nightmarer—by things like this and neglect of a hard-eyed alcoholic oldtime chorusgirl maid the curtains had now absorbed all the iron they could take and hung stiff and even the dust in them was iron, if you shook them they'd crack and fall in tatters to the floor and spatter like wings of iron on the bong and the dust would fly into your nose like filings of steel and choke you to death, so I never touched them. My little room at 6 in the comfy dawn (at 4:30) and before me all that time, that fresh-eyed time for a little coffee to boil water on my hot plate, throw some coffee in, stir it, French style, slowly carefully pour it in my white tin cup, throw sugar in (not California beet sugar like I should have been using but New Orleans cane sugar, because beet racks I carried from Oakland out to Watsonville many's the time, a 80-car freight train with nothing but gondolas loaded with sad beets looking like the heads of decapitated women)—ah me how but it was a hell and now I had the whole thing to myself, and make my raisin toast by sitting it on a little wire I'd especially bent to place over the hotplate, the toast crackled up, there, I spread the margarine on the still red hot toast and it too would crackle and sink in golden, among burnt raisins and this was my toast—then two eggs gently slowly fried in soft margarine in my little skidrow frying pan about half as thick as a dime in fact less a little piece of tiny tin you could bring on a camp trip—the eggs slowly fluffed in there and swelled from butter steams and I threw garlic salt on them, and when they were ready the yellow of them had been slightly filmed with a cooked white at the top from the tin cover I'd put over the frying pan, so now they were ready, and out they came, I spread them out on top of my already prepared potatoes which had been boiled in small pieces and then mixed with the bacon I'd already fried in small pieces, kind of raggely mashed bacon potatoes, with eggs on top steaming, and on the side lettuce, with peanut butter dab nearby on side.—I had heard that peanut butter and lettuce contained all the vitamins you should want, this after I had originally started to eat this combination because of the deliciousness and nostalgia of the taste—my breakfast ready at about 6:45 and as I eat already I'm dressing to go piece by piece and by the time the last dish is washed in the little sink at the boiling hot-water tap and I'm taking my lastquick slug of coffee and quickly rinsing the cup in the hot water spout and rushing to dry it and plop it in its place by the hot plate and the brown carton in which all the groceries sit tightly wrapped in brown paper, I'm already picking up my brakeman's lantern from where it's been hanging on the door handle and my tattered timetable's long been in my backpocket folded and ready to go, everything tight, keys, timetable, lantern, knife, handkerchief, wallet, comb, railroad keys, change and myself. I put the light out on the sad dab mad grub little diving room and hustle out into the fog of the flow, descending the creak hall steps where the old men are not yet sitting with Sunday morn papers because still asleep or some of them I can now as I leave hear beginning to disfawdle to wake in their rooms with their moans and yorks and scrapings and horror sounds, I'm going down the steps to work, glance to check time of watch with clerk cage clock—a hardy two or three oldtimers sitting already in the dark brown lobby under the tockboom clock, toothless, or grim, or elegantly mustached—what thought in the world swirling in them as they see the young eager brakeman bum hurrying to his thirty dollars of the Sunday—what memories of old homesteads, built without sympathy, hornyhanded fate dealt them the loss of wives, childs, moons—libraries collapsed in their time—oldtimers of the telegraph wired wood Frisco in the fog gray top time sitting in their brown sunk sea and will be there when this afternoon my face flushed from the sun, which at eight'll flame out and make sunbaths for us at Redwood, they'll still be here the color of paste in the green underworld and still reading the same editorial over again and won't understand where I've been or what for or what—I have to get out of there or suffocate, out of Third Street or become a worm, it's alright to live and bed-wine in and play the radio and cook little breakfasts and rest in but O my I've got to tog now to work, I hurry down Third to Townsend for my 7:15 train—it's 3 minutes to go, I start in a panic to jog, goddam it I didn't give myself enough time this morning, I hurry down under the Harrison ramp to the Oakland-Bay Bridge, down past Schweibacker-Frey the great dim red neon printshop always spectrally my father the dead executive I see there, I run and hurry past the beat Negro grocery stores where I buy all my peanut butter and raisin bread, past the redbrick railroad alley now mist and wet, across Townsend, the train is leaving!

Fatuous railroad men, the conductor old John J. Coppertwang 35 years pure service on ye olde S.P. is there in the gray Sunday morning with his gold watch out peering at it, he's standing by the engine yelling up pleasantries at old hoghead Jones and young fireman Smith with the baseball cap is at the fireman's seat munching sandwich—"We'll how'd ye like old Johnny O yestiddy, I guess he didn't score so many touchdowns like we thought." "Smith bet six dollars on the pool down in Watsonville and said he's rakin' in thirty four." "I've been in that Watsonville pool—." They've been in the pool of life fleartiming with one another, all the long poker-playing nights in brownwood railroad places, you can smell the mashed cigar in the wood, the spittoon's been there for more than 750,099 yars and the dog's been in and out and these old boys by old shaded brown light have bent and muttered and young boys too with their new brakeman passenger uniform the tie undone the coat thrown back the flashing youth smile of happy fatuous well-fed goodjobbed careered futured pensioned hospitalized taken-care-of railroad men—35, 40 years of it and then they get to be conductors and in the middle of the night they've been for years called by the Crew Clerk yelling "Cassady? It's the Maximush localized week do you for the right lead" but now as old men all they have is a regular job, a regular train, conductor of the 112 with goldwatch is helling up his pleasantries at all fire dog crazy Satan hoghead Willis why the wildest man this side of France and Frankincense, he was known once to take his engine up that steep grade—7:15, time to pull, as I'm running thru the station hearing the bell jangling and the steam chuff they're pulling out, O I come flying out on the platform and forget momentarily or that is never did know what track it was and whirl in confusion a while wondering what track and can't see no train and this is the time I lose there, 5, 6, 7 seconds when the train tho underway is only slowly upchugging to go and a man a fat executive could easily run up and grab it but when I yell to Assistant Stationmaster "Where's 112?" and he tells me the last track which is the track I never dreamed I run to it fast as I can go and dodge people à la Columbia halfback and cut into track fast as off-tackle where you carry the ball with you to the left and feint with neck and head and push of ball as tho you're gonna throw yourself all out to fly around that left end and everybody psychologically chuffs with you that way and suddenly you contract and you like whiff of smoke are buried in the hole in tackle, cutback play, you're flying into the hole almost before you yourself know it, flying into the track I am and there's the train about 30 yards away even as I look picking up tremendously momentum the kind of momentum I would have been able to catch if I'd a looked a second earlier—but I run, I know I can catch it. Standing on the back platform are the rear brakeman and an old deadheading conductor ole Charley W. Jones, why he had seven wives and six kids and one time out at Lick no I guess it was Coyote he couldn't seen on account of the steam and out he come and found his lantern in the igloo regular anglecock of my herald and they gave him fifteen benefits so now there he is in the Sunday har har owlala morning and he and young rear man watch incredulously this student brakeman running like a crazy trackman after their departing train. I feel like yelling "Make your airtest now make your airtest now!" knowing that when a passenger pulls out just about at the first crossing east of the station they pull the air a little bit to test the brakes, on signal from the engine, and this momentarily slows up the train and I could manage it, and could catch it, but they're not making no airtest the bastards, and I hek knowing I'm going to have to run like a sonofabitch. But suddenly I get embarrassed thinking what are all the people of the world gonna say to see a man running so devilishly fast with all his might sprinting thru life like Jesse Owens just to catch a goddam train and all of them with their hysteria wondering if I'll get killed when I catch the back platform and blam, I fall down and go boom and lay supine across the crossing, so the old flagman when the train has flowed by will see that everything lies on the earth in the same stew, all of us angels will die and we don't ever know how or our own diamond, O heaven will enlighten us and open your youeeeeeoueee—open our eyes, open our eyes—I know I won't get hurt, I trust my shoes, hand grip, feet, solidity of yipe and cripe of gripe and grip and strength and need no mystic strength to measure the musculature in my rib rack—but damn it all it's a social embarrassment to be caught sprinting like a maniac after a train especially with two men gaping at me from rear of train and shaking their heads and yelling I can't make it even as I halfheartedly sprint after them with open eyes trying to communicate that I can and not for them to get hysterical or laugh, but I realize it's all too much for me, not the run, not the speed of the train which anyway two seconds after I gave up the complicated chase did indeed slow down at the crossing in the airtest before chugging up again for good and Bay Shore. So I was late for work, and old Sherman hated me and was about to hate me more.

The ground I would have eaten in solitude, cronch—the railroad earth, the flat stretches of long Bay Shore that I have to negotiate to get to Sherman's bloody caboose on track 17 ready to go with pot pointed to Redwood and the morning's 3-hour work—I get off the bus at Bay Shore Highway and rush down the little street and turn in—boys riding the pot of a switcheroo in the yardgoat day come yelling by at me from the headboards and footboards "Come on down ride with us" otherwise I would have been about 3 minutes even later to my work but now I hop on the little engine that momentarily slows up to pick me up and it's alone not pulling anything but tender, the guys have been up to the other end of the yard to get back on some track of necessity—that boy will have to learn to flag himself without nobody helping him as many's the time I've seen some of these young goats think they have everything but the plan is late, the word will have to wait, the massive arboreal thief with the crime of the kind, and air and all kinds of ghouls—ZONKed! made tremendous by the flare of the whole prime and encrudalatures of all kinds—San Franciscos and shroudband Bay Shores the last and the last furbelow of the eek plot pall prime tit top work oil twicks and wouldn't you?—the railroad earth I would have eaten alone, cronch, on foot head bent to get to Sherman who ticking watch observes with finicky eyes the time to go to give the hiball sign get on going it's Sunday no time to waste the only day of his long seven-day-a-week worklife he gets a chance to rest a little bit at home when "Eee Christ" when "Tell that sonofabitch student this is no party picnic damn this shit and throb tit you tell them something and how do you what the hell expect to underdries out tit all you bright tremendous trouble anyway, we's LATE" and this is the way I come rushing up late. Old Sherman is sitting in the crummy over his switch lists, when he sees me with cold blue eyes he says "You know you're supposed to be here 7:30 don't you so what the hell you doing gettin' in here at 7:50 you're twenty goddam minutes late, what the fuck you think this your birthday?" and he gets up and leans off the rear bleak platform and gives the high sign to the enginemen up front we have a cut of about 12 cars and they say it easy and off we go slowly at first, picking up momentum to the work, "Light that goddam fire" says Sherman he's wearing brandnew workshoes just about bought yestiddy and I notice his clean coveralls that his wife washed and set on his chair just that morning probably and I rush up and throw coal in the potbelly flop and take a fusee and two fusees and light them crack em Ah fourth of the July when the angels would smile on the horizon and all the racks where the mad are lost are returned to us forever from Lowell of my soul prime and single meditatee long-song hope to heaven of prayers and angels and of course the sleep and interested eye of images and but now we detect the missing buffoon there's the poor goodman rear man ain't even on the train yet and Sherman looks out sulkily the back door and sees his rear man waving from fifteen yards aways to stop and wait for him and being an old railroad man he certainly isn't going to run or even walk fast, it's well understood, conductor Sherman's got to get up off his switch-list desk chair and pull the air and stop the goddam train for rear man Arkansaw Charley, who sees this done and just come up lopin' in his flop overalls without no care, so he was late too, or at least had gone gossiping in the yard office while waiting for the stupid head brakeman, the tagman's up in front on the presumably pot. "First thing we do is pick up a car in front at Redwood so all's you do get off at the crossing and stand back to flag, not too far." "Don't I work the head end?" "You work the hind end we got not much to do and I wanta get it done fast," snarls the conductor. "Just take it easy and do what we say and watch and flag." So it's peaceful Sunday morning in California and off we go, tack-a-tick, lao-tichi-couch, out of the Bay Shore yards, pause momentarily at the main line for the green, ole 71 or ole whatever been by and now we get out and go swamming up the tree valleys and town vale hollows and main street crossing parking-lot lastnight attendant plots and Stanford lots of the world—to our destination in the Poo which I can see, and, so to while the time I'm up in the cupolo and with my newspaper dig the latest news on the front page and also consider and make notations of the money I spent already for this day Sunday absolutely not jot spent a nothing—California rushes by and with sad eyes we watch it reel the whole bay and the discourse falling off to gradual gils that ease and graduate to Santa Clara Valley then and the fig and behind is the fog immemoriates while the mist closes and we come running out to the bright sun of the Sabbath Californiay—

At Redwood I get off and standing on sad oily ties of the brakie railroad earth with red flag and torpedoes attached and fusees in backpocket with timetable crushed against and I leave my hot jacket in crummy standing there then with sleeves rolled up and there's the porch of a Negro home, the brothers are sitting in shirtsleeves talking with cigarettes and laughing and little daughter standing amongst the weeds of the garden with her playpail and pigtails and we the railroad men with soft signs and no sound pick up our flower, according to same goodman train order that for the last entire lifetime of attentions ole conductor industrial worker harlotized Sherman has been reading carefully son so's not to make a mistake:

> "Sunday morning October 15 pick up flower
> car at Redwood, Dispatcher M.M.S."

WORKING

Christ in Concrete
Pietro Di Donato

March whistled stinging snow against the brick walls and up the gaunt girders. Geremio, the foreman, swung his arms about, and gaffed the men on.

Old Nick, the "Lean," stood up from over a dust-flying brick pile, and tapped the side of his nose.

"Master Geremio, the devil himself could not break his tail any harder than we here."

Burly Vincenzo of the walrus moustache, and known as the "Snoutnose," let fall the chute door of the concrete hopper and sang over in the Lean's direction: "Mari-Annina's belly and the burning night will make of me once more a milk-mouthed stripling lad . . ."

The Lean loaded his wheelbarrow and spat furiously. "Sons of two-legged dogs . . . despised of even the devil himself! Work! Sure! For America beautiful will eat you and spit your bones into the earth's hole! Work!" And with that his wiry frame pitched the barrow violently over the rough floor.

Snoutnose waved his head to and fro and with mock pathos wailed, "Sing on, oh guitar of mine . . ."

Short, cherry-faced Joe Chiappa, the scaffoldman, paused with hatchet in hand and tenpenny spike sticking out from small dice-like teeth to tell the Lean as he went by, in a voice that all could hear, "Ah, father of countless chicks, the old age is a carrion!"

Geremio chuckled and called to him: "Hey, little Joe, who are you to talk? You and big-titted Cola can't even hatch an egg, whereas the Lean has just to turn the doorknob of his bedroom and old Philomena becomes a balloon!"

Coarse throats tickled and mouths opened wide in laughter.

Mike, the "Barrel-mouth," pretended he was talking to himself and yelled out in his best English . . . he was always speaking English while the rest carried on in their native Italian: "I don't know myself, but somebodys whose gotta bigga buncha keeds and he alla times talka from somebodys elsa!"

Geremio knew it was meant for him and he laughed. "On the tomb of Saint Pimplelegs, this little boy my wife is giving me next week shall be the last! Eight hungry little Christians to feed is enough for any man."

Joe Chiappa nodded to the rest. "Sure, Master Geremio had a telephone call from the next bambino. Yes, it told him it had a little bell there instead of a rosebush . . . It even told him its name!"

"Laugh, laugh all of you," returned Geremio, "but I tell you that all my kids must be boys so that they someday will be big American builders. And then I'll help them to put the gold away in the basements for safe keeping!"

A great din of riveting shattered the talk among the fast-moving men. Geremio added a handful of "Honest" tobacco to his corncob, puffed strongly, and cupped his hands around the bowl for a bit of warmth. The chill day caused him to shiver, and he thought to himself, "Yes, the day is cold, cold . . . but who am I to complain when the good Christ himself was crucified?

"Pushing the job is all right (when has it been otherwise in my life?) but this job frightens me. I feel the building wants to tell me something: just as one Christian to another. I don't like this. Mr. Murdin tells me, 'Push it up!' That's all he knows. I keep telling him that the underpinning should be doubled and the old material removed from the floors, but he keeps the inspector drunk and . . . 'Hey, Ashes-ass! Get away from under that pilaster! Don't pull the old work. Push it away from you or you'll have a nice present for Easter if the wall falls on you!' . . . Well, with the help of God I'll see this job through. It's not my first, nor the . . . 'Hey, Patsy number two! Put more cement in that concrete; we're putting up a building, not an Easter cake!' "

Patsy hurled his shovel to the floor and gesticulated madly. "The padrone Murdin-sa tells me, 'Too much, too much! Lil' bit is plenty!' And you tell me I'm stingy! The rotten building can fall after I leave!"

Six floors below, the contractor called: "Hey Geremio! Is your gang of dagos dead?"

Geremio cautioned to the men: "On your toes, boys. If he writes out slips, someone won't have big eels on the Easter table."

The Lean cursed that "the padrone could take the job and shove it . . . !"

Curly-headed Sandino, the roguish, pigeon-toed scaffold-man, spat a clod of tobacco-juice and hummed to his own music.

"Yes, certainly yes to your face, master padrone . . . and behind, this to you and all your kind!"

The day, like all days, came to an end. Calloused and bruised bodies sighed, and numb legs shuffled towards shabby railroad flats. . . .

"Ah, *bella casa mia*. Where my little freshets of blood, and my good woman await me. Home where my broken back will not ache so. Home where midst the monkey chatter of my *piccolinos* I will float off to blessed slumber with my feet on the chair and the head on the wife's soft full breast."

These great child-hearted ones leave each other without words or ceremony, and as they ride and walk home, a great pride swells the breast. . . .

"Blessings to Thee, oh Jesus. I have fought winds and cold. Hand to hand I have locked dumb stones in place and the great building rises. I have earned a bit of bread for me and mine."

The mad day's brutal conflict is forgiven, and strained limbs prostrate themselves so that swollen veins can send the yearning blood coursing and pulsating deliciously as though the body mountained leaping streams.

The job alone remained behind . . . and yet, they too, having left the bigger part of their lives with it. The cold ghastly beast, the Job, stood stark, the eerie March wind wrapping it in sharp shadows of falling dusk.

That night was a crowning point in the life of Geremio. He bought a house! Twenty years he had helped to mould the New World. And now he was to have a house of his own! What mattered that it was no more than a wooden shack? It was his own!

He had proudly signed his name and helped Annunziata to make her X on the wonderful contract that proved them owners. And she was happy to think that her next child, soon to come, would be born under their own rooftree. She heard the church chimes, and cried to the children: "Children, to bed! It is near midnight. And remember, shut-mouth to the *paesanos!* Or they will send the evil eye to our new home even before we put foot."

The children scampered off to the icy yellow bedroom where three slept in one bed and three in the other. Coltishly and friskily they kicked about under the covers; their black iron-cotton stockings not removed . . . what! and freeze the peanut-little toes?

Said Annunziata, "The children are so happy, Geremio; let them be, for even I would a Tarantella dance." And with that she turned blushing. He wanted to take her on her word. She patted his hands, kissed them, and whispered, "Our children will dance for us . . . in the American style some day."

Geremio cleared his throat and wanted to sing. "Yes, with joy I could sing in a richer feeling than the great Caruso." He babbled little old country couplets and circled the room until the tenant below tapped the ceiling.

Annunziata whispered: "Geremio, to bed and rest. Tomorrow is a day for great things . . . and the day on which our Lord died for us."

The children were now hard asleep. Heads under the cover, over . . . moist noses whistling, and little damp legs entwined.

In bed Geremio and Annunziata clung closely to each other. They mumbled figures and dates until fatigue stilled their thoughts. And with chubby Johnnie clutching fast his bottle and warmed between them . . . life breathed heavily, and dreams entertained in far, far worlds, the nation-builder's brood.

But Geremio and Annunziata remained for a while staring into darkness, silently.

"Geremio?"

"Yes?"

"This job you are now working. . . ."

"So?"

"You used always to tell me about what happened on the jobs . . . who was jealous, and who praised. . . ."

"You should know by now that all work is the same. . . ."

"Geremio. The month you have been on this job, you have not spoken a word about the work . . . And I have felt that I am walking in a dream. Is the work dangerous? Why don't you answer . . . ?"

Job loomed up damp, shivery gray. Its giant members waiting.

Builders quietly donned their coarse robes, and waited.

Geremio's whistle rolled back into his pocket and the symphony of struggle began.

Trowel rang through brick and slashed mortar rivets were machine-gunned fast with angry grind Patsy number one check Patsy number two check the Lean three check Vincenzo four steel bellowed back at hammer donkey engines coughed purple Ashes-ass Pietro fifteen chisel point intoned stone thin steel whirred and wailed through wood liquid stone flowed with dull rasp through iron veins and hoist screamed through space Carmine the Fat twenty-four and Giacomo Sangini check . . . The multitudinous voices of a civilization rose from the surroundings and welded with the efforts of the Job.

To the intent ear, Nation was voicing her growing pains, but, hands that create are attached to warm hearts and not to calculating minds. The Lean as he fought his burden on looked forward to only one goal, the end. The barrow he pushed, he did not love. The stones that brutalized his palms, he did not love. The great God Job, he did not love. He felt a searing bitterness and a fathomless consternation at the queer consciousness that inflicted the ever mounting weight of structure that he HAD TO! HAD TO! raise above his shoulders! When, when and where would the last stone be? Never . . . did he bear his toil with the rhythm of song! Never . . . did his gasping heart knead the heavy mortar with lilting melody! A voice within him spoke in wordless language.

The language of worn oppression and the despair of realizing that his life had been left on brick piles. And always, there had been hunger and her bastard, the fear of hunger.

Murdin bore down upon Geremio from behind and shouted:

"Goddamnit, Geremio, if you're givin' the men two hours off today with pay, why the hell are they draggin' their tails? And why don't you turn that skinny old Nick loose, and put a young wop in his place?"

"Now, listen-a to me, Mister Murdin—"

"Don't give me that! And bear in mind that there are plenty of good barefoot men in the streets who'll jump for a day's pay!"

"Padrone—padrone, the underpinning gotta be make safe and—"

"Lissenyawopbastard! If you don't like it, you know what you can do!"

And with that he swung swaggering away.

The men had heard, and those who hadn't knew instinctively.

The new home, the coming baby, and his whole background, kept the fire from Geremio's mouth and bowed his head. "Annunziata speaks of scouring the ashcans for the children's bread in case I didn't want to work on a job where . . . But am I not a man, to feed my own with these hands? Ah, but day will end and no boss in the world can then rob me of the joy of my home!"

Murdin paused for a moment before descending the ladder.

Geremio caught his meaning and jumped to, nervously directing the rush of work . . . No longer Geremio, but a machine-like entity.

The men were transformed into single, silent, beasts. Snout-nose steamed through ragged moustache whip-lashing sand into mixer Ashes-ass dragged under four by twelve beam Lean clawed wall knots jumping in jaws masonry crumbled dust billowed thundered choked. . . .

At noon, Geremio drank his wine from an old-fashioned magnesia bottle and munched a great pepper sandwich . . . no meat on Good Friday. Said one, "Are some of us to be laid off? Easter is upon us and communion dresses are needed and . . ."

That, while Geremio was dreaming of the new house and the joys he could almost taste. Said he: "Worry not. You should know Geremio." It then all came out. He regaled them with his wonderful joy of the new house. He praised his wife and children one by one. They listened respectfully and returned him well wishes and blessings. He went on and on. . . . "Paul made a radio—all by himself, mind you! One can hear Barney Google and many American songs! How proud he."

The ascent to labor was made, and as they trod the ladder, heads turned and eyes communed with the mute flames of the brazier whose warmth they were leaving, not with willing heart, and in that fleeting moment, the breast wanted so, so much to speak of hungers that never reached the tongue.

About an hour later, Geremio called over to Pietro: "Pietro, see if Mister Murdin is in the shanty and tell him I must see him! I will convince him that the work must not go on like this . . . just for the sake of a little more profit!"

Pietro came up soon. "The padrone is not coming up. He was drinking from a large bottle of whisky and cursed in American words that if you did not carry out his orders—"

Geremio turned away disconcerted, stared dumbly at the structure and mechanically listed in his mind's eye the various violations of construction safety. An uneasy sensation hollowed him. The Lean brought down an old piece of wall and the structure palsied. Geremio's heart broke loose and outthumped the floor's vibrations, a rapid wave of heat swept him and left a chill touch in its wake. He looked about to the men, a bit frightened. They seemed usual, life-size, and moved about with the methodical deftness that made the moment then appear no different than the task of toil had ever been.

Snoutnose's voice boomed into him. "Master Geremio, the concrete is rea—dy!"

"Oh, yes, yes, Vincenz." And he walked gingerly towards the chute, but, not without leaving behind some part of his strength, sending out his soul to wrestle with the limbs of Job, who threatened in stiff silence. He talked and joked with Snoutnose. Nothing said anything, nor seemed wrong. Yet a vague uneasiness was to him as certain as the foggy murk that floated about Job's stone and steel.

"Shall I let the concrete down now, Master Geremio?"

"Well, let me see—no, hold it a minute. Hey, Sandino! tighten the chute cables!"

Snoutnose straightened, looked about, and instinctively rubbed the sore small of his spine. "Ah," sighed he, "all the men feel as I—yes, I can tell. They are tired but happy that today is Good Friday and we quit at three o'clock . . ." And he swelled in human ecstasy at the anticipation of food, drink, and the hairy flesh-tingling warmth of wife, and then, extravagant rest. In truth, they all felt as Snoutnose, although perhaps with variations on the theme.

It was the Lean only who had lived, and felt otherwise. His soul, accompanied with time, had shredded itself in the physical war to keep the physical alive. Perhaps he no longer had a soul, and the corpse continued from momentum. May he not be the Slave, working on from the birth of Man—He of whom it was said, "It was not for Him to reason"? And probably He who, never asking, taking, nor vaunting, created God and the creatable? Nevertheless, there existed in the Lean a sense of oppression suffered, so vast that the seas of time could never wash it away.

Geremio gazed about and was conscious of seeming to understand many things. He marveled at the strange feeling which permitted him to sense the familiarity of life. And yet— all appeared unreal, a dream pungent and nostalgic. Life, dream, reality, unreality, spiraling ever about each other.

"Ha," he chuckled, "how and from where do these thoughts come?"

Snoutnose had his hand on the hopper latch and was awaiting the word from Geremio. "Did you say something, Master Geremio?"

"Why, yes, Vincenz, I was thinking—funny! A—yes, what is the time—yes, that is what I was thinking."

"My American can of tomatoes says ten minutes from two o'clock. It won't be long now, Master Geremio."

Geremio smiled. "No, about an hour . . . and then, home."

"Oh, but first we stop at Mulberry Street, to buy their biggest eels, and the other finger-licking stuffs."

Geremio was looking far off, and for a moment happiness came to his heart without words, a warm hand stealing over. Snoutnose's words sang to him pleasantly, and he nodded.

"And Master Geremio, we ought really to buy the seafruits with the shells—you know, for the much needed steam they put into the—"

He flushed despite himself and continued. "It is true, I know it—especially the juicy clams . . . uhmn, my mouth waters like a pump."

Geremio drew on his unlit pipe and smiled acquiescence. The men around him were moving to their tasks silently, feeling of their fatigue, but absorbed in contemplations the very same as Snoutnose's. The noise of labor seemed not to be noise, and as Geremio looked about, life settled over him a gray concert—gray forms, atmosphere, and gray notes . . . Yet his off-tone world felt so near, and familiar.

"Five minutes from two," swished through Snoutnose's moustache.

Geremio automatically took out his watch, rewound, and set it. Sandino had done with the cables. The tone and movement of the scene seemed to Geremio strange, differently strange, and yet, a dream familiar from a timeless date. His hand went up in motion to Vincenzo. The molten stone gurgled low, and then with heightening rasp. His eyes followed the stone-cementy pudding, and to his ears there was no other sound than its flow. From over the roofs somewhere, the tinny voice of *Barney Google* whined its way, hooked into his consciousness and kept itself a revolving record beneath his skull-plate.

"Ah, yes, Barney Google, my son's wonderful radio machine . . . wonderful Paul." His train of thought quickly took in his family, home and hopes. And with hope came fear. Something within asked, "Is it not possible to breathe God's air without fear dominating with the pall of unemployment? And the terror of production for Boss, Boss and Job? To rebel is to lose all of the very little. To be obedient is to choke. Oh, dear Lord, guide my path."

Just then, the floor lurched and swayed under his feet. The slipping of the underpinning below rumbled up through the undetermined floors.

Was he faint or dizzy? Was it part of the dreamy afternoon? He put his hands in front of him and stepped back, and looked up wildly. "No! No!"

The men poised stricken. Their throats wanted to cry out and scream but didn't dare. For a moment they were a petrified and straining pageant. Then the bottom of their world gave way. The building shuddered violently, her supports burst with the crackling slap of wooden gunfire. The floor vomited upward. Geremio clutched at the air and shrieked agonizingly. "Brothers, what have we done? Ahhh-h, children of ours!" With the speed of light, balance went sickeningly awry and frozen men went flying explosively. Job tore down upon them madly. Walls, floors, beams became whirling, solid, splintering waves crashing with detonations that ground man and material in bonds of death.

The strongly shaped body that slept with Annunziata nights and was perfect in all the limitless physical quantities, thudded as a worthless sack amongst the giant debris that crushed fragile flesh and bone with centrifugal intensity.

Darkness blotted out his terror and the resistless form twisted, catapulted insanely in its directionless flight, and shot down neatly and deliberately between the empty wooden forms of a foundation wall pilaster in upright position, his blue swollen face pressed against the form and his arms outstretched, caught securely through the meat by the thin round bars of reinforcing steel.

The huge concrete hopper that was sustained by an independent structure of thick timber, wavered a breath or so, its heavy concrete rolling uneasily until a great sixteen-inch wall caught it squarely with all the terrific verdict of its dead weight and impelled it downward through joists, beams and masonry, until it stopped short, arrested by two girders, an arm's length above Geremio's head; the gray concrete gushing from the hopper mouth, and sealing up the mute figure.

Giacomo had been thrown clear of the building and dropped six floors to the street gutter, where he lay writhing.

The Lean had evinced no emotion. When the walls descended, he did not move. He lowered his head. One minute later he was hanging in mid-air, his chin on his chest, his eyes tearing loose from their sockets, a green foam bubbling from his mouth and his body spasming, suspended by the shreds left of his mashed arms pinned between a wall and a girder.

A two-by-four hooked little Joe Chiappa up under the back of his jumper and swung him around in a circle to meet a careening I-beam. In the flash that it lifted his frozen cherubic face, its shearing edge sliced through the top of his skull.

When Snoutnose cried beseechingly, "Saint Michael!" blackness enveloped him. He came to in a world of horror. A steady stream, warm, thick, and sickening as hot wine bathed his face and clogged his nose, mouth, and eyes. The nauseous syrup that pumped over his face, clotted his moustache red and drained into his mouth. He gulped for air, and swallowed the rich liquid scarlet. As he breathed, the pain shocked him to oppressive semi-consciousness. The air was wormingly alive with cries, screams, moans and dust, and his crushed chest seared him with a thousand fires. He couldn't see, nor breathe enough to cry. His right hand moved to his face and wiped at the gelatinizing substance, but it kept coming on, and a heartbreaking moan wavered about him, not far. He wiped his eyes in subconscious despair. Where was he? What kind of a dream was he having? Perhaps he wouldn't wake up in time for work, and then what? But how queer; his stomach beating him, his chest on fire, he sees nothing but dull red, only one hand moving about, and a moaning in his face!

The sound and clamor of the rescue squads called to him from far off.

Ah, yes, he's dreaming in bed, and far out in the streets, engines are going to a fire. Oh poor devils! Suppose his house were on fire? With the children scattered about in the rooms he could not remember! He must do his utmost to break out of this dream! He's swimming under water, not able to raise his head and get to the air. He must get back to consciousness to save his children!

He swam frantically with his one right hand, and then felt a face beneath its touch. A face! It's Angelina alongside of him! Thank God, he's awake! He tapped her face. It moved. It felt cold, bristly, and wet. "It moves so. What is this?" His fingers slithered about grisly sharp bones and in a gluey, stringy, hollow mass, yielding as wet macaroni. Gray light brought sight, and hysteria punctured his heart. A girder lay across his chest, his right hand clutched a grotesque human mask, and suspended almost on top of him was the twitching, faceless body of Joe Chiappa. Vincenzo fainted with an inarticulate sigh. His fingers loosed and the bodyless-headless face dropped and fitted to the side of his face while the drippings above came slower and slower.

The rescue men cleaved grimly with pick and axe.

Geremio came to with a start . . . far from their efforts. His brain told him instantly what had happened and where he was. He shouted wildly. "Save me! Save me! I'm being buried alive!"

He paused exhausted. His genitals convulsed. The cold steel rod upon which they were impaled froze his spine. He shouted louder and louder. "Save me! I am hurt badly! I can be saved, I can—save me before it's too late!" But the cries went no farther than his own ears. The icy wet concrete reached his chin. His heart was appalled. "In a few seconds I shall be entombed. If I can only breathe, they will reach me. Surely they will!" His face was quickly covered, its flesh yielding to the solid, sharp-cut stones. "Air! Air!" screamed his lungs as he was completely sealed. Savagely, he bit into the wooden form pressing upon his mouth. An eighth of an inch of its surface splintered off. Oh, if he could only hold out long enough to bite even the smallest hole through to air! He must! There can be no other way! He is responsible for his family! He cannot leave him like this! He didn't want to die! This could not be the answer to life! He had bitten halfway through when his teeth snapped off to the gums in the uneven conflict. The pressure of the concrete was such, and its effectiveness so thorough, that the wooden splinters, stumps of teeth, and blood never left the choking mouth.

Why couldn't he go any farther?

Air! Quick! He dug his lower jaw into the little hollowed space and gnashed in choking agonized fury. "Why doesn't it go through? Mother of Christ, why doesn't it give? Can there be a notch, or two-by-four stud behind it? Sweet Jesu! No! No! Make it give. . . . Air! Air!"

He pushed the bone-bare jaw maniacally; it splintered,

cracked, and a jagged fleshless edge cut through the form, opening a small hole to air. With a desperate burst the lung-prisoned air blew an opening through the shredded mouth and whistled back greedily a gasp of fresh air. He tried to breathe, but it was impossible. The heavy concrete was settling immutably, and its rich cement-laden grout ran into his pierced face. His lungs would not expand, and were crushing in tighter and tighter under the settling concrete.

"Mother mine—mother of Jesu-Annunziata—children of mine—dear, dear, for mercy, Jesu-Giuseppe e 'Maria," his blue-foamed tongue called. It then distorted in a shuddering coil and mad blood vomited forth. Chills and fire played through him and his tortured tongue stuttered, "Mercy, blessed Father—salvation, most kind Father—Saviour—Saviour of His children help me—adored Saviour—I kiss your feet eternally—you are my Lord—there is but one God—you are my God of infinite mercy—Hail Mary divine Virgin—our Father who art in heaven hallowed be thy—name—our Father —my Father," and the agony excruciated with never-ending mount, "our Father—Jesu, Jesu, soon Jesu, hurry dear Jesu Jesu! Je-sssu . . . !" His mangled voice trebled hideously, and hung in jerky whimperings.

The unfeeling concrete was drying fast, and shrinking into monolithic density. The pressure temporarily de-sensitized sensation; leaving him petrified, numb, and substanceless. Only the brain remained miraculously alive.

"Can this be death? It is all too strangely clear. I see nothing nor feel nothing, my body and senses are no more, my mind speaks as it never did before. Am I or am I not Geremio? But I am Geremio! Can I be in the other world? I never was in any other world except the one I knew of; that of toil, hardship, prayer . . . of my wife who awaits with child for me, of my children and the first home I was to own. Where do I begin in this world? Where do I leave off? Why? I recall only a baffled life of cruelty from every direction. And hope was always as painful as fear, the fear of displeasing, displeasing the people and ideas whom I could never understand; laws, policemen, priests, bosses, and a rag with colors waving on a stick. I never did anything to these things. But what have I done with my life? Yes, my life! No one else's! Mine—mine—MINE—Geremio! It is clear. I was born hungry, and have always been hungry for freedom—life! I married and ran away to America so as not to kill and be killed in Tripoli for things they call 'God and Country.' I've never known the freedom I wanted in my heart. There was always an arm upraised to hit at me. What have I done to them? I did not want to make them toil for me. I did not raise my arm to them. In my life I could never breathe, and now without air, my mind breathes clearly for me. Wait! There has been a terrible mistake! A cruel crime! The world is not right! Murderers! Thieves! You have hurt me and my kind, and have taken my life from me! I have long felt it—yes, yes, yes, they have cheated me with flags, signs and fear . . . I say you can't take my life! I want to live! My life! To tell the cheated to rise and fight! Vincenz! Chiappa! Nick! Men! Do you hear me? We must follow the desires within us for the world has been taken from us; we, who made the world! Life!"

Feeling returned to the destroyed form.

"Ahhh-h, I am not dead yet. I knew it—you have not done with me. Torture away! I cannot believe you, God and Country, no longer!" His body was fast breaking under the concrete's closing wrack. Blood vessels burst like mashed flower stems. He screamed. "Show yourself now, Jesus. Now is the time! Save me! Why don't you come! Are you there! I cannot stand it—ohhh, why do you let it happen—it is bestial—where are you! Hurry, hurry, hurry! You do not come! You make me suffer, and what have I done! Come, come—come now—now save me, save me now! Now, now, now! If you are God, save me!"

The stricken blood surged through a weltering maze of useless pipes and exploded forth from his squelched eyes and formless nose, ears and mouth, seeking life in the indifferent stone.

"Aie—aie, aie—devils and Saints—beasts! Where are you—quick, quick, it is death and I am cheated—cheat—ed! Do you hear, you whoring bastards who own the world? Ohhh-ohhh aie-aie—haha-haha!" His bones cracked mutely and his sanity went sailing distorted in the limbo of the subconscious.

With the throbbing tones of an organ in the hollow background, the fighting brain disintegrated and the memories of a baffled lifetime sought outlet.

He moaned the simple songs of barefoot childhood, scenes flashed desperately on and off in disassociated reflex, and words and parts of words came pitifully high and low from his inaudible lips, the hysterical mind sang cringingly and breathlessly, "Jesu my Lord my God my all Jesu my Lord my God my all

Jesu my Lord my God my all Jesu my Lord my God my all," and on as the whirling tempo screamed now far, now near, and came in soul-sickening waves as the concrete slowly contracted and squeezed his skull out of shape.

The Man Who Went to Chicago
Richard Wright

When I rose in the morning the temperature had dropped below zero. The house was as cold to me as the Southern streets had been in winter. I dressed, doubling my clothing. I ate in a restaurant, caught a streetcar, and rode south, rode until I could see no more black faces on the sidewalks. I had now crossed the boundary line of the Black Belt and had entered the territory where jobs were perhaps to be had from white folks. I walked the streets and looked into shop windows until I saw a sign in a delicatessen: PORTER WANTED.

I went in and a stout white woman came to me.

"Vat do you vant?" she asked.

The voice jarred me. She's Jewish, I thought, remembering with shame the obscenities I used to shout at Jewish storekeepers in Arkansas.

"I thought maybe you needed a porter," I said.

"Meester 'Offman, he eesn't here yet," she said. "Vill you vait?"

"Yes, ma'am."

"Seet down."

"No, ma'am, I'll wait outside."

"But eet's cold out zhere," she said.

"That's all right," I said.

She shrugged. I went to the sidewalk. I waited for half an hour in the bitter cold, regretting that I had not remained in the warm store, but unable to go back inside. A bald, stoutish white man went into the store and pulled off his coat. Yes, he was the boss man . . .

"Zo you vant a job?" he asked.

"Yes, sir," I answered, guessing at the meaning of his words.

"Vhere you vork before?"

"In Memphis, Tennessee."

"My brudder-in-law vorked in Tennessee vonce," he said.

I was hired. The work was easy, but I found to my dismay that I could not understand a third of what was said to me. My slow Southern ears were baffled by their clouded, thick accents. One morning Mrs. Hoffman asked me to go to a neighboring store—it was owned by a cousin of hers—and get a can of chicken *à la* king. I had never heard the phrase before and I asked her to repeat it.

"Don't you know nosing?" she demanded of me.

"If you would write it down for me, I'd know what to get," I ventured timidly.

"I can't vite!" she shouted in a sudden fury. "Vat kinda boy iss you?"

I memorized the separate sounds that she had uttered and went to the neighboring store.

"Mrs. Hoffman wants a can Cheek Keeng Awr Lar Keeng," I said slowly, hoping he would not think I was being offensive.

"All vite," he said, after staring at me a moment.

He put a can into a paper bag and gave it to me; outside in the street I opened the bag and read the label: Chicken *à la* King. I cursed, disgusted with myself. I knew those words. It had been her thick accent that had thrown me off. Yet I was not angry with her for speaking broken English; my English, too, was broken. But why could she not have taken more patience? Only one answer came to my mind. I was black and she did not care. Or so I thought . . . I was persisting in reading my present environment in the light of my old one. I reasoned thus: though English was my native tongue and America my native land, she, an alien, could operate a store and earn a living in a neighborhood where I could not even live. I reasoned further that she was aware of this and was trying to protect her position against me.

It was not until I had left the delicatessen job that I saw how grossly I had misread the motives and attitudes of Mr. Hoffman and his wife. I had not yet learned anything that would have helped me to thread my way through these perplexing racial relations. Accepting my environment at its face value, trapped by my own emotions, I kept asking myself what had black people done to bring this crazy world upon them?

The fact of the separation of white and black was clear to me; it was its effect upon the personalities of people that stumped and dismayed me. I did not feel that I was a threat to anybody; yet, as soon as I had grown old enough to think, I had learned that my entire personality, my aspirations, had long ago been discounted; that, in a measure, the very meaning of the words I spoke could not be fully understood.

And when I contemplated the area of No Man's Land into which the Negro mind in America had been shunted I wondered if there had ever been in all human history a more corroding and devastating attack upon the personalities of men than the idea of racial discrimination. In order to escape the racial attack that went to the roots of my life, I would have gladly accepted any way of life but the one in which I found myself. I would have agreed to live under a system of feudal oppression, not because I preferred feudalism but because I felt that feudalism made use of a limited part of a man, defined man, his rank, his function in society. I would have consented to live under the most rigid type of dictatorship, for I felt that dictatorships, too, defined the use of men, however degrading that use might be.

While working as a porter in Memphis I had often stood aghast as a friend of mine had offered himself to be kicked by the white men; but now, while working in Chicago, I was learning that perhaps even a kick was better than uncertainty . . . I had elected, in my fevered search for honorable adjustment to the American scene, not to submit and in doing so I had embraced the daily horror of anxiety, of tension, of eternal disquiet. I could now sympathize with—though I could never bring myself to approve—those tortured blacks who had given up and had gone to their white tormentors and had said: "Kick me, if that's all there is for me; kick me and let me feel at home, let me have peace!"

Color-hate defined the place of black life as below that of white life; and the black man, responding to the same dreams as the white man, strove to bury within his heart his awareness of this difference because it made him lonely and afraid. Hated by whites and being an organic part of the culture that hated him, the black man grew in turn to hate in himself that which others hated in him. But pride would make him hate his self-hate, for he would not want whites to know that he was so thoroughly conquered by them that his total life was conditioned by their attitude; but in the act of hiding his self-hate, he could not help but hate those who evoked his self-hate in him. So each part of his day would be consumed in a war with himself, a good part of his energy would be spent in keeping control of his unruly emotions, emotions which he had not wished to have, but could not help having. Held at bay by the hate of others, preoccupied with his own feelings, he was continuously at war with reality. He became inefficient, less able to see and judge the objective world. And when he reached that state, the white people looked at him and laughed and said:

"Look, didn't I tell you niggers were that way?"

To solve this tangle of balked emotion, I loaded the empty part of the ship of my personality with fantasies of ambition to keep it from toppling over into the sea of senselessness. Like any other American, I dreamed of going into business and making money; I dreamed of working for a firm that would allow me to advance until I reached an important position; I even dreamed of organizing secret groups of blacks to fight all whites . . . And if the blacks would not agree to organize, then they would have to be fought. I would end up again with self-hate, but it was now a self-hate that was projected outward upon other blacks. Yet I knew—with that part of my mind that the whites had given me—that none of my dreams were possible. Then I would hate myself for allowing my mind to dwell upon the unattainable. Thus the circle would complete itself.

Slowly I began to forge in the depths of my mind a mechanism that repressed all the dreams and desires that the Chicago streets, the newspapers, the movies were evoking in me. I was going through a second childhood; a new sense of the limit of the possible was being born in me. What could I dream of that had the barest possibility of coming true? I could think of nothing. And, slowly, it was upon exactly that nothingness that my mind began to dwell, that constant sense of wanting without having, of being hated without reason. A dim notion of what life meant to a Negro in America was coming to consciousness in me, not in terms of external events, lynchings, Jim Crowism, and the endless brutalities, but in terms of crossed-up feeling, of emotional tension. I sensed that Negro life was a sprawling land of unconscious suffering, and there were but few Negroes who knew the meaning of their lives, who could tell their story.

Word reached me that an examination for postal clerk was impending and at once I filed an application and waited. As the date for the examination drew near, I was faced with another problem. How could I get a free day without losing my job? In the South it would have been an unwise policy for a Negro to have gone to his white boss and asked for time to take an examination for another job. It would have implied that the Negro did not like to work for the white boss, that he felt he was not receiving just consideration and, inasmuch as most jobs that Negroes held in the South involved a personal, paternalistic relationship, he would have been risking an argument that might have led to violence.

I now began to speculate about what kind of man Mr.

Hoffman was, and I found that I did not know him; that is, I did not know his basic attitude toward Negroes. If I asked him, would he be sympathetic enough to allow me time off with pay? I needed the money. Perhaps he would say: "Go home and stay home if you don't like this job!" I was not sure of him. I decided, therefore, that I had better not risk it. I would forfeit the money and stay away without telling him.

The examination was scheduled to take place on a Monday; I had been working steadily and I would be too tired to do my best if I took the examination without benefit of rest. I decided to stay away from the shop Saturday, Sunday, and Monday. But what could I tell Mr. Hoffman? Yes, I would tell him that I had been ill. No, that was too thin. I would tell him that my mother had died in Memphis and that I had gone down to bury her. That lie might work.

I took the examination and when I came to the store on Tuesday, Mr. Hoffman was astonished, of course.

"I didn't sink you vould ever come back," he said.

"I'm awfully sorry, Mr. Hoffman."

"Vat happened?"

"My mother died in Memphis and I had to go down and bury her," I lied.

He looked at me, then shook his head.

"Rich, you lie," he said.

"I'm not lying," I lied stoutly.

"You vanted to do somesink, zo you zayed ervay," he said, shrugging.

"No, sir. I'm telling you the truth," I piled another lie upon the first one.

"No. You lie. You disappoint me," he said.

"Well, all I can do is tell you the truth," I lied indignantly.

"Vy didn't you use the phone?"

"I didn't think of it," I told a fresh lie.

"Rich, if your mudder die, you vould tell me," he said.

"I didn't have time. Had to catch the train," I lied yet again.

"Vhere did you get the money?"

"My aunt gave it to me," I said, disgusted that I had to lie and lie again.

"I don't vant a boy vat tells lies," he said.

"I don't lie," I lied passionately to protect my lies.

Mrs. Hoffman joined in and both of them hammered at me.

"Ve know. You come from ze Zouth. You feel you can't tell us ze truth. But ve don't bother you. Ve don't feel like people in ze Zouth. Ve treat you nice, don't ve?" they asked.

"Yes, ma'am," I mumbled.

"Zen vy lie?"

"I'm not lying," I lied with all my strength.

I became angry because I knew that they knew that I was lying. I had lied to protect myself, and then I had to lie to protect my lie. I had met so many white faces that would have violently disapproved of my taking the examination that I could not have risked telling Mr. Hoffman the truth. But how could I tell him that I had lied because I was so unsure of myself? Lying was bad, but revealing my own sense of insecurity would have been worse. It would have been shameful, and I did not like to feel ashamed.

Their attitudes had proved utterly amazing. They were taking time out from their duties in the store to talk to me, and I had never encountered anything like that from whites before. A Southern white man would have said: "Get to hell out of here!" or "All right, nigger. Get to work." But no white people had ever stood their ground and probed at me, questioned me at such length. It dawned upon me that they were trying to treat me as an equal, which made it even more impossible for me ever to tell them that I had lied, why I had lied. I felt that if I confessed I would be giving them a moral advantage over me that would have been unbearable.

"All vight, zay and vork," Mr. Hoffman said. "I know you're lying, but I don't care, Rich."

I wanted to quit. He had insulted me. But I liked him in spite of myself. Yes, I had done wrong; but how on earth could I have known the kind of people I was working for? Perhaps Mr. Hoffman would have gladly consented for me to take the examination; but my hopes had been far weaker than my powerful fears.

Working with them from day to day and knowing that they knew I had lied from fear crushed me. I knew that they pitied me and pitied the fear in me. I resolved to quit and risk hunger rather than stay with them. I left the job that following Saturday, not telling them that I would not be back, not possessing the heart to say good-by. I just wanted to go quickly and have them forget that I had ever worked for them.

After an idle week, I got a job as a dishwasher in a North Side café that had just opened. My boss, a white woman, directed me in unpacking barrels of dishes, setting up new tables, painting, and so on. I had charge of serving breakfast; in the late afternoon I carted trays of food to patrons in the hotel who did not want to come down to eat. My wages were fifteen dollars a week; the hours were long, but I ate my meals on the job.

The cook was an elderly Finnish woman with a sharp, bony face. There were several white waitresses. I was the only Negro in the café. The waitresses were a hard, brisk lot, and I was keenly aware of how their attitudes contrasted with those of Southern white girls. They had not been taught to keep a gulf between me and themselves; they were relatively free of the heritage of racial hate.

One morning as I was making coffee, Cora came forward with a tray loaded with food and squeezed against me to draw a cup of coffee.

"Pardon me, Richard," she said.

"Oh, that's all right," I said in an even tone.

But I was aware that she was a white girl and that her body was pressed closely against mine, an incident that had never happened to me before in my life, an incident charged with the memory of dread. But she was not conscious of my blackness or of what her actions would have meant in the South. And had I not been born in the South, her trivial act would have been as unnoticed by me as it was by her. As she stood close to me, I could not help thinking that if a Southern white girl had wanted to draw a cup of coffee, she would have commanded me to step aside so that she might not come in contact with me. The work of the hot and busy kitchen would have had to cease for the moment so that I could have taken my tainted body far enough away to allow the Southern white girl a chance to get a cup of coffee. There lay a deep, emotional safety in knowing that the white girl who was now leaning carelessly against me was not thinking of me, had no deep, vague, irrational fright that made her feel that I was a creature to be avoided at all costs.

One summer morning a white girl came late to work and rushed into the pantry where I was busy. She went into the women's room and changed her clothes; I heard the door open and a second later I was surprised to hear her voice:

"Richard, quick! Tie my apron!"

She was standing with her back to me and the strings of her apron dangled loose. There was a moment of indecision on my part, then I took the two loose strings and carried them around her body and brought them again to her back and tied them in a clumsy knot.

"Thanks a million," she said, grasping my hand for a split second, and was gone.

I continued my work, filled with all the possible meanings that the tiny, simple, human event could have meant to any Negro in the South where I had spent most of my hungry days.

I did not feel any admiration or any hate for the girls. My attitude was one of abiding and friendly wonder. For the most part I was silent with them, though I knew that I had a firmer grasp of life than most of them. As I worked I listened to their talk and perceived its puzzled, wandering, superficial fumbling with the problems and facts of life. There were many things they wondered about that I could have explained to them, but I never dared.

During my lunch hour, which I spent on a bench in a near-by park, the waitresses would come and sit beside me, talking at random, laughing, joking, smoking cigarettes. I learned about their tawdry dreams, their simple hopes, their home lives, their fear of feeling anything deeply, their sex problems, their husbands. They were an eager, restless, talkative, ignorant bunch, but casually kind and impersonal for all that. They knew nothing of hate and fear, and strove instinctively to avoid all passion.

I often wondered what they were trying to get out of life, but I never stumbled upon a clue, and I doubt if they themselves had any notion. They lived on the surface of their days; their smiles were surface smiles, and their tears were surface tears. Negroes lived a truer and deeper life than they, but I wished that Negroes, too, could live as thoughtlessly, serenely, as they. The girls never talked of their feelings; none of them possessed the insight or the emotional equipment to understand themselves or others. How far apart in culture we stood! All my life I had done nothing but feel and cultivate my feelings; all their lives they had done nothing but strive for petty goals, the trivial material prizes of American life. We shared a common tongue, but my language was a different language from theirs.

It was in the psychological distance that separated the races that the deepest meaning of the problem of the Negro lay for me. For these poor, ignorant white girls to have understood my life would have meant nothing short of a vast revolution in theirs. And I was convinced that what they needed to make them complete and grown-up in their living was the inclusion in their personalities of a knowledge of lives such as I lived and suffered containedly.

As I, in memory, think back now upon those girls and their lives I feel that for white America to understand the significance of the problem of the Negro will take a bigger and tougher America than any we have yet known. I feel that America's past is too shallow, her national character too superficially optimistic, her very morality too suffused with color hate for her to accomplish so vast and complex a task. Culturally the Negro represents a paradox: Though he is an organic part of the nation, he is excluded by the entire tide and direction of American culture. Frankly, it is felt to be right to exclude him, and it is felt to be wrong to admit him freely. Therefore if, within the confines of its present culture, the nation ever seeks to purge itself of its color hate, it will find itself at war with itself, convulsed by a spasm of emotional and moral confusion. If the nation ever finds itself examining its real relation to the Negro, it will find itself doing infinitely more than that; for the anti-Negro attitude of whites represents but a tiny part—though a symbolically significant one—of the moral attitude of the nation. Our too-young and too-new America, lusty because it is lonely, aggressive because it is afraid, insists upon seeing the world in terms of good and bad, the holy and the evil, the high and the low, the white and the black; our America is frightened by fact, by history, by processes, by necessity. It hugs the easy way of damning those whom it cannot understand, of excluding those who look different; and it salves its conscience with a self-draped cloak of righteousness. Am I damning my native land? No; for I, too, share these faults of character! And I really do not think that America, adolescent and cocksure, a stranger to suffering and travail, an enemy of passion and sacrifice, is ready to probe into its most fundamental beliefs.

I knew that not race alone, not color alone, but the daily values that gave meaning to life stood between me and those white girls with whom I worked. Their constant outwardlooking, their mania for radios, cars, and a thousand other trinkets, made them dream and fix their eyes upon the trash of life, made it impossible for them to learn a language that could have taught them to speak of what was in theirs or others' hearts. The words of their souls were the syllables of popular songs.

The essence of the irony of the plight of the Negro in America, to me, is that he is doomed to live in isolation, while those who condemn him seek the basest goals of any people on the face of the earth. Perhaps it would be possible for the

Negro to become reconciled to his plight if he could be made to believe that his sufferings were for some remote, high, sacrificial end; but sharing the culture that condemns him, and seeing that a lust for trash is what blinds the nation to his claims, is what sets storms to rolling in his soul.

Though I had fled the pressure of the South, my outward conduct had not changed. I had been schooled to present an unalteringly smiling face and I continued to do so despite the fact that my environment allowed more open expression. I hid my feelings and avoided all relationships with whites that might cause me to reveal them.

Tillie, the Finnish cook, was a tall, ageless, red-faced, raw-boned woman with long snow-white hair, which she balled in a knot at the nape of her neck. She cooked expertly and was superbly efficient. One morning as I passed the sizzling stove, I thought I heard Tilly cough and spit, but I saw nothing; her face, obscured by steam, was bent over a big pot. My senses told me that Tillie had coughed and spat into that pot, but my heart told me that no human being could possibly be so filthy. I decided to watch her. An hour or so later I heard Tillie clear her throat with a grunt, saw her cough and spit into the boiling soup. I held my breath; I did not want to believe what I had seen.

Should I tell the boss lady? Would she believe me? I watched Tillie for another day to make sure that she was spitting into the food. She was; there was no doubt of it. But who would believe me if I told them what was happening? I was the only black person in the café. Perhaps they would think that I hated the cook. I stopped eating my meals there and bided my time.

The business of the café was growing rapidly and a Negro girl was hired to make salads. I went to her at once.

"Look, can I trust you?" I asked.

"What are you talking about?" she asked.

"I want you to say nothing, but watch that cook."

"For what?"

"Now, don't get scared. Just watch the cook."

She looked at me as though she thought I was crazy; and, frankly, I felt that perhaps I ought not say anything to anybody.

"What do you mean?" she demanded.

"All right," I said. "I'll tell you. That cook spits in the food."

"What are you saying?" she asked aloud.

"Keep quiet," I said.

"Spitting?" she asked me in a whisper. "Why would she do that?"

"I don't know. But watch her."

She walked away from me with a funny look in her eyes. But half an hour later she came rushing to me, looking ill, sinking into a chair.

"Oh, God, I feel awful!"

"Did you see it?"

"She *is* spitting in the food!"

"What ought we do?" I asked.

"Tell the lady," she said.

"She wouldn't believe me," I said.

She widened her eyes as she understood. We were black and the cook was white.

"But I can't work here if she's going to do that," she said.

"Then you tell her," I said.

"She wouldn't believe me either," she said.

She rose and ran to the women's room. When she returned she stared at me. We were two Negroes and we were silently asking ourselves if the white boss lady would believe us if we told her that her expert white cook was spitting in the food all day long as it cooked on the stove.

"I don't know," she wailed, in a whisper, and walked away.

I thought of telling the waitresses about the cook, but I could not get up enough nerve. Many of the girls were friendly with Tillie. Yet I could not let the cook spit in the food all day. That was wrong by any human standard of conduct. I washed dishes, thinking, wondering; I served breakfast, thinking, wondering; I served meals in the apartments of patrons upstairs, thinking, wondering. Each time I picked up a tray of food I felt like retching. Finally the Negro salad girl came to me and handed me her purse and hat.

"I'm going to tell her and quit, goddamn," she said.

"I'll quit too, if she doesn't fire her," I said.

"Oh, she won't believe me," she wailed, in agony.

"You tell her. You're a woman. She might believe you."

Her eyes welled with tears and she sat for a long time; then she rose and went abruptly into the dining room. I went to the door and peered. Yes, she was at the desk, talking to the boss lady. She returned to the kitchen and went into the pantry; I followed her.

"Did you tell her?" I asked.

"Yes."

"What did she say?"

"She said I was crazy."

"Oh, God!" I said.

"She just looked at me with those gray eyes of hers," the girl said. "Why would Tillie do that?"

"I don't know," I said.

The boss lady came to the door and called the girl; both of them went into the dining room. Tillie came over to me; a hard cold look was in her eyes.

"What's happening here?" she asked.

"I don't know," I said, wanting to slap her across the mouth.

She muttered something and went back to the stove, coughed, and spat into a bubbling pot. I left the kitchen and went into the back areaway to breathe. The boss lady came out.

"Richard," she said.

Her face was pale. I was smoking a cigarette and I did not look at her.

"Is this true?"

"Yes, ma'am."

"It couldn't be. Do you know what you're saying?"

"Just watch her," I said.

"I don't know," she moaned.

She looked crushed. She went back into the dining room, but I saw her watching the cook through the doors. I watched both of them, the boss lady and the cook, praying that the cook would spit again. She did. The boss lady came into the kitchen and stared at Tillie, but she did not utter a word. She burst into tears and ran back into the dining room.

"What's happening here?" Tillie demanded.

No one answered. The boss lady came out and tossed Tillie her hat, coat, and money.

"Now, get out of here, you dirty dog!" she said.

Tillie stared, then slowly picked up her hat, coat, and the money; she stood a moment, wiped sweat from her forehead with her hand, then spat—this time on the floor. She left.

Nobody was ever able to fathom why Tillie liked to spit into the food.

Brooding over Tillie, I recalled the time when the boss man in Mississippi had come to me and had tossed my wages to me and said:

"Get out, nigger! I don't like your looks."

And I wondered if a Negro who did not smile and grin was

as morally loathsome to whites as a cook who spat into the food.

The following summer I was called for temporary duty in the post office, and the work lasted into the winter. Aunt Cleo succumbed to a severe cardiac condition and, hard on the heels of her illness, my brother developed stomach ulcers. To rush my worries to a climax, my mother also became ill. I felt that I was maintaining a private hospital. Finally, the postoffice work ceased altogether and I haunted the city for jobs. But when I went into the streets in the morning I saw sights that killed my hope for the rest of the day. Unemployed men loitered in doorways with blank looks in their eyes, sat dejectedly on front steps in shabby clothing, congregated in sullen groups on street corners, and filled all the empty benches in the parks of Chicago's South Side.

Luck of a sort came when a distant cousin of mine, who was a superintendent for a Negro burial society, offered me a position on his staff as an agent. The thought of selling insurance policies to ignorant Negroes disgusted me.

"Well, if you don't sell them, somebody else will," my cousin told me. "You've got to eat, haven't you?"

During that year I worked for several burial and insurance societies that operated among Negroes, and I received a new kind of education. I found that the burial societies, with some exceptions, were mostly "rackets." Some of them conducted their business legitimately, but there were many that exploited the ignorance of their black customers.

I was paid under a system that netted me fifteen dollars for every dollar's worth of new premiums that I placed upon the company's books, and for every dollar's worth of old premiums that lapsed I was penalized fifteen dollars. In addition, I was paid a commission of ten per cent on total premiums collected, but during the Depression it was extremely difficult to persuade a black family to buy a policy carrying even a dime premium. I considered myself lucky if, after subtracting lapses from new business, there remained fifteen dollars that I could call my own.

This "gambling" method of remuneration was practiced by some of the burial companies because of the tremendous "turnover" in policyholders, and the companies had to have a constant stream of new business to keep afloat. Whenever a black family moved or suffered a slight reverse in fortune, it usually let its policy lapse and later bought another policy from some other company.

Each day now I saw how the Negro in Chicago lived, for I visited hundreds of dingy flats filled with rickety furniture and ill-clad children. Most of the policyholders were illiterate and did not know that their policies carried clauses severely restricting their benefit payments, and, as an insurance agent, it was not my duty to tell them.

After tramping the streets and pounding on doors to collect premiums, I was dry, strained, too tired to read or write. I hungered for relief and, as a salesman of insurance to many young black girls, I found it. There were many comely black housewives who, trying desperately to keep up their insurance payments, were willing to make bargains to escape paying a ten-cent premium. I had a long, tortured affair with one girl by paying her ten-cent premium each week. She was an illiterate black child with a baby whose father she did not know. During the entire period of my relationship with her, she had but one demand to make of me: she wanted me to take her to a circus. Just what significance circuses had for her, I was never able to learn.

After I had been with her one morning—in exchange for the dime premium—I sat on the sofa in the front room and began to read a book I had with me. She came over shyly.

"Lemme see that," she said.

"What?" I asked.

"That book," she said.

I gave her the book; she looked at it intently. I saw that she was holding it upside down.

"What's in here you keep reading?" she asked.

"Can't you really read?" I asked.

"Naw," she giggled. "You know I can't read."

"You can read *some*," I said.

"Naw," she said.

I stared at her and wondered just what a life like hers meant in the scheme of things, and I came to the conclusion that it meant absolutely nothing. And neither did my life mean anything.

"How come you looking at me that way for?"

"Nothing."

"You don't talk much."

"There isn't much to say."

"I wished Jim was here," she sighed.

"Who's Jim?" I asked, jealous. I knew that she had other men, but I resented her mentioning them in my presence.

"Just a friend," she said.

I hated her then, then hated myself for coming to her.

"Do you like Jim better than you like me?" I asked.

"Naw. Jim just likes to talk."

"Then why do you be with me, if you like Jim better?" I asked, trying to make an issue and feeling a wave of disgust because I wanted to.

"You all right," she said, giggling. "I like you."

"I could kill you," I said.

"What?" she exclaimed.

"Nothing," I said, ashamed.

"Kill me, you said? You crazy, man," she said.

"Maybe I am," I muttered, angry that I was sitting beside a human being to whom I could not talk, angry with myself for coming to her, hating my wild and restless loneliness.

"You oughta go home and sleep," she said. "You tired."

"What do you ever think about?" I demanded harshly.

"Lotta things."

"What, for example?"

"You," she said, smiling.

"You know I mean just one dime to you each week," I said.

"Naw, I thinka lotta you."

"Then what do you think?"

" 'Bout how you talk when you talk. I wished I could talk like you," she said seriously.

"Why?" I taunted her.

"When you gonna take me to a circus?" she demanded suddenly.

"You ought to be in a circus," I said.

"I'd like it," she said, her eyes shining.

I wanted to laugh, but her words sounded so sincere that I could not.

"There's no circus in town," I said.

"I bet there is and you won't tell me 'cause you don't wanna take me," she said, pouting.

"But there's no circus in town, I tell you!"

"When will one come?"

"I don't know."

"Can't you read it in the papers?" she asked.

"There's nothing in the papers about a circus."

"There is," she said. "If I could read, I'd find it."

I laughed, and she was hurt.

"There *is* a circus in town," she said stoutly.

"There's no circus in town," I said. "But if you want to learn to read, then I'll teach you."

She nestled at my side, giggling.

"See that word?" I said, pointing.

"Yeah."

"That's an 'and,'" I said.

She doubled, giggling.

"What's the matter?" I asked.

She rolled on the floor, giggling.

"What's so funny?" I demanded.

"You," she giggled. "You so funny."

I rose.

"The hell with you," I said.

"Don't you go and cuss me now," she said. "I don't cuss you."

"I'm sorry," I said.

I got my hat and went to the door.

"I'll see you next week?" she asked.

"Maybe," I said.

When I was on the sidewalk, she called to me from a window.

"You promised to take me to a circus, remember?"

"Yes." I walked close to the window. "What is it you like about a circus?"

"The animals," she said simply.

I felt that there was a hidden meaning, perhaps, in what she had said, but I could not find it. She laughed and slammed the window shut.

Each time I left her I resolved not to visit her again. I could not talk to her; I merely listened to her passionate desire to see a circus. She was not calculating; if she liked a man, she just liked him. Sex relations were the only relations she had ever had; no others were possible with her, so limited was her intelligence.

Most of the other agents also had their bought girls and they were extremely anxious to keep other agents from tampering with them. One day a new section of the South Side was given to me as a part of my collection area, and the agent from whom the territory had been taken suddenly became very friendly with me.

"Say, Wright," he asked, "did you collect from Ewing on Champlain Avenue yet?"

"Yes," I answered, after consulting my book.

"How did you like her?" he asked, staring at me.

"She's a good-looking number," I said.

"You had anything to do with her yet?" he asked.

"No, but I'd like to," I said laughing.

"Look," he said. "I'm a friend of yours."

"Since when?" I countered.

"No, I'm really a friend," he said.

"What's on your mind?"

"Listen, that gal's sick," he said seriously.

"What do you mean?"

"She's got the clap," he said. "Keep away from her. She'll lay with anybody."

"Gee, I'm glad you told me," I said.

"You had your eye on her, didn't you?" he asked.

"Yes, I did," I said.

"Leave her alone," he said. "She'll get you down."

That night I told my cousin what the agent had said about Miss Ewing. My cousin laughed.

"That gal's all right," he said. "That agent's been fooling around with her. He told you she had a disease so that you'd be scared to bother her. He was protecting her from you."

That was the way the black women were regarded by the black agents. Some of the agents were vicious; if they had claims to pay to a sick black woman and if the woman was able to have sex relations with them, they would insist upon it, using the claims money as a bribe. If the woman refused, they would report to the office that the woman was a malingerer. The average black woman would submit because she needed the money badly.

As an insurance agent it was necessary for me to take part in one swindle. It appears that the burial society had originally issued a policy that was—from their point of view—too liberal in its provisions, and the officials decided to exchange the policies then in the hands of their clients for other policies carrying stricter clauses. Of course, this had to be done in a manner that would not allow the policyholder to know that his policy was being switched—that he was being swindled. I did not like it, but there was only one thing I could do to keep from being a party to it: I could quit and starve. But I did not feel that being honest was worth the price of starvation.

The swindle worked in this way. In my visits to the homes of the policyholders to collect premiums, I was accompanied by the superintendent who claimed to the policyholder that he was making a routine inspection. The policyholder, usually an illiterate black woman, would dig up her policy from the bottom of a trunk or chest and hand it to the superintendent. Meanwhile I would be marking the woman's premium book, an act which would distract her from what the superintendent was doing. The superintendent would exchange the old policy for a new one which was identical in color, serial number, and beneficiary, but which carried smaller payments. It was dirty work and I wondered how I could stop it. And when I could think of no safe way I would curse myself and the victims and forget about it. (The black owners of the burial societies were leaders in the Negro communities and were respected by whites.)

When I reached the relief station, I felt that I was making a public confession of my hunger. I sat waiting for hours, resentful of the mass of hungry people about me. My turn finally came and I was questioned by a middle-class Negro woman who asked me for a short history of my life. As I waited, I became aware of something happening in the room. The black men and women were mumbling quietly among themselves; they had not known one another before they had come here, but now their timidity and shame were wearing off and they were exchanging experiences. Before this they had lived as individuals, each somewhat afraid of the other, each seeking his own pleasure, each stanch in that degree of Americanism that had been allowed him. But now life had tossed them together, and they were learning to know the sentiments of their neighbors for the first time; their talking was enabling them to sense the collectivity of their lives, and some of their fear was passing.

Did the relief officials realize what was happening? No. If they had, they would have stopped it. But they saw their "clients" through the eyes of their profession, saw only what their "science" allowed them to see. As I listened to the talk, I could see black minds shedding many illusions. These people now knew that the past had betrayed them, had cast them out; but they did not know what the future would be like, did not know what they wanted. Yes, some of the things that the Communists said were true; they maintained that there came times in history when a ruling class could no longer rule. And now I sat looking at the beginnings of anarchy. To permit the birth of this new consciousness in these people was proof that those who ruled did not quite know what they were doing, assuming that they were trying to save themselves and their class. Had they understood what was happening, they would never have allowed millions of perplexed and defeated people to sit together for long hours and talk, for out of their talk was rising a new realization of life. And once this new conception of themselves had formed, no power on earth could alter it.

I left the relief station with the promise that food would be sent to me, but I also left with a knowledge that the relief officials had not wanted to give to me. I had felt the possibility of creating a new understanding of life in the minds of people rejected by the society in which they lived, people to whom the Chicago *Tribune* referred contemptuously as the "idle" ones, as though these people had deliberately sought their present state of helplessness.

Who would give these people a meaningful way of life? Communist theory defined these people as the molders of the future of mankind, but the Communist speeches I had heard in the park had mocked that definition. These people, of course, were not ready for a revolution; they had not abandoned their past lives by choice, but because they simply could not live the old way any longer. Now, what new faith would they embrace? The day I begged bread from the city officials was the day that showed me I was not alone in my loneliness; society had cast millions of others with me. But how could I be with them? How many understood what was happening? My mind swam with questions that I could not answer.

I was slowly beginning to comprehend the meaning of my environment; a sense of direction was beginning to emerge from the conditions of my life. I began to feel something more powerful than I could express. My speech and manner changed. My cynicism slid from me. I grew open and questioning. I wanted to know.

If I were a member of the class that rules, I would post men in all the neighborhoods of the nation, not to spy upon or club rebellious workers, not to break strikes or disrupt unions, but to ferret out those who no longer respond to the system under which they live. I would make it known that the real danger does not stem from those who seek to grab their share of wealth through force, or from those who try to defend their property through violence, for both of these groups, by their affirmative acts, support the values of the system under which they live. The millions that I would fear are those who do not dream of the prizes that the nation holds forth, for it is in them, though they may not know it, that a revolution has taken place and is biding its time to translate itself into a new and strange way of life.

I feel that the Negroes' relation to America is symbolically peculiar, and from the Negroes' ultimate reactions to their trapped state a lesson can be learned about America's future. Negroes are told in a language they cannot possibly misunderstand that their native land is not their own; and when, acting upon impulses which they share with whites, they try to assert a claim to their birthright, whites retaliate with terror, never pausing to consider the consequences should the Negroes give up completely. The whites never dream that they would face a situation far more terrifying if they were confronted by Negroes who made no claims at all than by those who are buoyed up by social aggressiveness. My knowledge of how Negroes react to their plight makes me declare that no man can possibly be individually guilty of treason, that an insurgent act is but a man's desperate answer to those who twist his environment so that he cannot fully share the spirit of his native land. Treason is a crime of the State.

Christmas came and I was once more called to the post office for temporary work. This time I met many young white men and we discussed world happenings, the vast armies of unemployed, the rising tide of radical action. I now detected a change in the attitudes of the whites I met; their privations were making them regard Negroes with new eyes, and, for the first time, I was invited to their homes.

When the work in the post office ended, I was assigned by the relief system as an orderly to a medical research institute in one of the largest and wealthiest hospitals in Chicago. I cleaned operating rooms, dog, rat, mice, cat, and rabbit pans, and fed guinea pigs. Four of us Negroes worked there and we occupied an underworld position, remembering that we must restrict ourselves—when not engaged upon some task—to the basement corridors, so that we would not mingle with white nurses, doctors, or visitors.

The sharp line of racial division drawn by the hospital authorities came to me the first morning when I walked along an underground corridor and saw two long lines of women coming toward me. A line of white girls marched past, clad in starched uniforms that gleamed white; their faces were alert, their step quick, their bodies lean and shapely, their shoulders erect, their faces lit with the light of purpose. And after them came a line of black girls, old, fat, dressed in ragged gingham, walking loosely, carrying tin cans of soap powder, rags, mops, brooms . . . I wondered what law of the universe kept them from being mixed? The sun would not have stopped shining had there been a few black girls in the first line, and the earth would not have stopped whirling on its axis had there been a few white girls in the second line. But the two lines I saw graded social status in purely racial terms.

Of the three Negroes who worked with me, one was a boy about my own age, Bill, who was either sleepy or drunk most of the time. Bill straightened his hair and I suspected that he kept a bottle hidden somewhere in the piles of hay which we fed to the guinea pigs. He did not like me and I did not like him, though I tried harder than he to conceal my dislike. We had nothing in common except that we were both black and lost. While I contained my frustration, he drank to drown his. Often I tried to talk to him, tried in simple words to convey to him some of my ideas, and he would listen in sullen silence. Then one day he came to me with an angry look on his face.

"I got it," he said.

"You've got what?" I asked.

"This old race problem you keep talking about," he said.

"What about it?"

"Well, it's this way," he explained seriously. "Let the government give every man a gun and five bullets, then let us all start over again. Make it just like it was in the beginning. The ones who come out on top, white or black, let them rule."

His simplicity terrified me. I had never met a Negro who was so irredeemably brutalized. I stopped pumping my ideas into Bill's brain for fear that the fumes of alcohol might send him reeling toward some fantastic fate.

The two other Negroes were elderly and had been employed in the institute for fifteen years or more. One was Brand, a short, black, morose bachelor; the other was Cooke, a tall, yellow, spectacled fellow who spent his spare time keeping track of world events through the Chicago *Tribune*. Brand and Cooke hated each other for a reason that I was never able to determine, and they spent a good part of each day quarreling.

When I began working at the institute, I recalled my adolescent dream of wanting to be a medical research worker. Daily I saw young Jewish boys and girls receiving instruction in chemistry and medicine that the average black boy or girl could never receive. When I was alone, I wandered and poked my fingers into strange chemicals, watched intricate machines trace red and black lines on ruled paper. At times I paused and stared at the walls of the rooms, at the floors, at the wide desks at which the white doctors sat; and I realized—with a feeling that I could never quite get used to—that I was looking at the world of another race.

My interest in what was happening in the institute amused the three other Negroes with whom I worked. They had no curiosity about "white folks' things," while I wanted to know if the dogs being treated for diabetes were getting well; if the rats and mice in which cancer had been induced showed any signs of responding to treatment. I wanted to know the principle that lay behind the Aschheim-Zondek tests that were made with rabbits, the Wassermann tests that were made with guinea pigs. But when I asked a timid question I found that even Jewish doctors had learned to imitate the sadistic method of humbling a Negro that the others had cultivated.

"If you know too much, boy, your brains might explode," a doctor said one day.

Each Saturday morning I assisted a young Jewish doctor in slitting the vocal cords of a fresh batch of dogs from the city pound. The object was to devocalize the dogs so that their howls would not disturb the patients in the other parts of the hospital. I held each dog as the doctor injected Nembutal into its veins to make it unconscious; then I held the dog's jaws open as the doctor inserted the scalpel and severed the vocal cords. Later, when the dogs came to, they would lift their heads to the ceiling and gape in a soundless wail. The sight became lodged in my imagination as a symbol of silent suffering.

To me Nembutal was a powerful and mysterious liquid, but when I asked questions about its properties I could not obtain a single intelligent answer. The doctor simply ignored me with:

"Come on. Bring me the next dog. I haven't got all day."

One Saturday morning, after I had held the dogs for their vocal cords to be slit, the doctor left the Nembutal on a bench. I picked it up, uncorked it, and smelled it. It was odorless. Suddenly Brand ran to me with a stricken face.

"What're you doing?" he asked.

"I was smelling this stuff to see if it had any odor," I said.

"Did you really smell it?" he asked me.

"Yes."

"Oh, God!" he exclaimed.

"What's the matter?" I asked.

"You shouldn't've done that!" he shouted.

"Why?"

He grabbed my arm and jerked me across the room.

"Come on!" he yelled, snatching open the door.

"What's the matter?" I asked.

"I gotta get you to a doctor 'fore it's too late," he gasped.

Had my foolish curiosity made me inhale something dangerous?

"But—Is it poisonous?"

"Run, boy!" he said, pulling me. "You'll fall dead."

Filled with fear, with Brand pulling my arm, I rushed out of the room, raced across a rear areaway, into another room, then down a long corridor. I wanted to ask Brand what symptoms I must expect, but we were running too fast. Brand finally stopped, gasping for breath. My heart beat wildly and my blood pounded in my head. Brand then dropped to the concrete floor, stretched out on his back, and yelled with laughter, shaking all over. He beat his fists against the concrete; he moaned, giggled, he kicked.

I tried to master my outrage, wondering if some of the white doctors had told him to play the joke. He rose and wiped tears from his eyes, still laughing. I walked away from him. He knew that I was angry and he followed me.

"Don't get mad," he gasped through his laughter.

"Go to hell," I said.

"I couldn't help it," he giggled. "You looked at me like you'd believe anything I said. Man, you was scared."

He leaned against the wall, laughing again, stomping his feet. I was angry, for I felt that he would spread the story. I knew that Bill and Cooke never ventured beyond the safe bounds of Negro living, and they would never blunder into anything like this. And if they heard about this, they would laugh for months.

"Brand, if you mention this, I'll kill you," I swore.

"You ain't mad?" he asked, laughing, staring at me through tears.

Sniffing, Brand walked ahead of me. I followed him back into the room that housed the dogs. All day, while at some task, he would pause and giggle, then smother the giggling with his hand, looking at me out of the corner of his eyes, shaking his head. He laughed at me for a week. I kept my temper and let him amuse himself. I finally found out the properties of Nembutal by consulting medical books; but I never told Brand.

One summer morning, just as I began work, a young Jewish boy came to me with a stop watch in his hand.

"Dr._____ wants me to time you when you clean a room," he said. "We're trying to make the institute more efficient."

"I'm doing my work, and getting through on time," I said.

"This is the boss's order," he said.

"Why don't you work for a change?" I blurted, angry.

"Now, look," he said. "*This* is my work. Now *you* work."

I got a mop and pail, sprayed a room with disinfectant, and scrubbed at coagulated blood and hardened dog, rat, and rabbit feces. The normal temperature of a room was ninety, but, as the sun beat down upon the skylights, the temperature rose above a hundred. Stripped to my waist, I slung the mop, moving steadily like a machine, hearing the boy press the button on the stop watch as I finished cleaning a room.

"Well, how is it?" I asked.

"It took you seventeen minutes to clean that last room," he said. "That ought to be the time for each room."

"But that room was not very dirty," I said.

"You have seventeen rooms to clean," he went on as though I had not spoken. "Seventeen times seventeen make four hours and forty-nine minutes." He wrote upon a little pad. "After lunch, clean the five flights of stone stairs. I timed a boy who scrubbed one step and multiplied that time by the number of steps. You ought to be through by six."

"Suppose I want relief?" I asked.

"You'll manage," he said and left.

Never had I felt so much the slave as when I scoured those stone steps each afternoon. Working against time, I would wet five steps, sprinkle soap powder, and then a white doctor or a nurse would come along and, instead of avoiding the soapy steps, would walk on them and track the dirty water onto the steps that I had already cleaned. To obviate this, I cleaned but two steps at a time, a distance over which a ten-year-old child could step. But it did no good. The white people still plopped their feet down into the dirty water and muddied the other clean steps. If I ever really hotly hated unthinking whites, it was then. Not once during my entire stay at the institute did a single white person show enough courtesy to avoid a wet step. I would be on my knees, scrubbing, sweating, pouring out what limited energy my body could wring from my meager diet, and I would hear feet approaching. I would pause and curse with tense lips:

"These sonofabitches are going to dirty these steps again, goddamn their souls to hell!"

Sometimes a sadistically observant white man would notice that he had tracked dirty water up the steps, and he would look back down at me and smile and say:

"Boy, we sure keep you busy, don't we?"

And I would not be able to answer.

The feud that went on between Brand and Cooke continued. Although they were working daily in a building where scientific history was being made, the light of curiosity was never in their eyes. They were conditioned to their racial "place," had learned to see only a part of the whites and the white world; and the whites, too, had learned to see only a part of the lives of the blacks and their world.

Perhaps Brand and Cooke, lacking interests that could absorb them, fuming like children over trifles, simply invented their hate of each other in order to have something to feel deeply about. Or perhaps there was in them a vague tension stemming from their chronically frustrating way of life, a pain whose cause they did not know; and, like those devocalized dogs, they would whirl and snap at the air when their old pain struck them. Anyway, they argued about the weather, sports, sex, war, race, politics, and religion; neither of them knew much about the subjects they debated, but it seemed that the less they knew the better they could argue.

The tug of war between the two elderly men reached a climax one winter day at noon. It was incredibly cold and an icy gale swept up and down the Chicago streets with blizzard force. The door of the animal-filled room was locked, for we always insisted that we be allowed one hour in which to eat and rest. Bill and I were sitting on wooden boxes, eating our lunches out of paper bags. Brand was washing his hands at the sink. Cooke was sitting on a rickety stool, munching an apple and reading the Chicago *Tribune*.

Now and then a devocalized dog lifted his nose to the ceiling and howled soundlessly. The room was filled with many rows of high steel tiers. Perched upon each of these tiers were layers of steel cages containing the dogs, rats, mice, rabbits, and guinea pigs. Each cage was labeled in some indecipherable scientific jargon. Along the walls of the room were long charts with zigzagging red and black lines that traced the success or failure of some experiment. The lonely piping of guinea pigs floated unheeded about us. Hay rustled as a rabbit leaped restlessly about in its pen. A rat scampered around in its steel prison. Cooke tapped the newspaper for attention.

"It says here," Cooke mumbled through a mouthful of apple, "that this is the coldest day since 1888."

Bill and I sat unconcerned. Brand chuckled softly.

"What in hell you laughing about?" Cooke demanded of Brand.

"You can't believe what that damn *Tribune* says," Brand said.

"How come I can't?" Cooke demanded. "It's the world's greatest newspaper."

Brand did not reply; he shook his head pityingly and chuckled again.

"Stop that damn laughing at me!" Cooke said angrily.

"I laugh as much as I wanna," Brand said. "You don't know what you talking about. The *Herald-Examiner* says it's the coldest day since 1873."

"But the *Trib* oughta know," Cooke countered. "It's older'n that *Examiner*."

"That damn *Trib* don't know nothing!" Brand drowned out Cooke's voice.

"How in hell you know?" Cooke asked with rising anger.

The argument waxed until Cooke shouted that if Brand did not shut up he was going to "cut his black throat."

Brand whirled from the sink, his hands dripping soapy water, his eyes blazing.

"Take that back," Brand said.

"I take nothing back! What you wanna do about it?" Cooke taunted.

The two elderly Negroes glared at each other. I wondered if the quarrel was really serious, or if it would turn out harmlessly as so many others had done.

Suddenly Cooke dropped the Chicago *Tribune* and pulled a long knife from his pocket; his thumb pressed a button and a gleaming steel blade leaped out. Brand stepped back quickly and seized an ice pick that was stuck in a wooden board above the sink.

"Put that knife down," Brand said.

"Stay 'way from me, or I'll cut your throat," Cooke warned.

Brand lunged with the ice pick. Cooke dodged out of range. They circled each other like fighters in a prize ring. The cancerous and tubercular rats and mice leaped about in their cages. The guinea pigs whistled in fright. The diabetic dogs bared their teeth and barked soundlessly in our direction. The Aschheim-Zondek rabbits flopped their ears and tried to hide in the corners of their pens. Cooke now crouched and sprang forward with the knife. Bill and I jumped to our feet, speechless with surprise. Brand retreated. The eyes of both men were hard and unblinking; they were breathing deeply.

"Say, cut it out!" I called in alarm.

"Them damn fools is really fighting," Bill said in amazement.

Slashing at each other, Brand and Cooke surged up and down the aisles of steel tiers. Suddenly Brand uttered a bellow and charged into Cooke and swept him violently backward. Cooke grasped Brand's hand to keep the ice pick from sinking into his chest. Brand broke free and charged Cooke again, sweeping him into an animal-filled steel tier. The tier balanced itself on its edge for an indecisive moment, then toppled.

Like kingpins, one steel tier lammed into another, then they all crashed to the floor with a sound as of the roof falling. The whole aspect of the room altered quicker than the eye could follow. Brand and Cooke stood stock-still, their eyes fastened upon each other, their pointed weapons raised; but they were dimly aware of the havoc that churned about them.

The steel tiers lay jumbled; the doors of the cages swung open. Rats and mice and dogs and rabbits moved over the floor in wild panic. The Wassermann guinea pigs were squealing as though judgment day had come. Here and there an animal had been crushed beneath a cage.

All four of us looked at one another. We knew what this meant. We might lose our jobs. We were already regarded as black dunces; and if the doctors saw this mess they would take it as final proof. Bill rushed to the door to make sure that it was locked. I glanced at the clock and saw that it was 12:30. We had one half-hour of grace.

"Come on," Bill said uneasily. "We got to get this place cleaned."

Brand and Cooke stared at each other, both doubting.

"Give me your knife, Cooke," I said.

"Naw! Take Brand's ice pick *first*," Cooke said.

"The hell you say!" Brand said. "Take his knife *first*!"

A knock sounded at the door.

"Sssssh," Bill said.

We waited. We heard footsteps going away. We'll all lose our jobs, I thought.

Persuading the fighters to surrender their weapons was a difficult task, but at last it was done and we could begin to set things right. Slowly Brand stooped and tugged at one end of a steel tier. Cooke stooped to help him. Both men seemed to be acting in a dream. Soon, however, all four of us were working frantically, watching the clock.

As we labored we conspired to keep the fight a secret; we agreed to tell the doctors—if any should ask—that we had not been in the room during our lunch hour; we felt that that lie would explain why no one had unlocked the door when the knock had come.

We righted the tiers and replaced the cages; then we were faced with the impossible task of sorting the cancerous rats and mice, the diabetic dogs, the Aschheim-Zondek rabbits, and the Wassermann guinea pigs. Whether we kept our jobs or not depended upon how shrewdly we could cover up all evidence of the fight. It was pure guesswork, but we had to try to put the animals back into the correct cages. We knew that certain rats or mice went into certain cages, but we did not know *what* rat or mouse went into *what* cage. We did not know a tubercular mouse from a cancerous mouse—the white doctors had made sure that we would not know. They had never taken time to answer a single question; though we worked in the institute, we were as remote from the meaning of the experiments as if we lived in the moon. The doctors had laughed at what they felt was our childlike interest in the fate of the animals.

First we sorted the dogs; that was fairly easy, for we could remember the size and color of most of them. But the rats and mice and guinea pigs baffled us completely.

We put our heads together and pondered, down in the underworld of the great scientific institute. It was a strange scientific conference; the fate of the entire medical research institute rested in our ignorant, black hands.

We remembered the number of rats, mice, or guinea pigs—we had to handle them several times a day—that went into a given cage, and we supplied the number helter-skelter from those animals that we could catch running loose on the floor. We discovered that many rats, mice, and guinea pigs were missing—they had been killed in the scuffle. We solved that problem by taking healthy stock from other cages and putting them into cages with sick animals. We repeated this process until we were certain that, numerically at least, all the animals with which the doctors were experimenting were accounted for.

The rabbits came last. We broke the rabbits down into two general groups: those that had fur on their bellies and those that did not. We knew that all those rabbits that had shaven bellies—our scientific knowledge adequately covered this point because it was our job to shave the rabbits—were undergoing the Aschheim-Zondek tests. But in what pen did a given rabbit belong? We did not know. I solved the problem very simply. I counted the shaven rabbits; they numbered seventeen. I counted the pens labeled "Aschheim-Zondek," then proceeded to drop a shaven rabbit into each pen at random. And again we were numerically successful. At least white America had taught us how to count . . .

Lastly we carefully wrapped all the dead animals in newspapers and hid their bodies in a garbage can.

At a few minutes to one the room was in order; that is, the kind of order that we four Negroes could figure out. I unlocked the door and we sat waiting, whispering, vowing secrecy, wondering what the reaction of the doctors would be.

Finally a doctor came, gray-haired, white-coated, spectacled, efficient, serious, taciturn, bearing a tray upon which sat a bottle of mysterious fluid and a hypodermic needle.

"My rats, please."

Cooke shuffled forward to serve him. We held our breath. Cooke got the cage which he knew the doctor always called for at that hour and brought it forward. One by one, Cooke took out the rats and held them as the doctor solemnly injected the mysterious fluid under their skins.

"Thank you, Cooke," the doctor murmured.

"Not at all, sir," Cooke mumbled with a suppressed gasp.

When the doctor had gone we looked at one another, hardly daring to believe that our secret would be kept. We were so anxious that we did not know whether to curse or laugh. Another doctor came.

"Give me A-Z rabbit number 14."

"Yes, sir," I said.

I brought him the rabbit and he took it upstairs to the operating room. We waited for repercussions. None came.

All that afternoon the doctors came and went. I would run into the room—stealing a few seconds from my step-scrubbing —and ask what progress was being made and would learn that the doctors had detected nothing. At quitting time we felt triumphant.

"They won't ever know," Cooke boasted in a whisper.

I saw Brand stiffen. I knew that he was aching to dispute

Cooke's optimism, but the memory of the fight he had just had was so fresh in his mind that he could not speak.

Another day went by and nothing happened. Then another day. The doctors examined the animals and wrote in their little black books, in their big black books, and continued to trace red and black lines upon the charts.

A week passed and we felt out of danger. Not one question had been asked.

Of course, we four black men were much too modest to make our contribution known, but we often wondered what went on in the laboratories after that secret disaster. Was some scientific hypothesis, well on its way to validation and ultimate public use, discarded because of unexpected findings on that cold winter day? Was some tested principle given a new and strange refinement because of fresh, remarkable evidence? Did some brooding research worker—those who held stop watches and slopped their feet carelessly in the water of the steps I tried so hard to keep clean—get a wild, if brief, glimpse of a new scientific truth? Well, we never heard . . .

I brooded upon whether I should have gone to the director's office and told him what had happened, but each time I thought of it I remembered that the director had been the man who had ordered the boy to stand over me while I was working and time my movements with a stop watch. He did not regard me as a human being. I did not share his world. I earned thirteen dollars a week and I had to support four people with it, and should I risk that thirteen dollars by acting idealistically? Brand and Cooke would have hated me and would have eventually driven me from the job had I "told" on them. The hospital kept us four Negroes as though we were close kin to the animals we tended, huddled together down in the underworld corridors of the hospital, separated by a vast psychological distance from the significant processes of the rest of the hospital—just as America had kept us locked in the dark underworld of American life for three hundred years—and we had made our own code of ethics, values, loyalty.

Pete: A Quarter Ahead
John Rechy

There was a youngman I had seen often around Times Square. Like me, he was there almost every night; and like me, too, he was, I knew, hustling. I would learn later his name is Pete. Although each of us had noticed the other—and it was obvious—we avoided pointedly more than glancing at each other whenever we met: He was very cocky, a wiseass; and, I figured, I struck him much the same way.

One night I saw him by the subway entrance on 42nd Street talking to an older man dressed in black. It was a warm night. After a series of wintry ones, the warmth returned miraculously and the street is crowded tonight, each person clutching for one last taste of a springlike night. . . . They're glancing at me, Pete and the older man. They talk some more, the older man nods yes, and Pete swaggers up to me. He said: "That score digs you, spote—" (He said sport like that: "spote.") "—he'll lay ten bucks on you—and itll be like cuhrazy," rolling his eyes. Pete's in his early 20s, not tall, very well built, dark; knowing eyes, sometimes moody, dreamy. Hes wearing an army fatigue cap rakishly almost over his eyes, so that he has to hold his chin up to look at you. . . . I turned and looked at the black-dressed man, and he smiled broadly at me, walked toward us. If he had worn a white collar, he would have looked like a priest. Pete says to me: "This is Al," indicating the older man, pats my shoulder—"Later, spote"—and disappears jauntily into the street, almost bouncing into the crowd.

"I havent seen you before—youre new?" the man in black was saying. He didnt wait for an answer: If he asks too many questions, he exposes himself to the possibility that he will get an entirely different answer from the one he wants to hear and it will shatter his sexdream.

I went around the corner with the black-dressed Al, down from 42nd Street—wordlessly—to a large room in an apartment house. "I dont live here," he explained as he opened the door into an almost-bare room: a bed, a table, two chairs. "I just keep this place—well—as a Convenience." He asked me to take my clothes off, but, "Not the pants, theyll do," he tells me. He went to a large closet, and brought out some clothes. Theres a black leather jacket with stars like a general, eagled motorcycle cap, engineer boots with gleaming polished buckles. He left the closet door open, and I could see, hanging neatly, other similar clothes—different sizes, I knew. On the floor were at least seven pairs of engineer boots, all different sizes. "Ive reached the point," Al said, "where I can tell the exact size by just glancing at the person, on the street. . . . Here, put these on." I did, and they fitted. "Fine!" he said. "Now lets go." Im startled. "Where?" I asked him. "Outside," the man says, then noticing me hesitating suspiciously: "I just want us to take a little walk. Dont worry—I'll pay you."

That night, for about an hour, I walked with him through Times Square, from block to block in that area, into the park, silently—just walked. A couple of times I was tempted to leave, walk away with his clothes—but Im curious and I need the money. At the end of the hour we returned to the room, I removed the clothes. He didnt touch me once. He hands me $10.00. I looked at him surprised. I thought somehow I had disappointed him, and I felt grossly rejected. "Thats all," he said; he smiles. "You were fine, just fine," he says, sensing whats troubling me. "But, you see," he said, rather wistfully, "thats *all* I want; to be seen along Times Square with a youngman in those clothes."

A few minutes later, I was back on 42nd Street, and Pete was still there, slouched outside the spaghetti place. He smiled at me. "Some scene, huh?" he said.

"Did he give you anything for it?" I ask him.

"What do *you* think, spote? He gives me five bucks for everyone I get him. I meet him once every two, three weeks. He spots someone he digs, I introduce him. Hes too shy to talk to anyone, so I do it for him, and he lays some bread on me—and I dont have to do nothing," he says smartly.

"Did you ever go with him—*spote?*" I said.

"Oh, sure!" He laughed. "And thats all he digs, spote. He dresses everyone he goes with in that motorcycle drag—and it bugs him for me to call it that. Then he walks around with them. Hardly anybody ever walks away with his clothes— theyre too curious. Hes hung up on that drag, thats how he gets his Kicks. . . . Oh, sure, I been with him." Then proudly —his gaze shifting back and forth from me to the street, pegging people—he adds. "I'm the only cat he walked around with *two* nights—*in a row!*"

Pete was a familiar figure in that world of Times Square. With his slouched army fatigue cap and his thick shaggy army jacket which he had dyed brown, his bouncing walk—it was easy to spot him in any crowd.

After that first night, I would meet him often, never by arrangement, but always at about the same time, around the same place. We would hang around together for a while, and then, compulsively, we'd split. Often, minutes later, we would meet again standing in the same place.

Although he wasn't much older than I—but because, as he told me, he'd been hustling the streets since he was 16—Pete liked to play the jaded, all-knowing street hustler, explaining to me how to make out. He had a series of rules: Walk up to people, dont wait to be asked; if you do, you may wait all day. Forget about the vice squad, and you'll never get caught. A quick score in a toilet for a few bucks can be worth more than a big one that takes all day. Stand at the urinal long after youre through pissing. At the slightest indication of interest from someone in one of the cubicles, go up to him quickly before he gets any free ideas and say. "I'll make it with you for twenty." But go for much less if you have to.

As we sat in Bickford's in the cold light, he told me without embarrassment that once he'd gone for 75¢. "It was a slow day," he explained, "and I had only four bits, just enough to make the flix. I thought, Do I buy a Hotdog or make the flix and try to score? It was raining—no one on the streets. So I made the flix. No scores. Then someone wants to give me 75¢, and Im in the balcony anyway, so I let him. Hell, man," he adds pragmatically, "I was a quarter ahead—I could still have that Hotdog." And he goes on: "Youll learn; sometimes youll stand around all day and wait for a 15-buck score, a 10-buck score, even a deuce—all day—so, hell, take what comes, spote —so long as it dont louse up all your time—but always ask for the highest. Ask for Twenty. That way they think they got a Bargain."

Part of Pete's technique as a hustler was to tell the men he'd been with that he knew other youngmen like himself, and if they wanted, he would fix them up. Like a social secretary, he kept mental dates when he'd meet certain people. If he still didnt have someone for the score, they would walk around

Times Square until the man spotted someone he wanted. Pete would make the introductions—as he had that night with me and the black-dressed Al—and would get a few bucks for it. . . . There was one problem, Pete explained: As the score got to know more and more people, he'd dispense with Pete's services.

Occasionally, we sat in the automat, talking for a long time, bragging, exaggerating last night's Big Score. Soon it would turn bitter cold, he warned me (and, already, the wind raked the streets savagely), and the hustling would become more difficult; the competition on the streets keener. "You can shack up with someone permanent, though," he told me, looking at me curiously as if he were trying to find out something about me; "but me," he added hurriedly, "I dont dig that scene—I guess Im too Restless."

He made it, instead, from place to place, week to week, night to night. Or, he told me, he'd stay in one of the all-night movies. Sometimes he would rent a room off Seventh Avenue where they knew him. "And if you aint got a pad any time, spote," he said, "you can pad there too." Then he changed the subject quickly. "I dig feeling Free all the time," he said suddenly, stretching his arms.

And I could understand those feelings. Alone, I, too, felt that Enormous freedom. Yet . . . there was always a persistent sensation of guilt: a strong compulsion to spend immediately whatever money I had scored.

I still lived in that building on 34th Street, its mirrored lobby a ghost of its former elegance.

I paid $8.50 a week for the room. Opposite my window, in another wing of the same building, lived an old man who coughed all night. Sometimes he kept me awake. Sometimes it was the old, old woman who staggered up and down the hallway whistling, checking to see that no one had left the water running in the bathrooms or the gas burning in the community kitchen. At times it was Gene de Lancey—the woman with the demented eyes I had met the first day in the hallway—who kept me up. Once she had been Beautiful—she had sighingly shown me pictures of herself, *then!*—now she was sadly faded, and her eyes burned with the knowledge. She seldom went out, although I did see her on the street one late afternoon, shielding her face with her hand. She'd knock on my door sometimes early in the morning, often as I had just walked in: I would wonder if she listened for me to come in.

I would open the door, and shes standing there in a Japanese kimono. "Lambie-pie," she'd say in a childish whimper, "I just couldnt sleep, I just gotta have a cigarette and talk— Steve's asleep—" That was her present husband. "—and I knew you wouldnt mind, sweetie." She would sit and talk into the morning, with such passion, such lonesomeness, that I couldnt bring myself to ask her to leave. She would tell me about how everyone she had ever loved had left her: her mother, dead—her father, constantly sending her to boarding schools as a girl—her two previous husbands, Gone—her son, disappeared. "Theres no love in this harsh world," she lamented. "Everybody's hunting for Something—but what?" When, finally, she would get up, she would kiss me on the cheek and leave quickly. . . .

I mentioned her to Pete, and he says: "Great, man, she sounds like a swinging nympho—lets make it with her together sometime!"

Like the rest of us on that street—who played the male role with other men—Pete was touchy about one subject: his masculinity. In Bickford's one afternoon, a goodlooking masculine youngman walked in, looked at us, walked out again hurriedly. "That cat's queer," Pete says, glaring at him. "I used to see him and I thought he was hustling, and one day he tried to put the make on me in the flix. It bugged me, him thinking I was queer or something. I told him fuck off, I wasnt gonna make it for free." He was moodily silent for a long while, and then he said almost belligerently. "Whatever a guy does with other guys, if he does it for money, that dont make him queer. Youre still straight. It's when you start doing it for free, with other young guys, that you start growing wings.". . .

And because this is such a big thing in That life, youll hear untrue stories from almost everyone whos paid someone about the person hes paid. It's a kind of petty vindication, to put down the hustler's masculinity—whether correctly or not—at the same time that they seek it out.

Standing on the street, Pete would always come on about the young girls that would breeze by like flowers, the wind lapping at their skirts coyly. . . .

I found out Pete can be vengeful. I saw him in Bryant Park and he was fuming. The manager of a moviehouse one block away had refused to let him in. (I had seen the manager—a skinny, tall, nervous, gaunt, pale-faced man. The theater is one of the gayest in New York. Late at night men stand leaning along the stairways, waiting.) "Hes a queer," Pete said angrily, "he dont give a fuck what goes on so long as it dont go on for money—thats why he wouldnt let me in." Later, Pete tells everyone the place is *crawling* with plainclothes vice squad, ready to raid it: Stay Away! And the theater balcony was almost empty for weeks.

He also told me that another hustler had taken a score from right under his nose in the park, and Pete went around telling people the other hustler had the clap. . . . "Make it anyway you can," he said when he finished telling me that, "and when you cant make it, get even."

He knew almost everyone on the street who paid. He would point them out to me. "See that blond pale kid? He pimps for this old guy: real swank pad, too. And, man, what a weirdo that old guy is. Dig: he pays by the hour, and talks, talks, talks!—hes a teacher or something—laid up in bed from an accident. I used to fall asleep—I'd wear sunglasses—and he never knew the difference, just kept on talking. . . ."

At least once I regretted not listening to Pete's advice.

"See that one over there?" he said, pointing to a harmless-looking middle-aged man in a raincoat. "Stay away from him, spote, hes psycho."

But remembering what he had told everyone about the theater whose manager wouldnt let him in, and remembering what he'd done to the hustler whod taken his score in the park, I figured this may be some kind of revenge on the man for whatever reason. The man looked entirely harmless, and I went with him.

After we had made a very ordinary scene—and I still hadnt got any money from him—his composure changed suddenly into savage rage. Before I knew it, he had pulled a knife on me. I dashed out, down the creaking steps. Like a demon—his shadow flung grotesquely down the stairs—he stands at the landing shouting:

"God! Damn! You! *God damn all of you!*"

I also learned not always to trust Pete.

One sharply cold windy Sunday afternoon—the clouds sweeping the newyork sky like sheets—I saw him coming toward me where I was standing. "You wanna score?" he says. "See that old cat over there?" He pointed to a small mousy man a few feet away. "He wants us both to come over to his house. Hes only good for five," he explained, adding quickly when he saw me hesitating: "but most of the time he'll lay more if he digs you. . . . Cummon, man," he coaxed me. "Lets go with him. It's a draggy day anyhow. And anyway, we get to eat there real good." He adds, smiling secretly. "And we dont have to do much. Oh, hes Special!" Remembering the man I had walked around Times Square with, wearing a jacket and cap, I began to laugh. "Not that," Pete says, "we wont be walking around Times Square in leather."

Without going to him, Pete motions yes to the man, who goes down the steps, into the subway. Pete and I follow. I was walking fast, to catch up with the man. "Cool it," Pete explains. "I know where we get off." Without glancing back, the man gets in one of the cars, and we got in another. "He doesnt want anyone to see him leaving with guys," Pete said. I had been through this before: Unlike the black-dressed Al, who walked you around for an hour through Times Square, some scores dont want to be seen leaving the street with a younger man. "He lives in—hold on—*Queens!*" Pete laughed. "And dig this, spote: I think he teaches at Queens College. They even got a school now," he says, shaking his head.

We got off at Queens Plaza, and followed the man to a large apartment house. We waited at the corner for a few minutes, and then we walked into the lobby. It's a moderate-priced apartment house, very quiet, softly lighted. We reached the second floor, and along the hallway, a door was open slightly. There stood the little man beaming at us sweetly. He had taken off his coat, and he was wearing a gayly colored apron now.

"Hello, hello, hello!" he chirped merrily. "Im so glad you boys could come. I was hardly expecting—"

Pete whispered to me (I couldnt see how the man could help but hear him, but possibly neither cared): "Play it Cool and go along with it." At times Pete seemed to have an enormous tolerance for the quirks of the people he knew: a tolerance which could instantly turn into intolerance when he felt he'd been had.

"Itll be just a few minutes, boys," the old man announced, "and then we'll have a Lovely dinner. You boys must be famished, and I just happen to have some Very Nice Steaks. Now," he says, and his voice trembles slightly, "you boys get—uh—

Comfortable." He stood watching us intently. I glanced at Pete, and he had begun to unbutton his shirt.

"Do what I do," he told me, but I was strangely embarrassed suddenly, because by then Pete was taking off all his clothes. "Come on, man," he says to me, annoyed. "You wanna score or dont you?" (Again, I knew the man, his gaze nailed on us, could hear him, and I realized conclusively this didnt matter.) "This cat's pretty swinging people if he digs you," Pete goes on, "and we can come back and have 'dinner.' " He laughed again. "Come on."

I finally did. Pete sat on the couch, glancing at a comic book. He was completely unembarrassed. I sat on a chair looking at a magazine. The man returned to the kitchen, humming gayly. "It'll be just a few more minutes, now boys—" He turned at the door and looks fondly at Pete. "Petey-boy," he said, "I do believe youve been gaining a few pounds—you should have more salads, less starches. . . . You boys dont know how to care for yourselves, but we'll fix that. . . . And you, my boy—" turning now to me like a doting mother "—you could stand a bit more weight—just a few more pounds, not much—and we'll fix that too." He disappeared into the kitchen, and I could hear dishes rattle.

I glanced up abruptly, and Pete is looking at me over the comic book. He smiles broadly.

Soon, the meal was served, on a small, carefully set table in the dining room. We were summoned by a tinkling little bell which the man jingled. I had never eaten like this before, and I start to put my pants on. Pete said no, emphatically, reminding me we're in the presence of "cool people" and I should play along. We sat at the table—just Pete and myself, facing each other. The man flutters in and out of the kitchen like a butterfly, returning, serving us lovingly, rearranging the silver, the glasses—standing back to see that they were Just Right. There was no place for him. He brought a chair and set it away from the table. He sat there, staring raptly as we ate. Completely unself-consciously Pete ate his food. I dropped my fork a couple of times, and the man rushed into the kitchen to get me a clean one. Finally we had finished, and the man places a cake before us, gives us a large portion. "And there's ice cream!" he announced joyously. "Vanilla?" he asked. Pete said, "Chocolate." I took vanilla. "All boys love cake and ice cream," the man said knowingly, and by then I was enjoying it. I even ate more cake.

"Now a nice rest," the man said. His voice shook slightly, as when he asked us to get "Comfortable." We went into the bedroom, where there were twin beds. Pete lay in one, I lay in the other. The man came in with a chair, which he stations between the two beds. "Now take a long rest," he said. Pete is looking at me steadily, as if to remind me to play along; winks—then pretends to fall asleep immediately. He even snored a couple of times. I lay in bed, my eyes supposedly closed, but I was glancing at the man: He sat on the chair, his chin propped on his hands: staring fixedly from one to the other; occasionally his face would brighten up benevolently like a mother watching over her adored children. . . .

After about 15 minutes, he "woke" us, and we sat in the bedroom, on one bed, Pete and I, and played checkers, while the man watched us with the fascinated attention of a child enjoying a cartoon. Pete couldnt play checkers, and we sat there merely moving them back and forth.

"We'll have to go now, Mom," Pete said finally. I looked at him startled. Had he called him "Mom"? Pete nods at me, indicating I must do the same. I couldnt bring myself to call him "Mom." The old man looked at me with a hurt look.

"We'll have to go now, Mom," Pete repeated. He gives me an exasperated look.

"Oh, must you?" the man said. "Im so sorry you cant stay longer." He removed the apron, rubbed his hands on it, folded it neatly, and he went into the kitchen. Pete follows him. I can hear voices. Then Pete returns, hands me $5.00. "You fucked up, spote," he told me, shaking his head. "You didnt call him Mom. Just five bucks. When hes real happy, he lays ten." He shook his head regretfully. "But we can come again, and if youre cool we'll score more. Why—didnya—call—him—Mom?"

A week later, alone, I ran into the same man. This time he knew me and he came and talked to me. "Do you have a young friend whod like to come up and have dinner with us?" he asked me. "I havent seen Petey-boy here today," he said, glancing around for him. "If you find another nice youngman, we'll have a lovely dinner, and youll each be $10.00 richer." "Ten?" I said. "Why, child," he said somewhat indignantly, "I *always* give ten." From my expression, he understood what had happened. "That Pete!" he said, and I thought he was going to stamp his foot. "Hes done it to me again. Why, I bet he only gave you five." I felt embarrassed to admit I'd been taken, and I said, no, he'd given me ten. "Well, Im relieved!" the man said. "Hes done that before, you know—gives his young friend only five, and keeps fifteen. But what can I do? It embarrasses me so, when Ive first met a youngman, to give him the money. Idont reallyknow whattodo." Then he smiles Tolerantly. "But Petey is a lovely youngman—only—only—" He frowns slightly. "—only I wish he wouldnt call me Mom."

When I saw Pete again, one night in Bryant Park, I mentioned the money to him. He looked at his feet, pretending—I was sure he was pretending—embarrassment. "You gotta learn not to trust no one too much," he mumbled. Then he reached for his wallet, brought out three dollars. "Thats all I got now," he said, sighing ("What Am I Going To Do Now?!"). "Here, take em," he said. I did, and he stared at me in surprise. "Youre learning, spote," he said.

A few days later I got even with him.

I told him I knew a girl who wanted to be a stripper. I had met her not too long ago in the lobby of an apartment house I had just scored in. Her name was Flip, and she asked me to come up with her—just like that. She shows me sexy pictures of herself, turning me on. She was very pretty, very young. To the groaning sounds of "Night Train" she began to do a strip—then stopped coquettishly; tells me poutingly shes sorry, she cant go all the way: "You see, zoll—" (Thats how she said doll.) "—little Flip's got the mean rag on." Suddenly I realized without doubt that Flip was a man. She was the first dragqueen I had ever been with. I didnt let her know I had found out, and she went ahead and did what she told me she liked anyway. . . . When it was over, she says: "If you know any other cute zolls, tell them about me. Im always Ready, zoll."

When I told Pete about Flip (leaving out that she was actually a dragqueen), she too sounded like a nympho to him. "I gotta meet that chick," he told me—and later, I took him to her apartment. "We'll all three make it together," he said enthusiastically, "it's Sexier that way." And although he kept insisting as we stood outside Flip's door that I should stay, I said I had something else to do.

"Just ring the bell," I told him. "She wont even ask who you are. She'll just let you in."

I waited on the steps until I saw him ring the bell. The door opened. I heard Flip squeal: "Ooo, you are a zoll!"

That night I expected perversely to see an indignant Pete. But when I saw him, he said: "Man!—what a great Lay that chick is!" . . .

I felt very smug—and very surprised.

Then, one day—in the midst of that cold bitter winter, when the snow cut across the streets like an icy knife and the wind shrieked like something from Hell—one day, the memory of my Mother—accentuated by the long painfully written three-times-a-week letters without punctuation asking when I would be Back, asking me to promise not to get into trouble—that memory seized me with a racking violence—and I decided to put down Times Square again—a pattern of guilt which would recur periodically. I got a job, with a Foundation dedicated to Spreading The Greatness of The American Way of Life. And I kept away from The Streets. At night I would stay home or go to the movies—but not on 42nd Street or The Others. But —again—that job lasted only briefly, and impulsively, I quit. The cold air outside struck me like my lost freedom, regained. That very night I was back on Times Square.

"Where you been, spote?" Pete said. "I thought you got busted or something, I looked around for you. Dont split like that again, hear?" For the first time since I had known him, we shook hands.

After that, I saw him more and more often. Sometimes— having scored—we would meet afterwards and sit in the automat at 42nd and Park Avenue (this appealed to him as Classier). He told me he was staying in the room which the black-dressed Al rented to keep his motorcycle clothes in. "He dont dig anyone staying there," Pete told me, "but I finally conned him into letting me."

Yet, although I saw Pete at least once a day now, there was still the urgency, on both our parts, to split abruptly—to get away from each other.

Occasionally, we would go see "Mom." And the initial embarrassment I had felt was completely gone: It was always the same scene, the man never touched either of us, he merely sat staring. Once he even took a picture of us at the table.

By now Pete had learned how to play checkers. And one afternoon, strangely—as Pete and I sat on the bed playing checkers for much longer than we ever had before, as if there had been no third party, no "performance," actually enjoying it—with startling suddenness "Mom" abandoned his role as watcher, as doting mother, and nervously, claiming A Huge Headache, he asked us to leave. He folded the board hurriedly and abruptly dumped the checkers into their box.

As we left, he almost slammed the door.

"What bugged him?" Pete asked; then, shrugging, dismissing it, "I guess he did have a bad headache—shes kinda weird, anyway. . . . Fuck-im."

We didnt go back.

Now the nights began to warm up. It's that magnificent interlude in New York between winter and spring, when you feel the warmth stirring, and you remember that the dreadful naked trees will inevitably sprout tiny green buds, soon. Everyone rushes into the parks, the streets—and you even forget that, very soon, summer will come scorchingly, dropping from the sky like a blanket of steam. . . .

"I dont feel like fuckin around today," Pete told me one afternoon. He seemed pensive. "Lets just make the flix, spote —and forget all about trying to score."

We saw a double feature—one, a French movie about Lesbians in a girls' school. When we got outside, it was dark, the sky beaded wondrously with spring stars. "You really believe two chicks could dig each other that tough?" Pete asked me. I answer, "Sure." I was wondering what had prompted such amazing, for him, naïveté. "It sure seems strange," he went on. "Dig: I can see guys making it with each other—sure —for money—but— . . . Well, it sure seems strange, just digging each other like that—and those two chicks, man, they were both beautiful." We were standing outside. Even the lights on the signs seemed livelier in the warm air.

I didnt have any place to go, but I said, "Later," to Pete. This is how it had always been before. "No, wait," he says, "dont split—unless you got something to do." "Nothing," I said. "Lets stick together," he said. "I just dont feel like fuckin around tonight," he said moodily.

We went to a cafeteria on the same block and ate. The drifting youngmen were in there, sitting at the tables sipping coffee, staring at the older men who walked in. "Sometimes this whole scene bugs me," Pete said. "I guess maybe I should split—leave New York—go somewhere else: L.A., maybe. You wanna know something? I been in the East all my life— New Jersey—New York. . . ." He stared dreamily out the window. "Lets go to Washington Square!" he said abruptly.

In a few minutes, by subway, we were there.

In Washington Square there were many people. In the center, around the fountain, the young painters and their girlfriends clustered; some had baby carriages. They seemed very happy. And I felt the same. I was sure it was the approaching warm weather. . . . One youngman with a beard played a guitar and sang softly in Spanish. Pete and I sat by the fountain, listening. Soon, we got up, walked around the west side— toward the "meat rack"—the gay part of the park. There, it was as if someone had hung a line of marionettes on the railing: the lonesome young homosexuals, legs dangling, looking, waiting for that one-night's sexual connection. . . . "This wouldnt be a good place for scoring tonight anyway," Pete says, "theres too many out for free fun." But we sit there too, silently.

Next to us, a Negro queen has nervously stationed herself —a screamingly effeminate youngman in a candy-striped shirt: twisting her neck haughtily, looking around her in pretended disdain. Soon a couple of her white "sisters" swish by, two equally effeminate youngmen. They stand talking to the Negro queen, gossiping breathlessly. Now theyre talking about gowns. "It was Fabulous!" said the Negro queen, "I dressed like the Queen of Sheba, and honey, I Mean To Tell You, I looked *Real!*"

"Wasnt thuh Queen of Shayba white?" says one of the white queens, a fiercely blond one, affecting a thick Southern accent.

The Negro queen's eyes open Wide. "Are you trying to dish me, Mary?" she says angrily.

"Honey," said the blond one, "all Ah asked was a simple question. Wasnt thuh Queen of Shayba White? For all Ah know, you *painted* youhself White."

"Mary," says the Negro queen, ready to spring from the railing, "I may not be the Queen of Sheba, *exactly,* but I am The Queen of This Meat Rack—and I'll prove it to any nelly-assed queen that wants to try me."

"Youretoomuch," says the blond one airily. "Why! whoevuh heard of a nigguh *Queen?*"

In one instant, the Negro queen jumps off the railing, grabs the blond one by her thin shoulders and shakes her back and forth until she begins to sob, trying tearfully to tear herself away from the Negro queen. Finally, the Negro queen lets go, and the blond one rushes off wailing:

"Mothuh-fuckuh, if we wuz in The South, Ahd show you whos Queen of thuh Meat Rack!" . . .

Pete said moodily: "She shoudnuh called her a nigger."

A fat zero-policeman comes by swinging his stick like a baton: "Move on, move on," he says. "Yes, sir, officer, sir," Pete says, raising his middle finger up at the cop as he passes by. . . . We move on, and it was beginning to get cool—the hint of spring withdrawing teasingly. We walk again through Washington Square. The guitarist with the beard has left, and we sit on a bench.

Sitting there with Pete, a great Loneliness overwhelmed me. Was it the sky? So like a Texas sky at night—the stars flung prodigiously in the expansive blackness. Or the sudden breathtaking memory of my Mother miles away? Her love radiates that great distance toward me stifling me. . . . Or was it the sudden change in the park?

The youngmen and girls had left—the older people were gone from the benches too. Now there remain only the hunting young homosexuals looking for a partner. They sit momentarily on benches, move away, stand restlessly. One sat near us. "You figure he thinks we're queer?" Pete asked me indignantly—and then he stared him away. . . . I wondered if the franticness of their search was overwhelming Pete as it was me; he was strangely silent. . . . Two youngmen walked by. Previously I had seen them standing a few feet apart, on the walk, moving slowly closer to each other. Then they had talked briefly—now they walked away together, speaking softly. They were both young, both goodlooking. I saw them smile at each other: For them, this night's search was over—not for money—but for a mutual, if fleeting, sharing. Staring after them, Pete says: "They coulda fooled me, even. They looked like hustlers, dont they? And I bet theyre gonna make it with each other."

We move along Fifth Avenue, past a dimlit bar in a hotel. Through the windows we see a woman playing the piano. A man is leaning over her, her lips move in a song, she slides closer to him. . . . We pause for a while, and then we continue walking—into Union Square now, where we stand listening to a man in a tight suit heatedly hollering about what a blight Union Square is. "Perverts and tramps!" he yells. And a little old tramp staggers up to him, he reeks of wine, his nose like a red lightbulb—and he shakes his old finger unsteadily at the man yelling out damnation and says: clearly: "Listenere, you—you jes listenere: Theres gonna be hobos! homos! and momos! in Our Park long after youve grown deaf and dumb!"

"Hey, spote," says Pete to me, "whats a momo?"

"I dont know, I guess he just made it up."

"Thats cute," says Pete. "Homos, hobos and—and—what?"

"Momos," I said.

"Yeah: Momos. Hey! Maybe *we're* momos!" he laughs.

Weve reached 34th Street, the corner of the Armory on Park Avenue.

"Heres where I live," I told Pete now.

"Can I come up and talk a while?" he asked me, rushing the words together.

"Im tired," I said quickly.

"Cummon," he insisted, "it's early yet—or you can come up with me Im still staying at Al's with all the motorcycle jackets. Come up there, I got a pint of juice, we'll kill it."

"It's too far," I told him.

He looked hurt.

"Okay. Lets go to my place," I said hurriedly.

There is still a doorman in the building where I lived: a Negro from Jamaica: a clinging relic, like the mirrored lobby, of its sadly gone elegance: Beyond the lobby and the doorman—who sits in a little room, nodding asleep through the night—the building is seedy two-room apartments and gray rooms—layers of wallpaper make the walls soft like quilts; the plumbing rattles; steam gives out on the coldest days. . . . We went up in the complaining elevator, into the apartment, broken up, in turn, into smaller apartments, tiny rooms. I turned on the light.

"This is nice," Pete said, looking at the dingy room. One thing was colorful: a Mexican blanket which my mother had sent me. . . . "I wish I had a place of my own," Pete says. "You know, I actually been thinking of getting a small apartment—with someone, maybe—you know, split the rent—it wouldnt be much that way. . . . You like living alone, spote?"

I pretended I hadnt heard him. . . . But long before that night when I had resolved to explore this world not with one person but with many, I had become aware that there was something about someone getting too close to me which suffocated me. . . .

"Maybe," Pete says, going on, "maybe—you know—I was just thinking—shacking up with another guy for a while—we could hustle together, really make the scores. It wouldnt be hard: I know lots of scores. Theyd stop digging me; dig you; so on—I mean, whoever it was, we would keep going like that.

. . . I was even thinking—Christ—well—that fuckin street—it bugs me—sometimes I get nightmares about those toilets—I mean, all those fags—and—well, if I got a job, even—and split the rent with someone—well—"

"It's past midnight," I said interrupting him.

For a long while there seems to be nothing to say. Im aware of a smothering self-consciousness between us. I wanted him to leave. It was the first time anyone other than the curious men and women in the other rooms had been in this room with me.

"Can I stay here tonight?" I heard him ask clearly.

In a kind of panic, I want to say no. "Yes," I answered.

The lights are out now. The darkness seems very real, like a third person waiting. I lay on the very edge of one side of the bed, and he lay on the very edge of the other. A long time passed. Hours.

"Are you asleep?" he asked me.

"No—I cant sleep."

"Me neither," he says. "Maybe I should go." But he didnt move.

More silence.

And then I felt his hand, lightly, on mine.

Neither of us moved. Moments passed like that. And now his hand closes over mine, tightly.

And that was all that happened.

The man in the other wing of the building, on the other side of my window, began to cough very early, and I got up hurriedly and dressed. "I have to go out," I told Pete.

"Me, too," he said. "I have to see someone."

We avoided looking at each other. "I'll see you around The Street," he said at the door. "Man," he says—but his voice was forced, as mine was, "I got a real tough score lined up today—hes worth Twenty."

"Later," I said.

"Later—spote," he said.

I saw him again, many times—in the movie theaters, in Bryant Park, on Times Square. We would say hello to each other, stop, talk casually: He would exaggerate his scores, I would exaggerate mine. But we were never together for long any more. "I have to score," one of us would say, and we'd split.

Soon we wouldnt stop to talk to each other when we met.

We would say hello, rush on. . . . And then one day, one stifling summer day, I saw him bouncing along the street in my direction. I turned sharply, pretended to be looking at some movie posters; and glancing back once, briefly, I noticed that he—for the same reason I had turned away, to avoid meeting —had crossed to the other side of the street.

In a While Crocodile
William Eastlake

The Prince came to the Indian country in '34 or '35. His title was no accident of blood nor fantasy nor imaginative appellation of some trader in the area. The title had been conferred on him by all, earned by him for doing something better than anybody in the world. He blew a horn. He blew the horn better than anybody in the world. His kingdom in the South had been overrun. But the vanquished were unvanquished. They left the South, New Orleans mostly, when their world fell, when corruption rode in on a slick, facile beat infecting everywhere. They left the South but they remembered, they endured, until they died in some hovel. They endured, their gold trumpet still there, their scepter still borne in the dust, and sometimes singing.

Like The Prince who wandered to Indian country to die in an unclaimed hogan. Before death The Weaver, who lived hard by, could hear the quick jerk of sweet music flow out over the quiet land, rhythmic and gay and sometimes sad.

The Prince had been on his way to Denver, he thought, from Albuquerque, but he was on his way to nowhere. He was one of the dispossessed, the unwanted, the wanderers over the unsinging land.

"One of those who had secret dreams. He would not corrupt. One of those who knew who he was," the trader said.

"Yes, of course," the city man who had come so far said. "I don't want any philosophy. I'm paid to get the facts. Did he die of starvation?"

"Why?"

"We're making a TV of his life," the man said.

"Maybe."

"Maybe," the man who had come so far and dressed in city clothes said. "Maybe. The editor won't settle for maybe. I got to get the facts. I pay well."

"That may very well be," the trader said.

"All right," the city man said. "I could pay what it's worth."

"Maybe he did," the trader said. "Maybe he died of starvation. What would that be worth?"

"I'm going to level with you," the city man said. He wore a pork-pie hat with a narrow brim snapped down over a harried, small-featured baby face. "I'm going to level with you." The baby-faced city man stared around the trading post at the goods and the Indians against the wall. "We'll pay what it's worth if he died of starvation, for example, and you gave it to us, we'll send you a check for what it's worth."

"It's worth nothing," the trader said.

"All right," the city man said. "I'm going to level with you. I want to succeed."

The trader was dressed like the Indians in jeans with a big Stetson pushed back above a long and slanting face. Absent-minded in back of the long counter and leaning forward, he waited for the city man to continue his sentence.

"I want to succeed," the city man repeated. "That's all. I want to succeed. Offering you money doesn't seem to work, so I'm giving it to you straight. I want to succeed."

"Congratulations," the trader said, and he went back to trying to figure out how an adding machine works when it's busted.

"But I've failed," the city man said.

"Congratulations anyway," the trader said.

"Listen," the city man said. "I was going to bluff it through. This is my first assignment but I was going to act like an old vet, toss some money around and things like that. Did I hurt your feelings?"

The trader shook his head no.

"I'd like to get back to Albuquerque and call the wife and say look who succeeded."

The trader was mixed up with the adding machine.

"The company flew me out here in a luxurious Constellation Transcontinental Mainliner and they put me up at the Albuquerque Hilton, rented me a Drive-Ur-Self car, no questions asked. Today I'm dead. You sure I didn't hurt your feelings?"

The trader shook his head no.

"You mind if I talk to the Indians?"

"There's no law against talking to the Indians."

"Do they speak English?"

"They speak some of all foreign languages. Yes, they speak English," the trader said. "But don't tell them you want to succeed."

"Thank you," the city man said.

"And talk to the one on the end of the bench, the one with the turquoise ring. He was his friend."

"Did you know The Prince?" the city man said to the Indian without any niceties.

"Yes," the Indian said.

"Did he die of starvation?"

"Maybe," the Indian said.

"The name is Russell," the city man said.

"Congratulations," the Indian said.

"I've come a long way," the city man with the pork hat said, "to get the scoop on The Prince. And all I get is maybe. The editors won't think much of that."

"That's too bad," the Indian said.

"The Prince is a famous man now," the city man said. "They're playing his music again. Everyone wants to know about him. I've come a long way to find out. You might say I represent a hundred million people." The city man paused and watched the Indian for the effect. "Yes, I might say it—"

"Say it," the Indian said.

The city man got up and walked back to the trader.

"I'm not getting anywhere. I'm dead," he said. "Just tell me, did The Prince come out here and starve to death? I can build from that."

"Work on that Indian you just talked to," the trader said. "They call him The Weaver. He's an artist. They were friends, The Prince and The Weaver. They were artists."

"Yes, but I can't build on that," the city man said. "The Prince must have come in your post."

"Yes."

"Did he have anything to trade?"

"No. Nothing."

"What do the Indians trade?"

"In season, wool. Most of the year their turquoise jewelry. I keep the jewelry until they redeem it."

"He had a trumpet," the city man said. "Why didn't he pawn that?"

"Because I wouldn't take it," the trader said.

"Why?"

"Because I figure with the Indians the jewelry is their wealth, their beauty. With his trumpet—"

"It was his life," Russell said.

"Maybe," the trader said.

"But you loaned him money without taking the trumpet?"

"Some."

"Listen, I'm doing all right," the city man said.

"You always will."

"I mean I'm getting somewhere," Russell said. "Now did he finally die of starvation?"

"Maybe."

"That's no help."

"He came in '34, I think, or '35."

"We know that."

"It was a rainy night. I don't know how he got here. Some salesman, I guess, who went back to Albuquerque. He hung around the post till it closed. I couldn't see him standing out on that muddy road with no cars. It was dirt then."

"It still is."

"No. Gravel."

"Gravel?"

"I took him to a hogan. He was a tall, bent man with small alert eyes, graying hair under a wide preacher hat. Carried a brief case with socks, new shirt and such. He was a clean old man. In the other hand he carried the instrument. It was in a black case. I knew that's what it was because when I left him there, had only gotten away maybe fifty yards, it started."

"What was that?"

"This thing he had in the case. I just stood there in the rain, maybe fifteen minutes, listening, not knowing I was soaking wet. Then I realized I was surrounded by Indians listening, too."

"Then he did die of starvation?"

"No. Not then. That is, he became a thing with the Indians—his music anyway. They fed him for months, almost years, and then he had a house—a hogan—for the first time in maybe ten years. Then one night the Indians burned it down."

"Then he didn't die of starvation. He was—?"

"No," the trader said.

"But why burn his house down? Oh, of course," the city man said. "I see."

"What do you see?"

"He was a Negro."

"No," the trader said. "I mean, the Indians didn't know that, didn't care. They thought maybe he was some new kind of a white man. They'd never seen a black before and they thought he was some new kind of a white man."

"And you never told them?"

"What was there to tell them?"

"I see," the city man said. "I'll accept that. But what did he die of? You say he didn't get burned in the house."

"No. He played on that thing while the hogan burned, helped them start the fire, then played on that thing while the house burned. Then they built him another."

"What was wrong with the one they burned?"

"A Navaho had died in it. Evil spirits. That's why it was vacant, why it was available for him to move in and why it was burned."

"I see. Then he didn't die there?"

"No," the trader said. "He became a thing with the Indians, played at all their festivals. He was their new kind of a white man. The first white man they had discovered who was black. They knew he was a white man because that's the way he acted, dressed, the language he spoke, but they knew he was a new kind of white man because he was black——"

"And made sweet music."

"Yes," the trader said.

"He was a genius. We know that now. A little late."

"A little late."

"But the Indians knew it because they, too, were primitive, could understand the clear, simple, honest note——"

"You reach," the trader said.

"Maybe we don't reach enough," the city man said. "Anyway, they'll take care of that in the office. But what happened then? When did he die of starvation?"

"Who said he died of starvation?" The trader moved down the counter.

"You didn't deny it," the city man said, following.

"I didn't say it either," the trader said.

"You mind if I try the Indian again?"

"Go ahead," the trader said.

When the city man sat down, the Indian called The Weaver got up and went over to the window. His round dark face was without expression.

I'm dead, the city man thought. You can't approach an Indian. You can't approach an Indian or a king or a genius. You can't get anything out of those kinds of people. They got a world all of their own. Why did they have to send me on this kind of assignment to the damn Indians? I'm dead. I'll never succeed. I wonder how The Prince got close to the Indians. I guess he had something they wanted to buy. Well, they won't buy money, I found that out. What did he have, what did The Prince have they wanted to buy? Art. That covers too much. That means nothing. That's awful vague. Better, it was his music that got around all languages, all customs, all cultures, all differences. What have I got? Nothing. I'm dead. I'll never get around them. I'll never succeed.

The city man thought a bit about all the money the company had put out to send him here to the end of the world.

I must have something. The wife says I've got something. The company says I've got something. Well, it certainly isn't brains and it certainly isn't good looks. Well, what else is there? Will power. That's what I got—will power. If God forgot you on everything else, you can always pick up plenty of will power around the place. And stick-to-itness and perseverance, keeping my nose clean and hitting the line hard. That's what I got. I got nothing.

The city man turned to the Indian next to him. "Yes I have. I've got patience, that's what I've got. Patience."

"Congratulations," the Indian said.

The Weaver who had gone over to the window to avoid the city man looked out over the far country and thought: How can you tell it to a man like that? How can you tell him about the man who knew who he was? How can you tell him about The Prince? Who but another artist would understand the loneliness and the separateness of wanting to belong but needing to belong on your own terms? Who would understand? Who would understand that he had to live at the end of the world because the end of the world was the only place the people understood? Now it's different, from what the city man says some people understand now all over the world and they want to make a picture. But who understood back there? No one understood back there. That's why people have to go to the end of the world because at times people don't understand in the middle of the world. Well, why not change? Why not come down to earth? I guess it's because the earth's not right. When the earth is right, people like The Prince will come down to it. How did he say it? "I will sweat it out." That's what The Prince said. That doesn't sound much like a prince talking but he said it, just that way. He said other things too, like, "It's got to be clean, Jackson. It's got to be true, Jackson. You got to feel it, Jackson. It's got to be right or it's not worth it. Give me some skin, Indian." The city man wouldn't understand that but the city man wanted to know about starvation. Yes, The Prince starved to death but maybe not in the way a city man would understand. He wants the facts, but what good are the facts without feeling?

"Listen," the city man said. "I got a proposition." He had joined the Indian at the window and he pulled down on his narrow-brimmed oval hat. The Indian noticed that the city man had a green and red feather in the band from no bird that ever lived.

"My proposition is this." He reached into a green leather brief case and brought out strings of bright beads. He placed the bright beads along the counter, draping some of them so they hung down over the edge in all their gaudy glass brilliance. The city man stepped back away from them to admire them and envy the ones that were going to get them and wonder whether he could afford to part with them and furrowed his brow at the terrific expense of giving away this chief's ransom. When he had used up all these expressions and more, he said: "I give you these in return for the facts about The Prince."

The trader translated to some of the Indians that did not follow, and all the Indians mumbled among themselves for a long minute.

"I'm waiting," the city man said. "Is it a deal?"

The Indians ignored him, continuing to mumble.

"I've got to have a decision," the city man said.

The Indians stopped their conference now.

"Well, what is it?" the city man said.

"They want to know where you got them."

"It's a collection formerly owned by a man named Woolworth. That's who I got them from."

The Indians mumbled again among themselves before the trader announced their decision.

"They say for you to blow the whistle on that guy Woolworth. He sold you a pile of glass."

"Well, that's what I read," the city man said. "Indians will trade anything for beads."

"Manhattan Island," the trader said. "New York City maybe, but nothing they think worth while. Not for glass."

"All right, touché. You win," the city man said. "But I've got another proposition. My proposition is this," the city man said. "I've got patience. I'll stay around here for years if necessary, badgering you people. It's the ultimate weapon. I hope you people don't make me use it."

The Indians were silent.

The city man took off his hat, examined it, flicked his feather, and put it on again. Then he watched the Indians a long moment before he went over to the counter and came back with his green cowhide brief case from which he withdrew a book with the title *Hommes et Problèmes du Jazz.*

"I've got another proposition," the city man said. "You understand that?" He held up the book. "You understand what that says?"

"Yes." The Indian nodded from a hooded glance.

"Oh," the city man said. "You're not supposed to. I was going to translate what this man said about The Prince's music in exchange for your facts."

"I learned a few words at Indian boarding school," The Weaver said. "Not too much."

"Enough probably to correct me. No, I've got another proposition." The city man took off his hat and drummed on it, then he touched the bright feather of no bird with a preening motion. "Supposing I could bring The Prince back—back to life. Would you give me the facts then?"

"Yes," The Weaver said, knowing he was risking nothing. "I buried him."

"And I shall make him rise again," the city man said.

All the silent, imperturbable Indians who looked straight ahead into infinity, seeing and hearing nothing, all smiled now. All tapped their feet and moved their eyes, and all the squaws sitting under the counter shook their heads and winked and touched each other, looked at the city man and then away again, embarrassed.

"He shall rise again," the city man repeated.

"When?" The Weaver said.

"Now," the city man said. "Follow me."

All the Indians trooped out in file after the city man with a feather. They followed him to the car while he got another case, a red one this time. Now he had a green and a red case in either arm and a green and red feather in his hat.

"Where did he live?" he said.

The Weaver pointed to the hogan under the purple brow of a near blue mesa. The Indians followed the bright feathered hat of the city man through the gray sage and stark greasewood, the beavertail and the cholla cactus. Now they went through the piñon, clumped and huddled, the line of file of the Indians swinging with the lead of the city man. Now they were in the flat country, the land of grama and sand and infinity and occasionally this.

"What's that?" the city man said.

"Arroyo," The Weaver said. All the Indians now stood at

the edge of the canyon that separated them from the hogan.

"Impossible to cross here," The Weaver said. "We can cross five miles down."

"Then it might be too late," the city man said. "Might lose the tip."

"The what?"

"The audience," the city man said. "Follow me." He crossed his green and red cases in front of him and got down on his rear and slid down the bank. At the bottom he got up running. When he reached the opposite bank, he ran right up it, full at it, then he fell and scrambled, clawed his way to the top, the red and green cases finally flung over the top and the man following, slowly pulling himself up on a greasewood root.

"There," the man hollered loud across the arroyo. "Don't just watch. Follow me."

The Indians settled for just watching, standing there along the edge of the canyon. If he was going to produce The Prince, they could see from here.

"All right," the city man said, and he turned and walked toward the hogan, entered it and soon reappeared without the red and green cases and without The Prince.

"Now," the city man said and he kicked the hogan and out came The Prince, not in the flesh but as the Indians, the world, remembered him.

The Indians piled down the bank now and ran up the other side, not even scrambling but running upright on the impossible angle. Now they stood panting, listening, in front of the city man. The city man took off his hat, drummed on it and preened the feather.

"It's a phonograph," The Weaver said.

"But it's him, The Prince." The city man put on his hat. "He's come back," he said.

The Weaver listened now to the cool, solid truth of an alone trumpet blasting clearly and rich through the long Indian country.

"Yes," The Weaver said. "It's him."

A note hung now, wavered, and then blew loud and clear.

"Yes. Yes," The Weaver said.

"That's all a man is," the city man said. "What he does. This is what he did. This is The Prince. The Prince had patience."

"Yes," The Weaver said.

The music started to walk now and sing, led by the big trumpet, then hushed, muted now before it shattered brilliantly like colored glass exploding in the sun.

"A man doesn't die now," the city man said. "Not some men. They can always come back when the world is ready, when the world is right. Patience."

The music shifted now to a weird, steady beat, the trumpet sliding in and out tenderly, then suddenly clean and brave.

"Some people don't die any more." The city man took out a pack of cigarettes and offered them around, but the Indians were listening. "If he has honor and patience, he can come back. He can live forever."

"Yes, yes," The Weaver said. "But listen."

"Do I win?" the city man said.

"Man is more powerful than death. Yes. Anything. But listen."

"Thank you," the city man said.

Late that night, back at the post, the city man gave The Weaver a large album of records marked "The Prince."

"Keep these," he said. "And the machine, too. You can bring him back any time you want."

"I didn't think there were any records of his."

"Not for a long time," the city man said. "But you only have to find some busted old ones in New Orleans, piece them together and make a million copies."

"Is that what they did?"

"Two million," the city man said.

"That's nice. That's very nice," The Weaver said. "Thank you."

"And now, did he die of starvation?" the city man said.

"Yes," The Weaver said. "It was a long hard winter that winter. There wasn't much a man, an Indian, could do against such a long, hard, cold winter. But he played against it and he was winning as far as we were concerned. But he couldn't stand it. With all the hunger he had seen in his own people, he had never seen anything like what happens to an Indian in a long, hard, cold winter. He sold his trumpet to a trader from Aztec, bought food from him and fed us all. Not our trader. Our trader was out of food, but he bought food from Aztec and fed us all. Then he starved to death. You understand how a man with food could starve to death?"

"I think so."

"Without his trumpet to blow. It was his life."

"Yes."

"Is that enough?"

"I think we can build with that."

"Will you do it honestly?"

"We will try to do it honestly."

The city man rose now, put on his pork hat and proffered his hand toward The Weaver. The Weaver looked at it and then up at the ceiling. The city man pulled down on his hat then held out his hand again.

"Give me some skin, Indian."

The Weaver took his hand slowly now, but he took it. They stared into each other's eyes a brief second, the pressure between their hands increasing.

"Patience. Now I go," the city man said, turning and walking to the door. Before he closed it he said, "See you later, alligator."

The Weaver went into the back room where the sheep hides hung and where the Indians and the trader were listening to the record. He had a whole book of the records in his arms. He walked out of the room again, conscious of his riches. He went over to the window and raised the book to his lips and kissed The Prince. Then he watched out the window as the city man's car, running beneath the big mesa became a speck soon to disappear. Now he said, toward the speck and smiling —"In a while, crocodile."

A New Day
Charles Wright

"I'm caught. Between the devil and the deep blue sea." Lee Mosely laughed and made a V for victory sign and closed the front door against a potpourri of family voices, shouting good wishes and tokens of warning.

The late, sharp March air was refreshing and helped cool his nervous excitement but his large hands were tight fists in his raincoat pockets. All morning he had been socking one fist into the other, running around the crowded, small living room like an impatient man waiting for a train, and had even screamed at his mother, who had recoiled as if he had sliced her heart with a knife. Andy, his brother-in-law, with his whine of advice. "Consider . . . Brother . . ."

Consider your five stair-step children. Consider the sweet, brown babe switching down the subway steps ahead of me. What would she say? Lee wondered.

Of course, deep down in his heart, he wanted the job, wanted it desperately. The job seemed to hold so much promise, and really he was getting nowhere fast, not a God damn place in the year and seven weeks that he had been shipping clerk at French-American Hats. But that job, too, in the beginning had held such promise. He remembered how everyone had been proud of him.

Lee Mosely was a twenty-five-year-old Negro, whose greatest achievement had been the fact that he had graduated twenty-fourth in his high school class of one hundred and twenty-seven. This new job that he was applying for promised the world, at least as much of the world as he expected to get in one hustling lifetime. But he wouldn't wear his Ivy League suits and unloosen his tie at ten in the morning for coffee and doughnuts. He would have to wear a uniform, and mouth a grave Yes mam and No mam. What was worse, his future boss was a Southern white woman, and he had never said one word to a Southern white woman in his life, had never expected to either.

"It's honest work, ain't it?" his mother had said. "Mrs.

Davies ain't exactly a stranger. All our people down home worked for her people. They were mighty good to us and you should be proud to work for her. Why, you'll even be going overseas and none of us ain't been overseas except Joe and that was during the big war. Lord knows, Mrs. Davies pays well."

Lee had seen her picture once in the *Daily News,* leaving the opera, furred and bejeweled, a waxen little woman with huge, gleaming eyes, who faced the camera with pouting lips as if she were on the verge of spitting. He had laughed because it seemed strange to see a society woman posing as if she were on her way to jail.

Remembering, he laughed now and rushed up the subway steps at Columbus Circle.

Mrs. Maude T. Davies had taken a suite in a hotel on Central Park South for the spring, a spring that might well be two weeks or a year. Lee's Aunt Ella in South Carolina had arranged the job, a very easy job. Morning and afternoon drives around Central Park. The hotel's room service would supply the meals, and Lee would personally serve them. The salary was one hundred and fifty dollars a week, and it was understood that Lee could have the old, custom-built Packard on days off.

"Lord," Lee moaned audibly and sprinted into the servants' entrance of the hotel.

Before ringing the doorbell, he carefully wiped his face with a handkerchief that his mother had ironed last night and inspected his fingernails, cleared his throat, and stole a quick glance around the silent, silk-walled corridor.

He rang the doorbell, whispered "damnit," because the buzzing sound seemed as loud as the sea in his ears.

"Come in," a husky female voice shouted and Lee's heart exploded in his ears. His armpits began to drip.

But he opened the door manfully, and entered like a boy who was reluctant to accept a gift, his highly polished black shoes sinking into layers of apple-green carpet.

He raised his head slowly and saw Mrs. Davies sitting in a yellow satin wing chair, bundled in a mink coat and wearing white gloves. A flowered scarf was tied neatly around her small, oval head.

"I'm Lee Mosely. Sarah's boy. I came to see about a job."

Mrs. Davies looked at him coldly and then turned toward the bedroom.

"Muffie," she called, and then sat up stiffly, clasping her

gloved hands. "You go down to the garage and get the car. Muffie and I will meet you in the lobby."

"Yes mam," Lee said, executing a nod that he prayed would serve as a polite bow. He turned smartly like a soldier and started for the door.

Muffie, a Yorkshire terrier bowed in yellow satin, trotted from the bedroom and darted between Lee's legs. His bark was like an old man coughing. Lee moaned, "Lord," and noiselessly closed the door.

He parked the beige Packard ever so carefully and hopped out of the car as Mrs. Davies emerged from the hotel lobby.

Extending his arm, he assisted Mrs. Davies from the curb.

"Thank you," she said sweetly. "Now, I expect you to open and close the car door but I'm no invalid. Do you understand?"

"Yes mam. I'm sorry."

"Drive me through the park."

Muffie barked. Lee closed the door and then they drove off as the sun skirted from behind dark clouds.

There were many people in the park and it was like a spring day except for the chilled air.

"We haven't had any snow in a long time," Lee said, making conversation. "Guess spring's just around the corner."

"I know that," Mrs. Davies said curtly.

And that was the end of their conversation until they returned to the hotel, twenty minutes later.

"Put the car away," Mrs. Davies commanded. "Don't linger in the garage. The waiter will bring up lunch shortly and you must receive him."

Would the waiter ever come? Lee wondered, pacing the yellow and white tiled serving pantry. Should he or Mrs. Davies phone down to the restaurant? The silence and waiting was unbearable. Even Muffie seemed to be barking impatiently.

The servant entrance bell rang and Mrs. Davies screamed, "Lee!" and he opened the door quickly and smiled at the pale, blue-veined waiter, who did not return the smile. He had eyes like a dead fish, Lee thought, rolling in the white covered tables. There was a hastily scrawled note which read: "Miss Davies food on top. Yours on bottom."

Grinning, Lee took his tray from under the bottom shelf, and was surprised to see two bottles of German beer. He set his tray on the pantry counter and took a quick peep at Mrs. Davies's tossed salad, one baby lamb chop. There was a split of champagne in a small iced bucket.

"Lord," he marveled, and rolled the white covered table into the living room.

"Where are you eating, mam?" Lee asked, pleased because his voice sounded so professional.

"Where?" Mrs. Davies boomed. "In this room, boy!"

"But don't you have a special place?" Lee asked, relieved to see a faint smile on the thin lips.

"Over by the window. I like the view. It's almost as pretty as South Carolina. Put the yellow wing over there too. I shall always dine by the window unless I decide otherwise. Understand?"

"Yes mam." Lee bowed and rolled the table in front of the floor-to-ceiling wall of windows. Then he rushed over and picked up the wing chair as if it were a loaf of bread.

He seated Mrs. Davies and asked gravely: "Will that be all, mam?"

"Of course!"

Exiting quickly, Lee remembered what his uncle Joe had said about V-day. "Man. When they tell us the war is over, I just sat down in the foxhole and shook my head."

And Lee Mosely shook his head and entered the serving pantry, took a deep breath of relief which might well have been a prayer.

He pulled up a leather-covered fruitwood stool to the pantry counter and began eating his lunch of fried chicken, mashed potatoes, gravy and tossed salad. He marveled at the silver domes covering the hot, tasty food, amused at his distorted reflection in the domes. He thanked God for the food and the good job. True, Mrs. Davies was sharp-tongued, a little funny, but she was nothing like the Southern women he had seen in the movies and on television and had read about in magazines and newspapers. She was not a part of Negro legends, of plots, deeds, and mockery. She was a wealthy woman named Mrs. Maude T. Davies.

Yeah, that's it, Lee mused in the quiet and luxury and warmth of the serving pantry.

He bit into a succulent chicken leg and took a long drink of the rich, clear-tasting German beer.

And then he belched. Mrs. Maude T. Davies screamed: "Nigger!"

I still have half a chicken leg left, Lee thought. He continued eating, chewing very slowly, but it was difficult to swallow. The chicken seemed to set on the valley of his tongue like glue.

So there was not only the pain of digesting but the quicksand sense of rage and frustration, and something else, a nameless something that had always started ruefully at the top of his skull like a windmill.

He knew he had heard *that* word, although the second lever of his mind kept insisting loudly that he was mistaken.

So he continued eating with difficulty his good lunch.

"Nigger boy!" Mrs. Davies repeated, a shrill command, strangely hot and tingling like the telephone wire of the imagination, the words entering through the paneled pantry door like a human being.

Lee Mosely sweated very hard summer and winter. Now, he felt his blood congeal, freeze, although his anger, hot and dry came bubbling to the surface. Saliva doubled in his mouth and his eyes smarted. The soggy chicken was still wedged on his tongue and he couldn't swallow it nor spit it out. He had never cried since becoming a man and thought very little of men who cried. But for the love of God, what could he do to check his rage, helplessness?

"Nigger!" Mrs. Davies screamed again, and he knew that some evil, white trick had come at last to castrate him. He had lived with this feeling for a long time and it was only natural that his stomach and bowels grumbled as if in protest.

And then like the clammy fear that evaporates at the crack of day, Lee's trembling left hand picked up the bottle of beer and he brought it to his lips and drank. He sopped the bread in the cold gravy. He lit a cigarette and drank the other bottle of German beer.

A few minutes later, he got up and went into the living room.

Mrs. Davies was sitting very erect and elegant in the satin chair, and had that snotty *Daily News* photograph expression, Lee thought bitterly.

"Mrs. Davies," he said politely, clearly, "did you call me?"

"Yes," Mrs. Maude T. Davies replied, like a jaded, professional actress. Her smile was warm, pleased, amused. "Lee, you and I are going to get along very well together. I like people who think before they answer."

An Act of Prostitution
James Alan McPherson

When he saw the woman the lawyer put down his pencil and legal pad and took out his pipe.

"Well," he said. "How do you want to play it?"

"I wanna get outta here," the whore said. "Just get me outta here."

"Now get some sense," said the lawyer, puffing on the pipe to draw in the flame from the long wooden match he had taken from his vest pocket. "You ain't got a snowball's chance in hell."

"I just want out," she said.

"You'll catch hell in there," he said, pointing with the stem of his pipe to the door which separated them from the main courtroom. "Why don't you just get some sense and take a few days on the city."

"I can't go up there again," she said. "Those dike matrons in Parkville hate my guts because I'm wise to them. They told me last time they'd really give it to me if I came back. I can't do no time up there again."

"Listen," said the lawyer, pointing the stem of his pipe at her this time, "you ain't got a choice. Either you cop a plea or I don't take the case."

"*You* listen, you two-bit Jew shyster." The whore raised her voice, pointing her very chubby finger at the lawyer. "*You* ain't got no choice. The judge told you to be my lawyer and you got to do it. I ain't no dummy, you know that?"

"Yeah," said the lawyer. "You're a real smarty. That's why you're out on the streets in all that snow and ice. You're a real smarty all right."

"You chickenshit," she said. "I don't want you on my case anyway, but I ain't got no choice. If you was any good, you wouldn't be working the sweatboxes in this court. I ain't no dummy."

"You're a real smarty," said the lawyer. He looked her up and down: a huge woman, pathetically blonde, big-boned and absurd in a skirt sloppily crafted to be mini. Her knees were ruddy and the flesh below them was thick and white and flabby. There was no indication of age about her. Like most whores, she looked at the same time young but then old, possibly as old as her profession. Sometimes they were very old but seemed to have stopped aging at a certain point so that ranking them chronologically, as the lawyer was trying to do, came hard. He put his pipe on the table, on top of the police affidavit, and stared at her. She sat across the room, near the door in a straight chair, her flesh oozing over its sides. He watched her pull her miniskirt down over the upper part of her thigh, modestly, but with the same hard, cold look she had when she came in the room. "You're a real smarty," he commented, drawing on his pipe and exhaling the smoke into the room.

The fat woman in her miniskirt still glared at him. "Screw you, Yid!" she said through her teeth. "Screw your fat mama and your chubby sister with hair under her arms. Screw your brother and your father and I hope they should go crazy playing with themselves in pay toilets."

The lawyer was about to reply when the door to the consultation room opened and another man came into the small place. "Hell, Jimmy," he said to the lawyer, pretending to ignore the woman, "I got a problem here."

"Yeah?" said Jimmy.

The other man walked over to the brown desk, leaned closer to Jimmy so that the woman could not hear and lowered his voice. "I got this kid," he said. "A nice I-talian boy that grabbed this Cadillac outta a parking lot. Now he only done it twice before and I think the Judge might go easy if he got in a good mood before the kid goes on, this being Monday morning and all."

"So?" said Jimmy.

"So I was thinking," the other lawyer said, again lowering his voice and leaning much closer and making a sly motion with his head to indicate the whore on the chair across the room. "So I was thinking. The Judge knows Philomena over there. She's here almost every month and she's always good for a laugh. So I was thinking, this being Monday morning and all and with a cage-load of nigger drunks out there, why not put her on first, give the old man a good laugh and then put my I-talian boy on. I know he'd get a better deal that way."

"What's in it for me?" said Jimmy, rapping the ashes from his pipe into an ashtray.

"Look, I done *you* favors before. Remember that Chinaman? Remember the tip I gave you?"

Jimmy considered while he stuffed tobacco from a can into his pipe. He lit the pipe with several matches from his vest pocket and considered some more. "I don't mind, Ralph," he said. "But if she goes first the Judge'll get a good laugh and then he'll throw the book at her."

"What the hell, Jimmy?" said Ralph. He glanced over at the whore who was eying them hatefully. "Look, buddy," he went on, "you know who that is? Fatso Philomena Brown. She's up here almost every month. Old Bloom knows her. I tell you, she's good for a laugh. That's all. Besides, she's married to a nigger anyway."

"Well," said Jimmy. "So far she ain't done herself much good with me. She's a real smarty. She thinks I'm a Jew."

"There you go," said Ralph. "Come on, Jimmy. I ain't got much time before the Clerk calls my kid up. What you say?"

Jimmy looked over at his client, the many pounds of her rolled in great logs of meat under her knees and around her belly. She was still sneering. "O.K." He turned his head back to Ralph. "O.K., I'll do it."

"Now look," said Ralph, "this is how we'll do. When they call me up I'll tell the Clerk I need more time with my kid for consultation. And since you follow me on the docket you'll get on pretty soon, at least before I will. Then after everybody's had a good laugh, I'll bring my I-talian on."

"Isn't *she* Italian?" asked Jimmy, indicating the whore with a slight movement of his pipe.

"Yeah. But she's married to a nigger."

"O.K.," said Jimmy, "we'll do it."

"What's that?" said the whore, who had been trying to listen all this time. "What are you two kikes whispering about anyway? What the hell's going on?"

"Shut up," said Jimmy, the stem of his pipe clamped far back in his mouth so that he could not say it as loud as he wanted. Ralph winked at him and left the room. "Now listen," he said to Philomena Brown, getting up from his desk and walking over to where she still sat against the wall. "If you got a story, you better tell me quick because we're going out there soon and I want you to know I ain't telling no lies for you."

"I don't want you on my case anyway, kike," said Philomena Brown.

"It ain't what *you* want. It's what the old man out there says you gotta do. Now if you got a story let's have it *now*."

"I'm a file clerk. I was just looking for work."

"Like *hell!* Don't give *me* that shit. When was the last time you had your shots?"

"I ain't never had none," said Mrs. Brown.

Now they could hear the Clerk, beyond the door, calling the Italian boy into court. They would have to go out in a few minutes. "Forget the story," he told her. "Just pull your dress down some and wipe some of that shit off your eyes. You look like hell."

"I don't want you on the case, Moses," said Mrs. Brown.

"Well you got me," said Jimmy. "You got me whether you want me or not." Jimmy paused, put his pipe in his coat pocket, and then said: "And my name is *Mr. Mulligan!*"

The woman did not say anything more. She settled her weight in the chair and made it creak.

"Now let's get in there," said Jimmy.

II

The Judge was in his Monday morning mood. He was very ready to be angry at almost anyone. He glared at the Court Clerk as the bald, seemingly consumptive man called out the names of six defendants who had defaulted. He glared at the group of drunks and addicts who huddled against the steel net of the prisoners' cage, gazing toward the open courtroom as if expecting mercy from the rows of concerned parties and spectators who sat in the hot place. Judge Bloom looked as though he wanted very badly to spit. There would be no mercy this Monday morning and the prisoners all knew it.

"*Willie Smith!* Willie Smith! Come into Court!" the Clerk barked.

Willie Smith slowly shuffled out of the prisoners' cage and up to the dirty stone wall, which kept all but his head and neck and shoulders concealed from the people in the musty courtroom.

From the bench the Judge looked down at the hung-over Smith.

"You know, I ain't never seen him sitting down in that chair," Jimmy said to one of the old men who came to court to see the daily procession, filling up the second row of benches, directly behind those reserved for court-appointed lawyers. There were at least twelve of these old men, looking almost semi-professional in faded gray or blue or black suits with shiny knees and elbows. They liked to come and watch the fun. "Watch old Bloom give it to this nigger," the same old man leaned over and said into Jimmy Mulligan's ear. Jimmy nodded without looking back at him. And after a few seconds he wiped his ear with his hand, also without looking back.

The Clerk read the charges: Drunkenness, Loitering, Disorderly Conduct.

"You want a lawyer, Willie?" the Judge asked him. Judge Bloom was now walking back and forth behind his bench, his arms gravely folded behind his back, his belly very close to pregnancy beneath his black robe. "The Supreme Court says I have to give you a lawyer. You want one?"

"No sir," the hung-over Smith said, very obsequiously.

"Well, what's your trouble?"

"Nothing."

"You haven't missed a Monday here in months."

"Yes sir."

"All that money you spend on booze, how do you take care of your family?"

Smith moved his head and shoulders behind the wall in a gesture that might have been a shuffle.

"When was the last time you gave something to your wife?"

"Last Friday."

"You're a liar. Your wife's been on the City for years."

"I help," said Smith, quickly.

"You help, all right. You help her raise her belly and her income every year."

The old men in the second row snickered and the Judge eyed them in a threatening way. They began to stifle their chuckles. Willie Smith smiled.

"If she has one more kid she'll be making more than me," the Judge observed. But he was not saying it to Smith. He was looking at the old men.

Then he looked down at the now bashful, smiling Willie Smith. "You want some time to sleep it off or you want to pay?"

"I'll take the time."

"How much you want, Willie?"

"I don't care."

"You want to be out for the weekend, I guess."

Smith smiled again.

"Give him five days," the Judge said to the Clerk. The Clerk wrote in his papers and then said in a hurried voice: "Defendant Willie Smith, you have been found guilty by this court of being drunk in a public place, of loitering while in this condition, and of disorderly conduct. This court sentences you to five days in the House of Correction at Bridgeview and one month's suspended sentence. You have, however, the right to appeal in which case the suspended sentence will not be allowed and the sentence will then be thirty-five days in the House of Correction."

"You want to appeal, Willie?"

"Naw sir."

"See you next week," said the Judge.

"Thank you," said Willie Smith.

A black fellow in a very neatly pressed Army uniform came on next. He stood immaculate and proud and clean-shaven with his cap tucked under his left arm while the charges were read. The prosecutor was a hard-faced black police detective, tieless, very long-haired in a short-sleeved white shirt with wet armpits. The detective was tough but very nervous. He looked at his notes while the Clerk read the charges. The Judge, bald and wrinkled and drooping in the face, still paced behind his bench, his nose twitching from time to time, his arms locked behind the back. The soldier was charged with assault and battery with a dangerous weapon on a police officer; he remained standing erect and silent, looking off into the space behind the Judge until his lawyer, a plump, greasy black man in his late fifties, had heard the charge and motioned for him to sit. Then he placed himself beside his lawyer and put his cap squarely in front of him on the table.

The big-bellied black detective managed to get the police officer's name, rank and duties from him, occasionally glancing over at the table where the defendant and his lawyer sat, both hard-faced and cold. He shuffled through his notes, paused, looked up at the Judge, and then said to the white officer: "Now, Officer Bergin, would you tell the Court in your own words what happened?"

The white policeman put his hands together in a prayer-like gesture on the stand. He looked at the defendant whose face was set and whose eyes were fixed on the officer's hands. "We was on duty on the night of July twenty-seventh driving around the Lafayette Street area when we got a call to proceed to the Lafayette Street subway station because there was a crowd gathering there and they thought it might be a riot. We proceeded there, Officer Biglow and me, and when we got there sure enough there was a crowd of colored people running up and down the street and making noise and carrying on.

We didn't pull our guns because they been telling us all summer not to do that. We got out of the car and proceeded to join the other officers there in forming a line so's to disperse the crowd. Then we spotted that fellow in the crowd."

"Who do you mean?"

"That fellow over there." Officer Bergin pointed to the defendant at the table. "That soldier, Irving Williams."

"Go on," said the black detective, not turning to look at the defendant.

"Well, he had on this red costume and a cape, and he was wearing this big red turban. He was also carrying a big black shield right outta Tarzan and he had that big long cane waving it around in the air."

"Where is that cane now?"

"We took it off him later. That's it over there."

The black detective moved over to his own table and picked up a long brown leather cane. He pressed a small button beneath its handle and then drew out from the interior of the cane a thin, silver-white rapier, three feet long.

"Is this the same cane?"

"Yes sir," the white officer said.

"Go on, Officer."

"Well, he was waving it around in the air and he had a whole lot of these colored people behind him and it looked to me that he was gonna charge the police line. So me and Tommy left the line and went in to grab him before he could start something big. That crowd was getting mean. They looked like they was gonna try something big pretty soon."

"Never mind," said the Judge. He had stopped walking now and stood at the edge of his elevated platform, just over the shoulder of the officer in the witness box. "Never mind what you thought, just get on with it."

"Yes sir." The officer pressed his hands together much tighter. "Well, Tommy and me, we tried to grab him and he swung the cane at me. Caught me right in the face here." He pointed his finger to a large red and black mark under his left eye. "So then we hadda use force to subdue him."

"What did you do, Officer?" the black detective asked.

"We hadda use the sticks. I hit him over the head once or twice, but not hard. I don't remember. Then Tommy grabbed his arms and we hustled him over to the car before these other colored people with him tried to grab us."

"Did he resist arrest?"

"Yeah. He kicked and fought us and called us lewd and

lascivious names. We hadda handcuff him in the car. Then we took him down to the station and booked him for assault and battery."

"Your witness," said the black detective without turning around to face the other lawyer. He sat down at his own table and wiped his forehead and hands with a crumpled white handkerchief. He still looked very nervous but not as tough.

"May it please the Court," the defendant's black lawyer said slowly, standing and facing the pacing Judge. "I move . . ." And then he stopped because he saw that the Judge's small eyes were looking over his head, toward the back of the courtroom. The lawyer turned around and looked, and saw that everyone else in the room had also turned their heads to the back of the room. Standing against the back walls and along the left side of the room were twenty-five or so stern-faced, cold-eyed black men, all in African dashikies, all wearing brightly colored hats, and all staring at the Judge and the black detective. Philomena Brown and Jimmy Mulligan, sitting on the first bench, turned to look too, and the whore smiled but the lawyer said, "Oh hell," aloud. The men, all big, all bearded and tight-lipped, now locked hands and formed a solid wall of flesh around almost three-quarters of the courtroom. The Judge looked at the defendant and saw that he was smiling. Then he looked at the defendant's lawyer, who still stood before the Judge's bench, his head down, his shoulders pulled up towards his head. The Judge began to pace again. The courtroom was very quiet. The old men filling the second rows on both sides of the room leaned forward and exchanged glances with each other up and down the row. "Oh hell," Jimmy Mulligan said again.

Then the Judge stopped walking. "Get on with it," he told the defendant's lawyer. "There's justice to be done here."

The lawyer, whose face was now very greasy and wet, looked up at the officer, still standing in the witness box, but with one hand now at his right side, next to his gun.

"Officer Bergin," said the black lawyer. "I'm not clear about something. Did the defendant strike you *before* you asked him for the cane or *after* you attempted to take it from him?"

"Before. It was before. Yes sir."

"You *did* ask him for the cane, then?"

"Yes sir. I asked him to turn it over."

"And what did he do?"

"He hit me."

"But if he hit you before you asked for the cane, then it

must be true that you asked him for the cane *after* he had hit you. Is that right?"

"Yes sir."

"In other words, after he had struck you in the face you were still polite enough to keep your hands off him and ask for the weapon."

"Yes sir. That's what I did."

"In other words, he hit you twice. Once, *before* you requested the cane and once *after* you requested it."

The officer paused. "No sir," he said quickly. "He only hit me once."

"And when was that again?"

"I thought it was before I asked for the cane but I don't know now."

"But you did ask for the cane before he hit you?"

"Yeah." The officer's hands were in prayer again.

"Now, Officer Bergin, did he hit you *because* you asked for the cane or did he hit you in the process of giving it to you?"

"He just hauled off and hit me with it."

"He made no effort to hand it over?"

"No, no sir. He hit me."

"In other words, he struck you the moment you got close enough for him to swing. He did not hit you as you were taking the cane from him?"

The officer paused again. Then he said: "No sir." He touched his face again, then put his right hand down to the area near his gun again. "I asked him for the cane and he hauled off and hit me in the face."

"Officer, are you telling this court that you did not get hit until you tried to take the cane away from this soldier, this Vietnam veteran, or that he saw you coming and immediately began to swing the cane?"

"He swung on me."

"Officer Bergin, did he swing on you, or did the cane accidentally hit you while you were trying to take it from him?"

"All I know is that he *hit me*." The officer was sweating now.

"Then you don't know just when he hit you, before or after you tried to take the cane from him, do you?"

The black detective got up and said in a very soft voice: "I object."

The black lawyer for the defendant looked over at him contemptuously. The black detective dropped his eyes and tightened his belt, and sat down again.

"That's all right," the oily lawyer said. Then he looked at the officer again. "One other thing," he said. "Was the knife still inside the cane or drawn when he hit you?"

"We didn't know about the knife till later at the station."

"Do you think that a blow from the cane by itself could kill you?"

"Object!" said the detective. But again his voice was low.

"Jivetime Uncle Tom motherfucker!" someone said from the back of the room. "Shave that Afro off your head!"

The Judge's eyes moved quickly over the men in the rear, surveying their faces and catching what was in all their eyes. But he did not say anything.

"The prosecution rests," the black detective said. He sounded very tired.

"The defense calls the defendant, Irving Williams," said the black lawyer.

Williams took the stand and waited, head high, eyes cool, mouth tight, militarily, for the Clerk to swear him in. He looked always toward the back of the room.

"Now Mr. Williams," his lawyer began, "tell this court in your own words the events of the night of July twenty-seventh of this year."

"I had been to a costume party." Williams' voice was slow and deliberate and resonant. The entire courtroom was tense and quiet. The old men stared, stiff and erect, at Irving Williams from their second-row benches. Philomena Brown settled her flesh down next to her lawyer, who tried to edge away from touching her fat arm with his own. The tight-lipped Judge Bloom had reassumed the pacing behind his bench.

"I was on leave from the base," Williams went on, "and I was coming from the party when I saw this group of kids throwing rocks. Being in the military and being just out of Vietnam, I tried to stop them. One of the kids had that cane and I took it from him. The shield belongs to me. I got it in Taiwan last year on R and R. I was trying to break up the crowd with my shield when this honkie cop begins to beat me over the head with his club. Police brutality. I tried to tell . . ."

"That's enough," the Judge said. "That's all I want to hear." He eyed the black men in the back of the room. "This case isn't for my court. Take it upstairs."

"If Your Honor pleases," the black lawyer began.

"I don't," said the Judge. "I've heard enough. Mr. Clerk, make out the papers. Send it upstairs to Cabot."

"This court has jurisdiction to hear this case," the lawyer said. He was very close to being angry. "This man is in the service. He has to ship out in a few weeks. We want a hearing today."

"Not in my court you don't get it. Upstairs, and that's *it!*"

Now the blacks in the back of the room began to berate the detective. "Jivetime cat! Handkerchief-head flunky! Uncle Tom motherfucker!" they called. "We'll get *you*, baby!"

"Get them out of here," the Judge told the policeman named Bergin. "Get them the hell out!" Bergin did not move. "Get them the hell out!"

At that moment Irving Williams, with his lawyer behind him, walked out of the courtroom. And the twenty-five bearded black men followed them. The black detective remained sitting at the counsel table until the Clerk asked him to make way for counsel on the next case. The detective got up slowly, gathered his few papers, tightened his belt again and moved over, his head held down, to a seat on the right side of the courtroom.

"Philomena Brown!" the Clerk called. "Philomena Brown! Come into Court!"

The fat whore got up from beside Jimmy Mulligan and walked heavily over to the counsel table and lowered herself into one of the chairs. Her lawyer was talking to Ralph, the Italian boy's counsel.

"Do a good job, Jimmy, please," Ralph said. "Old Bloom is gonna be awful mean now."

"Yeah," said Jimmy. "I got to really work on him."

One of the old men on the second row leaned over the back of the bench and said to Jimmy: "Ain't that the one that's married to a nigger?"

"That's her," said Jimmy.

"She's gonna catch hell. Make sure they give her hell."

"Yeah," said Jimmy. "I don't see how I'm gonna be able to try this with a straight face."

"Do a good job for me, please, Jimmy," said Ralph. "The kid's name is Angelico. Ain't that a beautiful name? He ain't a bad kid."

"Don't you worry, I'll do it." Then Jimmy moved over to the table next to his client.

The defendant and the arresting officer were sworn in. The arresting officer acted for the state as prosecutor and its only witness. He had to refer to his notes from time to time while the Judge paced behind his bench, his head down, ponderous and impatient. Then Philomena Brown got in the witness box and rested her great weight against its sides. She glared at the Judge, at the Clerk, at the officer in the box on the other side, at Jimmy Mulligan, at the old men smiling up and down the second row, and at everyone in the courtroom. Then she rested her eyes on the officer.

"Well," the officer read from his notes. "It was around one-thirty A.M. on the night of July twenty-eighth. I was working the night duty around the combat zone. I come across the defendant there soliciting cars. I had seen the defendant there soliciting cars on previous occasions in the same vicinity. I had then on previous occasions warned the defendant there about such activities. But she kept on doing it. On that night I come across the defendant soliciting a car full of colored gentlemen. She was standing on the curb with her arm leaning up against the door of the car and talking with these two colored gentlemen. As I came up they drove off. I then arrested her, after informing her of her rights, for being a common street-walker and a public nuisance. And that's all I got to say."

Counsel for the whore waived cross-examination of the officer and proceeded to examine her.

"What's your name?"

"Mrs. Philomena Brown."

"Speak louder so the Court can hear you, Mrs. Brown."

She narrowed her eyes at the lawyer.

"What is your religion, Mrs. Brown?"

"I am a Roman Catholic. Roman Catholic born."

"Are you presently married?"

"Yeah."

"What is your husband's name?"

"Rudolph Leroy Brown, Jr."

The old men in the second row were beginning to snicker and the Judge lowered his eyes to them. Jimmy Mulligan smiled.

"Does your husband support you?"

"Yeah. We get along all right."

"Do *you* work, Mrs. Brown?"

"Yeah. That's how I make my living."

"What do you do for a living?"

"I'm a file clerk."

"Are you working now?"

"No. I lost my job last month on account of a bad leg I got. I couldn't move outta bed."

The men in the second row were grinning and others in the audience joined them in muffled guffaws and snickerings.

"What were you doing on Beaver Avenue on the night of July twenty-eighth?"

"I was looking for a job."

Now the entire court was laughing and the Judge glared out at them from behind his bench as he paced, his arms clasped behind his back.

"Will you please tell this court, Mrs. Brown, how you intended to find a job at that hour?"

"These two guys in a car told me they knew where I could find some work."

"As a file clerk?"

"Yeah. What the hell else do you think?"

There was here a roar of laughter from the court, and when the Judge visibly twitched the corners of his usually severe mouth, Philomena Brown saw it and began to laugh too.

"Order! Order!" the Clerk shouted above the roar. But he was laughing.

Jimmy Mulligan bit his lip. "Now, Mrs. Brown, I want you to tell me the truth. Have you ever been arrested before for prostitution?"

"Hell no!" she fired back. "They had me in here a coupla times but it was all a fluke. They never got nothing on me. I was framed, right from the start."

"How old are you, Mrs. Brown?"

"Nineteen."

Now the Judge stopped pacing and stood next to his chair. His face was dubious: very close and very far away from smiling. The old men in the second row saw this and stopped laughing, awaiting a cue from him.

"That's enough of this," said the Judge. "I know you. You've been up here seven times already this year and it's still summer. I'm going to throw the book at you." He moved over to the left end of the platform and leaned down to where a husky, muscular woman Probation Officer was standing. She had very short hair and looked grim. She had not laughed with the others. "Let me see her record," said the Judge. The manly Probation Officer handed it up to him and then they talked together in whispers for a few minutes.

"All right, *Mrs. Brown*," said the Judge, moving over to the right side of the platform near the defendant's box and pointing his finger at her. "You're still on probation from the last time you were up here. I'm tired of this."

"I don't wanna go back up there, Your Honor," the whore said. "They hate me up there."

"You're going back. That's it! You got six months on the State. Maybe while you're there you can learn how to be a file clerk so you can look for work during the day."

Now everyone laughed again.

"Plus you get a one-year suspended sentence on probation."

The woman hung her head with the gravity of this punishment.

"Maybe you can even learn a *good* profession while you're up there. Who knows? Maybe you could be a ballerina dancer."

The courtroom roared with laughter. The Judge could not control himself now.

"And another thing," he said. "When you get out, keep off the streets. You're obstructing traffic."

Such was the spontaneity of laughter from the entire courtroom after the remark that the lawyer Jimmy Mulligan had to wipe the tears from his eyes with his finger and the short-haired Probation Officer smiled, and even Philomena Brown had to laugh at this, her final moment of glory. The Judge's teeth showed through his own broad grin, and Ralph, sitting beside his Italian, a very pretty boy with clean, blue eyes, patted him on the back enthusiastically between uncontrollable bursts of laughter.

For five minutes after the smiling Probation Officer led the fat whore in a miniskirt out of the courtroom, there was the sound of muffled laughter and occasional sniffles and movements in the seats. Then they settled down again and the Judge resumed his pacings and the Court Clerk, very slyly wiping his eyes with his sleeve, said in a very loud voice: "Angelico Carbone! Angelico Carbone! Come into Court!"

A Policeman's Journal
T. Mike Walker

January 4

To begin a new year and a new life simultaneously, I woke up at six o'clock this morning, showered, shaved, and shit, brushed my teeth, and walked nude through the still dark hall of my house to the yellow cube of my kitchen, where I sliced two ripe bananas which I drowned in milk and sugar and gulped while listening to KJAZ on the FM and read, for perhaps the tenth time in two days, a letter from the Mayor congratulating me on passing the physical and mental exams and instructing me to report to the Hall of Justice at eight o'clock sharp for induction into the Police Department. I searched the raised gilt letterhead and bold black type and machine-stamped signature for some clue to the future, but the words said Nothing, formally, Nothing, with artificial warmth, Nothing, grammatically and cautiously—as bureaucratic messages have a tendency to do. Between the lines there was an immense whiteness, an emptiness which hinted Nothing. I finally crumpled it up and threw it in the trash-burner of the stove.

After working as a clerk-typist for the Police Department for a year during the day while going to college at night, I knew for certain only that now, at last, I would be able to go to college in the daytime and work at night—to finish college at last, and eventually to teach. I silently thanked Lieutenant Matches, who had been my boss in the Bureau of Identification, for suggesting that I try to double my salary and double my fun by joining the Department officially, rather than continue to slave as a "civilian" for $345 a month. My starting salary as a cop would be $765 a month, with raises every year; and since my wife Ann is pregnant with our second child, Matches didn't have to ask me twice. Even though my entire mental set is opposed to the business of police work, my life was such that I was no longer entirely free to choose.

Just so the record will be straight, I should say now that I am twenty-one, a father, a student of English, and terribly in debt. When I walked down the hall to the bedroom where Ann slept, soft and round beneath blankets which rose and fell like breath over her swollen stomach, slipping on my freshly starched and ironed white shirt and only tie and only suit, I felt a sense of anticipation and dread. But I shined my shoes with a cynical smile on my lips, knowing that the gleaming black leather would reflect my concern for trivia and would certainly impress whoever might care to be impressed by Nothing-neatly-done. After adjusting my simple tieclasp—a paperclip stolen from my old job with the Police Department —I pulled back the covers and kissed Ann on the forehead, then went into my daughter Pam's room, stumbling over toys in the half darkness, and kissed her too.

When I finally left the house, the sun was just beginning to burn the morning fog from the top of the Berkeley hills across the bay and the air was sharp with the taste of frost. I wiped moisture from the windshield of my car and drove down Army Street to the Freeway, then over to North Beach and the old Hall of Justice on Kearny Street. I parked in front of the Compass Bookstore on Clay, where my friend of the past year Martin J., the owner, a small, weathered, ex-merchant marine, had been trying for the past three months to talk me out of joining the Force. I locked the car and walked around the corner, up the marble stairs to the main floor of the Hall of Justice, which was both familiar and foreign to me this morning.

There were already several young men dressed in dark suits who leaned, comfortable and smug, against the marble walls in the large central hallway near the elevators, smoking cigarettes or chewing gum, talking quietly to each other like old friends. I didn't recognize any of them and felt terribly shy, though I suspected they were recipients of letters like the one I had burned. I said good morning instead to Henry Lew, the middle-aged Chinese elevator operator, who winked and called me "officer" and offered as a joke to take me up to the fifth floor Bureau of Identification as usual, as he had been doing for the past year. I declined and walked over to the blind newsvendor's stand and helped him open for the day, then thumbed through paperback books and magazines, stealing glances at the growing groups of young men who greeted each other with shouts of goodwill and warm handshakes. I felt alien, estranged, out of it; something kept stretching the skin around the edges of my eyes, trying to pull them around to the back of my head. I felt lonesome and awkward and loaded my pipe for protection, puffing on it until I gained enough courage to walk over to a group where I was the tallest person—being six foot three, and lean and pretty tough and healthy, since I had spent my lunch hours exercising on a City Prison mattress on the roof of the building for the past few months, getting brown. I asked them for the time and introduced myself, and within seconds I was shaking hands and trying to remember names and accepting a cigarette and my eyes snapped back into place again. I was in it, but not yet of it.

At eight o'clock sharp we were ushered into a courtroom on the main floor where we filed into hardbacked rows of wooden seats, shuffling our feet and coughing self-consciously until the Deputy Chief, dressed in a plain blue business suit, came out of the judge's chambers and delivered a five-minute warm-up speech of almost-welcome which ended with a threat, warning us that when we walked back out of that room we would no longer be merely citizens, but *servants*, not merely men, but *Police*-men, upholders of Law, Morality, and God's Inflexible Will. I smiled smugly to myself; I would not be intimidated by abstractions. Still, I trembled inwardly when he spoke of the need for religious unity among the brothers on the force, despite our varying creeds, and I had a vision of us tramping the streets armed not with revolvers and clubs, but with Bibles with which to bob burglars on their beans, and somehow the idea cheered me. Better than bullets!

Then the photographers from the town's three major newspapers entered the courtroom and set up their tripods, adjusting light meters and lenses, and a captain, all jowls and flab, stepped quivering onto the platform in front of the judge's bench. His heavy cheeks jiggled as he cleared his throat and adjusted his heavily gold-braided blue uniform over his paunchy form. He paused to polish his glasses on his sleeve, staring myopically over his bulbous nose at the crowd of men. His face was red and pockmarked with broken blood vessels and thin blue veins. His lips were moist and trembled against each other like globs of spit, but when he finally spoke his voice was strong, sharp, and edged with anger as he barked *"Attention!"* We leaped to our feet and stood as rigidly as rows of erections in front of our chairs.

The door to the judge's chambers opened again, and a short redheaded man stalked into the room, glittering and swaggering in his uniform like a one-man parade. His pale square face was freckled, and his small blue eyes gazed unblinking at us like two gray stones. His body was square and stocky, his movements measured and dramatic. He paused near the front of the platform with one hand resting on the table, nodded at the Captain and the Deputy Chief with a quick snap of his head, and fixed his attention completely on us.

"At ease, men," he snapped, and we collapsed suddenly, as if we had all ejaculated simultaneously. I whipped out my notebook and pen and glanced around. Every face was turned toward the Chief as he swept us with his cold gray gaze, meeting the glance of each man as if challenging us to deny his power, which no one did. The room was silent. One of the reporters coughed.

"Men," the Chief said, his voice choked with emotion, "I want first of all to congratulate you on passing the rigorous tests which allowed you to enter this, your chosen profession. Only one-tenth of the men who apply for this profession meet our high standards, and you men should be proud that you qualified. This is a profession. I want you to remember that. And you're here because you choose to be here."

His eyebrows lowered heavily at this point, and his face flushed dark.

"If any of you plan on thinking of it in any other way than as a *lifetime dedication*, you might as well leave this room now, because, men, the second after you are sworn in this morning, your lives will have changed *profoundly*. I can't impress this on you strongly enough. The eyes of the world will be upon you. Your mothers, your sisters, your wives and families and friends will suddenly be critical of your every act. Some will respect you, some will fear you, and that respect and that fear must be *earned*. Others will expect special favors, but *there will be no special favors*. Is that clear? I expect you to act as exemplary figures. I expect you to behave like the men you are and bring nothing but credit upon yourselves and your brothers on the force. And I'm here before you, by God, to see that you do!"

He slammed his fist on the table and took a step toward us, threatening, punching a finger in my direction.

"So let's get a few things straight right now. I'm here to make sure you toe the line, and it's a narrow line. The minute any one of you steps across that line, for any reason, I'll break you. Men, I'm a fair person. I believe in justice. If you go by the Book, if you're right in what you do, you'll find me behind you one hundred percent. But if you're wrong . . . God help you, because nobody else will. You read the papers. You know what's going on. You know that just this morning I came from a meeting where I was forced to break a man because he stepped over that line. It's bad business, men. What are his children going to say, now that he's disgraced, now that his picture is all over the front pages of every paper in town? Where can he get a job? So get this through your heads right now. I'm the boss. Nobody else. Each and every one of you will get your orders directly from me, down through the chain of command, which is only right. I will not stand for even minor infractions of the rules. Because they're *good* rules, men. You're going to be given the Rule Book before you leave here today, and I want you to memorize it, to live by it, to make it henceforth your second Bible."

He nodded to the reporters, who moved to the front of the stage with their cameras. I noticed that the Captain had been glowering at me throughout the speech, and I tucked my notebook back in my pocket and tried to look intimidated and frightened. The Chief turned on his toe and jerked his head again. The Captain sprang from his seat and brought the Chief a Bible, which he placed on the table. The Chief looked at us skeptically.

"I want you to know that if any of you thinks he disagrees with what I have said here, or if for *any* reason you have had second thoughts about this profession and have changed your mind, leave now. The door is open, and no repercussions will follow you, no stigma will be attached for doing it, and no questions will be asked. Right now you are free men, but the minute you take this oath you give up many of your rights as citizens, you give up your autonomy. Then it will be too late."

He glanced slowly around the room, and although there was some shuffling, some self-conscious coughing, nobody moved toward the door, which one of the Chief's assistants held open, smugly waiting. I thought of the money and held my tongue. The Chief nodded his head and the door was closed. The Captain shouted *"At-ten-tion!"*, each syllable popping like a firecracker, and we jumped to our feet and raised our right hands and repeated the oath after the Chief. Flashbulbs popped and fizzled. Then we filed forward to shake the Chief's hand, to measure the strength of his freckled fingers, to receive our Rule Books and badges and callbox keys from the Captain and an assistant, to be instructed tersely to proceed directly to the Police Academy in Golden Gate Park for further instructions. We were given an hour to get there.

I lit a cigarette in the hallway, shoved the Rule Book under my arm, dropped the callbox key into my coat pocket, and examined my badge, my new identity, no longer a name or a person with a will of his own, but Number Ninety-Seven. I turned the tarnished silver seven-pointed star in my hands and ran the tips of my fingers over the raised black letters which spelled out the name of the city in a semicircle above the number, with Police Department stamped in black below. I wondered how many other men had worn this badge before me and what they had been like and why they had given it up to me, and I sighed and dropped my new self into the pocket with the key and moved with my now-brothers who were yet strangers into the fourth day of this new year, which was stranger still. I had been reborn.

As I walked to my car, I decided to drop in on Martin J. in the Compass Bookstore and share part of this first morning with him, but Martin was bent suspiciously over a book at the counter in the dim back of the store and squinted at me over the rims of his glasses as I walked back to him and sat down on a stool. I fished my badge out of my pocket and slapped it down on the counter.

"You're under arrest, Martin. So talk with me for a minute."

Martin shook his head in disgust and pushed the badge toward me with disdain. He wiped his fingers on his shirt and ran his tongue over his lips.

"So? You have a number now and you feel pretty smug? I have a number too, did I ever show you?" He rolled back his shirtsleeve and held up his wrist to reveal a number tattooed neatly on his right wrist. "I'd rather have a name," he said. "You want coffee?"

"I *need* coffee," I said.

"So wait." He scooted back into his cramped kitchen to reappear in a moment with two demitasse cups and a steaming Turkish coffeepot of burnished brass.

He poured carefully to keep the thick muck on the bottom while I told him about the indoctrination ceremony and read from my notes, laughing at the way the Chief had tried to intimidate us through fear. But Martin sipped his coffee and glowered at me in silence. I spoke of the silly games we humans play and how we've constructed a hierarchy of fear from the Chief of Police and Mayor on down to the city janitors, but finally Martin lifted his hand a fraction of an inch and cut me off abruptly with a snort.

"Listen," he said, "I want to tell you something. You've been a *gendarme* for how long, ten minutes now? And already you sound like a fool. *Don't prejudge*. You don't know what you're talking about. A word of advice: Shut up and look around you, keep your eyes open and your mouth shut and remember everything. What you're talking now, it's just so much *dreck*. What do you know about fear? You're twenty-one, an American. I'll tell you, you've got that notebook there. If you write in it every day, keep a journal of your experiences, you might learn something. Maybe you'll even learn someday what fear *really* is if you're lucky. Who knows? Maybe more. But whatever else life is, it's not a game, Danny. It's life and death every minute, and if you don't pay attention, if you don't remember who you are all the time, that game will swallow you up the first time you turn your head. Watch out! I tell you this for your own good, even though I know you don't believe me. Men are weak, but those who work and who make it into high places the hard way like your Chief —do you even know what 'the hard way' is, you *schmuck?* —they're going to snap their fingers under your smart-aleck nose and make you jump through hoops whether you like it or not. What do they care about your 'education,' these men? What do they care about what you think? You're an instrument to them, a tool, and it's easy to give in to them, to compromise yourself, your beliefs, your dreams even. Watch out! I've warned you enough, but like most young people you listened with your ass instead of your ears, your ego instead of your heart. I only hope you survive. More coffee?"

He poured for me, and lit a nickel cigar, leaning back on his swivel chair, appraising me critically, as if viewing me for the first time. His hair was gray, peppered with black, and his gray mustache dipped over the edge of his cup as he sipped the thick black coffee. His anger seemed to subside for a few seconds, and he lifted his demitasse to mine and grinned suddenly, saying, "To Danny Tanner . . . may he survive!" But my mood was low and sober now, and the store smelled like leather and dust and ink and seemed to press against my brain. It was getting late and my day had hardly begun. I finished my coffee, thanked Martin, and left for the Academy.

The sun was burning away the haze that clung to the top of Twin Peaks, and my breath made ghosts in the brisk winter air as I climbed into my car and drove toward Golden Gate Park. I parked on Fulton Street, a block from the Academy, and walked toward the squat adobe structure fronted by a swatch of green lawn and a flagpole. The roof was an angle of thick red tile, and the open door was like a mouth between two windows which seemed to watch me like eyes as I approached. I pushed through two glass doors and then two large oak doors behind them into a classroom with perhaps fifty desks, a blackboard on the far wall behind a raised platform which held a lectern and a chair, a wall of windows on the left, and a long bulletin board on the right with official notices and wanted posters tacked to it. Against the back wall stood a large glass case which contained zip guns, enormous knives, brass knuckles, burglary tools, chains taped at one end, and wooden maces with spikes, all taken away from juveniles and displayed as an ominous warning.

A door at the rear led to the locker room. As I walked in, I found myself in a queue of men who were moving around a row of tables where revolvers, handcuffs, flashlights, holsters, and uniforms were on display. Another row of smiling men in suits and ties efficiently wrote in their order books, trying, like all salesmen, to sell us more than we could possibly need or use while we were still dazed by our new existence. And ignorant.

Lieutenant Matches had warned me not to buy any more than the bare essentials for the first year, to wait and see if I liked the job before I committed myself to much equipment. When my turn came I picked the cheapest revolver, a Smith and Wesson .38 which, although it cost only sixty dollars, could easily kill sixty thousand men if properly used. I picked through a display of arm-holsters, upside-down holsters, righthanded holsters, lefthanded holsters, groin holsters, flip-top holsters, etc., until I found a plain black simple old-fashioned low-slung hip holster that I liked. I moved on to a table full of handcuffs, where an argument raged between two salesmen and half a dozen cops over whether the heavier handcuffs were better, because they could be used as weapons in a pinch and could break the bridge of a man's nose if properly swung during riots or fights, or the lighter ones, because they were less of a burden to carry and just as strong but more expensive and lousy weapons.

Across the room, one fairly tall dark-haired boy with a long jaw and a crewcut grinned as he tried on a hat which was so small it sat high on his bristly hair and refused to respond to his tuggings.

Finally we were herded into the lecture room where we were seated alphabetically, as in high school. I wound up in the back of the room, a position I had always despised because I didn't feel obliged to pay much attention there; I felt, in fact, sneaky, and frequently had been sneaky in the past, but there was no appealing their decision. I found myself sitting next to the boy who had tried on the hat, Gene P., and we discovered that we were both married, that we both had children, that we had both been to college for a few years, and that we were both Superior Beings, far above the rest of the members of the class, and were comforted, I think, to find that we were not quite so alone.

The jowly Captain who had introduced the Chief earlier in the day reappeared at the lectern, scowling at us. He warned us not to wear our weapons until after we had been instructed in their proper use, and reminded us that while we were policemen *in fact*, we were not yet policemen in any other way, and that we were on one year's probation and could be dropped from the roll at any time without explanation, warning, or the possibility of appeal. He then told us to stay out of trouble, to stay at home at night where we belonged, to stay out of bars where Trouble lurked, to stay out of women unless we were married—in which case we were to stay out of other women, and he cited several humorously horrible examples of ex-policemen who hadn't, including the case of the man the Chief had fired that morning—and finally instructed us to be at the Police pistol range at Lake Merced near the zoo in the morning at 7:45 A.M. sharp, to wear old clothes and warm coats because it would be cold. At noon we were dismissed.

I declined an offer to have a beer with Gene, said good-bye at the door, and walked back to my car carrying my new equipment which, counting my uniform, came to a modest $375, which meant that I would have to last out the job a month at least, if only to pay for it all. I threw it in the back seat, except for the revolver, which I removed from its box. The tough plastic curve of the handle fit neatly into the palm of my hand, and I ran my fingers over the sleek steel-blue muzzle and listened to the clicks of the trigger as I revolved the chamber with one finger and held back the hammer with my thumb, just as I had watched John Wayne do a thousand times in the movies. This could kill a man, I mused, and the thought stayed with me for the rest of the day. It could kill a man, yes. But not by itself. It needed a human being to pull the trigger, a human brain to aim it, a human heart to hate enough to murder, and I wondered if I was capable of such an act. For the first time I realized that this was, as Martin warned, anything *but* a game!

Cry for Me
William Melvin Kelley

This is about my Uncle Wallace, who most of you know by his last name—Bedlow—because that's all they ever put on his records. I only got one of his albums myself. It has a picture of him on it, sitting, holding his two guitars, wearing his white dinner jacket, his mouth wide open and his eyes squinted shut. The name of the album is: *Bedlow—Big Voice Crying in the Wilderness* and I got it in particular because it has the only two songs he sang that I really like: *Cotton Field Blues* and *John Henry*. Besides that, I don't much like folk songs or folk singers. But I liked Uncle Wallace all right.

I guess I should tell you about the first time I met Uncle Wallace; this was even before he was folk singing, or maybe before any of us *knew* it. We just knew he was a relative, my old man's brother, come North from the South.

That was in June of 1957. We went to Pennsylvania Station to meet him. He sent us a telegram; there wasn't enough time for him to write a letter because, he told us later, he only decided to come two days before he showed up.

So we went to the station, and the loud-speaker called out his train from down South. A *whole* bunch of colored people got off the train, all looking like somebody been keeping it a secret from them they been free for a hundred years, all bulgy-eyed and confused, carrying suitcases and shopping bags and boxes and little kids.

My old man was craning his neck, looking to find Uncle Wallace. None of us would-a recognized him because when my old man come North twenty years ago he didn't bring but one picture of Uncle Wallace and that was of him when he was about seven. But my old man been back South once and saw Uncle Wallace a man. He would recognize him all right.

But I heard my old man say to my mother, "Don't see him yet."

And then we did see him; we could not-a missed him because he come rumbling out the crowd—the size of a black Grant's Tomb with a white dinner jacket draped over it (he had the jacket even then, having won it in some kind-a contest driving piles, or cutting wood)—and punched my old man square in the chops so he flew back about twenty feet, knocking over this little redcap, and springing all the locks on the four suitcases he was carrying, scattering clothes in all directions like a flock of pigeons in Central Park you tossed a rock at.

My old man is about six-five and two-fifty and works in heavy construction and I ain't never seen anyone hit him, let alone knock him off his feet, and I thought sure he'd go nuts and get mad, but he didn't; he started to laugh, and Uncle Wallace stood over him and said: "How you doing, Little Brother? I see you ain't been keeping up your strength. Use to have more trouble with you when I was six." And he reached out his hand to my old man, who got up, and even though he was on his feet still looked like he was lying down because Uncle Wallace was at least a head taller.

My old man said, "Never could beat you, Wallace. Pa's the only man could." And I remember figuring how to be able to do that, my Grandpa Mance Bedlow must-a been close to eight feet tall and made of some kind of fireproof metal.

Then my old man turned to us and said: "I'd like you to meet my family. This is my wife, Irene." He pointed at my mother. "And this is Mance; we call him Little Brother." He pointed at my brother. "And this is my first-born, Carlyle junior." And he pointed at me and I reached up my hand to Uncle Wallace before I realized he'd probably crush it. He took it, but didn't crush it at all, just squeezed it a little and smiled, looking down at me out tiny, red eyes in his black-moon face.

So we took Uncle Wallace home to the Bronx.

My old man got him a job with the same construction company he worked for, and the foreman, he'd send them both up on the girders and give them enough work for eight men and they'd get it done, and then they'd come home and Uncle Wallace'd watch television until one and then go to sleep. He never seen it before and it knocked him out.

He hadn't seen anything of New York but our house and the building he and my old man was practically putting up single-handed. That's why one Friday night, my old man said: "Carlyle, why don't you take old Wallace downtown and show him the city?"

I really didn't want to go; I mean, that's *nowhere,* getting stuck with a man could be your father, but I went.

First I took him to Harlem near where we used to live and we said hello to some of my old friends who was standing in front of a bar, watching the girls swishing by in dresses where you could see everything, either because the dresses was so tight over what they should-a been covering, or because there wasn't no dress covering the other parts. I guess Uncle Wallace liked that pretty much because everybody was colored and where we live in the Bronx, everybody is Italian. So in Harlem, he must-a felt at home.

Then we went to Times Square. I don't think he liked that too much, too big and noisy for him, him being right out of a cotton field. I was about to take him home, but then I said: "Hey, Uncle Wallace, you ever seen a queer?"

He looked down at me. "What's that, Carlyle?"

I was about to laugh because I figured maybe he ain't seen a queer, but I would-a thought *everybody* knew what they was. But then I decided just to explain—I knew how strong he was, but hadn't been knowing him long enough to know how fast he got mad. So I just told him what a queer was.

He looked down at me blank and sort of stupid. "No stuff?"

"I wouldn't lie to you, Uncle Wallace." I took him by the arm. "Come on, I'll show you some queers."

That's why we went to Greenwich Village.

It was comical to see him looking at his first queer, who was as queer as a giraffe sitting on a bird's nest. Uncle Wallace just gaped like he seen a farmer hitch a chipmunk to a plow, then turned to me. "Well, I'll be lynched, Carlyle!"

After that we walked around past the handbag and sandal shops and the coffee houses and dug the queers and some girls in sort of black underwear, and then all of a sudden, he wasn't with me no more. I turned all the way around, a little scared because if he would-a got his-self lost, I'd never see him again. He was halfway back up the block, his head way above everybody else's like he was standing on a box, and a look on his face like he been knocked up side his head with a cast-iron Cadillac. I ran back up to him, but by the time I got to where he been standing, he was most down some steps leading into a cellar coffee shop called *The Lantern*. I called to him but he must-a not heard me over the singing that was coming from inside. He was already at the door and a cross-eyed little blond girl was telling him to put a dollar in the basket she was tending. So I followed him down, paid my dollar, and caught up to him. "Hey, Uncle Wallace, what's the matter?"

He put his hand on my shoulder, grabbing it tight so I could hear the bones shift around. "Hush, boy." And then he turned to this little lit-up stage and there was this scrawny yellow Negro sitting on a stool playing the guitar and singing some folk song. He was wearing a green shirt open to his belly button, and a pair of tight black pants. What a queer!

The song he was singing was all about how life is tough—he looked like the toughest day he ever spent was when his boy friend didn't serve him breakfast in bed—and how when you're picking cotton, the sun seems to be as big as the whole sky. The last line was about how he'd pick all the cotton in the world and not plant no more and wouldn't have to work again and how he'd finally win out over the sun. When he finished, everybody snapped their fingers, which is what they do in the Village instead of clap.

Then he said: "And now, ladies and gentlemen, this next piece is another from the collection of Francis Mazer, a song he found during his 1948 trip through the South. A blues called *Wasn't That a Man*." He struck a chord and started to sing: something about a Negro who swum a flooded, raging river with his two sons and his wife tied on his back. He sang it very fast so all the words ran together.

Uncle Wallace listened through one chorus, his eyes narrowing all the time until they about disappeared, and then he was moving, like a black battleship, and I grabbed his coat so he wouldn't make a fool of his-self in front of all them white folks, but then I just let him go. It was his business if he wanted to act like a nigger, and I couldn't stop him anyway. So I just stood there watching him walk in the dark between the little tables and looming out in the spotlight, burying the yellow Negro in his shadow.

Uncle Wallace reached out and put his hand around the neck of the guitar and the notes choked off. His hand must-a gone around the neck about three times.

The yellow Negro looked up at him, sort of shook. "I beg your pardon?"

"Brother, you better start begging somebody's pardon for what you doing to that song. You sings it all wrong."

Then a bald man in a shirt with the points of the collar all twisted and bent come up and patted Uncle Wallace on the back, hard. "Come on, buddy. Let's move out."

Uncle Wallace about-faced and looked way down at him. "Brother, next time you come up behind me and touch me, you'll find yourself peeping at me out of that guitar."

The bald man took a step back. Uncle Wallace looked at the

yellow Negro again. "Now, look-a-here, colored brother, you can't sing my songs that way. You sing them like I made them up or don't sing them at all. And if you *do* sing them your way, then you may just never sing again, ever." He was still holding the neck of the guitar.

"Your songs? You didn't write these songs," the yellow Negro said. "They grew up out of the Rural Southern Negro Culture."

"Go on, nigger! They grew up out-a me. That song you was just singing now, about the man and the river, I wrote that song about my very own Daddy."

A couple people in the audience started to sit up and listen. But that little yellow flit of a Negro didn't believe it. "I tell you, these songs were collected in 1948 by Francis Mazer, and there's no telling how long they've been sung. I heard the original tapes myself."

Uncle Wallace's eyes went blank for a second. Then he said: "What this Francis Mazer look like? He a little old gray-haired man with a game leg?"

That stopped the yellow Negro for a while. "Yessss." He held onto the word like he didn't want to let it out.

"Sure enough, I remember him. He was a mighty sweet old gentleman, told me all he wanted to do was put my songs on a little strip of plastic. I asked him if he meant to write *all* my songs on that small space. He said I got him wrong, that the machine he had with him would make a record of them. And I said for him to go on. I was playing a dance and the folks was happy and I sang from Friday night until the next afternoon, and that little gentleman stood by just putting them spools in his machine and smiling. And when I got done he give me thirty dollars, U.S. currency, and I went out and bought me some new strings and a plow too." Uncle Wallace stopped and shook his head. "Mighty sweet old gentleman. And you say his name was Mazer?"

"This has gone far enough!" The yellow Negro was real ticked off now, sort of cross like a chick. "Arthur, get him out of here." He was talking to the bald man.

Uncle Wallace looked at the bald man too, sort of menacing. Then he looked at the yellow Negro. "I don't want you singing my songs *at all*." Then he just walked away, out of the lights and it was like the sun come up on the yellow Negro all at once.

But the bald man wouldn't let it stop there and said: "Hey, you, mister, wait!" He was talking to Uncle Wallace, who didn't stop because (he told me later) he never in his life got called *Mister* by no white man, so he thought the bald man was talking to someone else.

The bald man run after him and was about to put his hand on his shoulder, but remembered what Uncle Wallace said before and hot-footed it around in front of him and started to talk, backing up. "I'm Arthur Friedlander. I own this place. If you're what you say you are, then I'd like you to sing some songs."

That stopped Uncle Wallace, who told me once he'd sing for anybody, even a president of a White Citizens' Council, if he got asked. So he came to a halt like a coal truck at a sudden red light and looked down on Mister Friedlander and said: "You want me to sing?"

And Mister Friedlander said: "If you can. Sure, go on."

"But I ain't brung my guitars."

"He'll let you use his. Go on." He reached out sort of timid, like at a real mean dog, and took Uncle Wallace's arm and started to lead him back to the lights.

The yellow Negro, he didn't really want to give up his guitar, but I guess he figured Mister Friedlander would fire him if he didn't, so he left it resting against the stool and stormed off the stage.

Uncle Wallace and Mister Friedlander went up there and Uncle Wallace picked up the guitar and ran his fingers over the strings. It looked like he was holding a ukulele.

Mister Friedlander looked at the audience and said: "*The Lantern* takes pleasure in presenting a new folk singer." He realized he didn't know Uncle Wallace's name and turned around.

"Bedlow," Uncle Wallace said, sort-a shy.

"Bedlow," said Mister Friedlander to the audience.

A couple people giggled and a couple others snapped their fingers, but they was joking. Uncle Wallace whacked the guitar again, and all of a sudden music come out of it. I was surprised because way down deep I thought sure Uncle Wallace was just a fool. He didn't play right off, though, just hit it a couple times and started to talk:

"That song the other fellow was playing, I wrote that when my Daddy died, for his funeral. That was 1947. It's all about how when I was a boy we had a flood down home and where we was living got filled up with water. There was only one safe, high spot in that country—an island in mid-river. But none of us could swim but my Daddy, so he tied me and my brother on his back and my Mama, she hung on and he swum the whole parcel of us over. So everybody remembered that and when he was taken I made a song about it to sing over his trench . . ." He hit another chord, but still didn't sing yet, just stopped.

"Say," he said, "anybody got another guitar?"

Some folks started mumbling about him being a fake and stalling and a couple of them laughed. I was thinking maybe they was right.

A white boy with a beard come up with a guitar case and opened it and reached over a guitar to Uncle Wallace and so now he had two guitars. I thought he didn't like the yellow Negro's guitar, but he started to get them in the same tune—hitting one and then the other. And when he judged they was all right, he put one on his left knee, with his left hand around the neck like anybody would hold a guitar, and then put the other one on his right knee and grabbed the neck of that one with his right hand. His arms was way out and he looked like he was about to fly away. Then he clamped his fingers down on the strings of them both so hard and so fast they both sounded, not just a little noise, but a loud chord like an organ in church, or two men playing guitars. Then he started to stamp his feet and clamp his fingers and you could hear the blues get going and then he was singing . . .

Well, not really, because the most you could say about his voice was that it was on key, and it was sure loud! It wasn't deep and hollow, or high and sweet. It didn't even sound like singing. In fact, I don't think anybody ever heard him sing or really listened to him. It wasn't a voice you heard or listened to; it was a voice you swallowed, because it always seemed to upset your stomach. I heard him sing lots of times and it was always the same: not hearing anything, but feeling kind of sick, like you been drinking a gallon of wine, and the wine was fighting you inside, grabbing at your belly and twisting it around so you wanted to yell out, but didn't because you was scared the wine might take offense and tear you to pieces. And when he stopped and the grabbing stopped, you'd feel all weak and terrible, like maybe you would feel if you gotten a date with a girl you thought might give you some tail and you been thinking about it all day in school and then you went out with her and when you took her home, her folks was out, and so she took you inside and you *did* get some tail and now that it was all over, you wished she'd run inside and not given you anything because then it wouldn't be all over now and you'd still have it to look forward to. But pretty soon he'd start singing again and everything would be like it was before, feeling sick, and wishing you was *still* sick when you didn't feel sick no more.

So that's the way it was that Friday in the Village; that's the way it always was. And the people was always the same. When he got through grabbing at them, no one snapped their fingers; no one ordered anything. The cooks come out the kitchen and the waitresses sat down with the customers. People come down the steps and paid their money and managed to get into a seat before he reached out and caught them, and when the seats was all gone—because nobody left—people kept coming until they was standing and sitting in the aisles, packed right to the doors, and even on the stage with him, nobody moving or making a sound, just getting sick in the stomach and hating it and loving it all at the same time.

So Uncle Wallace sang right until Saturday morning at four. And then we went home and I slept all day.

That was how we found out what Uncle Wallace was, or did. But for a while after he sang that Friday, he didn't sing no more. It was like before: Uncle Wallace going to work, him and my old man building their building, coming home, and Uncle Wallace gassing himself on TV until one, then going to sleep.

But then the phone call came from Mister Friedlander and I answered it. He sounded real tired and said: "Hello? Is this the Bedlow residence? Do you have someone living with you or know of someone named Bedlow who sings folk songs?"

And when I answered the questions Yes, there was a silence and then I could hear sobbing on the other end of the line and through all the sobbing, him saying, "Thank God. Thank God," for about five minutes.

So at first I was about to hang up because I heard of guys calling up and cursing at women and all that mess, but then he said: "Who am I talking to?" I told him. "You were with that man who sang in my place four weeks ago? *The Lantern?* I'm Arthur Friedlander." So I said Hello, because I remembered him. He asked me what Uncle Wallace was to me and I told him.

"Carlyle," he said, "I've been trying to find your uncle for three weeks. I called Bedfords and Bradfords for the first two. It's like this, kid, every night a hundred people come into the place and ask for him and I have to say he isn't here and they get so mad they go away. He's ruining me! Where's your uncle now?"

I told him Uncle Wallace was at work.

"Listen, kid, there's a five in it for you if you can get him down here tonight by seven-thirty. And tell him I'll pay him thirty—no, make that fifty a week."

I said I could only *try* like I figured it might be hard to get Uncle Wallace to sing. Mister Friedlander give me his number and told me to call him back when I had an answer and hung up.

When Uncle Wallace come home, I said: "That man you sang for a month ago?—he wants you to come again . . . for money." I didn't have to add the money part because I could tell by his face, he was ready to go.

So I called back Mister Friedlander and told him we was coming. I said that to get Uncle Wallace to sing, which he hadn't wanted to do, I had to say Mister Friedlander was paying him seventy-five dollars a week.

Mister Friedlander didn't even seem surprised. He just said, "But you got him to come?"

"Yes, sir," I said.

"Good boy! I'm giving you ten dollars instead of five." Which is what I figured he'd do if I told him I had trouble.

When we turned the corner into *The Lantern*'s block there was a riot going on, with a hundred people, maybe even a thousand there, not all Village people neither. A whole bunch of them was in suits, and fur coats, and jewels. Man, if I been a pickpocket I could-a retired on what I could-a got there that night. And there was cops in their green cars with flashing lights going off and on, and on horses. Folks was pushing each other into the gutter and throwing punches. I looked up at Uncle Wallace and said: "Hey, we better split. We ain't got nothing to do with this, and you know how cops pick on colored folks."

"But I promised the man I'd sing, Carlyle," he said. But I could tell it wasn't that: he just wanted to sing, promise or no promise.

So we tried to sneak around behind all the rioting to get into *The Lantern*. And we most made it, but someone said: "Is that him?"

And someone answered: "Got to be."

I poked Uncle Wallace and said: "Now we really better get out-a here. These white folks think you done something."

"What?" he asked.

"I don't know, but we better get out-a here, *now*." And I grabbed his arm and started to pull him away, out-a there. I could tell he didn't want to go; he wanted to sing, but I figured I had to keep him out-a jail if I could.

Then someone started to yell at us to stop and I turned around to see how big they was and if there was more than we could handle, because either Uncle Wallace could flatten them or we could outrun them. But it was Mister Friedlander, chugging up the stairs, yelling.

We stopped.

He got to us and said, "What's wrong?"

"They think Uncle Wallace did something. He didn't do nothing. We just got here. We don't know nothing about this riot."

"Come inside. I'll explain," Mister Friedlander said. So we went down the stairs and inside, and he locked the door.

The place was jammed! There was more people there than that first Friday night.

Mister Friedlander said: "After you called, I put a sign in the window saying: *Bedlow here tonight*. Those people, they're here to see him. That's what the riot is." Then he asked me if I read that New York Sunday paper which weighs so much and ain't got no funnies. I told him No.

"Well, that Friday night your Uncle Wallace was here, there was a guy here from that paper. And the next Sunday he wrote an article—wait, I'll show you." So he ran behind the counter and come out with this page of a newspaper that he got magnified around forty times and pasted on cardboard. At the top of the page was this title: *Big Voice Crying in the Wilderness*.

The article under it was about Uncle Wallace. It told all about that other Friday night and said that Uncle Wallace was a voice speaking for all the colored folks and that to hear him was to understand the pain of discrimination and segregation and all that kind of stuff, which seemed like a lot of B-S to me because I didn't understand Uncle Wallace hardly myself; I didn't understand why he sang folk songs when he could sing rock-and-roll or jazz. So how the hell could he by *my* voice or the voice of anybody like me? But that's what this writer said anyway.

When I looked up from the story I must-a been frowning, or maybe looked like I didn't get it, because Mister Friedlander grabbed me by the shoulders and shook me. "Don't you see? Your uncle is the hottest thing to hit New York since the Chicago Fire. He's a fad!"

And all the time he was telling me this, Uncle Wallace was standing by the window looking out at the people, not realizing this was all about him. That was when I started to dig something about him I never had before, and when I started to really like him and decided I'd have to look after him, even though he was old enough and big enough and smart enough to look after his-self: Uncle Wallace was innocent. To him you didn't sing for money, or for people even, but because you wanted to. And I guess the most important thing was that he wasn't some guy singing about love who never loved, or hard work who never worked hard, because he done all that, loved women and picked cotton and plowed and chopped trees. And even though he was in show business, he wasn't at all like anybody else in it. He was more real somehow.

Anyway, I could say he was better that night than he was before, but that wouldn't be really honest because I didn't dig his music so I don't know if he was better or not. I think the people liked him better, but I can't be sure of *that* either because when he finished, they was in so much pain, they never snapped their fingers for him, just sat staring, sad and hurting like before.

After he sung three sets and was sitting back in the kitchen drinking gin and fruit juice, this man come in with Mister Friedlander. "Bedlow, this is A. V. Berger. He wants to speak to you a minute."

This Mister Berger was five feet tall—tops—but weighed close to three hundred pounds, with black hair, straight and greasy. He was wearing a black wool suit—this was in midsummer now—with a vest and a scarf, which was black wool too. And the English this man spoke was fantabulous! I can only *try* to copy it. He hemmed and hawed a lot too so it sounded like:

"Mister Bedlow, (hem) I'm a concert producer. And (hem) I have been watching you perform. It seems quite likely that (hem) I can use you in a concert (hem) I'm staging at Carnegie Hall." He stopped there. I could see he was looking for Uncle Wallace to jump in the air and clap his hands. I knew what Carnegie Hall was, but I bet Uncle Wallace didn't. Mister Berger thought Uncle Wallace was playing it cagey.

"Mister Bedlow, (hem) I'm prepared to offer you a good price to appear in the show."

"What's it to be? A dance?" Uncle Wallace said. "Sure, I'll play for a dance. That's what I done down home."

"No, Mister Bedlow. You (hem) misunderstand. This will be a concert."

"Like what?" He turned to me. "Like what, Carlyle?"

"A concert, Uncle Wallace. That's when a whole lot of folks come and just sit and listen to you sing."

"You mean just like here?"

"No, Uncle Wallace. It's like a church." I was thinking about how the seats was arranged, but he didn't get me.

"But I don't sing church music, Carlyle. My songs is too dirty for church. They never let me sing in no church." He looked back at Mister Berger. "What kind-a church you running, mister, that they sing my kind-a songs in there?"

"(hem) I don't run a church, Mister Bedlow." Mister Berger looked sort-a bleak and confused.

"No, Uncle Wallace, it ain't in no church," I said. "It's in a big hall and they want you to sing for a couple thousand people."

"No stuff?"

"Yeah, sure," I said.

"That's (hem) right," said Mister Berger.

"Go on, Bedlow," chimed in Mister Friedlander.

So he did.

But that concert wasn't until October and Mister Berger asked him to appear in early July, so there was a lot of time in between, when Uncle Wallace was making all his records.

And there was that damn movie. It was about this plantation family and all their problems in the Civil War. It wasn't really such a bad movie, but Uncle Wallace made it worse. I mean, he was the best thing in it, but after he was on the screen you couldn't look at the movie no more.

The movie would be going on all right and then would come Uncle Wallace's scene. He be sitting on this log in raggedy clothes and they *even* had a bandana around his head. You know how they make movies about colored people in Hollywood; the slaves act like slavery was the best God-damn thing ever happened to them and all they did all day was sit around on logs and sing and love Old Master, instead of breaking their asses in his cotton field and waiting for the chance to run away or slit Old Master's throat wide open. But that wasn't the worst. Dig this! They made him sing *John Henry*. But it didn't matter. They didn't know Uncle Wallace. He started playing and singing, and when he got through, you had the feeling old John Henry wasn't no idiot after all. I mean, I heard some guy sing that song once and I said to myself: what an idiot this John Henry must-a been, killing his-self to beat a machine when he could-a joined a union, like my old man's, and made twice the money and kept the machine out.

But when Uncle Wallace sang *John Henry* you didn't feel that way. You felt like old John Henry was trapped and he had to do what he did, like when a fellow says your Mama screws for syphilitic blind men, you got to hit him; you don't think about it; it don't even matter if he joking or not, you just got to hit him even if he beats all hell out-a you. Well, that's what Uncle Wallace did to you.

So when them white folks come back on the screen with their dumb problems, and started kissing it up, you could see they was cardboard; you could see they was acting, and you got up and left out of there because you had to see real people again, and even when you got out in the street you sort-a felt like the people *out there* wasn't real neither, so what you did was go back in and stand in the lobby until the next showing, when Uncle Wallace come on again for his two minutes and you'd go in and see him. Then you'd walk out again to the lobby. There was always a whole lot of folks out there, waiting like you and not looking at you because you was as cardboardy to them as they was to you, and you'd wait for his two minutes again, and like that all day until you got too hungry to see.

After he made the movie he come back East and it was October and it was time for the concert at Carnegie Hall. And I guess you know what happened at the concert, but I'll tell it again and also some things I felt about it.

Mister Berger had-a told Uncle Wallace to play it cool and save his best until last, which meant that Uncle Wallace was to come out and sing a couple songs with only one guitar and then—bingo!—lay the two guitars on them. So they fixed me up in a tux and when the time come, I paraded out and give him the other guitar.

Uncle Wallace was tuning the second guitar when a voice come whispering up from the dark in the front row. "Hey, nigger, you the same one, ain't you."

Uncle Wallace squinted down, and there in the front row with all them rich white folks was this dark little Negro. There was a woman with him and a whole bunch of little kids, all shabby-looking, all their eyes shining like a row of white marbles.

"The same as what?" Uncle Wallace said.

And the voice come back. "The same fellow what played at a East Willson café in 1948."

"Yeah, I played there that year."

"There was one night in particular, when a cripple white man was taping you, and we all danced until the next day."

"Sure, it was!" Uncle Wallace snapped his fingers. "I remember you. You was with a *pretty* girl."

"You right, man. Here she is; my wife." He turned to the woman. "Honey, get up and meet Mister Bedlow." She did, and Uncle Wallace leaned over the edge of the stage and shook her hand. "Say, you know, I bought these big money seats because I wanted my kids to see you up close. Them is them." He pointed at the row of kids. "The oldest one, he's Bedlow. I named him after you because me and the wife wasn't getting on so good until that night." It was like they was all alone in that great big place, just those two down-home Negroes talking over old times. "And them others is Booker, Carver, Robeson, Robinson, and Bunche."

"Man, you do me proud. Pleased to meet you all. Say, you want to come up here and sit with me?"

"Now, you do *me* proud." So they all come up on stage like a row of ducks.

Then Uncle Wallace started to play and the littlest kid, that was Bunche—he was about three—he sat there for about one minute and then I saw him jump on his feet and start to do these wild little steps, just his feet moving like little pistons. Then the man got up and asked his wife to dance, and the next thing I knew, everybody was dancing—even me; I danced right out on stage—and all the rich white folks was on their feet in the aisles and their wives was hugging strangers, black and white, and taking off their jewelry and tossing it in the air and all the poor people was ignoring the jewelry, was dancing instead, and you could see everybody laughing like crazy and having the best old time ever. Colored folks was teaching white folks to dance, and white folks was dancing with colored folks, and all the seats was empty and people was coming on stage to dance. Then the other singers backstage come out and started to back up Uncle Wallace and we was all dancing, all of us, and over all the noise and laughing you could hear Uncle Wallace with his two guitars. You could hear him over the whole thing.

Then the air changed; you could feel it. It wasn't just air any more, it started to get sweet-tasting to breathe, like perfume, and the people started to run down the aisles toward the stage, and everybody on the stage started to dance in toward Uncle Wallace, and everybody, *everybody* in the whole place was sobbing and crying and tears was pouring down their cheeks and smearing their make-up and making their eyes red and big. I could hear Uncle Wallace singing louder than ever. The people was rushing toward him. They was all crying and smiling too like people busting into a trance in church and it seemed like everybody in the place was on stage, trying to get near enough to touch him, grab his hand and shake it and hug him and kiss him even. And then the singing stopped.

I pushed my way through the crowd up to his chair. The first thing I seen was his two guitars all tore up and smashed and the strings busted. Uncle Wallace was sitting in his chair, slumped over, his face in his lap. And this was real strange; he looked like an old, punctured black balloon, deflated and all. There wasn't a mark on him, but he was dead all right.

Mister Berger called in a whole bunch of doctors, but they just stood around shaking their heads. They couldn't figure out how he'd died. One of them said, "There isn't nothing wrong with him, except he's dead."

Now I know this'll sound lame to you, but I don't think anything killed him except maybe at that second, he'd done everything that he ever wanted to do; he'd taken all them people, and sung to them, and made them forget who they was, and what they come from, and remember only that they was people. So he'd seen all he wanted to see and there was no use going on with it. I mean, he'd made it. He got over.

It's kind of like that girl I was telling you about—the one who'd promised you some tail, and when you got it, you was sorry, because then you'd still have it to look forward to? Well, I think it's like that: getting tail and coming out of her house and there ain't nothing but pussycats and garbage cans in the street, and it's lonely and late and you wished you hadn't done it, but then you shrug and say to yourself: "Hell, man, you did, and that's it." And there ain't nothing to do but leave, because it's finished. But then there's something else. You're walking along and all at once you smile, and maybe even laugh, and you say: "Man, that was some *good* tail!" And it's a nice memory to walk home with.

DYING

Laughs, Etc.
James Leo Herlihy

Tom, don't you think I should tell Ceil and Harry about Friday night? Well, *I* do.

It was truly one of those I mean like (quote) great nights (underscore). And it came about with no help whatever, it just took place. That's East Village, I mean it's not the East Seventies. Things can still happen here, thank God we moved.

To wit: We have these really darling kids upstairs—three Boys. (Don't ask me what the "arrangements" are!) One of them, the blond, with hair down to here and eyes that see other worlds, is sweet on me. Strictly Oedipus-type thing, I mean it's not *voulez-vous coucher,* he wants to be in my *lap!*

Which I, Gloria of the barren marriage, see no harm in.

Tom, Tom, Tom, I'm not blaming *anybody* for the barren marriage, Ceil and Harry know we've chosen it thus, they know you're just bursting with seed. Pretty please, I'm trying to tell something, Tom, is nothing sacred?

Anyway!

I'm sitting here, gagging with boredom, at ten-thirty Friday night: Tom asleep in that chair, much as you see him now, mouth slightly open. *Very* attractive. Oh, Gloria wasn't bored. She was embalmed!

When *rap-rap-rap* on her chamber door, it's the blond one, Could he have some ice cubes, please. Looking like an archangel and his name is Michael! Can you bear it?

Nor can I.

So, just on an impulse, No, I said, I won't let you have a single cube, but you may have a drink.

Oh but, said he, finger pointing toward Heaven, I have these friends up there.

Ah well, the more angels the better, Go fetch them, I said. And while he was upstairs fetching I telephoned the liquor store.

Oh. Oh thank you, Tom, for that wonderfully salty contribution to my tale. Ceil and Harry are so grateful to hear all about the liquor bill. Now back to sleep, don't exhaust yourself, and we'll just see if I can't somehow manage to limp through without all this detailed assistance.

So.

I no more than hang up the phone when the parade begins. This lovely airborne parade. Angels and archangels. Cherubim and seraphim. All manner of winged creature, lighting gracefully on the furniture.

Slight hyperbole here: there were only three actually. Three Boys.

And this curious girl.

A dreadful little stump of a thing named Jo-Anne. All hair and horn rims. Truly. All you could see was its smock, its little fists, with ud-cray galore under its fingernails, *ça va sans dire*, and the most formidable hair. Virtually you could not see its face without trespassing. I haven't to this day the faintest notion of what the child looked like.

And yet, in retrospect, she managed, without speaking so much as a word that anyone heard, mind you, she saw to it that she became the star of the evening. Truly! This unappetizing little bitch!

Wait! Wait! I have to tell things in my own way.

All right: I knew she'd been living up there with The Three, because I'd been seeing her for a couple of weeks, darting about the halls with pathetic little grocery bags. Making Herself Useful, I suppose. It seems Michael the Archangel had found her in the street in front of the Dom one morning at dawn, just sitting there inside of all this hair, and brought her home to make a little sister of her. Apparently they adore having little sisters.

(And mothers, a-ha-ha.)

So at one point, on ze glorious Friday night, Michael follows me to what we laughingly call the bar, that sad little tea wagon there, and wants to know what I think of his Jo-Anne. And I said, Michael, I haven't even seen her yet, what is all that hair about?

He looked at me with these ghost-blue eyes (Ceil, you'd faint!), and he said, perfectly serious, Jo-Anne's in hiding. From herself.

Oh, you idiot, Harry, of course I didn't laugh. What *am* I? Granted, inside, in here where it counts, I was splitting. But not a flicker did I show.

Then Michael said, Gloria, I hope you'll try to bring her out, will ya? Try to get to know her a little? She's very worthwhile, she has all kinds of original thoughts, insights, ideas, she has her own little window on the world.

(Window! I thought; what the poor thing needs is a periscope!)

In any case, I was distinctly uneager, shall we say, to enter that red, unwashed wigwam. Treasure trove or no.

But anyway there we all were, having our otherwise memorable and splendid Friday night: one of the Boys was doing perfectly thrilling things with his hands, an entire puppet show without puppets, *unbelievably* touching. And it was all wonderfully gay.

But a little too much so for Tom. Gay he doesn't mind if it's mixed, *un peu*. So I get on the blower once more and call Tom *deuxième*, who stage-manages at this coffeehouse over here, you know the one, Café Something, off-off-off-*off*-Broadway?

Seconds later in traipses he with the entire cast of this terribly integrated revue. And then Tom, my Tom, Tom *première*, really perks up. Tom likes Africans. Oh, he does he does he does! When I'm suntanned he can't keep his hands to himself. The dark shadow of Mama or something!

Oh look! Look! That brought him to life again! The sound of his own libido always does it. I have the most self-referencing husband in the world, I wish there were a contest I could enter him in.

Back to sleep, tiger.

Well now, with all this utter variety going on all over the place, I think—selfless being that I am—of all my dear square friends uptown. And I want them with me. I want them to see that Life Can Be Beautiful. So, on the blower again, dialing my fingies right down to the knuckles. *Come at once!* I shout to all and sundry; laughs, etc., at Gloria's. And Tom's.

I did call you!

Tom, how many times in all did I call Ceil and Harry? Eight, or was it only twenty?

Well, if people are mad enough to entomb themselves at the cinema on the first really brilliant night of the summer . . .

It was glorious. It was balmly. It was heaven replete with angels. All you could smell was life—and perhaps a little pot, ha-ha. We threw open that door to the fire escape, every window in the place, even the skylight, and let everyone flow at will.

Talk about heterogeneous! We had everything. Plus these

performers. Oh, I grant you the revue itself stunk! (But isn't that always the way? By the time anything gets on the boards in this town, it's packaged to extinction.) But the kids! Themselves! The talent could kill you! I won't tell you about this one singer, not yet, I'm *saving* that! You'll die.

Where am I, for godsake?

Oh yes, the gnome. Jo-Anne.

At odd intervals throughout the evening or shall I say night, out of the corner of my eye, I catch its little act.

Nothing.

In short, it sits. A perfect lump. Inside of itself. Occasionally Michael goes over to it, puts his angel nose inside this disastrous hair and whispers to it. It whispers back. He puts his arm around it. He takes it to the roof for a breath of air. He guides it across the room to meet someone. He gives it a Coca-Cola.

(*Nota bene:* It doesn't drink hard liquor. Oh, no, not at all, my dears! Nothing so simple! *Wait* till you hear what's coming up!)

Now let's do a little montage of time pressing on: Me, this very matron you see before you, doing a watusi with the puppeteer (and quite good actually); Michael, trying to get his little catatonic to dance; Tom here, trying to get a little something *else* going on the roof.

He didn't hear that, just as well, I'd better whisper: Yes, my Tom, Tom *première, not* cohabiting with Africans on the fire escape, and *not* very pleased about it. No thank you, said Miss Ghana. A stunning thing she was, too, *imperial*, and quite an artist of the put-down apparently. Tom doesn't know I had a full report.

What, Tom? Nothing, baby, you're just sensitive. Now nod off for Mama; that's it.

Isn't he heaven?

So! Emergency time! Michael, the guardian angel of the gnome, backs Mama into the bedroom! Yes, *me!* Too good to be true, surely!

Alas it *was* too good to be true: he didn't want Gloria, he wanted money.

Thirty-five smackeroos. Which is not thirty-five cents, need I add.

Good heavens, Michael, replied I, that's a great deal of money.

Oh, but he simply *had* to have it!

Frankly, he didn't look like he was kidding either, he was white as a sheet.

I said, Michael, are you in some kind of trouble?

No, but a friend of mine is, he said.

(Big light flashes on.)

Jo-Anne? I said.

Yes, she's sick, she's very sick. She's got to have some (and there was ever-so-tiny a pause) some attention! he said. She's got to have some *attention!*

(*Kleig* lights flash on.)

Drugs? I said.

Michael nodded.

H? I said.

H, he said.

And you want *me* to put up the thirty-five dollars to get her through this one?

You've got to, he said.

I've got to, I thought. My back went up. I adore this boy, but I don't *got to* anything of the kind. My poor Tom here works like a Trojan for thirty-five dollars, I felt guilty enough pouring out his good liquor for these young snot-noses. Which they swill happily, all the while I'm sure silently putting down Tom for being such a square as to actually practice anything so dreary as the law so he can come *up* with the money to finance a party. For them.

Frankly, it made me cross.

But Gloria did not blow her cool. All she said was, Michael darling, why have I got to? *I* can't afford such expensive vices myself, why must I support Jo-Anne's?

Because she's beautiful, he said. Because she's a human being. Because she's dying.

Dear Michael, I said, get her to a doctor at once if she's dying, don't come to me!

He said, Doctors file reports and Jo-Anne's too young to have her life ruined.

Well, yes, I said, there is a question of legality, isn't there. And you're asking me to involve myself? Please, I urged him, get the girl to a doctor!

(To be perfectly honest, I wanted her out of my house.)

He said he bet I wasn't so worried about legality at income tax time, or when I wanted an abortion. (He had me there! But of course the two things are not comparable!)

In any case he was furious, he absolutely *turned* on me!

Screw doctors, he said, screw cops, screw legislators, screw society! All she needs right now is one human being.

With which he turned on his heel and left the room.

I, of course, was the enemy.

Well, I went into ze dainty powder room and did what I could with a little cold water applied to the face. I'm damned, I said, if my night's going to be wrecked by that hirsute little junkie! Oh, I felt sorry for her, God knows, but there was just one teensy little question: *Whose* problem was it? Mine?

The answer to that didn't seem *too* tricky to me, so I went in and poured myself a good stiff one.

As a matter of fact, I think I'll fill this thing up right now.

Oh, would you, Harry? Thank you. Right to the top, and not too much ice.

No no no, the Scotch, damn it!

I did not shout.

So! Another montage. *Le temps marche,* it's now Saturday A.M., party still in progress.

I only remember seeing Michael once more, he was passing through the dining room saying, Is there a human being in the house, is there a human being in the house—looking bitter and grave and fugitive from Heaven; and that's the last I saw of him. Until . . .

Oh, but I know what's next: this song thing!

I won't be able to do justice to it, it's one of those things where you have to be there.

But I'll try:

At some juncture or other—I'm none too clear about time sequences—I came out of the bathroom and heard this fabulous silence. Everybody, all these young, wild things, standing stock-still, not uttering a sound. Well, well, wonders me, what's going on here?

Then I heard!

This singer was out on the fire escape. Singing to the rooftops.

You know that song from *Fantasticks:* try to remember a something September when nights are something and something is something else?

Well, this boy, an Italian, one of those three angels from above, with the most glorious tenor voice!

No! No, I'm wrong! *Not* really glorious! *Not* a great voice!

Merely perfect! Perfect for *that* song at *that* moment on *that* fire escape on *that* Friday night.

And everybody knew it. There was this enormous, collective

sharing of something truly magical, and not a soul was excluded.

But that's not all. Something happened to top it.

You know where the end of the song goes: *Follow follow follow?*

Well! Just as he got to that part, there was a new voice! A woman's. We don't know where she was. We don't know who she was. We couldn't even see her. She was in some other building, way-way-way across the courtyards, leaning out of some dirty little window I suppose. And when our tenor was through, she picked it up in her sad little penny whistle of a voice; she sang: *Follow follow follow.*

I cried. Me, who doesn't cry any more. I cried. I'm crying now!

Everybody did. It was as if we were all seven, and pure again, and taking our first Holy Communion. Together. There was this feeling of the Oneness of humanity, the sort of thing Dostoevski raved about.

Excuse me, let me blow this nose.

Honestly, Ceil and Harry, I just adore this neighborhood. *So* it's noisy, *so* it's bearded and unwashed, *so* there are no taxis. You *take* all that, because it's alive!

Even if you are held responsible for murdering all the junkies. Don't you love that kind of thinking? It's terribly popular now. Some Negro playwright started it: the claim is that I, Gloria, personally adjusted the rope around every black neck that's been strung up in the U.S.A. for the last one hundred years. And of course it follows that this same dreadful Gloria is responsible for shelling out thirty-five smackeroos to save the life of every drug fiend in Manhattan!

Madly logical, don't you think?

Tom and I are strictly from Squaresville, we happen to think charity starts right here, we sort of look after each other first and foremost, don't we, sleeping beauty?

Never mind, dear, not important.

What?

The girl? Jo-Anne?

Well, I *said!*

Harry, *I did!*

Didn't I? Well, I know I did, I must have, that's what I've been going on and on about.

Forgive me, then, I *thought* I *said:* the poor little thing did indeed die.

Tom and I felt wretched, as you can imagine.

She died the next afternoon. I guess they were trying to do the withdrawal bit upstairs, you know, home style? And it just plain did not work.

I saw Michael in the hall that evening and he delivered the bare facts, looking—you guessed it, homesick for Paradise—and *so* tragic. And pointedly *not* saying I told you so.

I still adore him. It's just that once in a while he makes me a teensy bit cross.

Daddy Wolf
James Purdy

You aren't the first man to ask me what I am doing so long in the phone booth with the door to my flat open and all. Let me explain something, or if you want to use the phone, I'll step out for a minute, but I am trying to get Operator to reconnect me with a party she just cut me off from. If you're not in a big hurry would you let me just try to get my party again.

See I been home 2 days now just looking at them 2 or 3 holes in the linoleum in my flat, and those holes are so goddam big now—you can go in there and take a look—those holes are so goddam big that I bet my kid, if he was still here, could almost put his leg through the biggest one.

Maybe of course the rats don't use the linoleum holes as entrances or exits. They could come through the calcimine in the wall. But I kind of guess and I bet the super for once would back me up on this, the rats are using the linoleum holes. Otherwise what is the meaning of the little black specks in and near each hole in the linoleum. I don't see how you could ignore the black specks there. If they were using the wall holes you would expect black specks there, but I haven't found a single one.

The party I was just talking to on the phone when I got cut off was surprised when I told her how the other night after my wife and kid left me I came in to find myself staring right head-on at a fat, I guess a Mama rat, eating some of my uncooked cream of wheat. I was so took by surprise that I did not see which way she went out. She ran, is all I can say, the minute I come into the room.

I had no more snapped back from seeing the Mama rat when a teeny baby one run right between my legs and disappeared ditto.

I just stood looking at my uncooked cream of wheat knowing I would have to let it go to waste.

It was too late that evening to call the super or anybody and I know from a lot of sad experience how sympathetic he would be, for the rats, to quote him, is a *un-avoidable probability* for whatever party decides to rent one of these you-know-what linoleum apartments.

If you want something better than some old you-know-what linoleum-floor apartments, the super says, *you got the map of Newyorkcity to hunt with.*

Rats and linoleum go together, and when you bellyache about rats, remember you're living on linoleum.

I always have to go to the hall phone when I get in one of these states, but tonight instead of calling the super who has gone off by now anyhow to his night job (he holds down 2 jobs on account of, he says, the high cost of chicken and peas), I took the name of the first party my finger fell on in the telephone book.

This lady answered the wire.

I explained to her the state I was in, and that I was over in one of the linoleum apartments and my wife and kid left me.

She cleared her throat and so on.

Even for a veteran, I told her, this is rough.

She kind of nodded over the phone in her manner.

I could feel she was sort of half-friendly, and I told her how I had picked her name out from all the others in the telephone book.

It was rough enough, I explained to her, to be renting an apartment in the linoleum district and to not know nobody in Newyorkcity, and then only the other night after my wife and kid left me this Mama rat was in here eating my uncooked cream of wheat, and before I get over this, her offspring run right between my legs.

This lady on the wire seemed to say *I see* every so often but I couldn't be sure on account of I was talking so fast myself.

I would have called the super of the building, I explained to her, in an emergency like this, but he has 2 jobs, and as it is after midnight now he is on his night job. But it would be just as bad in the daytime as then usually he is out inspecting the other linoleum apartments or catching up on his beauty sleep and don't answer the door or phone.

When I first moved into this building, I told her, I had to pinch myself to be sure I was actually seeing it right. I seen all the dirt before I moved in, but once I was in, I really SEEN: all the traces of the ones who had been here before, people who had died or lost their jobs or found they was the wrong race or something and had had to vacate all of a sudden before they could clean the place up for the next tenant. A lot of them left in such a hurry they just give you a present of some of their belongings and underwear along with their dirt. But then after one party left in such a hurry, somebody else from somewhere moved in, found he could not make it in Newyorkcity, and lit out somewhere or maybe was taken to a hospital in a serious condition and never returned.

I moved in just like the others on the linoleum.

Wish you could have seen it then. Holes everywhere and that most jagged of the holes I can see clear over here from the phone booth is where the Mama rat come through, which seems now about 3,000 years ago to me.

I told the lady on the phone how polite she was to go on listening and I hoped I was not keeping her up beyond her bedtime or from having a nightcap before she did turn in.

I don't object to animals, see. If it had been a Mama bird, say, which had come out of the hole, I would have had a start, too, as a Mama bird seldom is about and around at that hour, not to mention it not nesting in a linoleum hole, but I think I feel the way I do just because you think of rats along with neglect and lonesomeness and not having nobody near or around you.

See my wife left me and took our kid with her. They could not take any more of Newyorkcity. My wife was very scared of disease, and she had heard the radio in a shoe-repair store telling that they were going to raise the V.D. rate, and she said to me just a few hours before she left, *I don't think I am going to stay on here, Benny, if they are going to have one of them health epidemics*. She didn't have a disease, but she felt she would if the city officials were bent on raising the V.D. rate. She said it would be her luck and she would be no exception to prove the rule. She packed and left with the kid.

Did I feel sunk with them gone, but Jesus it was all I could do to keep on here myself. A good number of times at night I did not share my cream of wheat with them. I told them to prepare what kind of food they had a yen for and let me eat my cream of wheat alone with a piece of warmed-over oleo and just a sprinkle of brown sugar on that.

My wife and kid would stand and watch me eat the cream of wheat, but they was entirely indifferent to food. I think it was partly due to the holes in the linoleum, and them knowing what was under the holes of course.

We have only the one chair in the flat, and so my kid never had any place to sit when I was to home.

I couldn't help telling this party on the phone then about my wife and DADDY WOLF.

I was the one who told my wife about DADDY WOLF and the TROUBLE PHONE in the first place, but at first she said she didn't want any old charity no matter if it was money or advice or just encouraging words.

Then when things got so rough, my wife did call DADDY WOLF. I think the number is CRack 8-7869 or something like that, and only ladies can call. You phone this number and say DADDY WOLF, *I am a lady in terrible trouble. I am in one of the linoleum apartments, and just don't feel I can go on another day. Mama rats are coming in and out of their holes with their babies, and all we have had to eat in a month is cream of wheat.*

DADDY WOLF would say he was listening and to go on, and then he would ask her if she was employed anywhere.

DADDY WOLF, *yes and no. I just do not seem to have the willpower to go out job-hunting any more or on these house-to-house canvassing jobs that I have been holding down lately, and if you could see this linoleum flat, I think you would agree,* DADDY WOLF, *that there is very little incentive for me and Benny.*

Then my wife would go on about how surprised we had both been, though she was the only one surprised, over the high rate of V.D. in Newyorkcity.

You see, DADDY WOLF, *I won't hold a thing back, I have been about with older men in order to tide my husband over this rough financial situation we're in. My husband works in the mitten factory, and he just is not making enough for the three of us to live on. He has to have his cream of wheat at night or he would not have the strength to go back to his day-shift, and our linoleum apartment costs 30 smackers a week.*

I leave the kid alone here and go out to try and find work, DADDY WOLF, *but I'm telling you, the only job I can find for a woman of my education and background is this house-to-house cavassing of Queen Bee royal jelly which makes older women look so much more appealing, but I hardly sell more than a single jar a day and am on my feet 12 hours at a stretch.*

The kid is glad when I go out to sell as he can have the chair to himself then. You see when I and his Daddy are home he either has to sit down on my lap, if I am sitting, or if his Daddy is sitting, just stand because I won't allow a little fellow like him to sit on that linoleum, it's not safe, and his Daddy will not let him sit on his lap because he is too dead-tired from the mitten factory.

That was the way she explained to DADDY WOLF on the TROUBLE PHONE, and that went on every night, night after night, until she left me.

DADDY WOLF always listened, I will give him credit for that. He advised Mabel too: *go to Sunday school and church and quit going up to strange men's hotel rooms. Devote yourself only to your husband's need, and you don't ever have to fear the rise in the V.D. rate.*

My wife, though, could just not take Newyorkcity. She was out selling that Queen Bee royal jelly every day, but when cold weather come she had only a thin coat and she went out less and less and that all added up to less cream of wheat for me in the evening.

It is funny thing about cream of wheat, you don't get tired of it. I think if I ate, say, hamburger and chop suey every night, I would get sick and tired of them. Not that I ever dine on them. But if I did, I would—get sick and tired, I mean. But there's something about cream of wheat, with just a daub of warm oleo on it, and a sprinkle of brown sugar that makes you feel you might be eatin' it for the first time.

My wife don't care for cream of wheat nearly so much as I do.

Our kid always ate with the old gentleman down the hall with the skullcap. He rung a bell when it was supper time, and the kid went down there and had his meal. Once in a while, he brought back something or other for us.

It's funny talking to you like this, Mister, and as I told this lady I am waiting to get re-connected with on the phone, if I didn't know any better I would think either one of you was DADDY WOLF on the TROUBLE PHONE.

Well, Mabel left me, then, and took the kid with her.

It was her silly fear of the V.D. rate that really made her light out. She could have stayed here indefinitely. She loved this here city at first. She was just crazy about Central Park.

Newyorkcity was just the place for me to find work in. I had a good job with the Singer sewing-machine people in one of their spare-parts rooms, then I got laid off and was without a thing for over 6 months and then was lucky to find this job at the mitten factory. I raise the lever that sews the inner lining to your mittens.

I don't think it is Mabel and the kid leaving me so much

sometimes as it is the idea of that Mama rat coming through the holes in the linoleum that has got me so down-in-the-dumps today. I didn't even go to the mitten factory this A.M., and I have, like I say, got so down-in-the-dumps I almost felt like calling DADDY WOLF myself on the TROUBLE PHONE like she did all the time. But knowing he won't talk to nobody but ladies, as a kind of next-best-thing I put my finger down haphazard on top of this lady's name in the phone book, and I sure appreciated having that talk with her.

See DADDY WOLF would only talk with my wife for about one and a half minutes on account of other women were waiting to tell him their troubles. He would always say *Go back to your affiliation with the Sunday school and church of your choice, Mabel, and you'll find your burdens lighter in no time.*

DADDY said the same thing to her every night, but she never got tired hearing it, I guess.

DADDY WOLF told Mabel she didn't have to have any fear at all of the V.D. rate on account of she was a married woman and therefore did not have to go out for that relationship, but if she ever felt that DESIRE coming over her when her husband was gone, to just sit quiet and read an uplifting book.

Mabel has not had time, I don't think, to write me yet, taking care of the kid and all, and getting settled back home, and I have, well, been so goddam worried about everything. They are talking now about a shut-down at the mitten factory so that I hardly as a matter of fact have had time to think about my wife and kid, let alone miss them. There is, as a matter of fact, more cream of wheat now for supper, and I splurged today and bought a 5-pound box of that soft brown sugar that don't turn to lumps, which I wouldn't ever have done if they was still here.

The old gent down the hall with the skullcap misses my kid, as he almost entirely kept the boy in eats.

He never speaks to me in the hall, the old man. They said, I heard this somewhere, he don't have linoleum on his floor, but carpets, but I have not been invited in to see.

This building was condemned two years ago, but still isn't torn down, and the old man is leaving as soon as he can find the right neighborhood for his married daughter to visit him in.

Wait a minute. No, I thought I seen some action from under that one hole there in the linoleum.

Excuse me if I have kept you from using the phone with my talk but all I can say is you and this lady on the phone have been better for me tonight than DADDY WOLF on the TROUBLE PHONE ever was for my wife.

Up until now I have usually called the super when I was in one of these down-moods, but all he ever said was *Go back where you and Mabel got your own people and roots, Benny. You can't make it here in a linoleum apartment with your background and education.*

He has had his eyes opened—the super. He has admitted himself that he never thought Mabel and me could stick it out this long. (He don't know she is gone.)

But I won't give up. I WILL NOT give up. Mabel let a thing like the hike in the V.D. rates chase her out. I tried to show her that that was just statistics, but she always was superstitious as all get-out.

I judge when this scare I've had about the Mama rat dies down and I get some sleep and tomorrow if I go back to the mitten factory I will then really and truly begin to miss Mabel and the kid. The old man down the hall already misses the kid. That kid ate more in one meal with him than Mabel and me eat the whole week together. I don't begrudge it to him, though, because he was growing.

Well, Mister, if you don't want to use the phone after all, I think I will try to have Operator re-connect me with that party I got disconnected from. I guess as this is the hour that Mabel always called DADDY WOLF I have just automatically caught her habit, and anyhow I sure felt in the need of a talk.

Do you hear that funny clicking sound? Here, I'll hold you the receiver so as you can hear it. Don't go away just yet: I think Operator is getting me that party again, so stick around awhile yet.

No, they cut us off again, hear? there is a bad connection or something.

Well, like I say, anyhow Mabel and the kid did get out of here, even if it was superstition. Christ, when I was a boy I had every one of those diseases and it never did me no hurt. I went right into the army with a clean bill of health, Korea, home again, and now Newyorkcity.

You can't bullshit me with a lot of statistics.

Mabel, though, goddam it, I could knock the teeth down her throat, running out on me like this and taking the kid.

WHERE IS THAT GODDAM OPERATOR?

Hello. Look, Operator, what number was that I dialed and talked so long? Re-connect me please. That number I just got through talking with so long. I don't know the party's name or number. Just connect me back, will you please. This here is an emergency phone call, Operator.

Judgement Day
Flannery O'Connor

Tanner was conserving all his strength for the trip home. He meant to walk as far as he could get and trust to the Almighty to get him the rest of the way. That morning and the morning before, he had allowed his daughter to dress him and had conserved that much more energy. Now he sat in the chair by the window—his blue shirt buttoned at the collar, his coat on the back of the chair, and his hat on his head—waiting for her to leave. He couldn't escape until she got out of the way. The window looked out on a brick wall and down into an alley full of New York air, the kind fit for cats and garbage. A few snow flakes drifted past the window but they were too thin and scattered for his failing vision.

The daughter was in the kitchen washing dishes. She dawdled over everything, talking to herself. When he had first come, he had answered her, but that had not been wanted. She glowered at him as if, old fool that he was, he should still have had sense enough not to answer a woman talking to herself. She questioned herself in one voice and answered herself in another. With the energy he had conserved yesterday letting her dress him, he had written a note and pinned it in his pocket. IF FOUND DEAD SHIP EXPRESS COLLECT TO COLEMAN PARRUM, CORINTH, GEORGIA. Under this he had continued: COLEMAN SELL MY BELONGINGS AND PAY THE FREIGHT ON ME & THE UNDERTAKER. ANYTHING LEFT OVER YOU CAN KEEP. YOURS TRULY T. C. TANNER. P.S. STAY WHERE YOU ARE. DON'T LET THEM TALK YOU INTO COMING UP HERE. IT'S NO KIND OF PLACE. It had taken him the better part of thirty minutes to write the paper; the script was wavery but decipherable with patience. He controlled one hand by holding the other on top of it. By the time he had got it written, she was back in the apartment from getting her groceries.

Today, he was ready. All he had to do was push one foot in front of the other until he got to the door and down the steps. Once down the steps, he would get out of the neighborhood. Once out of it, he would hail a taxi cab and go to the freight yards. Some bum would help him onto a car. Once he got in the freight car, he would lie down and rest. During the night the train would start South, and the next day or the morning after, dead or alive, he would be home. Dead or alive. It was being there that mattered; the dead or alive did not.

If he had had good sense he would have gone the day after he arrived; better sense and he would not have arrived. He had not got desperate until two days ago when he had heard his daughter and son-in-law taking leave of each other after breakfast. They were standing in the front door, she seeing him off for a three-day trip. He drove a long distance moving van. She must have handed him his leather headgear. "You ought to get you a hat," she said, "a real one."

"And sit all day in it," the son-in-law said, "like him in there. Yah! All he does is sit all day with that hat on. Sits all day with that damn black hat on his head. Inside!"

"Well you don't even have you a hat," she said. "Nothing but that leather cap with flaps. People that are somebody wear hats. Other kinds wear those leather caps like you got on."

"People that are somebody!" he cried. "People that are somebody! That kills me! That really kills me!" The son-in-law had a stupid muscular face and a yankee voice to go with it.

"My daddy is here to stay," his daughter said. "He ain't going to last long. He was somebody when he was somebody. He never worked for nobody in his life but himself and had people—other people—working for him."

"Yah? Niggers is what he had working for him," the son-in-law said. "That's all. I've worked a nigger or two myself."

"Those were just nawthun niggers you worked," she said, her voice suddenly going lower so that Tanner had to lean forward to catch the words. "It takes brains to work a real nigger. You got to know how to handle them."

"Yah so I don't have brains," the son-in-law said.

One of the sudden, very occasional, feelings of warmth for the daughter came over Tanner. Every now and then she said something that might make you think she had a little sense stored away somewhere for safe keeping.

"You got them," she said. "You don't always use them."

"He has a stroke when he sees a nigger in the building," the son-in-law said, "and she tells me . . ."

"Shut up talking so loud," she said. "That's not why he had the stroke."

There was a silence. "Where you going to bury him?" the son-in-law asked, taking a different tack.

"Bury who?"

"Him in there."

"Right here in New York," she said. "Where do you think? We got a lot. I'm not taking that trip down there again with nobody."

"Yah. Well I just wanted to make sure," he said.

When she returned to the room, Tanner had both hands gripped on the chair arms. His eyes were trained on her like the eyes of an angry corpse. "You promised you'd bury me there," he said. "Your promise ain't any good. Your promise ain't any good. Your promise ain't any good." His voice was so dry it was barely audible. He began to shake, his hands, his head, his feet. "Bury me here and burn in hell!" he cried and fell back into his chair.

The daughter shuddered to attention. "You ain't dead yet!" She threw out a ponderous sigh. "You got a long time to be worrying about that." She turned and began to pick up parts of the newspaper scattered on the floor. She had grey hair that hung to her shoulders and a round face, beginning to wear. "I do every last living thing for you," she muttered, "and this is the way you carry on." She stuck the papers under her arm and said, "And don't throw hell at me. I don't believe in it. That's a lot of hardshell Baptist hooey." Then she went into the kitchen.

He kept his mouth stretched taut, his top plate gripped between his tongue and the roof of his mouth. Still the tears flooded down his cheeks; he wiped each one furtively on his shoulder.

Her voice rose from the kitchen. "As bad as having a child. He wanted to come and now he's here, he don't like it."

He had not wanted to come.

"Pretended he didn't but I could tell. I said if you don't want to come I can't make you. If you don't want to live like decent people there's nothing I can do about it."

"As for me," her higher voice said, "when I die that ain't the time I'm going to start getting choosey. They can lay me in the nearest spot. When I pass from this world I'll be considerate of them that stay in it. I won't be thinking of just myself."

"Certainly not," the other voice said. "You never been that selfish. You're the kind that looks out for other people."

"Well I try," she said, "I try."

He laid his head on the back of the chair for a moment and the hat tilted down over his eyes. He had raised three boys and her. The three boys were gone, two in the war and one to the devil and there was nobody left who felt a duty toward him but her, married and childless, in New York City like Mrs. Big and ready when she came back and found him living the way he was to take him back with her. She had put her face in the door of the shack and had stared, expressionless, for a second. Then all at once she had screamed and jumped back.

"What's that on the floor?"

"Coleman," he said.

The old Negro was curled up on a pallet asleep at the foot of Tanner's bed, a stinking skin full of bones, arranged in what seemed vaguely human form. When Coleman was young, he had looked like a bear; now that he was old he looked like a monkey. With Tanner it was the opposite; when he was young he had looked like a monkey but when he got old, he looked like a bear.

The daughter stepped back onto the porch. There were the bottoms of two cane chairs tilted against the clapboard but she declined to take a seat. She stepped out about ten feet from the house as if it took that much space to clear the odor. Then she had spoken her piece.

"If you don't have any pride I have and I know my duty and I was raised to do it. My mother raised me to do it if you didn't. She was from plain people but not the kind that likes to settle in with niggers."

At that point the old Negro roused up and slid out the door, a doubled-up shadow which Tanner just caught sight of gliding away.

She had shamed him. He shouted so they both could hear. "Who you think cooks? Who you think cuts my firewood and empties my slops? He's paroled to me. That no-good scoundrel has been on my hands for thirty years. He ain't a bad nigger."

She was unimpressed. "Whose shack is this anyway?" she had asked. "Yours or his?"

"Him and me built it," he said. "You go on back up there. I wouldn't come with you for no million dollars or no sack of salt."

"It looks like him and you built it. Whose land is it on?"

"Some people that live in Florida," he said evasively. He had known then that it was land up for sale but he thought it was too sorry for anyone to buy. That same afternoon he had found out different. He had found out in time to go back with her. If he had found out a day later, he might still be there, squatting on the doctor's land.

When he saw the brown porpoise-shaped figure striding across the field that afternoon, he had known at once what had happened; no one had to tell him. If that nigger had owned the whole world except for one runty rutted peafield and he acquired it, he would walk across it that way, beating the weeds aside, his thick neck swelled, his stomach a throne for his gold watch and chain. Doctor Foley. He was only part black. The rest was Indian and white.

He was everything to the niggers—druggist and undertaker and general counsel and real estate man and sometimes he got the evil eye off them and sometimes he put it on. Be prepared, he said to himself, watching him approach, to take something off him, nigger though he be. Be prepared, because you ain't got a thing to hold up to him but the skin you come in, and that's no more use to you now than what a snake would shed. You don't have a chance with the government against you.

He was sitting on the porch in the piece of straight chair tilted against the shack. "Good evening, Foley," he said and nodded as the doctor came up and stopped short at the edge of the clearing, as if he had only just that minute seen him though it was plain he had sighted him as he crossed the field.

"I be out here to look at my property," the doctor said. "Good evening." His voice was quick and high.

Ain't been your property long, he said to himself. "I seen you coming," he said.

"I acquired this here recently," the doctor said and proceeded without looking at him again to walk around to one side of the shack. In a moment he came back and stopped in front of him. Then he stepped boldly to the door of the shack and put his head in. Coleman was in there that time too, asleep. He looked for a moment and then turned aside. "I know that nigger," he said. "Coleman Parrum—how long does it take him to sleep off that stump liquor you all make?"

Tanner took hold of the knobs on the chair bottom and held them hard. "This shack ain't in your property. Only on it, by my mistake," he said.

The doctor removed his cigar momentarily from his mouth. "It ain't my mis-take," he said and smiled.

He had only sat there, looking ahead.

"It don't pay to make this kind of mis-take," the doctor said.

"I never found nothing that paid yet," he muttered.

"Everything pays," the Negro said, "if you knows how to make it," and he remained there smiling, looking the squatter up and down. Then he turned and went around the other side of the shack. There was a silence. He was looking for the still.

Then would have been the time to kill him. There was a gun inside the shack and he could have done it as easy as not, but, from childhood, he had been weakened for that kind of violence by the fear of hell. He had never killed one, he had always handled them with his wits and with luck. He was known to have a way with niggers. There was an art to handling them. The secret of handling a nigger was to show him his brains didn't have a chance against yours; then he would jump on your back and know he had a good thing there for life. He had had Coleman on his back for thirty years.

Tanner had first seen Coleman when he was working six of them at a saw mill in the middle of a pine forest fifteen miles from nowhere. They were as sorry a crew as he had worked, the kind that on Monday they didn't show up. What was in the air had reached them. They thought there was a new Lincoln elected who was going to abolish work. He managed them with a very sharp penknife. He had had something wrong with his kidney then that made his hands shake and he had taken to whittling to force that waste motion out of sight. He did not intend them to see that his hands shook of their own accord and he did not intend to see it himself or to countenance it. The knife had moved constantly, violently, in his quaking hands and here and there small crude figures—that he never looked at again and could not have said what they were if he had—dropped to the ground. The Negroes picked them up and took them home; there was not much time between them and darkest Africa. The knife glittered constantly in his hands. More than once he had stopped short and said in an off-hand voice to some half-reclining, head-averted Negro, "Nigger, this knife is in my hand now but if you don't quit wasting my time and money, it'll be in your gut shortly." And the Negro would begin to rise—slowly, but he would be in the act—before the sentence was completed.

A large black loose-jointed Negro, twice his own size, had begun hanging around the edge of the saw mill, watching the others work and when he was not watching, sleeping, in full view of them, sprawled like a gigantic bear on his back. "Who is that?" he had asked. "If he wants to work, tell him to come here. If he don't, tell him to go. No idlers are going to hang around here."

None of them knew who he was. They knew he didn't want to work. They knew nothing else, not where he had come from, nor why, though he was probably brother to one, cousin to all of them. He had ignored him for a day; against the six of them he was one yellow-faced scrawny white man with shaky hands. He was willing to wait for trouble, but not forever. The next day the stranger came again. After the six Tanner worked had seen the idler there for half the morning, they quit and began to eat, a full thirty minutes before noon. He had not risked ordering them up. He had gone to the source of the trouble.

The stranger was leaning against a tree on the edge of the clearing, watching with half-closed eyes. The insolence on his face barely covered the wariness behind it. His look said, this ain't much of a white man so why he come on so big, what he fixing to do?

He had meant to say, "Nigger, this knife is in my hand now but if you ain't out of my sight . . ." but as he drew closer he changed his mind. The Negro's eyes were small and bloodshot. Tanner supposed there was a knife on him somewhere that he would as soon use as not. His own penknife moved, directed solely by some intruding intelligence that worked in his hands. He had no idea what he was carving, but when he reached the Negro, he had already made two holes the size of half dollars in the piece of bark.

The Negro's gaze fell on his hands and was held. His jaw slackened. His eyes did not move from the knife tearing recklessly around the bark. He watched as if he saw an invisible power working on the wood.

He looked himself then and, astonished, saw the connected rims of a pair of spectacles.

He held them away from him and looked through the holes past a pile of shavings and on into the woods to the edge of the pen where they kept their mules.

"You can't see so good, can you, boy?" he said and began scraping the ground with his foot to turn up a piece of wire. He picked up a small piece of haywire; in a minute he found another, shorter piece and picked that up. He began to attach these to the bark. He was in no hurry now that he knew what he was doing. When the spectacles were finished, he handed them to the Negro. "Put these on," he said. "I hate to see anybody can't see good."

There was an instant when the Negro might have done one thing or another, might have taken the glasses and crushed them in his hand or grabbed the knife and turned it on him. He saw the exact instant in the muddy liquor-swollen eyes when the pleasure of having a knife in this white man's gut was balanced against something else, he could not tell what.

The Negro reached for the glasses. He attached the bows carefully behind his ears and looked forth. He peered this way and that with exaggerated solemnity. And then he looked directly at Tanner and grinned, or grimaced, Tanner could not tell which, but he had an instant's sensation of seeing before him a negative image of himself, as if clownishness and captivity had been their common lot. The vision failed him before he could decipher it.

"Preacher," he said, "what you hanging around here for?" He picked up another piece of bark and began, without looking at it, to carve again. "This ain't Sunday."

"This here ain't Sunday?" the Negro said.

"This is Friday," he said. "That's the way it is with you preachers—drunk all week so you don't know when Sunday is. What you see through those glasses?"

"See a man."

"What kind of a man?"

"See the man make theseyer glasses."

"Is he white or black?"

"He white!" the Negro said as if only at that moment was his vision sufficiently improved to detect it. "Yessuh, he white!" he said.

"Well, you treat him like he was white," Tanner said. "What's your name?"

"Name Coleman," the Negro said.

And he had not got rid of Coleman since. You make a monkey out of one of them and he jumps on your back and stays there for life, but let one make a monkey out of you and all you can do is kill him or disappear. And he was not going to hell for killing a nigger. Behind the shack he heard the doctor kick over a bucket. He sat and waited.

In a moment the doctor appeared again, beating his way around the other side of the house, whacking at scattered clumps of Johnson grass with his cane. He stopped in the middle of the yard, about where that morning the daughter had delivered her ultimatum.

"You don't belong here," he began. "I could have you prosecuted."

Tanner remained there, dumb, staring across the field.

"Where's your still?" the doctor asked.

"If it's a still around here, it don't belong to me," he said and shut his mouth tight.

The Negro laughed softly. "Down on your luck, ain't you?" he murmured. "Didn't you used to own a little piece of land over acrost the river and lost it?"

He had continued to study the woods ahead.

"If you want to run the still for me, that's one thing," the doctor said. "If you don't, you might as well had be packing up."

"I don't have to work for you," he said. "The governmint ain't got around yet to forcing the white folks to work for the colored."

The doctor polished the stone in his ring with the ball of his thumb. "I don't like the governmint no bettern you," he said. "Where you going instead? You going to the city and get you a soot of rooms at the Biltmo' Hotel?"

Tanner said nothing.

"The day coming," the doctor said, "when the white folks IS going to be working for the colored and you mights well to git ahead of the crowd."

"That day ain't coming for me," Tanner said shortly.

"Done come for you," the doctor said. "Ain't come for the rest of them."

Tanner's gaze drove on past the farthest blue edge of the treeline into the pale empty afternoon sky. "I got a daughter in the north," he said. "I don't have to work for you."

The doctor took his watch from his watch pocket and looked at it and put it back. He gazed for a moment at the back of his hands. He appeared to have measured and to know secretly the time it would take everything to change finally upsidedown. "She don't want no old daddy like you," he said. "Maybe she say she do, but that ain't likely. Even if you rich," he said, "they don't want you. They got they own ideas. The black ones they rares and they pitches. I made mine," he said, "and I ain't done none of that." He looked again at Tanner. "I be back here next week," he said, "and if you still here, I know you going to work for me." He remained there a moment, rocking on his heels, waiting for some answer. Finally he turned and started beating his way back through the overgrown path.

Tanner had continued to look across the field as if his spirit had been sucked out of him into the woods and nothing was left on the chair but a shell. If he had known it was a question of this—sitting here looking out of this window all day in this no-place, or just running a still for a nigger, he would have run the still for the nigger. He would have been a nigger's white nigger any day. Behind him he heard the daughter come in from the kitchen. His heart accelerated but after a second he heard her plump herself down on the sofa. She was not yet ready to go. He did not turn and look at her.

She sat there silently a few moments. Then she began. "The trouble with you is," she said, "you sit in front of that window all the time where there's nothing to look out at. You need some inspiration and an out-let. If you would let me pull your chair around to look at the TV, you would quit thinking about morbid stuff, death and hell and judgement. My Lord."

"The Judgement is coming," he muttered. "The sheep'll be separated from the goats. Them that kept their promises from them that didn't. Them that did the best they could with what they had from them that didn't. Them that honored their father and their mother from them that cursed them. Them that . . ."

She heaved a mammoth sigh that all but drowned him out. "What's the use in me wasting my good breath?" she asked. She rose and went back in the kitchen and began knocking things about.

She was so high and mighty! At home he had been living in a shack but there was at least air around it. He could put his feet on the ground. Here she didn't even live in a house. She lived in a pigeon-hutch of a building, with all stripes of foreigner, all of them twisted in the tongue. It was no place for a sane man. The first morning here she had taken him sightseeing and he had seen in fifteen minutes exactly how it was. He had not been out of the apartment since. He never wanted to set foot again on the underground railroad or the steps that moved under you while you stood still or any elevator to the thirty-fourth floor. When he was safely back in the apartment again, he had imagined going over it with Coleman. He had to turn his head every few seconds to make sure Coleman was behind him. Keep to the inside or these people'll knock you down, keep right behind me or you'll get left, keep your hat on, you damn idiot, he had said, and

Coleman had come on with his bent running shamble, panting and muttering, What we doing here? Where you get this fool idea coming here?

I come to show you it was no kind of place. Now you know you were well off where you were.

I knowed it before, Coleman said. Was you didn't know it.

When he had been here a week, he had got a postcard from Coleman that had been written for him by Hooten at the railroad station. It was written in green ink and said, "This is Coleman—X—howyou boss." Under it Hooten had written from himself, "Quit frequenting all those nitespots and come on home, you scoundrel, yours truly, W. P. Hooten." He had sent Coleman a card in return, care of Hooten, that said, "This place is alrite if you like it. Yours truly, W. T. Tanner." Since the daughter had to mail the card, he had not put on it that he was returning as soon as his pension check came. He had not intended to tell her but to leave her a note. When the check came, he would hire himself a taxi to the bus station and be on his way. And it would have made her as happy as it made him. She had found his company dour and her duty irksome. If he had sneaked out, she would have had the pleasure of having tried to do it and to top that off, the pleasure of his ingratitude.

As for him, he would have returned to squat on the doctor's land and to take his orders from a nigger who chewed ten-cent cigars. And to think less about it than formerly. Instead he had been done in by a nigger actor, or one who called himself an actor. He didn't believe the nigger was any actor.

There were two apartments on each floor of the building. He had been with the daughter three weeks when the people in the next hutch moved out. He had stood in the hall and watched the moving-out and the next day he had watched a moving-in. The hall was narrow and dark and he stood in the corner out of the way, offering only a suggestion every now and then to the movers that would have made their work easier for them if they had paid any attention. The furniture was new and cheap so he decided the people moving in might be a newly married couple and he would just wait around until they came and wish them well. After a while a large Negro in a light blue suit came lunging up the stairs, carrying two canvas suitcases, his head lowered against the strain. Behind him stepped a young tan-skinned woman with bright copper-colored hair. The Negro dropped the suitcases with a thud in front of the door of the next apartment.

"Be careful, Sweetie," the woman said. "My make-up is in there."

It broke upon him then just what was happening.

The Negro was grinning. He took a swipe at one of her hips.

"Quit it," she said, "there's an old guy watching."

They both turned and looked at him.

"Had-do," he said and nodded. Then he turned quickly into his own door.

His daughter was in the kitchen. "Who you think's rented that apartment over there?" he asked, his face alight.

She looked at him suspiciously. "Who?" she muttered.

"A nigger!" he said in a gleeful voice. "A South Alabama nigger if I ever saw one. And got him this high-yeller, high-stepping woman with red hair and they two are going to live next door to you!" He slapped his knee. "Yes siree!" he said. "Damn if they ain't!" It was the first time since coming up here that he had had occasion to laugh.

Her face squared up instantly. "All right now you listen to me," she said. "You keep away from them. Don't you go over there trying to get friendly with him. They ain't the same around here and I don't want any trouble with niggers, you hear me? If you have to live next to them, just you mind your business and they'll mind theirs. That's the way people were meant to get along in this world. Everybody can get along if they just mind their business. Live and let live." She began to wrinkle her nose like a rabbit, a stupid way she had. "Up here everybody minds their own business and everybody gets along. That's all you have to do."

"I was getting along with niggers before you were born," he said. He went back out into the hall and waited. He was willing to bet the nigger would like to talk to someone who understood him. Twice while he waited, he forgot and in his excitement, spit his tobacco juice against the baseboard. In about twenty minutes, the door of the apartment opened again and the Negro came out. He had put on a tie and a pair of horn-rimmed spectacles and Tanner noticed for the first time that he had a small almost invisible goatee. A real swell. He came on without appearing to see there was anyone else in the hall.

"Haddy, John," Tanner said and nodded, but the Negro brushed past without hearing and went rattling rapidly down the stairs.

Could be deaf and dumb, Tanner thought. He went back

into the apartment and sat down but each time he heard a noise in the hall, he got up and went to the door and stuck his head out to see if it might be the Negro. Once in the middle of the afternoon, he caught the Negro's eye just as he was rounding the bend of the stairs again but before he could get out a word, the man was in his own apartment and had slammed the door. He had never known one to move that fast unless the police were after him.

He was standing in the hall early the next morning when the woman came out of her door alone, walking on high gold-painted heels. He wished to bid her good morning or simply to nod but instinct told him to beware. She didn't look like any kind of woman, black or white, he had ever seen before and he remained pressed against the wall, frightened more than anything else, and feigning invisibility.

The woman gave him a flat stare, then turned her head away and stepped wide of him as if she were skirting an open garbage can. He held his breath until she was out of sight. Then he waited patiently for the man.

The Negro came out about eight o'clock.

This time Tanner advanced squarely in his path. "Good morning, Preacher," he said. It had been his experience that if a Negro tended to be sullen, this title usually cleared up his expression.

The Negro stopped abruptly.

"I seen you move in," Tanner said. "I ain't been up here long myself. It ain't much of a place if you ask me. I reckon you wish you were back in South Alabama."

The Negro did not take a step or answer. His eyes began to move. They moved from the top of the black hat, down to the collarless blue shirt, neatly buttoned at the neck, down the faded galluses to the grey trousers and the high-top shoes and up again, very slowly, while some unfathomable dead-cold rage seemed to stiffen and shrink him.

"I thought you might know somewhere around here we could find us a pond, Preacher," Tanner said in a voice growing thinner but still with considerable hope in it.

A seething noise came out of the Negro before he spoke. "I'm not from South Alabama," he said in a breathless wheezing voice. "I'm from New York City. And I'm not no preacher! I'm an actor."

Tanner chortled. "It's a little actor in most preachers, ain't it?" he said and winked. "I reckon you just preach on the side."

"I don't preach!" the Negro cried and rushed past him as if a swarm of bees had suddenly come down on him out of nowhere. He dashed down the stairs and was gone.

Tanner stood there for some time before he went back in the apartment. The rest of the day he sat in his chair and debated whether he would have one more try at making friends with him. Every time he heard a noise on the stairs he went to the door and looked out, but the Negro did not return until late in the afternoon. Tanner was standing in the hall waiting for him when he reached the top of the stairs. "Good evening, Preacher," he said, forgetting that the Negro called himself an actor.

The Negro stopped and gripped the banister rail. A tremor racked him from his head to his crotch. Then he began to come forward slowly. When he was close enough he lunged and grasped Tanner by both shoulders. "I don't take no crap," he whispered, "off no wool-hat red-neck son-of-a-bitch peckerwood old bastard like you." He caught his breath. And then his voice came out in the sound of an exasperation so profound that it rocked on the verge of a laugh. It was high and piercing and weak. "And I'm not no preacher! I'm not even no Christian. I don't believe that crap. There ain't no Jesus and there ain't no God."

The old man felt his heart inside him hard and tough as an oak knot. "And you ain't black," he said. "And I ain't white!"

The Negro slammed him against the wall. He yanked the black hat down over his eyes. Then he grabbed his shirt front and shoved him backwards to his open door and knocked him through it. From the kitchen the daughter saw him blindly hit the edge of the inside hall door and fall reeling into the living-room.

For days his tongue appeared to be frozen in his mouth. When it unthawed it was twice its normal size and he could not make her understand him. What he wanted to know was if the government check had come because he meant to buy a bus ticket with it and go home. After a few days, he made her understand. "It came," she said, "and it'll just pay the first two weeks' doctor-bill and please tell me how you're going home when you can't talk or walk or think straight and you got one eye crossed yet? Just please tell me that?"

It had come to him then slowly just what his present situation was. At least he would have to make her understand that he must be sent home to be buried. They could have him shipped back in a refrigerated car so that he would keep for the trip. He didn't want any undertaker up here messing with him. Let them get him off at once and he would come in on the early morning train and they could wire Hooten to get Coleman and Coleman would do the rest; she would not even have to go herself. After a lot of argument, he wrung the promise from her. She would ship him back.

After that he slept peacefully and improved a little. In his dreams he could feel the cold early morning air of home coming in through the cracks of the pine box. He could see Coleman waiting, red-eyed, on the station platform and Hooten standing there with his green eyeshade and black alpaca sleeves. If the old fool had stayed at home where he belonged, Hooten would be thinking, he wouldn't be arriving on the 6:03 in no box. Coleman had turned the borrowed mule and cart so that they could slide the box off the platform onto the open end of the wagon. Everything was ready and the two of them, shut-mouthed, inched the loaded coffin toward the wagon. From inside he began to scratch on the wood. They let go as if it had caught fire.

They stood looking at each other, then at the box.

"That him," Coleman said. "He in there his self."

"Naw," Hooten said, "must be a rat got in there with him."

"That him. This here one of his tricks."

"If it's a rat he might as well stay."

"That him. Git a crowbar."

Hooten went grumbling off and got the crowbar and came back and began to pry open the lid. Even before he had the upper end pried open, Coleman was jumping up and down, wheezing and panting from excitement. Tanner gave a thrust upward with both hands and sprang up in the box. "Judgement Day! Judgement Day!" he cried. "Don't you two fools know it's Judgement Day?"

Now he knew exactly what her promises were worth. He would do as well to trust to the note pinned in his coat and to any stranger who found him dead in the street or in the boxcar or wherever. There was nothing to be looked for from her except that she would do things her way. She came out of the kitchen again, holding her hat and coat and rubber boots.

"Now listen," she said, "I have to go to the store. Don't you try to get up and walk around while I'm gone. You've been to the bathroom and you shouldn't have to go again. I don't want to find you on the floor when I get back."

You won't find me atall when you get back, he said to himself. This was the last time he would see her flat dumb face. He felt guilty. She had been good to him and he had been nothing but a nuisance to her.

"Do you want you a glass of milk before I go?" she asked.

"No," he said. Then he drew breath and said, "You got a nice place here. It's a nice part of the country. I'm sorry if I've give you a lot of trouble getting sick. It was my fault trying to be friendly with that nigger." And I'm a damned liar besides, he said to himself to kill the outrageous taste such a statement made in his mouth.

For a moment she stared as if he were losing his mind. Then she seemed to think better of it. "Now don't saying something pleasant like that once in a while make you feel better?" she asked and sat down on the sofa.

His knees itched to unbend. Git on, git on, he fumed silently. Make haste and go.

"It's great to have you here," she said. "I wouldn't have you any other place. My own daddy." She gave him a big smile and hoisted her right leg up and began to pull on her boot. "I wouldn't wish a dog out on day like this," she said, "but I got to go. You can sit here and hope I don't slip and break my neck." She stamped the booted foot on the floor and then began to tackle the other one.

He turned his eyes to the window. The snow was beginning to stick and freeze to the outside pane. When he looked at her again, she was standing there like a big doll stuffed into its hat and coat. She drew on a pair of green knitted gloves. "Okay," she said, "I'm gone. You sure you don't want anything?"

"No," he said, "go ahead on."

"Well so long then," she said.

He raised the hat enough to reveal a bald palely speckled head. The hall door closed behind her. He began to tremble with excitement. He reached behind him and drew the coat into his lap. When he got it on, he waited until he had stopped panting, then he gripped the arms of the chair and pulled himself up. His body felt like a great heavy bell whose clapper swung from side to side but made no noise. Once up, he remained standing a moment, swaying until he got his balance. A sensation of terror and defeat swept over him. He would never make it. He would never get there dead or alive. He pushed one foot forward and did not fall and his confidence returned. "The Lord is my shepherd," he muttered, "I shall not want." He began moving toward the sofa where he would have support. He reached it. He was on his way.

By the time he got to the door, she would be down the four flights of steps and out of the building. He got past the sofa and crept along by the wall, keeping his hand on it for support. Nobody was going to bury him here. He was as confident as if the woods of home lay at the bottom of the stairs. He reached the front door of the apartment and opened it and peered into the hall. This was the first time he had looked into it since the actor had knocked him down. It was dank-smelling and empty. The thin piece of linoleum stretched its moldy length to the door of the other apartment, which was closed. "Nigger actor," he said.

The head of the stairs was ten or twelve feet from where he stood and he bent his attention to getting there without creeping around the long way with a hand on the wall. He held his arms a little way out from his sides and pushed forward directly. He was half way there when all at once his legs disappeared, or felt as if they had. He looked down, bewildered, for they were still there. He fell forward and grasped the banister post with both hands. Hanging there, he gazed for what seemed the longest time he had ever looked at anything down the steep unlighted steps; then he closed his eyes and pitched forward. He landed upsidedown in the middle of the flight.

He felt presently the tilt of the box as they took it off the train and got it on the baggage wagon. He made no noise yet. The train jarred and slid away. In a moment the baggage wagon was rumbling under him, carrying him back to the station side. He heard footsteps rattling closer and closer to him and he supposed that a crowd was gathering. Wait until they see this, he thought.

"That him," Coleman said, "one of his tricks."

"It's a damn rat in there," Hooten said.

"It's him. Git the crowbar."

In a moment a shaft of greenish light fell on him. He pushed through it and cried in a weak voice, "Judgement Day! Judgement Day! You idiots didn't know it was Judgement Day, did you?

"Coleman?" he murmured.

The Negro bending over him had a large surly mouth and sullen eyes.

"Ain't any coal man, either," he said. This must be the wrong station, Tanner thought. Those fools put me off too soon. Who is this nigger? It ain't even daylight here.

At the Negro's side was another face, a woman's—pale, topped with a pile of copper-glinting hair and twisted as if she had just stepped in a pile of dung.

"Oh," Tanner said, "it's you."

The actor leaned closer and grasped him by the front of his shirt. "Judgement day," he said in a mocking voice. "Ain't no judgement day, old man. 'Cept this. Maybe this here judgement day for you."

Tanner tried to catch hold of a banister-spoke to raise himself but his hand grasped air. The two faces, the black one and the pale one, appeared to be wavering. By an effort of will he kept them focussed before him while he lifted his hand, as light as a breath, and said in his jauntiest voice, "Hep me up, Preacher. I'm on my way home!"

His daughter found him when she came in from the grocery store. His hat had been pulled down over his face and his head and arms thrust between the spokes of the banister; his feet dangled over the stairwell like those of a man in the stocks. She tugged at him frantically and then flew for the police. They cut him out with a saw and said he had been dead about an hour.

She buried him in New York City, but after she had done it she could not sleep at night. Night after night she turned and tossed and very definite lines began to appear in her face, so she had him dug up and shipped the body to Corinth. Now she rests well at night and her good looks have mostly returned.

A Pedestrian Accident
Robert Coover

Paul stepped off the curb and got hit by a truck. He didn't know what it was that hit him at first, but now, here on his back, under the truck, there could be no doubt. Is it me? he wondered. Have I walked the earth and come here?

Just as he was struck, and while still tumbling in front of the truck and then under the wheels, in a kind of funhouse gambado of pain and terror, he had thought: this has happened before. His neck had sprung, there was a sudden flash of light and a blaze roaring up in the back of his head. The hot—almost fragrant—pain: that was new. It was the *place* he felt he'd returned to.

He lay perpendicular to the length of the truck, under the trailer, just to the rear of the truck's second of three sets of wheels. All of him was under the truck but his head and shoulders. Maybe I'm being born again, he reasoned. He stared straight up, past the side of the truck, toward the sky, pale blue and cloudless. The tops of skyscrapers closed toward the center of his vision; now that he thought about it, he realized it was the first time in years he had looked up at them, and they seemed inclined to fall. The old illusion; one of them anyway. The truck was red with white letters, but his severe angle of vision up the side kept him from being able to read the letters. A capital "K," he could see that—and a number, yes, it seemed to be a "14." He smiled inwardly at the irony, for he had a private fascination with numbers: fourteen! He thought he remembered having had a green light, but it didn't really matter. No way to prove it. It would have changed by now, in any case. The thought, obscurely, troubled him.

"Crazy goddamn fool he just walk right out in fronta me no respect just burstin for a bustin!"

The voice, familiar somehow, guttural, yet falsetto, came from above and to his right. People were gathering to stare down at him, shaking their heads. He felt like one chosen. He tried to turn his head toward the voice, but his neck flashed hot again. Things were bad. Better just to lie still, take no chances. Anyway, he saw now, just in the corner of his eye, the cab of the truck, red like the trailer, and poking out its window, the large head of the truckdriver, wagging in the sunshine. The driver wore a small tweed cap—too small, in fact: it sat just on top of his head.

"Boy I seen punchies in my sweet time but this cookie takes the cake God bless the laboring classes I say and preserve us from the humble freak!"

The truckdriver spoke with broad gestures, bulbous eyes rolling, runty body thrusting itself in and out of the cab window, little hands flying wildly about. Paul worried still about the light. It was important, yet how could he ever know? The world was an ephemeral place, it could get away from you in a minute. The driver had a bent red nose and coarse reddish hair that stuck out like straw. A hard shiny chin, too, like a mirror image of the hooked nose. Paul's eyes wearied of the strain, and he had to stop looking.

"Listen lays and gentmens I'm a good Christian by Judy a decent hardworkin fambly man earnin a honest wage and got a dear little woman and seven yearnin younguns all my own seed *a responsible man* and goddamn that boy what he do but walk right into me and my poor ole truck!"

On some faces Paul saw compassion, or at least a neutral curiosity, an idle amusement, but on most he saw reproach. There were those who winced on witnessing his state and seemed to understand, but there were others—a majority— who jeered.

"He asked for it if you ask me!"

"It's the idler plays the fool and the workingman's to hang for it!"

"Shouldn't allow his kind out to walk the streets!"

"What is the use of running when you are on the wrong road?"

It worsened. Their shouts grew louder and ran together. There were orations and the waving of flags. Paul was wondering: had he been carrying anything? No, no. He had only— *wait!* a book? Very likely, but . . . ah well. Perhaps he was carrying it still. There was no feeling in his fingers.

The people were around him like flies, grievances were being aired, sides taken, and there might have been a brawl, but a policeman arrived and broke it up. "All right, everybody! Stand back, please!" he shouted. "Give this man some air! Can't you see he's been injured?"

At last, Paul thought. He relaxed. For a moment, he'd felt

himself in a strange and hostile country, but now he felt at home again. He even began to believe he might survive. Though really: had he ever doubted it?

"Everybody back, *back!*" The policeman was effective. The crowd grew quiet, and by the sound of their sullen shuffling, Paul guessed they were backing off. Not that he got more or less air by it, but he felt relieved just the same. "Now," said the policeman, gently but firmly, "what has happened here?"

And with that it all started up again, same as before, the clamor, the outrage, the arguments, the learned quotations, but louder and more discordant than ever. I'm hurt, Paul said. No one heard. The policeman cried out for order, and slowly, with his shouts, with his nightstick, with his threats, he reduced them again to silence.

One lone voice hung at the end: "—for the last time, Mister, *stop goosing me!*" Everybody laughed, released.

"Stop goosing her, sir!" the policeman commanded with his chin thrust firmly forward, and everybody laughed again.

Paul almost laughed, but he couldn't, quite. Besides, he'd just, with that, got the picture, and given his condition, it was not a funny one. He opened his eyes and there was the policeman bent down over him. He had a notebook in his hand.

"Now, tell me, son, what happened here?" The policeman's face was thin and pale, like a student's, and he wore a trim little tuft of black moustache under the pinched peak of his nose.

I've just been hit, Paul explained, by this truck, and then he realized that he probably didn't say it at all, that speech was an art no longer his. He cast his eyes indicatively toward the cab of the truck.

"Listen, I asked you what happened here! Cat got your tongue, young man?"

"Crazy goddam fool he just walk right out in fronta me no respect just burstin for a bustin!"

The policeman remained crouched over Paul, but turned his head up to look at the truckdriver. The policeman wore a brilliant blue uniform with large brass buttons. And gold epaulettes.

"Boy I seen punchies in my sweet time but this cookie takes the cake God bless the laboring classes I say and preserve us from the humble freak!"

The policeman looked down at Paul, then back at the truckdriver. "I know about truckdrivers," Paul heard him say.

"Listen lays and gentmens I'm a good Christian by Judy a decent hardworkin fambly man earnin a honest wage and got a dear little woman and seven yearnin younguns all my own seed *a responsible man* and goddamn that boy what he do but walk right into me and my poor ole trike. Truck, I mean."

There was a loose tittering from the crowd, but the policeman's frown and raised stick contained it. "What's your name, lad?" he asked, turning back to Paul. At first, the policeman smiled, he knew who truckdrivers were and he knew who Pauls were, and there was salvation of sorts in that smile, but gradually it faded. "Come, come, boy! Don't be afraid!" He winked, nudged him gently. "We're here to help you."

Paul, Paul replied. But, no, no doubt about it, it was jammed up in there and he wasn't getting it out.

"Well, if you won't help me, I can't help you," the policeman said pettishly and tilted his nose up. "Anybody here know this man?" he called out to the crowd.

Again a roar, a threatening tumult of words and sounds, shouts back and forth. It was hard to know if none knew him or if they all did. But then one voice, belted out above the others, came through: "Oh God in heaven! It's Amory! *Amory Westerman!*" The voice, a woman's, hysterical by the sound of it, drew near. "Amory! What . . . *what* have they *done* to you?"

Paul understood. It was not a mistake. He was astonished by his own acumen.

"Do you know this young man?" the policeman asked, lifting his notebook.

"What? Know him? Did Sarah know Abraham? Did Eve know Cain?"

The policeman cleared his throat uneasily. "Adam," he corrected softly.

"You know who you know, I know who I know," the woman said, and let fly with a low throaty snigger. The crowd responded with a belly laugh.

"But this young man—!" the policeman insisted, flustered.

"Who, you and Amory?" the woman cried. "I can't believe it!" The crowd laughed and the policeman bit his lip. "Amory! What new persecutions are these?" She billowed out above him: old, maybe even seventy, fat and bosomy, pasty-faced with thick red rouges, head haloed by ringlets of sparse orangish hair. "My poor Amory!" And down she came on him. Paul tried to duck, got only a hot flash in his neck for it. Her breath reeked of cheap gin. Help, said Paul.

"Hold, madame! Stop!" the policeman cried, tugging at the woman's sleeve. She stood, threw up her arms before her face, staggered backwards. What more she did, Paul couldn't see, for his view of her face was largely blocked by the bulge of her breasts and belly. There were laughs, though. "Everything in order here," grumped the policeman, tapping his notebook. "Now, what's your name, please . . . uh . . . miss, madame?"

"My name?" She twirled gracelessly on one dropsied ankle and cried to the crowd: *"Shall I tell?"*

"Tell! Tell! Tell!" shouted the spectators, clapping rhythmically. Paul let himself be absorbed by it; there was, after all, nothing else to do.

The policeman, rapping a pencil against his blue notebook to the rhythm of the chant, leaned down over Paul and whispered: ("I think we've got them on our side now!")

Paul, his gaze floating giddily up past the thin white face of the police officer and the red side of the truck into the horizonless blue haze above, wondered if alliance were really the key to it all. What *am* I without them? Could I even die? Suddenly, the whole world seemed to tip: his feet dropped and his head rose. Beneath him the red machine shot grease and muck, the host rioted above his head, the earth pushed him from behind, and out front the skyscrapers pointed, like so many insensate fingers, the path he must walk to oblivion. He squeezed shut his eyes to set right the world again—he was afraid he would slide down beneath the truck to disappear from sight forever.

"My name—!" bellowed the woman, and the crowd hushed, tittering softly. Paul opened his eyes. He was on his back again. The policeman stood over him, mouth agape, pencil poised. The woman's puffy face was sequined with sweat. Paul wondered what she'd been doing while he wasn't watching. "My name, officer, is Grundy."

"I beg your pardon?" The policeman, when nervous, had a way of nibbling his moustache with his lowers.

"Mrs. Grundy, dear boy, who did you think I was?" She patted the policeman's thin cheek, tweaked his nose. "But you can call me Charity, handsome!" The policeman blushed. She twiddled her index finger in his little moustache. "Kootchy-kootchy-koo!" There was a roar of laughter from the crowd.

The policeman sneezed. "Please!" he protested.

Mrs. Grundy curtsied and stooped to unzip the officer's fly. "Hello! Anybody home!"

"Stop that!" squeaked the policeman through the thunderous laughter and applause. Strange, thought Paul, how much I'm enjoying this.

"Come out, come out, wherever you are!"

"The story!" the policeman insisted through the tumult.

"Story? What—?"

"This young fellow," said the policeman, pointing with his pencil. He zipped up, blew his nose. "Mr., uh, Mr. Westerman . . . you said—"

"Mr. *Who?*" The woman shook her jowls, perplexed. She frowned down at Paul, then brightened. "Oh yes! Amory!" She paled, seemed to sicken. Paul, if he could've, would've smiled. "Good God!" she rasped, as though appalled at what she saw. Then, once more, she took an operatic grip on her breasts and staggered back a step. "O mortality! O fatal mischief! Done in! A noble man lies stark and stiff! Delenda est Carthago! *Sic transit glans mundi!*"

Gloria, corrected Paul. No, leave it.

"Squashed like a lousy bug!" she cried. "And at the height of his potency!"

"Now, wait a minute!" the policeman protested.

"The final curtain! The last farewell! The journey's end! Over the hill! The last muster!" Each phrase was answered by a happy shout from the mob. "Across the river! The way of all flesh! The last roundup!" She sobbed, then ballooned down on him again, tweaked his ear and whispered: ("How's Charity's weetsie snotkins, enh? Him fall down and bump his little putsy? Mumsy kiss and make well!") And she let him have it on the—well, sort of on the left side of his nose, left cheek, and part of his left eye: one wet enveloping sour blubbering kiss, and this time, sorrily, the policeman did not intervene. He was busy taking notes. Officer, said Paul.

"Hmmm," the policeman muttered, and wrote. "G-R-U-N-ah, ahem, Grundig, Grundig -D, yes, D-I-G. Now what did you—?"

The woman labored clumsily to her feet, plodded over behind the policeman, and squinted over his shoulder at the notes he was taking. "That's a 'Y' there, buster, a 'Y.'" She jabbed a stubby ruby-tipped finger at the notebook.

"Grundigy?" asked the policeman in disbelief. "What kind of a name is that?"

"No, no!" the old woman whined, her grand manner flung to the winds. "Grundy! Grundy! Without the '-ig,' don't you see? You take off your—"

"Oh, *Grundy!* Now I have it!" The policeman scrubbed the back end of his pencil in the notebook. "Darned eraser. About shot." The paper tore. He looked up irritably. "Can't we just make it Grundig?"

"Grundy," said the woman coldly.

The policeman ripped the page out of his notebook, rumpled it up angrily, and hurled it to the street. "All right, gosh damn it all!" he cried in a rage, scribbling: "Grundy. I have it. Now get on with it, lady!"

"Officer!" sniffed Mrs. Grundy, clasping a handkerchief to her throat. "Remember your place, or I shall have to speak to your superior!" The policeman shrank, blanched, nibbled his lip.

Paul knew what would come. He could read these two like a book. *I'm* the strange one, he thought. He wanted to watch their faces, but his streetlevel view gave him at best a perspective on their underchins. It was their crotches that were prominent. Butts and bellies: the squashed bug's-eye view. And that was strange, too: that he wanted to watch their faces.

The policeman was begging for mercy, wringing his pale hands. There were faint hissing sounds, wriggling out of the crowd like serpents. "Cut the shit, mac," Charity Grundy said finally, "you're overdoing it." The officer chewed his moustache, stared down at his notebook, abashed. "You wanna know who this poor clown is, right?" The policeman nodded. "Okay, are you ready?" She clasped her bosom again and the crowd grew silent. The police officer held his notebook up, the pencil poised. Mrs. Grundy snuffled, looked down at Paul, winced, turned away and wept. "Officer!" she gasped. *"He was my lover!"*

Halloos and cheers from the crowd, passing to laughter. The policeman started to smile, blinking down at Mrs. Grundy's body, but with a twitch of his moustache, he suppressed it.

"We met . . . just one year ago today. O fateful hour!" She smiled bravely, brushing back a tear, her lower lip quivering. Once, her hands clenched woefully before her face, she winked down at Paul. The wink nearly convinced him. Maybe I'm him after all. Why not? "He was selling seachests, door to door. I can see him now as he was then—" She paused to look down at him as he was now, and wrinkles of revulsion swept over her face. Somehow this brought laughter. She looked away, puckered her mouth and bugged her eyes, shook one hand limply from the wrist. The crowd was really with her.

"Mrs. Grundy," the officer whispered, "please . . ."

"Yes, there he was, chapfallen and misused, orphaned by the rapacious world, yet pure and undefiled, there: there at my door!" With her baggy arm, flung out, quavering, she indicated the door. "Bent nearly double under his impossible seachest, perspiration illuminating his manly brow, wounding his eyes, wrinkling his undershirt—"

"Careful!" cautioned the policeman nervously, glancing up from his notes. He must have filled twenty or thirty pages by now.

"In short, my heart went out to him!" Gesture of heart going out. "And though—alas!—my need for seachests was limited—"

The spectators somehow discovered something amusing in this and tittered knowingly. Mainly in the way she said it, he supposed. Her story in truth did not bother Paul so much as his own fascination with it. He knew where it would lead, but it didn't matter. In fact, maybe that *was* what fascinated him.

"—I invited him in. Put down that horrid seachest, dear boy, and come in here, I cried, come in to your warm and obedient Charity, love, come in for a cup of tea, come in and rest, rest your pretty little shoulders, your pretty little back, your pretty little . . ." Mrs. Grundy paused, smiled with a faint arch of one eyebrow, and the crowd responded with another burst of laughter. "And it *was* pretty little, okay," she grumbled, and again they whooped, while she sniggered throatily.

How was it now? he wondered. In fact, he'd been wondering all along.

"And, well, officer, that's what he did, he *did* put down his seachest—alas! sad to tell, right on my unfortunate cat Rasputin, dozing there in the day's brief sun, God rest his soul, his (again, alas!) somewhat homaloidal soul!"

She had a great audience. They never failed her, nor did they now.

The policeman, who had finally squatted down to write on his knee, now stood and shouted for order. "Quiet! *Quiet!*" His moustache twitched. "Can't you see this is a serious matter?" He's the funny one, thought Paul. The crowd thought so, too, for the laughter mounted, then finally died away. "And . . . and then what happened?" the policeman whispered. But they heard him anyway and screamed with delight, throwing up a new clamor in which could be distinguished several coarse paraphrases of the policeman's question. The officer's pale face flushed. He looked down at Paul with a brief commiserating smile, shrugged his shoulders, fluttering the epaulettes. Paul made a try at a never-mind kind of gesture, but, he supposed, without bringing it off.

"What happened next, you ask, you naughty boy?" Mrs. Grundy shook and wriggled. Cheers and whistles. She cupped her plump hands under her breasts and hitched her abundant hips heavily to one side. "You don't understand," she told the crowd. "I only wished to be a mother to the lad." Hoohahs and catcalls. "But I had failed to realize, in that fleeting tragic moment when he unburdened himself upon poor Rasputin, how I was wrenching his young and unsullied heart asunder! Oh yes, I know, I know—"

"This is the dumbest story I ever heard," interrupted the policeman finally, but Mrs. Grundy paid him no heed.

"I know I'm old and fat, that I've crossed the Grand Climacteric!" She winked at the crowd's yowls of laughter. "I know the fragrant flush of first flower is gone forever!" she cried, not letting a good thing go, pressing her wrinkled palms down over the soft swoop of her blimp-sized hips, peeking coyly over one plump shoulder at the shrieking crowd. The policeman stamped his foot, but no one noticed except Paul. "I know, I know—*yet:* somehow, face to face with little Charity, a primitive unnameable urgency welled up in his untaught loins, his pretty little—"

"*Stop it!*" cried the policeman, right on cue. "This has gone far enough!"

"And *you* ask what happened next? I shall tell you, officer! For why conceal the truth . . . from *you* of all people?" Though uneasy, the policeman seemed frankly pleased that she had put it this way. "Yes, without further discourse, he buried his pretty little head in my bosom—" (Paul felt a distressing sense of suffocation, though perhaps it had been with him all the while) "—and he tumbled me there, yes he did, there on the front porch alongside his seachest and my dying Rasputin, there in the sunlight, before God, before the neighbors, before Mr. Dunlevy the mailman who is hard of hearing, before the children from down the block passing on their shiny little—"

"Crazy goddamn fool he just walk right out in fronta me no respect just burstin for a bustin!" said a familiar voice.

Mrs. Grundy's broad face, now streaked with tears and mottled with a tense pink flush, glowered. There was a long and difficult silence. Then she narrowed her eyes, smiled faintly, squared her shoulders, touched a handkerchief to her eye, plunged the handkerchief back down her bosom, and resumed: "—Before, in short, the whole itchy eyes-agog world, a coupling unequaled in the history of Western concupiscence!" Some vigorous applause, which she acknowledged. "Assaulted, but —yes, I confess it—assaulted, but *aglow,* I reminded him of—"

"Boy I seen punchies in my sweet time but this cookie takes the cake God bless the laboring classes I say and preserve us from the humble freak!"

Swiveling his wearying gaze hard right, Paul could see the truckdriver waggling his huge head at the crowd. Mrs. Grundy padded heavily over to him, the back of her thick neck reddening, swung her purse in a great swift arc, but the truckdriver recoiled into his cab, laughing with a taunting cackle. Then, almost in the same instant, he poked his red-beaked head out again, and rolling his eyes, said: "Listen lays and gentmens I'm a good Christian by Judy a decent hardworkin fambly man earnin a honest wage and got a dear little woman and seven yearnin younguns all my own seed *a responsible—*"

"I'll responsible your ass!" hollered Charity Grundy and let fly with her purse again, but once more the driver ducked nimbly inside, cackling obscenely. The crowd, taking sides, was more hysterical than ever. Cheers were raised and bets taken.

Again the driver's waggling head popped out: "*—man and god—*" he began, but this time Mrs. Grundy was waiting for him. Her great lumpish purse caught him square on his bent red nose—*ka*-RAACKK!—and the truckdriver slumped lifelessly over the door of his cab, his stubby little arms dangling limp, reaching just below the top of his head. As best Paul could tell, the tweed cap did not drop off, but since his eyes were cramped with fatigue, he had to stop looking before the truckdriver's head ceased bobbing against the door.

Man and god! he thought. Of course! terrific! What did it mean? Nothing.

The policeman made futile little gestures of interference, but apparently had too much respect for Mrs. Grundy's purse to carry them out. That purse was big enough to hold a bowling ball, and maybe it did.

Mrs. Grundy, tongue dangling and panting furiously, clapped one hand over her heart and, with the handkerchief, fanned herself with the other. Paul saw sweat dripping down her legs. "And so—*foo!*—I . . . I—*puf!*—I reminded him of . . . of the—*whee!*—the cup of tea!" she gasped. She paused, swallowed, mopped her brow, sucked in a deep lungful of air, and exhaled it slowly. She cleared her throat. *"And so I reminded him of the cup of tea!"* she roared with a grand sweep of one powerful arm, the old style recovered. There was a general smattering of complimentary applause, which Mrs. Grundy acknowledged with a short nod of her head. "We went inside. The air was heavy with expectation and the unmistakable aroma of catshit. One might almost be pleased that Rasputin had yielded up the spirit—"

"Now JUST STOP IT!" cried the policeman. "THIS IS—"

"I poured some tea, we sang the now famous duet, '¡*Ciérrate la bragueta!* ¡*La bragueta está cerrada!*,' I danced for him, he—"

"ENOUGH, I SAID!" screamed the policeman, his little moustache quivering with indignation. "THIS IS ABSURD!"

You're warm, said Paul. But that's not quite it.

"Absurd?" cried Charity Grundy, aghast. *"Absurd?* You call my dancing *absurd?"*

"I . . . I didn't say—"

"Grotesque, perhaps, and yes, a bit awesome—but *absurd!"* She grabbed him by the lapels, lifting him off the ground. "What do you have against dancing, you worm? *What do you have against grace?"*

"P-please! Put me down!"

"Or is it, you don't believe I *can* dance?" She dropped him.

"N-no!" he squeaked, brushing himself off, straightening his epaulettes. "No! I—"

"Show him! Show him!" chanted the crowd.

The policeman spun on them. "STOP! IN THE NAME OF THE LAW!" They obeyed. "This man is injured. He may die. He needs help. It's no joking matter. I ask for your cooperation." He paused for effect. "That's better." The policeman stroked his moustache, preening a bit. "Now, ahem, is there a doctor present? A doctor, please?"

"Oh, officer, you're cute! You're *very* cute!" said Mrs. Grundy on a new tack. The crowd snickered. *"Is there a doctor present?"* she mimicked, *"a doctor, please?"*

"Now just cut it out!" the policeman ordered, glaring angrily across Paul's chest at Mrs. Grundy. "Gosh damn it now, you stop it this instant, or . . . or you'll see what'll happen!"

"Aww, you're *jealous!"* cried Mrs. Grundy. "And of poor little supine Rasputin! Amory, I mean." The spectators were in great spirits again, total rebellion threatening, and the police officer was at the end of his rope. "Well, *don't* be jealous, dear boy!" cooed Mrs. Grundy. "Charity tell you a weetsie bitty secret."

"*Stop!*" sobbed the policeman. Be careful where you step, said Paul below.

Mrs. Grundy leaned perilously out over Paul and got a grip on the policeman's ear. He winced, but no longer attempted escape. "That boy," she said, "*he humps terrible!*"

It carried out to the crowd and broke it up. It was her big line and she wambled about gloriously, her rouged mouth stretched in a flabby toothless grin, retrieving the pennies that people were pitching (Paul knew about them from being hit by them; one landed on his upper lip, stayed there, emitting that familiar dead smell common to pennies the world over), thrusting her chest forward to catch them in the cleft of her bosom. She shook and, shaking, jangled. She grabbed the policeman's hand and pulled him forward to share a bow with her. The policeman smiled awkwardly, twitching his moustache.

"You asked for a doctor," said an old but gentle voice.

The crowd noises subsided. Paul opened his eyes and discovered above him a stooped old man in a rumpled gray suit. His hair was shaggy and white, his face dry, lined with age. He wore rimless glasses, carried a black leather bag. He smiled down at Paul, that easy smile of a man who comprehends and assuages pain, then looked back at the policeman. Inexplicably, a wave of terror shook Paul.

"You wanted a doctor," the old man repeated.

"Yes! *Yes!*" cried the policeman, almost in tears. "Oh, thank God!"

"I'd rather you thanked the profession," the doctor said. "Now what seems to be the problem?"

"Oh, doctor, it's awful!" The policeman twisted the notebook in his hands, fairly destroying it. "This man has been struck by this truck, or so it would appear, no one seems to know, it's all a terrible mystery, and there is a woman, but now I don't see—? and I'm not even sure of his name—"

"No matter," interrupted the doctor with a kindly nod of his old head, "who he is. He is a man and that, I assure you, is enough for me."

"Doctor, that's so good of you to say so!" wept the policeman.

I'm in trouble, thought Paul. Oh boy, I'm really in trouble.

"Well, now, let us just see," said the doctor, crouching down over Paul. He lifted Paul's eyelids with his thumb and peered intently at Paul's eyes; Paul, anxious to assist, rolled them from side to side. "Just relax, son," the doctor said. He opened his black bag, rummaged about in it, withdrew a flashlight. Paul was not sure exactly what the doctor did after that, but he seemed to be looking in his ears. I can't move my head, Paul told him, but the doctor only asked: "Why does he have a penny under his nose?" His manner was not such as to insist upon an answer, and he got none. Gently, expertly, he pried Paul's teeth apart, pinned his tongue down with a wooden depressor, and scrutinized his throat. Paul's head was on fire with pain. "Ahh, yes," he mumbled. "Hum, hum."

"How . . . how is he, Doctor?" stammered the policeman, his voice muted with dread and respect. "Will . . . will he . . . ?"

The doctor glared scornfully at the officer, then withdrew a stethoscope from his bag. He hooked it in his ears, slipped the disc inside Paul's shirt and listened intently, his old head inclined to one side like a bird listening for worms. Absolute silence now. Paul could hear the doctor breathing, the policeman whimpering softly. He had the vague impression that the doctor tapped his chest a time or two, but if so, he didn't feel it. His head felt better with his mouth closed. "Hmmm," said the doctor gravely, "yes . . ."

"Oh, please! What *is* it, Doctor?" the policeman cried.

"What is it? *What is it?*" shouted the doctor in a sudden burst of rage. "I'll tell you *what is it!*" He sprang to his feet, nimble for an old man. "I cannot examine this patient while you're hovering over my shoulder and mewling like a goddamn schoolboy, *that's* what *is* it!"

"B-but I only—" stammered the officer, staggering backwards.

"And how do you expect me to examine a man half buried under a damned truck?" The doctor was in a terrible temper.

"But I—"

"Damn it! I'll but-I you, you idiot, if you don't remove this truck from the scene so that I can determine the true gravity of this man's injuries! *Have I made myself clear?*"

"Y-yes! But . . . but wh-what am I to *do?*" wept the police officer, hands clenched before his mouth. "I'm only a simple policeman, Doctor, doing my duty before God and count—"

"Simple, you said it!" barked the doctor. "I *told* you what to do, you God-and-cunt simpleton—*now get moving!*"

God and cunt! Did it again, thought Paul. Now what?

The policeman, chewing wretchedly on the corners of his notebook, stared first at Paul, then at the truck, at the crowd, back at the truck. Paul felt fairly certain now that the letter following the "K" on the truck's side was an "I." "Shall I . . . shall I pull him out from under—?" the officer began tentatively, thin chin aquiver.

"Good God, no!" stormed the doctor, stamping his foot. "This man may have a broken neck! Moving him would *kill* him, don't you see that, you sniveling birdbrain? Now, goddamn it, wipe your wretched nose and go wake up your— your accomplice up there, *and I mean right now!* Tell him to back his truck *off* this poor devil!"

"B-back it off—! But . . . but he'd have to run *over* him again! He—"

"Don't by God run-over-him-again *me,* you blackshirt hireling, *or I'll have your badge!"* screamed the doctor, brandishing his stethoscope.

The policeman hesitated but a moment to glance down at Paul's body, then turned and ran to the front of the truck. "Hey! Come on, you!" He whacked the driver on the head with his nightstick. Hollow *thunk!* "Up and at 'em!"

"—DAM THAT BOY WHAT," cried the truckdriver, rearing up wildly and fluttering his head as though lost, "HE DO BUT WALK RIGHT INTO ME AND MY POOR OLE TRICK! TRUCK, I MEAN!" The crowd laughed again, first time in a long time, but the doctor stamped his foot and they quieted right down.

"Now, start up that engine, you, right now! I mean it!" ordered the policeman, stroking his moustache back. He was getting a little of his old spit and polish back. He slapped the nightstick in his palm two or three times.

Paul felt the pavement under his back quake as the truckdriver started the motor. The white letters above him joggled in their red fields like butterflies. Beyond, the sky's blue had deepened, but white clouds now flowered in it. The skyscrapers had grayed, as though withdrawing information.

The truck's noise smothered the voices, but Paul did overhear the doctor and the policeman occasionally, the doctor ranting, the policeman imploring, something about mass and weight and vectors and direction. It was finally decided to go forward, since there were two sets of wheels up front and only one to the rear (a decent kind of humanism maintaining, after all, thought Paul), but the truckdriver apparently misunderstood, because he backed up anyway, and the middle set of wheels rolled up on top of Paul.

"Stop! STOP!" shrieked the police officer, and the truck motor coughed and died. "I ordered you to go *forward,* you pighead, not backward!"

The driver popped his head out the window, bulged his ping-pong-ball eyes at the policeman, then waggled his tiny hands in his ears and brayed. The officer took a fast practiced swing at the driver's big head (epaulettes, or no, he had a skill or two), but the driver deftly dodged it. He clapped his runty hands and bobbed back inside the cab.

"What oh *what* shall we ever do *now?*" wailed the officer. The doctor scowled at him with undisguised disgust. Paul felt like he was strangling, but he could locate no specific pain past his neck. "Dear lord above! There's wheels on each side of him and wheels in the middle!"

"Capital!" the doctor snorted. "Figure that out by yourself, or somebody help you?"

"You're making fun," whimpered the officer.

"AND YOU'RE MURDERING THIS MAN!" bellowed the doctor.

The police officer uttered a short anxious cry, then raced to the front of the truck again. Hostility welling in the crowd, Paul could hear it. "Okay, okay!" cried the officer. "Back up or go forward, *please,* I don't care, but hurry! HURRY!"

The motor started up again, there was a jarring grind of gears abrading, then slowly   slowly   slowly   the middle set of wheels backed down off Paul's body. There was a brief tense interim before the next set climbed up on him, hesitated as a ferris wheel hesitates at the top of its ambit, then sank down off him.

Some time passed.

He opened his eyes.

The truck had backed away, out of sight, out of Paul's limited range of sight anyway. His eyelids weighed closed. He remembered the doctor being huddled over him, shreds of his clothing being peeled away.

Much later, or perhaps not, he opened his eyes once more. The doctor and the policeman were standing over him, some other people too, people he didn't recognize, though he felt somehow he ought to know them. Mrs. Grundy, she was there; in fact, it looked for all the world as though she had set up a ticket booth and was charging admission. Some of the people were holding little children up to see, warm faces, tender, compassionate; more or less. Newsmen were taking his picture. "You'll be famous," one of them said.

"His goddamn body is like a mulligan stew," the doctor was telling a reporter.

The policeman shook his head. He was a bit green. "Do you think—?"

"Do I think what?" the doctor asked. Then he laughed, a thin raking old man's laugh. "You mean, do I think he's going to *die?*" He laughed again. "Good God, man, you can see for yourself! There's nothing left of him, he's a goddamn gallimaufry, and hardly an appetizing one at that!" He dipped his fingers into Paul, licked them, grimaced. "Foo!"

"I think we should get a blanket for him," the policeman said weakly.

"Of course you should!" snapped the doctor, wiping his stained hands on a small white towel he had brought out of his black bag. He peered down through his rimless spectacles at Paul, smiled. "Still there, eh?" He squatted beside him. "I'm sorry, son. There's not a damn thing I can do. Well, yes, I suppose I can take this penny off your lip. You've little use for it, eh?" He laughed softly. "Now, let's see, there's no function for it, is there? No, no, there it is." The doctor started to pitch it away, then pocketed it instead. The eyes, don't they use them for the eyes? "Well, that's better, I'm sure. But let's be honest: it doesn't get to the real problem, does it?" Paul's lip tickled where the penny had been. "No, I'm of all too little use to you there, boy. I can't even prescribe a soporific platitude. Leave that to the goddamn priests, eh? Hee hee hee! Oops, sorry, son! Would you like a priest?"

No thanks, said Paul.

"Can't get it out, eh?" The doctor probed Paul's neck. "Hmmm. No, obviously not." He shrugged. "Just as well. What could you possibly have to say, eh?" He chuckled drily, then looked up at the policeman who still had not left to search out a blanket. "Don't just stand there, man! Get this lad a priest!" The police officer, clutching his mouth, hurried away, out of Paul's eye-reach. "I know it's not easy to accept death," the doctor was saying. He finished wiping his hands, tossed the towel into his black bag, snapped the bag shut. "We all struggle against it, boy, it's part and parcel of being alive, this brawl, this meaningless gutterfight with death. In fact, let me tell you, son, it's *all* there is to life." He wagged his finger in punctuation, and ended by pressing the tip of it to Paul's nose. "That's the secret, *that's* my happy paregoric! Hee hee hee!"

KI, thought Paul. KI and 14. What could it have been? Never know now. One of those things.

"But death begets life, there's *that,* my boy, and don't you ever forget it! Survival and murder are synonyms, son, first flaw of the universe! Hee hee h—oh! Sorry, son! No time for puns! Forget I said it!"

It's okay, said Paul. Listening to the doctor had at least made him forget the tickle on his lip and it was gone.

"New life burgeons out of rot, new mouths consume old organisms, father dies at orgasm, mother dies at birth, only old Dame Mass with her twin dugs of Stuff and Tickle persists, suffering her long slow split into pure light and pure carbon! Hee hee hee! A tender thought! Don't you agree, lad?" The doctor gazed off into space, happily contemplating the process.

I tell you what, said Paul. Let's forget it.

Just then, the policeman returned with a big quilted comforter, and he and the doctor spread it gently over Paul's body, leaving only his face exposed. The people pressed closer to watch.

"Back! *Back!*" shouted the policeman. "Have you no respect for the dying? *Back, I say!*"

"Oh, come now," chided the doctor. "Let them watch if they want to. It hardly matters to this poor fellow, and even if it does, it can't matter for much longer. And it will help keep the flies off him."

"Well, doctor, if you think . . ." His voice faded away. Paul closed his eyes.

As he lay there among the curious, several odd questions plagued Paul's mind. He knew there was no point to them, but he couldn't rid himself of them. The book, for example: did he have a book? And if he did, what book, and what had happened to it? And what about the stoplight, that lost increment of what men call history, why had no one brought up the matter of the stoplight? And pure carbon he could understand, but as for light: what could its purity consist of? KI. 14. That impression that it had happened before. Yes, these were mysteries, all right. His head ached from them.

People approached Paul from time to time to look under the blanket. Some only peeked, then turned away, while others stayed to poke around, dip their hands in the mutilations.

There seemed to be more interest in them now that they were covered. There were some arguments and some occasional horseplay, but the doctor and policeman kept things from getting out of hand. If someone arrogantly ventured a Latin phrase, the doctor always put him down with some toilet-wall barbarism; on the other hand, he reserved his purest, most mellifluous toponymy for small children and young girls. He made several medical appointments with the latter. The police officer, though queasy, stayed nearby. Once, when Paul happened to open his eyes after having had them closed some while, the policeman smiled warmly down on him and said: "Don't worry, good fellow. I'm still here. Take it as easy as you can. I'll be here to the very end. You can count on me." Bullshit, thought Paul, though not ungratefully, and he thought he remembered hearing the doctor echo him as he fell off to sleep.

When he awoke, the streets were empty. They had all wearied of it, as he had known they would. It had clouded over, the sky had darkened, it was probably night, and it had begun to rain lightly. He could now see the truck clearly, off to his left. Must have been people in the way before.

MAGIC KISS LIPSTICK
IN
14
DIFFERENT SHADES

Never would have guessed. Only in true life could such things happen.

When he glanced to his right, he was surprised to find an old man sitting near him. Priest, no doubt. He had come after all . . . black hat, long grayish beard, sitting in the puddles now forming in the street, legs crossed. Go on, said Paul, don't suffer on my account, don't wait for me, but the old man remained, silent, drawn, rain glistening on his hat, face, beard, clothes: prosopopoeia of patience. The priest. Yet, something about the clothes: well, they were in rags. Pieced together and hanging in tatters. The hat, too, now that he noticed. At short intervals, the old man's head would nod, his eyes would cross, his body would tip, he would catch himself with a start, grunt, glance suspiciously about him, then back down at Paul, would finally relax again and recommence the cycle.

Paul's eyes wearied, especially with the rain splashing into them, so he let them fall closed once more. But he began suffering discomforting visions of the old priest, so he opened them again, squinted off to the left, toward the truck. A small dog, wiry and yellow, padded along in the puddles, hair drooping and bunching up with the rain. It sniffed at the tires of the truck, lifted its leg by one of them, sniffed again, padded on. It circled around Paul, apparently not noticing him, but poking its nose at every object, narrowing the distance between them with every circle. It passed close by the old man, snarled, completed another half-circle, and approached Paul from the left. It stopped near Paul's head—the wet-dog odor was suffocating—and whimpered, licking Paul's face. The old man did nothing, just sat, legs crossed, and passively watched. Of course . . . not a priest at all: an old beggar. Waiting for the clothes when he died. If he still had any. Go ahead and take them now, Paul told him, I don't care. But the beggar only sat and stared. Paul felt a tugging sensation from below, heard the dog growl. His whole body seemed to jerk upwards, sending another hot flash through his neck. The dog's hind feet were planted alongside Paul's head, and now and again the right paw would lose its footing, kick nervously at Paul's face, a buffeting counterpoint to the waves of hot pain behind his throat and eyes. Finally, something gave way. The dog shook water out of its yellow coat, and padded away, a fresh piece of flesh between its jaws. The beggar's eyes crossed, his head dipped to his chest, and he started to topple forward, but again he caught himself, took a deep breath, uncrossed his legs, crossed them again, but the opposite way, reached in his pocket and pulled out an old cigarette butt, molded it between his yellow fingers, put it in his mouth, but did not light it. For an instant, the earth upended again, and Paul found himself hung on the street, a target for the millions of raindarts somebody out in the night was throwing at him. There's nobody out there, he reminded himself, and that set the earth right again. The beggar spat. Paul shielded his eyes from the rain with his lids. He thought he heard other dogs. How much longer must this go on? he wondered. How much longer?

LOOKING AHEAD

The Watchers
Florence Engel Randall

From the moment Althea awoke that morning, she knew their building had been chosen. She knew it even before she saw the excitement in her husband's eyes as he handed her the official notice that had been put under their door.

"Well," he said, smiling at her while she read it, "what do you think of that?"

"I had a feeling, George," she said, "even before I opened my eyes, I had a feeling that this would happen today."

"We were due to be next," George said. "The setup here is about perfect for it."

"Will you be home early?" She watched him while he sipped his coffee.

"It won't start until late," he said. "It won't start until it gets dark. You know how these things are."

"Just the same," she said, "I couldn't bear it just sitting around and waiting for you. We have so much to do. We have to have dinner first and then change our clothes and find seats. We want to have good seats," she reminded him. "They won't reserve any for us, you know."

"Don't worry about it." He touched her cheek lightly with the back of his hand. "I'll be home in plenty of time."

"Do you have everything? I was never so scared in my life yesterday when I found your gun on the top of the dresser. I just couldn't believe my eyes. I wanted to run after you but I didn't know which route you had taken."

"I always carry a spare," he said. "You know that. I always keep a spare in my coat pocket. Why don't you trust me?"

"I know I'm being foolish," Althea said, kissing him good-bye. "Just be careful, that's all. I don't want you to be so sure of yourself that you'll get careless."

"You be careful," he said. "Do you have to go out today?"

She frowned. "I have to go marketing, and then I thought I'd go downtown and buy a new dress for tonight. All the women will be dressed up and I don't want to go looking like a frump."

"Watch out for the department stores," he reminded her. "They can be dangerous. Don't take any crowded elevators and check the dressing room before you try anything on."

She locked and double-locked the door after him, then fastened the chain before she had her own breakfast. Standing at the window while she drank her coffee, she thought how ridiculous it was the way they went through the same routine each morning as if the very fact that they had to take precautions was making them nervous. When they were first married two years ago, it would never have occurred to either of them that there was any reason for worry.

It must be because we're so much in love, she told herself, stacking the dishes in the washer. Love breeds its own vulnerability, its own fear.

When the signal flashed on the wall, Althea had just finished dressing. She watched it for a moment. It was their code, all right. Three lights in a row, the flickering pause, and then the slow, deliberate hold. She pressed the button that buzzed downstairs.

"Who is it?" she said, her mouth against the intercom.

"It's all right," said a woman's voice, clear and high and a bit too shrill. "I've already shown my identification to your doorman. I'm Sally Milford—Cary Milford's wife. My husband works in your husband's office."

"What do you want?" said Althea cautiously. "I'm much too busy to see anyone this morning. Besides, I'm on my way out." She bit her lip. George would be right if he scolded her for being careless. Why had she told this woman she was going out?

"I'll only take a moment of your time. It's important."

"Can't you tell me what it is over the intercom?"

"If I wanted to talk this way, I could have called you on the phone. I must see you. Please."

"All right," said Althea, reluctantly, knowing she was being foolish, "you can come up."

She checked her own gun even though she knew it was loaded and she palmed the small dagger—the one her mother had given her as a wedding present—the one with the jeweled handle.

"Things are so different now," her mother had said, sighing. She had lifted the dagger from the tissue paper and had studied it for a moment before she handed it to Althea. "In my day we could walk the streets without this sort of thing."

"That's not true," Althea reminded her. "You told me you used to wear stilt-like heels and you always carried a whistle in your purse."

"But that's not the same. It still wasn't like this," said her mother. "Did you know we weren't allowed to carry weapons?"

"You weren't?" said Althea, startled.

"That was before everyone realized that our laws were lagging behind our customs and public opinion. That was before the Citizen's Defense Act was passed."

"There is only one crime," Althea said firmly, "and that is to be a victim. Nothing makes sense otherwise."

"I suppose not." Her mother shook her head. "I guess I'm just being sentimental," she added wistfully. "Sometimes I miss the policemen we used to have. They would wear blue uniforms and they would drive around with sirens blaring and lights flashing. It seems a shame they became obsolete. Why I can even remember the time when we could take a walk in the park."

"In the park?" said Althea, incredulous. "You could actually do that?"

Now Althea bit her lip. There was no point in daydreaming. She stationed herself at the oneway peephole. The woman who now came within her range of vision was thin of face and well-dressed. She blinked her eyes nervously and hesitated before she knocked.

"Just a moment," said Althea. She unfastened the chain and the two locks, and then stepped back so that when the door opened she would be behind it. "Come in," she said.

"Where are you?"

"Right behind you," said Althea, her hand on her gun. "You're not very smart to walk right in like that, are you?"

"But I know who you are," said Sally Milford, her eyes wide with fright. "My husband and your husband are good friends."

"The first thing you have to learn," said Althea, "is not to trust anyone." She kicked the door shut. "Hold up your hands." She found a small acid gun in Sally's purse and a knife in the pocket of her jacket. "Just put them on the table," Althea directed, "and then sit down. Would you like some coffee?"

Sally shook her head. "Look," she said, her mouth trembling, "I wouldn't trouble you like this—I wouldn't have come at all if I didn't, in a way, know you. You see that, don't you?"

"No," said Althea firmly, "I don't see anything. Suppose you tell me what you want."

Sally clasped her hands on the edge of the table. "I have a brother-in-law who knows someone on the Board of Commissioners," she said, leaning forward in her eagerness, "and we heard that your apartment house has been chosen."

"These things are supposed to be a secret," Althea said sharply. "No one except the people involved is supposed to know. Don't you realize what can happen to you if they find out? And what can happen to me?"

"I'm sorry but I just couldn't help it. When I heard about it—all I could think was that I simply had to go. I have never been to a performance and, the way things look, I'll never have a chance."

"Where do you live?" Althea asked, putting the gun away.

"On the East Side. You know how safe it's getting to be over there. We haven't had an incident in months."

"That doesn't mean they won't choose your building eventually."

"Do you really think they will?"

"Why not?" said Althea.

"Then, in that case, why can't you make believe that we're visiting you or something? They do have special passes for visitors and then, when we're finally chosen, we could reciprocate. Cary and I could invite you and George. That way we could each see two performances."

"It wouldn't work," said Althea. "In the first place, we have the perfect setting for this sort of thing. That's why we picked this particular apartment building. We could have had a much better place to live but both George and I agreed that our best chance was being here. We had to wait two years for this day, and if they ever suspect that this was a put-up thing, you know what would happen to us."

"I suppose I was foolish to even hope." Sally stood up. "I thought it would work out."

"It won't," said Althea, feeling a sudden pity for her. "Believe me, Sally, it won't. I happen to know that Mrs. Tremont, who lives on the third floor, has her sister-in-law staying with her; that, of course, makes it possible for her sister-in-law to go tonight, but if she had just arrived today someone would be sure to report it and Mrs. Tremont would get into trouble."

"You said you were going out," said Sally. "Do you want a ride with me?"

"I'm going downtown," said Althea. "I thought I'd buy a new dress for tonight."

"I haven't been shopping in ages," said Sally. "Cary won't let me go without him and he's been much too busy on Saturdays. We could shop together and maybe have lunch."

"Just remember one thing," Althea warned as she reached for her coat and hat. "No matter what you say, I won't change my mind. You can spend the whole day with me if you like but I still won't change my mind."

"I know you're right," said Sally as they pressed the button for the elevator. "It's just that I'm glad to have some company on the subway."

"Are you still taking the subway?" Althea stared at her, amazed. "George insists that I take the bus. Not taxis—they're not too reliable anymore but a bus is still fine."

"It takes too long," said Sally. "The subway is much quicker. I have my own system. I never wait on a platform if I'm alone and I usually ride in the first car where the motorman is and, just in case anyone is following me, I change at every other stop."

"Now," said Althea, watching as the elevator stopped at their floor, "run!"

They pounded through the corridor and down one flight of steps. Then they rang for the elevator again. When it arrived, it was empty and they rode it the rest of the way down.

It turned out to be, Althea told George later, a rather pleasant day. With the two of them together, the shopping proved much easier. Sally stood watch while Althea tried on dresses and Althea stood guard while Sally shopped. When they finally parted, it was after four.

Althea took a bus uptown again and got off three blocks before her destination. She glanced behind to make sure she wasn't being followed; then she bought a steak at the meat market. Steak would be the quickest thing to cook for dinner and she didn't want to load her arms with too many packages. It was difficult enough carrying the dress, although she had insisted that the clerk put it in a shopping bag instead of a box. With a shopping bag she would feel less clumsy and have one hand free.

The doorman beamed at her when she entered the lobby.

"This is a great day for us," he said.

Althea nodded. "I bought a new dress," she told him happily, "a black sheath."

"I'll ride the elevator with you if you like," he offered generously. "Most of the tenants are home by now."

"You're not supposed to leave your post," Althea reminded him. "Anyone could come in while you were away. You know what happened to the last doorman we had?"

"You're right," he admitted. "For a moment I forgot."

"By the way," she whispered, "do you know who will be giving the performance?"

He shook his head. "No one knows," he said. "I've been asking but no one knows for sure. I think it's a young one. They usually are."

"You'd think those kids could learn," said Althea, ringing for the elevator. "My parents were pretty strict with me—I can tell you that."

"That's the best way," the doorman said. "You have to be firm with them. I always say that from the time they can walk, they can be taught. Now, you take that kid of Mrs. Hammond. You know the Hammonds on the fifth floor? He got his first slash today and was sent home from school in disgrace."

"Oh, no," said Althea, in horror. "He's only eleven. He's only allowed two more mistakes."

"The way Mrs. Hammond spanked him, he'll learn," the doorman said. "That'll never happen to him again, I can tell you that."

"Who was the other boy?"

"It was a girl," said the doorman. "A pretty little thing, I understand. Well, she'll get her first gold star for that."

"I got a gold star when I was twelve," said Althea, stepping into the elevator.

She rode it to the fourth floor and got out. She took the stairs the rest of the way, then stood before her own front door for a moment, listening. When she was positive it was safe, she inserted her key in the lock.

At precisely six o'clock George came home and, by seven thirty, they had finished dinner and were dressed.

"I'd like to go now," said Althea, impatiently.

"It won't get dark until eight," George said. "You know how it is this time of year. Even then, we'll have to wait a while."

"I can see the stands from here," said Althea, craning her neck as she peered out of the window. "People are beginning to arrive now. Please, darling, let's go."

"You're like a child," he said, hugging her. "Just an anxious little kid."

"I can't help it," she said. "I'm excited. Aren't you thrilled. George?"

"Come on," he said, indulgently. He looked at her, chic and lovely in her new black sheath. "No pockets," he said, shaking his head. "What made you buy a dress without any pockets? I didn't know they made them that way anymore."

"I'll only wear it when I'm with you," she said. "Besides, I have a knife in my purse."

"Just see that you keep it handy." He held the door for her. "I'm glad you used your head this morning."

"For a moment I was tempted," Althea confessed. "Sally seems like a sweet person and it might be fun if we could go there sometimes, but then I realized we'd be taking a chance."

"It doesn't pay to take chances," said George. "Otherwise you can end up giving the performance instead of watching it."

"The doorman told me it was a young one. Probably a girl."

"It usually is," said George.

"Do you know what she did?" Althea asked as they walked through the back of the lobby and out into the courtyard. "No one seems to know what she did."

"Probably something stupid," said George, looking around and waving to their neighbors. "You know, honey, you were right. The stands are filling up."

The stands had been placed next to their building. They were permanent, sturdily built of brick and stone, and erected when the building itself had been new. Optimistically every building had its stands ready for the day when it would be chosen, and Althea looked around proudly as she and George found seats in the second row.

Mr. and Mrs. Hammond were there and seated between them was their son, Timmy. Timmy's right arm was bandaged and he huddled close to his mother.

"I heard about it," said Althea, with sympathy. "I'm sure Timmy will never let it happen again."

"Because she was pretty. Because it was a girl," said Mrs. Hammond bitterly. "She called to him and he ran right over, leaving his knife in his pocket as if a knife ever did anybody any good in a pocket. Just because it was a little girl, he trusted her. But he's learned his lesson, haven't you, Timmy?" she said, slapping him across the face.

"No more," Timmy wept, putting his bandaged arm across his eyes. "Please, Mommy, don't hit me anymore."

He'll never amount to anything, Althea thought, staring at him in dismay. Only three chances and he's used up one already. He's too soft. When I have a child—

She thought about it for a moment, longing for a child but the apartment they were in was too small and they hadn't wanted to move until they had a chance at a performance. Maybe now—maybe now that they were finally spectators— perhaps now that the longed-for, dreamed-about moment had finally arrived, they could move to a larger place and she would have a child.

"You have to train them from the beginning," she whispered to George.

"Sure," he said, knowing what she meant. "It won't happen to us."

"It won't happen to us," she agreed, seeing the way George, even now, even at this moment of pleasure and relaxation, kept his hand in his pocket; George's hand curled over the bulge of his gun.

Althea leaned back. She had known, of course, what the stage setting would be but, just the same, sitting there, part of the expectant, eager audience, she had to admire its reality.

It represented a street scene. It could have been Althea's own street with its middle-class, red-brick buildings, the old-fashioned canopies extending from wide entrances to the edge of the curb. Behind the lighted windows of the buildings, Althea could see the people, all the families together, having dinner, watching television, reading, talking, laughing—all the people of the city settling down for the night.

In the center of the stage was a street lamp, still unlit although it was twilight now; on the far right, there was a fire hydrant. The first floor of the center building was occupied by a shop. The sign said, "ANTIQUES," and Althea could see the lovely things in the window—the paintings in the carved, ornate frames, the delicate crystal goblets, a curved brass bowl. Suddenly the street light went on, dominating the center of the stage with its soft, gentle glow.

The curtain is rising, thought Althea, taking a deep breath. She always loved that moment in the theatre, that magic moment when all the murmuring and the movement and the whispering stopped, the hush and wonder when the curtain rose and the stage lay there before them, the play ready to begin.

Someone somewhere in the back coughed and Althea drew a deep, sighing gasp of impatience.

The stage became alive. From the center building a man emerged, a nondescript man walking his dog at night. The dog tugged and the man whistled softly between his teeth as the two of them walked down the street. The stage became empty again and Althea clasped her hands in her lap, amazed to discover that they were shaking.

At the far right two shadows blurred, moved, took form. Now a girl and a boy strolled down the street. His arm was flung around her shoulders and, from the way she smiled at him, Althea knew they were in love. They moved slowly across the stage. They stopped before the antique shop and the girl pointed to the brass bowl and the boy nodded and gestured expansively, showing her there was nothing in the world he wouldn't get for her. They disappeared on the far left and the stage was empty again.

Althea unclasped her hands and, because her palms were wet, she rubbed them furtively together. Beside her she could hear the sound of George's breathing, slow, heavy, as if each breath were an effort.

Onstage, in the lighted backdrop, in the center building, some of the windows began to darken as if the occupants were retiring for the night.

It's getting late, thought Althea, watching. The lights are dimming all over the city. People are yawning and stretching and getting into bed and even the sounds of the distant traffic seem muted as if someone had muffled all the rolling wheels.

A shadow, part of the shadow of the building, almost part of the square shape of the center building, took on form, and Althea saw that it was a man, a man who had been there all the time, hiding there without her being conscious of his presence.

From the far right she could hear the clicking of high heels on the pavement. Someone else, she thought, will walk down this street this night.

There was a rustle and a stir in the stands.

"Please, Mommy," Timmy whispered. "I don't want to stay here."

"Oh, you'll stay all right," said Mrs. Hammond grimly.

"You just open your eyes wide. You watch everything, Timmy Hammond, if you know what's good for you."

"Be quiet down there," someone hissed. "Do you want to spoil everything?"

Althea gripped George's arm.

The footsteps grew louder and a girl came into view, entering downstage from the right. The shadow that was the man moved, and then became very still, waiting.

The girl moved across the stage. She paused under the street light. She touched the lamppost as if the feel of it under her fingers gave her some sort of reassurance. She hesitated, reluctant to leave the light.

Althea could see her clearly now. She was very young. She could be no more than nineteen—perhaps twenty. She wore a red suit and a little red beret with a feather stuck jauntily in it and her handbag was tucked under her arm. Her hair was blond and it tumbled loose over her shoulders.

Althea watched absorbed as the second figure moved again, the man crouching and then straightening as he ran toward the light, toward the girl in the red suit. At the clear view of his black-jacketed, black-clad figure, there was a sudden roar of applause. Althea clapped until her hands ached.

Out of the dark, into the light, he moved. The girl had her back toward him, not seeing him as the watchers saw him— sinuous, beautiful in his grace, tall, broad of shoulder, his hair allowed to grow long in back and his black cap set on the back of his head. The knife in his hand caught the light and sparkled.

He ran and then stopped. Deliberately, he stalked her. Professional that he was, he began to move slowly, coming down light on the balls of his feet.

The girl whirled around and, at the sight of him, she made a little whimpering sound in her throat. Her back now to the audience, she darted to the left and, as if they were part of a rigid dance pattern, the man stepped after her. She turned and ran to the right, her heels clicking frantically but he was there before her.

"Please," said the girl in the red suit. She darted back to the lamppost, back where the light was the brightest, where she could be seen most clearly. She turned and faced the backdrop, faced the buildings, the windows where the people were. Her right hand still clutched her purse, her left was now at her throat.

"Oh, please." Her voice rose to a keening wail of terror and anguish.

"Please," she screamed, her voice begging, her body begging. Then blindly she turned again and ran.

This cry in the night had awakened the sleepers. It had roused the dreamers. The darkened windows in the backdrop were illuminated again. Figures moved; there were silhouettes framed in the windows. The sleepers were awake. The dreamers had stopped dreaming and the city was alert and watching.

"Help me."

The city held its breath and listened.

"Please, help me."

But, Althea saw, she couldn't run far enough. She couldn't run fast enough. The man had her pinned against the wall now, pinned against the lighted, listening backdrop of the building and her handbag fell to the ground.

"I beg you." She was almost hidden by the man's bulk as he bent over her. "Won't someone help me?"

The man in the black jacket raised his arm and the knife flashed. The girl screamed in agony, her cheek now as crimson as her suit. Dodging under his arm, she ran again, the slowing rhythm of her clicking heels the only sound to be heard.

The man watched her for a moment. The quiet, lighted windows watched and the filled stands watched. The man stood very still as if he were resting and then, gracefully, quickly, easily, he caught her again.

That does it, thought Althea, her heart pounding; that does it.

The knife gleamed and Althea held her breath. The arm lifted. The black-draped arm lifted and fell, lifted and fell. The red suit crumpled, falling as if it were empty, the red suit only a splotch now on the pavement. Then the man moved toward the hushed, absorbed watchers.

And there he stood, bowing and smiling, the knife dripping red at his side. Over and over again he took his bow while they all gave him the ultimate, the supreme tribute of their silence.

The Police Band
Donald Barthelme

It was kind of the department to think up the Police Band. The original impulse, I believe, was creative and humanitarian. A better way of doing things. Unpleasant, bloody things required by the line of duty. Even if it didn't work out.

The Commissioner (the old Commissioner, not the one they have now) brought us up the river from Detroit. Where our members had been, typically, working the Sho Bar two nights a week. Sometimes the Glass Crutch. Friday and Saturday. And the rest of the time wandering the streets disguised as postal employees. Bitten by dogs and burdened with third-class mail.

What are our duties? we asked at the interview. Your duties are to wail, the Commissioner said. That only. We admired our new dark-blue uniforms as we came up the river in canoes like Indians. We plan to use you in certain situations, certain tense situations, to alleviate tensions, the Commissioner said. I can visualize great success with this new method. And would you play "Entropy." He was pale, with a bad liver.

We are subtle, the Commissioner said, never forget that. Subtlety is what has previously been lacking in our line. Some of the old ones, the Commissioner said, all they know is the club. He took a little pill from a little box and swallowed it with his Scotch.

When we got to town we looked at those Steve Canyon recruiting posters and wondered if we resembled them. Henry Wang, the bass man, looks like a Chinese Steve Canyon, right? The other cops were friendly in a suspicious way. They liked to hear us wail, however.

The Police Band is a very sensitive highly trained and ruggedly anti-Communist unit whose efficacy will be demonstrated in due time, the Commissioner said to the Mayor (the old Mayor). The Mayor took a little pill from a little box and said, We'll see. He could tell we were musicians because we were holding our instruments, right? Emptying spit valves, giving the horn that little shake. Or coming in at letter E with some sly emotion stolen from another life.

The old Commissioner's idea was essentially that if there was a disturbance on the city's streets—some ethnic group cutting up some other ethnic group on a warm August evening—the Police Band would be sent in. The handsome dark-green band bus arriving with sirens singing, red lights whirling. Hard-pressed men on the beat in their white hats raising a grateful cheer. We stream out of the vehicle holding our instruments at high port. A skirmish line fronting the angry crowd. And play "Perdido." The crowd washed with new and true emotion. Startled, they listen. Our emotion stronger than their emotion. A triumph of art over good sense.

That was the idea. The old Commissioner's *musical* ideas were not very interesting, because after all he was a cop, right? But his police ideas were interesting.

We had drills. Poured out of that mother-loving bus onto vacant lots holding our instruments at high port like John Wayne. Felt we were heroes already. Playing "Perdido," "Stumblin'," "Gin Song," "Feebles." Laving the terrain with emotion stolen from old busted-up loves, broken marriages, the needle, economic deprivation. A few old ladies leaning out of high windows. Our emotion washing rusty Rheingold cans and parts of old doors.

This city is too much! We'd be walking down the street talking about our techniques and we'd see out of our eyes a woman standing in the gutter screaming to herself about what we could not imagine. A drunk trying to strangle a dog somebody'd left leashed to a parking meter. The drunk and the dog screaming at each other. This city is too much!

We had drills and drills. It is true that the best musicians come from Detroit but there is something here that you have to get in your playing and that is simply the scream. We got that. The Commissioner, a sixty-three-year-old hippie with no doubt many graft qualities and unpleasant qualities, nevertheless understood that. When we'd play "ugly," he understood that. He understood the rising expectations of the world's peoples also. That our black members didn't feel like toting junk mail around Detroit forever until the ends of their lives. For some strange reason.

He said one of our functions would be to be sent out to play in places where people were trembling with fear inside their houses, right? To inspirit them in difficult times. This was the plan. We set up in the street. Henry Wang grabs hold of his instrument. He has a four-bar lead-in all by himself. Then the whole group. The iron shutters raised a few inches.

Shorty Alanio holding his horn at his characteristic angle (sideways). The reeds dropping lacy little fill-ins behind him. We're cooking. The crowd roars.

The Police Band was an idea of a very romantic kind. The Police Band was an idea that didn't work. When they retired the old Commissioner (our Commissioner), who it turned out had a little drug problem of his own, they didn't let us even drill anymore. We have never been used. His idea was a romantic idea, they said (right?), which was not adequate to the rage currently around in the world. Rage must be met with rage, they said. (Not in so many words.) We sit around the precinct houses, under the filthy lights, talking about our techniques. But I thought it might be good if you knew that the Department still has us. We have a good group. We still have emotion to be used. We're still here.

Tomorrow and Tomorrow and Tomorrow
Kurt Vonnegut, Jr.

The year was A.D. 2158 and Lou and Emerald Schwartz were whispering on the balcony outside Lou's family's apartment on the seventy-sixth floor of Building 257 in Alden Village, a New York housing development that covered what had once been known as Southern Connecticut. When Lou and Emerald had married, Em's parents had tearfully described the marriage as being between May and December; but now, with Lou one hundred and twelve and Em ninety-three, Em's parents had to admit that the match had worked out well.

But Em and Lou weren't without their troubles, and they were out in the nippy air of the balcony because of them.

"Sometimes I get so mad, I feel like just up and diluting his anti-gerasone," said Em.

"That'd be against Nature, Em," said Lou, "it'd be murder. Besides, if he caught us tinkering with his anti-gerasone, not only would he disinherit us, he'd bust my neck. Just because he's one hundred and seventy-two doesn't mean Gramps isn't strong as a bull."

"Against Nature," said Em. "Who knows what Nature's like anymore? Ohhhhh—I don't guess I could ever bring myself to dilute his anti-gerasone or anything like that, but, gosh, Lou, a body can't help thinking Gramps is never going to leave if somebody doesn't help him along a little. Golly—we're so crowded a person can hardly turn around, and Verna's dying for a baby, and Melissa's gone thirty years without one." She stamped her feet. "I get so sick of seeing his wrinkled old face, watching him take the only private room and the best chair and the best food, and getting to pick out what to watch on TV, and running everybody's life by changing his will all the time."

"Well, after all," said Lou bleakly, "Gramps *is* head of the family. And he can't help being wrinkled like he is. He was seventy before anti-gerasone was invented. He's going to leave, Em. Just give him time. It's his business. I know he's tough to live with, but be patient. It wouldn't do to do anything that'd rile him. After all, we've got it better'n anybody else, there on the daybed."

"How much longer do you think we'll get to sleep on the daybed before he picks another pet? The world's record's two months, isn't it?"

"Mom and Pop had it that long once, I guess."

"When *is* he going to leave, Lou?" said Emerald.

"Well, he's talking about giving up anti-gerasone right after the five-hundred-mile Speedway Race."

"Yes—and before that it was the Olympics, and before that the World's Series, and before that the Presidential Elections, and before that I-don't-know-what. It's been just one excuse after another for fifty years now. I don't think we're ever going to get a room to ourselves or an egg or anything."

"All right—call me a failure!" said Lou. "What can I do? I work hard and make good money, but the whole thing, practically, is taxed away for defense and old age pensions. And if it wasn't taxed away, where you think we'd find a vacant room to rent? Iowa, maybe? Well, who wants to live on the outskirts of Chicago?"

Em put her arms around his neck. "Lou, hon, I'm not calling you a failure. The Lord knows you're not. You just haven't had a chance to be anything or have anything because Gramps and the rest of his generation won't leave and let somebody else take over."

"Yeah, yeah," said Lou gloomily. "You can't exactly blame 'em, though, can you? I mean, I wonder how quick we'll knock off the anti-gerasone when we get Gramps' age."

"Sometimes I wish there wasn't any such thing as anti-gerasone!" said Emerald passionately. "Or I wish it was made out of something real expensive and hard-to-get instead of mud and dandelions. Sometimes I wish folks just up and died regular as clockwork, without anything to say about it, instead of deciding themselves how long they're going to stay around. There ought to be a law against selling the stuff to anybody over one hundred and fifty."

"Fat chance of that," said Lou, "with all the money and votes the old people've got." He looked at her closely. "You ready to up and die, Em?"

"Well, for heaven's sakes, what a thing to say to your wife. Hon! I'm not even one hundred yet." She ran her hands lightly over her firm, youthful figure, as though for confirmation. "The best years of my life are still ahead of me. But you can bet that when one hundred and fifty rolls around, old Em's going to pour her anti-gerasone down the sink, and quit taking up room, and she'll do it smiling."

"Sure, sure," said Lou, "you bet. That's what they all say. How many you heard of doing it?"

"There was that man in Delaware."

"Aren't you getting kind of tired of talking about him, Em? That was five months ago."

"All right, then—Gramma Winkler, right here in the same building."

"She got smeared by a subway."

"Then what was she doing carrying a six-pack of anti-gerasone when she got it?"

"That's just the way she picked to go," said Em.

Emerald shook her head wearily and covered her eyes. "I dunno, I dunno, I dunno. All I know is, something's just got to be done." She sighed. "Sometimes I wish they'd left a couple of diseases kicking around somewhere, so I could get one and go to bed for a little while. Too many people!" she cried, and her words cackled and gabbled and died in a thousand asphalt-paved, skyscraper-walled courtyards.

Lou laid his hand on her shoulder tenderly. "Aw, hon, I hate to see you down in the dumps like this."

"If we just had a car, like the folks used to in the old days," said Em, "we could go for a drive, and get away from people for a little while. Gee—if *those* weren't the days!"

"Yeah," said Lou, "before they'd used up all the metal."

"We'd hop in, and Pop'd drive up to a filling station and say, 'Fillerup!'"

"That *was* the nuts, wasn't it—before they'd used up all the gasoline."

"And we'd go for a carefree ride in the country."

"Yeah—all seems like a fairyland now, doesn't it, Em? Hard to believe there really used to be all that space between cities."

"And when we got hungry," said Em, "we'd find ourselves a restaurant, and walk in, big as you please and say, 'I'll have a steak and French-fries, I believe,' or, 'How are the pork chops today?'" She licked her lips, and her eyes glistened.

"Yeah man!" growled Lou. "How'd you like a hamburger with the works, Em?"

"Mmmmmmmm."

"If anybody'd offered us processed seaweed in those days, we would have spit right in his eye, huh, Em?"

"Or processed sawdust," said Em.

Doggedly, Lou tried to find the cheery side of the situation.

"Well, anyway, they've got the stuff so it tastes a lot less like seaweed and sawdust than it did at first; and they say it's actually better for us than what we used to eat."

"I felt fine!" said Em fiercely.

Lou shrugged. "Well, you've got to realize, the world wouldn't be able to support twelve billion people if it wasn't for processed seaweed and sawdust. I mean, it's a wonderful thing, really. I guess. That's what they say."

"They say the first thing that pops into their heads," said Em. She closed her eyes. "Golly—remember shopping, Lou? Remember how the stores used to fight to get our folks to buy something? You didn't have to wait for somebody to die to get a bed or chairs or a stove or anything like that. Just went in—bing!—and bought whatever you wanted. Gee whiz that was nice, before they used up all the raw materials. I was just a little kid then, but I can remember so plain."

Depressed, Lou walked listlessly to the balcony's edge, and looked up at the clean, cold, bright stars against the black velvet of infinity. "Remember when we used to be bugs on science fiction, Em? Flight seventeen, leaving for Mars, launching ramp twelve. 'Board! All non-technical personnel kindly remain in bunkers. Ten seconds . . . nine . . . eight . . . seven . . . six . . . five . . . four . . . three . . . two . . . *one! Main Stage! Barrrrrrooooom!*"

"Why worry about what was going on on Earth?" said Em, looking up at the stars with him. "In another few years, we'd all be shooting through space to start life all over again on a new planet."

Lou sighed. "Only it turns out you need something about twice the size of the Empire State Building to get one lousy colonist to Mars. And for another couple of trillion bucks he could take his wife and dog. *That's* the way to lick over-population—*emigrate!*"

"Lou—?"

"Hmmm?"

"When's the Five-Hundred-Mile Speedway Race?"

"Uh—Memorial Day, May thirtieth."

She bit her lip. "Was that awful of me to ask?"

"Not very, I guess. Everybody in the apartment's looked it up to make sure."

"I don't want to be awful," said Em, "but you've just got to talk over these things now and then, and get them out of your system."

"Sure you do. Feel better?"

"Yes—and I'm not going to lose my temper anymore, and I'm going to be just as nice to him as I know how."

"That's my Em."

They squared their shoulders, smiled bravely, and went back inside.

Gramps Schwartz, his chin resting on his hands, his hands on the crook of his cane, was staring irascibly at the five-foot television screen that dominated the room. On the screen, a news commentator was summarizing the day's happenings. Every thirty seconds or so, Gramps would jab the floor with his cane-tip and shout, "Hell! We did that a hundred years ago!"

Emerald and Lou, coming in from the balcony, were obliged to take seats in the back row, behind Lou's father and mother, brother and sister-in-law, son and daughter-in-law, grandson and wife, granddaughter and husband, great-grandson and wife, nephew and wife, grandnephew and wife, great-grandniece and husband, great-grandnephew and wife, and, of course, Gramps, who was in front of everybody. All, save Gramps, who was somewhat withered and bent, seemed by pre-anti-gerasone standards, to be about the same age—to be somewhere in their late twenties or early thirties.

"Meanwhile," the commentator was saying, *"Council Bluffs, Iowa, was still threatened by stark tragedy. But two hundred weary rescue workers have refused to give up hope, and continue to dig in an effort to save Elbert Haggedorn, one hundred and eighty-three, who has been wedged for two days in a . . ."*

"I wish he'd get something more cheerful," Emerald whispered to Lou.

"Silence!" cried Gramps. "Next one shoots off his big bazoo while the TV's on is gonna find hisself cut off without a dollar—" and here his voice suddenly softened and sweetened "when they wave that checkered flag at the Indianapolis Speedway, and old Gramps gets ready for the Big Trip Up Yonder." He sniffed sentimentally, while his heirs concentrated desperately on not making the slightest sound. For them, the poignancy of the prospective Big Trip had been dulled somewhat by its having been mentioned by Gramps about once a day for fifty years.

"Dr. Brainard Keyes Bullard," said the commentator, *"President of Wyandotte College, said in an address tonight that*

most of the world's ills can be traced to the fact that Man's knowledge of himself has not kept pace with his knowledge of the physical world."

"Hell!" said Gramps. "We said that a hundred years ago!"

"In Chicago tonight," said the commentator, *"a special celebration is taking place in the Chicago Lying-in Hospital. The guest of honor is Lowell W. Hitz, age zero. Hitz, born this morning, is the twenty-five-millionth child to be born in the hospital."* The commentator faded, and was replaced on the screen by young Hitz, who squalled furiously.

"Hell," whispered Lou to Emerald, "we said that a hundred years ago."

"I heard that!" shouted Gramps. He snapped off the television set, and his petrified descendants stared silently at the screen. "You, there, boy—"

"I didn't mean anything by it, sir," said Lou.

"Get me my will. You know where it is. You kids *all* know where it is. Fetch, boy!"

Lou nodded dully, and found himself going down the hall, picking his way over bedding to Gramps' room, the only private room in the Schwartz apartment. The other rooms were the bathroom, the living room, and the wide, windowless hallway, which was originally intended to serve as a dining area, and which had a kitchenette in one end. Six mattresses and four sleeping bags were dispersed in the hallway and living room, and the daybed, in the living room, accommodated the eleventh couple, the favorites of the moment.

On Gramps' bureau was his will, smeared, dog-eared, perforated, and blotched with hundreds of additions, deletions, accusations, conditions, warnings, advice, and homely philosophy. The document was, Lou reflected, a fifty-year diary, all jammed onto two sheets—a garbled, illegible log of day after day of strife. This day, Lou would be disinherited for the eleventh time, and it would take him perhaps six months of impeccable behavior to regain the promise of a share in the estate.

"Boy!" called Gramps.

"Coming, sir." Lou hurried back into the living room, and handed Gramps the will.

"Pen!" said Gramps.

He was instantly offered eleven pens, one from each couple.

"Not *that* leaky thing," he said, brushing Lou's pen aside. "Ah, there's a nice one. Good boy, Willy." He accepted Willy's pen. That was the tip they'd all been waiting for. Willy, then, Lou's father, was the new favorite.

Willy, who looked almost as young as Lou, though one hundred and forty-two, did a poor job of concealing his pleasure. He glanced shyly at the daybed, which would become his, and from which Lou and Emerald would have to move back into the hall, back to the worst spot of all by the bathroom door.

Gramps missed none of the high drama he'd authored, and he gave his own familiar role everything he had. Frowning and running his finger along each line, as though he were seeing the will for the first time, he read aloud in a deep, portentous monotone, like a bass tone on a cathedral organ:

"I, Harold D. Schwartz, residing in Building 257 of Alden Village, New York City, do hereby make, publish, and declare this to be my last Will and Testament, hereby revoking any and all former wills and codicils by me at any time heretofore made." He blew his nose importantly, and went on, not missing a word, and repeating many for emphasis—repeating in particular his ever-more-elaborate specifications for a funeral.

At the end of these specifications, Gramps was so choked with emotion that Lou thought he might forget why he'd gotten out the will in the first place. But Gramps heroically brought his powerful emotions under control, and, after erasing for a full minute, he began to write and speak at the same time. Lou could have spoken his lines for him, he'd heard them so often.

"I have had many heartbreaks ere leaving this vale of tears for a better land," Gramps said and wrote. "But the deepest hurt of all has been dealt me by—" He looked around the group, trying to remember who the malefactor was.

Everyone looked helpfully at Lou, who held up his hand resignedly.

Gramps nodded, remembering, and completed the sentence: "my great-grandson, Louis J. Schwartz."

"Grandson, sir," said Lou.

"Don't quibble. You're in deep enough now, young man," said Gramps, but he changed the trifle. And from there he went without a misstep through the phrasing of the disinheritance, causes for which were disrespectfulness and quibbling.

In the paragraph following, the paragraph that had belonged to everyone in the room at one time or another, Lou's name was scratched out and Willy's substituted as heir to the apartment and, the biggest plum of all, the double bed in the private bedroom. "So!" said Gramps, beaming. He erased the date at the foot of the will, and substituted a new one, including the time of day. "Well—time to watch the McGarvey Family." The McGarvey Family was a television serial that Gramps had been following since he was sixty, or for one hundred and twelve years. "I can't wait to see what's going to happen next," he said.

Lou detached himself from the group and lay down on his bed of pain by the bathroom door. He wished Em would join him, and he wondered where she was.

He dozed for a few moments, until he was disturbed by someone's stepping over him to get into the bathroom. A moment later, he heard a faint gurgling sound, as though something were being poured down the washbasin drain. Suddenly, it entered his mind that Em had cracked up, and that she was in there doing something drastic about Gramps.

"Em—!" he whispered through the panel. There was no reply, and Lou pressed against the door. The worn lock, whose bolt barely engaged its socket, held for a second, then let the door swing inward.

"Morty!" gasped Lou.

Lou's great-grandnephew, Mortimer, who had just married and brought his wife home to the Schwartz menage, looked at Lou with consternation and surprise. Morty kicked the door shut, but not before Lou had glimpsed what was in his hand— Gramps' enormous economy-size bottle of anti-gerasone, which had been half-emptied, and which Morty was refilling to the top with tap water.

A moment later, Morty came out, glared defiantly at Lou, and brushed past him wordlessly to rejoin his pretty bride.

Shocked, Lou didn't know what on earth to do. He couldn't let Gramps take the mousetrapped anti-gerasone; but if he warned Gramps about it, Gramps would certainly make life in the apartment, which was merely insufferable now, harrowing.

Lou glanced into the living room, and saw that the Schwartzes, Emerald among them, were momentarily at rest, relishing the botches that the McGarveys had made of *their* lives. Stealthily, he went into the bathroom, locked the door as well as he could, and began to pour the contents of Gramps' bottle down the drain. He was going to refill it with full-strength anti-gerasone from the twenty-two smaller bottles on the shelf. The bottle contained a half-gallon, and its neck was small, so it seemed to Lou that the emptying would take forever.

And the almost imperceptible smell of anti-gerasone, like Worcestershire sauce, now seemed to Lou, in his nervousness, to be pouring out into the rest of the apartment through the keyhole and under the door.

"Gloog-gloog-gloog-gloog-," went the bottle monotonously. Suddenly, up came the sound of music from the living room, and there were murmurs and the scraping of chair legs on the floor. *"Thus ends,"* said the television announcer, *"the 29,121st chapter in the life of your neighbors and mine, the McGarveys."* Footsteps were coming down the hall. There was a knock on the bathroom door.

"Just a sec," called Lou cheerily. Desperately, he shook the big bottle, trying to speed up the flow. His palms slipped on the wet glass, and the heavy bottle smashed to splinters on the tile floor.

The door sprung open, and Gramps, dumfounded, stared at the mess.

Lou grinned engagingly through his nausea, and, for want of anything remotely resembling a thought, he waited for Gramps to speak.

"Well, boy," said Gramps at last, "looks like you've got a little tidying up to do."

And that was all he said. He turned around, elbowed his way through the crowd, and locked himself in his bedroom.

The Schwartzes contemplated Lou in incredulous silence for a moment longer, and then hurried back to the living room, as though some of his horrible guilt would taint them, too, if they looked too long. Morty stayed behind long enough to give Lou a quizzical, annoyed glance. Then he, too, went into the living room, leaving only Emerald standing in the doorway.

Tears streamed over her cheeks. "Oh, you poor lamb—please don't look so awful. It was my fault. I put you up to this."

"No," said Lou, finding his voice, "really you didn't. Honest, Em, I was just—"

"You don't have to explain anything to me, hon. I'm on your side no matter what." She kissed him on his cheek, and whispered in his ear. "It wouldn't have been murder, hon. It wouldn't have killed him. It wasn't such a terrible thing to do. It just would have fixed him up so he'd be able to go any time God decided He wanted him."

"What's gonna happen next, Em?" said Lou hollowly. "What's he gonna do?"

Lou and Emerald stayed fearfully awake almost all night, waiting to see what Gramps was going to do. But not a sound came from the sacred bedroom. At two hours before dawn, the pair dropped off to sleep.

At six o'clock they arose again, for it was time for their generation to eat breakfast in the kitchenette. No one spoke to them. They had twenty minutes in which to eat, but their reflexes were so dulled by the bad night that they had hardly swallowed two mouthfuls of egg-type processed seaweed before it was time to surrender their places to their son's generation.

Then, as was the custom for whomever had been most recently disinherited, they began preparing Gramps' breakfast, which would presently be served to him in bed, on a tray. They tried to be cheerful about it. The toughest part of the job was having to handle the honest-to-God eggs and bacon and oleomargarine on which Gramps spent almost all of the income from his fortune.

"Well," said Emerald, "I'm not going to get all panicky until I'm sure there's something to be panicky about."

"Maybe he doesn't know what it was I busted," said Lou hopefully.

"Probably thinks it was your watch crystal," said Eddie, their son, who was toying apathetically with his buckwheat-type processed sawdust cakes.

"Don't get sarcastic with your father," said Em, "and don't talk with your mouth full, either."

"I'd like to see anybody take a mouthful of this stuff and *not* say something," said Eddie, who was seventy-three. He glanced at the clock. "It's time to take Gramps his breakfast, you know."

"Yeah, it is, isn't it," said Lou weakly. He shrugged. "Let's have the tray, Em."

"We'll both go."

Walking slowly, smiling bravely, they found a large semicircle of long-faced Schwartzes standing around the bedroom door.

Em knocked. "Gramps," she said brightly, "break-fast is rea-dy."

There was no reply, and she knocked again, harder.

The door swung open before her fist. In the middle of the

room, the soft, deep, wide, canopied bed, the symbol of the sweet by-and-by to every Schwartz, was empty.

A sense of death, as unfamiliar to the Schwartzes as Zoroastrianism or the causes of the Sepoy Mutiny, stilled every voice and slowed every heart. Awed, the heirs began to search gingerly under the furniture and behind the drapes for all that was mortal of Gramps, father of the race.

But Gramps had left not his earthly husk but a note, which Lou finally found on the dresser, under a paperweight which was a treasured souvenir from the 2000 World's Fair. Unsteadily, Lou read it aloud:

" 'Somebody who I have sheltered and protected and taught the best I know how all these years last night turned on me like a mad dog and diluted my anti-gerasone, or tried to. I am no longer a young man. I can no longer bear the crushing burden of life as I once could. So, after last night's bitter experience, I say goodbye. The cares of this world will soon drop away like a cloak of thorns, and I shall know peace. By the time you find this, I will be gone.' "

"Gosh," said Willy brokenly, "he didn't even get to see how the Five-Hundred-Mile Speedway Race was going to come out."

"Or the World's Series," said Eddie.

"Or whether Mrs. McGarvey got her eyesight back," said Morty.

"There's more," said Lou, and he began reading aloud again: " 'I, Harold D. Schwartz . . . do hereby make, publish and declare this to be my last Will and Testament, hereby revoking any and all former wills and codicils by me at any time heretofore made.' "

"No!" cried Willy. "Not another one!"

" 'I do stipulate,' " read Lou, " 'that all of my property, of whatsoever kind and nature, not be divided, but do devise and bequeath it to be held in common by my issue, without regard for generation, equally, share and share alike.' "

"Issue?" said Emerald.

Lou included the multitude in a sweep of his hand. "It means we all own the whole damn shootin' match."

All eyes turned instantly to the bed.

"Share and share alike?" said Morty.

"Actually," said Willy, who was the oldest person present, "it's just like the old system, where the oldest people head up things with their headquarters in here, and—"

"I like *that!*" said Em. "Lou owns as much of it as you do, and I say it ought to be for the oldest one who's still working. You can snooze around here all day, waiting for your pension check, and poor Lou stumbles in here after work, all tuckered out, and—"

"How about letting somebody who's never had any privacy get a little crack at it?" said Eddie hotly. "Hell, you old people had plenty of privacy back when you were kids. I was born and raised in the middle of the goddam barracks in the hall! How about—"

"Yeah?" said Morty. "Sure, you've all had it pretty tough, and my heart bleeds for you. But try honeymooning in the hall for a real kick."

"Silence!" shouted Willy imperiously. "The next person who opens his mouth spends the next six months by the bathroom. Now clear out of my room. I want to think."

A vase shattered against the wall, inches above his head. In the next moment, a free-for-all was underway, with each couple battling to eject every other couple from the room. Fighting coalitions formed and dissolved with the lightning changes of the tactical situation. Em and Lou were thrown into the hall, where they organized others in the same situation, and stormed back into the room.

After two hours of struggle, with nothing like a decision in sight, the cops broke in.

For the next half-hour, patrol wagons and ambulances hauled away Schwartzes, and then the apartment was still and spacious.

An hour later, films of the last stages of the riot were being televised to 500,000,000 delighted viewers on the Eastern Seaboard.

In the stillness of the three-room Schwartz apartment on the 76th floor of Building 257, the television set had been left on. Once more the air was filled with the cries and grunts and crashes of the fray, coming harmlessly now from the loudspeaker.

The battle also appeared on the screen of the television set in the police station, where the Schwartzes and their captors watched with professional interest.

Em and Lou were in adjacent four-by-eight cells, and were stretched out peacefully on their cots.

"Em—" called Lou through the partition, "you got a washbasin all your own too?"

"Sure. Washbasin, bed, light—the works. Ha! And we thought Gramps' room was something. How long's this been going on?" She held out her hand. "For the first time in forty years, hon, I haven't got the shakes."

"Cross your fingers," said Lou, "the lawyer's going to try to get us a year."

"Gee," said Em dreamily, "I wonder what kind of wires you'd have to pull to get solitary?"

"All right, pipe down," said the turnkey, "or I'll toss the whole kit and caboodle of you right out. And first one who lets on to anybody outside how good jail is ain't never getting back in!"

The prisoners instantly fell silent.

The living room of the Schwartz apartment darkened for a moment, as the riot scenes faded, and then the face of the announcer appeared, like the sun coming from behind a cloud. *"And now, friends,"* he said, *"I have a special message from the makers of anti-gerasone, a message for all you folks over one hundred and fifty. Are you hampered socially by wrinkles, by stiffness of joints and discoloration or loss of hair, all because these things came upon you before anti-gerasone was developed? Well, if you are, you need no longer suffer, need no longer feel different and out of things.*

"After years of research, medical science has now developed super-anti-gerasone! *In weeks, yes weeks, you can look, feel, and act as young as your great-great-grandchildren! Wouldn't you pay $5,000 to be indistinguishable from everybody else? Well, you don't have to. Safe, tested super-anti-gerasone costs you only dollars a day. The average cost of regaining all the sparkle and attractiveness of youth is less than fifty dollars.*

"Write now for your free trial carton. Just put your name and address on a dollar postcard, and mail it to 'Super,' Box 500,000, Schenectady, N. Y. Have you got that? I'll repeat it. 'Super.' Box . . ." Underlining the announcer's words was the scratching of Gramps' fountain-pen, the one Willy had given him the night before. He had come in a few minutes previous from the Idle Hour Tavern, which commanded a view of Building 257 across the square of asphalt known as the Alden Village Green. He had called a cleaning woman to come straighten the place up, and had hired the best lawyer in town to get his descendants a conviction. Gramps had then moved the daybed before the television screen so that he could watch from a reclining position. It was something he'd dreamed of doing for years.

"Schen-*ec*-ta-dy," mouthed Gramps. "Got it." His face had changed remarkably. His facial muscles seemed to have relaxed, revealing kindness and equanimity under what had been taut, bad-tempered lines. It was almost as though his trial package of *Super*-anti-gerasone had already arrived. When something amused him on television, he smiled easily, rather than barely managing to lengthen the thin line of his mouth a millimeter. Life was good. He could hardly wait to see what was going to happen next.

Selected Bibliography

William Melvin Kelley (1937–   )
A Different Drummer (1959); *Dancers on the Shore* (1962); *A Drop of Patience* (1965); *Dem* (1967); *Dunfords Travels Every Wheres* (1970).

Joseph Heller (1923–   )
Catch-22 (1961); *We Bombed in New Haven* (1968).

Jay Neugeboren (1938–   )
Big Man (1966); *Listen Ruben Fontanez* (1968); *Corky's Brother* (1969).

James Baldwin (1924–   )
Go Tell It on the Mountain (1953); *Notes of a Native Son* (1955); *The Amen Corner* (1955); *Giovanni's Room* (1956); *Going to Meet the Man* (1958); *Nobody Knows My Name* (1961); *Another Country* (1962); *The Fire Next Time* (1963); *Blues for Mister Charlie* (1964); *Tell Me How Long the Train's Been Gone* (1968).

Nelson Algren (1909–   )
The Neon Wilderness (1947); *The Man with the Golden Arm* (1949); *Chicago: City on the Make* (1951); *A Walk on the Wild Side* (1956); *Nelson Algren's Own Book of Lonesome Monsters* (1963).

Jeremy Larner (1937–   )
Drive, he said (1964); *The Addict in the Street* [ed.] (1965); *The Answer* (1969); *Nobody Knows* (1970).

LeRoi Jones (1934–   )
Preface to a Twenty Volume Suicide Note (1961); *Blues People* (1963); *The Dead Lecturer* (1964); *Two Plays: Dutchman and The Slave* (1964); *The System of Dante's Hell* (1965); *Home* (1966); *Tales* (1967); *The Baptism; The Toilet* (1967); *Black Music* (1968); *Black Magic Poetry* (1969); *In Our Terribleness* (1970).

Bernard Malamud (1914–   )
The Natural (1952); *The Assistant* (1957); *A New Life* (1961); *Idiots First* (1963); *The Fixer* (1966); *The Magic Barrel* (1967); *Pictures of Fidelman* (1969).

Harvey Swados (1920–   )
Out Went the Candle (1955); *On the Line* (1957); *Nights in the Gardens of Brooklyn* (1960); *False Coin* (1960); *A Radical's America* (1962); *A Story for Teddy and Others* (1965); *Standing Fast* (1970).

John Cheever (1912–   )
The Enormous Radio and Other Stories (1953); *The Wapshot Chronicle* (1957); *The Brigadier and the Golf Widow* (1964); *Bullet Park* (1969).

Leonard Michaels (1933–   )
Going Places (1969).

Jack Kerouac (1922–1969)
The Town and the City (1950); *On the Road* (1957); *The Subterraneans* (1958); *The Dharma Bums* (1958); *Doctor Sax* (1959); *Maggie Cassidy* (1959); *Visions of Cody* (1960); *Tristessa* (1960); *Big Sur* (1962); *Visions of Gerard* (1963); *Desolation Angels* (1965); *Vanity of Duluoz* (1968).

Pietro Di Donato (1911–   )
Christ in Concrete (1939); *The Penitent* (1962).

Richard Wright (1908–1960)
Uncle Tom's Children (1938); *Native Son* (1940); *Black Boy* (1945); *The Outsider* (1953); *Savage Holiday* (1954); *The Long Dream* (1958); *Eight Men* (1961).

John Rechy (1934–   )
City of Night (1963); *Numbers* (1967); *This Day's Death* (1969); *The Vampires* (1971).

William Eastlake (1917–   )
Go In Beauty (1956); *The Bronc People* (1958); *Portrait of An Artist with Twenty-Six Horses* (1963); *Castle Keep* (1965).

Charles Wright (1932–   )
The Messenger (1963); *The Wig* (1966).

James Alan McPherson (1943–   )
Hue and Cry (1967).

T. Mike Walker (1937–   )
Voices from the Bottom of the World: A Policeman's Journal (1970).

SELECTED BIBLIOGRAPHY

James Leo Herlihy (1927–)
Blue Denim, with William Noble (1958); *The Sleep of Baby Filbertson and Other Stories* (1959); *All Fall Down* (1960); *Midnight Cowboy* (1965); *The Story that Ends with a Scream* (1967); *The Season of the Witch* (1971).

James Purdy (1923–)
63: Dream Palace (1956); *Don't Call Me by My Right Name* (1956); *Color of Darkness* (1957); *Malcolm* (1960); *The Nephew* (1960); *Children Is All* (1962); *Cabot Wright Begins* (1964); *Eustace Chisholm and the Works* (1967); *Jeremy's Version* (1971).

Flannery O'Connor (1924–1964)
Wise Blood (1952); *A Good Man Is Hard to Find* (1955); *The Violent Bear it Away* (1960); *Everything that Rises Must Converge* (1965).

Robert Coover (1932–)
The Origin of the Brunists (1967); *The Universal Baseball Association, Inc., J. Henry Waugh, Prop.* (1968); *Pricksongs & Descants* (1969).

Florence Engel Randall (1917–)
Hedgerow (1967); *Place of Sapphires* (1969).

Donald Barthelme (1933–)
Come Back, Dr. Caligari (1964); *Snow White* (1967); *Unspeakable Practices, Unnatural Acts* (1968); *City Life* (1970).

Kurt Vonnegut, Jr. (1922–)
Player Piano (1952); *Cat's Cradle* (1963); *God Bless You, Mr. Rosewater, or Pearls Before Swine* (1965); *Sirens of Titan* (1967); *Welcome to the Monkey House* (1968); *Slaughterhouse-Five* (1969); *Mother Night* (1969); *Happy Birthday, Wanda June* (1970).

Not Included in the Bibliography:
Jon Lomberg (1947–): a graduate of Trinity College, Hartford, in 1969, now a painter living in Boston.

Woodie King, Jr. (1937–): playwright, actor, founder of Concept East Theatre, in 1965 became director of Cultural Arts Program of Mobilization For Youth in New York City.

Sondra Spatt lives in Manhattan, teaches English at Queens College, and has published short stories in several periodicals.

ABOUT THE EDITORS

SUSAN NEUNZIG CAHILL is co-editor of *The Urban Reader* (Prentice-Hall), a multi-media college anthology. TOM CAHILL is producer/director of "America the Motley: A Political Light Show," now touring American campuses. They have organized and taught in experimental programs at Queens College, Fordham University, and the Center for Humanistic Studies of Seton Hall University. For the past year they have lived in Dublin, collaborating on *Ireland: Writers and Places* (Scribner's, 1972), a study of environment and imagination.

SPECIAL OFFER: If you enjoyed this book and would like to have our catalog of over 1,400 other Bantam titles, just send your name and address and 25¢ (to help defray postage and handling costs) to: Catalog Department, Bantam Books, Inc., 414 East Golf Rd., Des Plaines, Ill. 60016.